The Musician and Maria Salcoiati

ANTHONY DAVID MORRIS

13-XII-2006

Sue -
Hope you enjoy the read
Care
Tony

Lindfield Press

Anthony David Morris

Published by Lindfield Press

Copyright © Anthony David Morris 1999–2006

Anthony David Morris has asserted his right
under the Copyright, Designs and Patents Act 1988
to be identified as the author of this work.

The photo of the author is © Jessica Morris 2006

Cover Design by Mandy Lampard
Typeset by Whoosh Design Graphics Ltd
sales@whooshdesign.co.uk   www.whooshdesign.co.uk

This book is sold subject to the condition that it shall not by way of
trade or otherwise, be lent, resold, hired out, or otherwise circulated
without the publisher's prior consent in any form of binding other
than that in which it is published and without a similar condition
including this condition being imposed on the subsequent purchaser.

This edition is a limited edition
published by Lindfield Press 2006.

Lindfield Press
PO Box 59205, London NW3 9EP
Email: lindfield_press@yahoo.co.uk

ISBN: 0-9554351-0-2
978-0-9554351-0-2

Printed and bound in England by Caric Press Limited
sales@caricpress.co.uk   www.caricpress.co.uk

In memory of my father

Monty Morris
1925–1999

Index

	Preface	
	Acknowledgments	
I	Arrival	1
II	Dream	14
III	Vows	35
IV	Harmony	51
V	Portents	69
VI	Departure	101
VII	Guidance	110
VIII	Declaration	129
IX	Preparations	143
X	Celebration	168
XI	Christmas	187
XII	Conflagration	207
XIII	Devotion	224
XIV	Adultery	234
XV	Reunion	252
XVI	Ambition	269
XVII	Conviction	289
XVIII	Seduction	311
XIX	Portrait	328
XX	Rescue	353
XXI	Settlement	370
XXII	Alone	393
XXIII	Betrayal	409
XXIV	Confession	435
XXV	Hibernation	456
XXVI	Recognition	460
XXVII	Awakening	468
	Addendum and Glossary	482

Preface

It was in August 1999 that I was staying in Florence with my wife, Ros. I had been there once before, as a student, nearly thirty years earlier. After my first visit, the city of the Medici had left an indelible impression on me, an impression that was reinforced and elevated on the second. There was much that I remembered and remembered well, the Uffizi in particular. Back then, with an open-ended itinerary, it took me two days to view the entirety of what the Uffizi had on display, two days of beautiful imagery that remained imprinted on my subconscious. Impatient to share those memories, we headed for the Uffizi on our first morning. In 1970 there had not been much of a queue for entry. In 1999, the forty-five minute wait intensified my anticipation.

We started by making our way through the galleries of the East Corridor at a relatively leisurely pace. Although we thought about leaving the rest of the gallery for another day, with limited time in the city, we may not have made been able to make it back for a second visit. We decided to continue on to view as much of the West Corridor as we could.

When we reached the Pontormo and Rosso Fiorentino Room the crowds were thinner. Two portraits drew my attention and held it. There seemed to be no logical reason why 'Ritratto di Musicisa' and 'Ritratto di Maria Salviati' were hanging next to each other in the most prominent position in the room. The musician was to the left and Maria Salviati was to the right. The face of each was inclined a little towards the other. In any event, I found it hard to turn my attention away from these two strangers who were staring at me from a distance of nearly five hundred years. The unnamed musician with a book of manuscripts on his lap looked as though he was about to make a change in his life. Holding what appears to be a holy book, Maria Salviati was beautiful in an ascetic way. A beatific look imbues the composition with a feeling of tranquility, yet, despite this, Pontormo conveys a sense that she was inwardly troubled, perhaps affected by self-doubt.

I felt as though I had been invited to be there to listen to their story. Unable to move away, I shut out the rest of the portraits that hung around them. I began to imagine what they might have to tell me and why these two portraits were hanging next to each other. After a while, I pulled a pen out of my shoulder bag and, opening the fly-page at the back of my Rough Guide, I hurriedly scribbled down some notes. That is how I started work on 'The Musician and Maria Salcoiati'. I did not know then that Maria Salviati was married to Giovanni dalle Bande Nere and was the mother of Cosimo I de Medici. I also did not know that the unknown musician was believed to be Francesco dell'Aiolle and that, although not signed, his portrait is also believed to have been painted by Pontormo. I subsequently learned that dell'Aiolle left Florence in 1518 to settle in Lyon. Whether or not dell'Aiolle could ever have met or known Maria Salviati is debatable, though, interestingly enough, they were both born in 1492, dell'Aiolle on 4th March and Maria Salviati on 12th July.

A few days later, we were staying in a small hotel outside of San Gimignano where I worked out the basic concept of the story that I initially resolved to write as a novella. My two earlier novels had failed to attract publishers. I did not then feel that I could make the emotional commitment needed to write a hundred thousand plus words again, only to see them condemned to ignominy.

By the following summer I completed the first version of 'The Musician and Maria Salcoiati', a twenty thousand word novella. I enjoyed the experience very much and those to whom I showed the work received it enthusiastically. They included Val Hudson, then head of non-fiction at HarperCollins (subsequently at Hodder Headline). Val was hugely complimentary about my writing and encouraged me to develop the novella into a novel. She determined to find me an agent/editor who could advise me on the project. That summer I started work on a full-blown outline and treatment for the novel that was completed by around early September 2000. Val then introduced me to a wonderful literary man by the name of Rivers Scott with whom I met on two or three occasions. He read my earlier novels, agreeing that they were perhaps best left in the drawer where I kept them, and critiqued the novella and my outline for the full-length novel of 'Maria'. Much of his advice was very valuable and in writing the novel, I made reference to the notes that I had taken of the meetings that we had in Autumn 2000.

At this point, Ros, a historian by training, then in between projects of her own, kindly started initial research for me on some of the things that I thought I ought to know about the period. Almost embarrassed to receive the encouragement of seasoned and knowledgeable professionals, I never started serious work on the novel. My energies were diverted by a number of issues at work that required my ongoing attention. 'The Musician and Maria Salcoiati' was consigned to the same drawer as my earlier writing, though, in truth, I never forgot about it.

In Spring 2003, through my work as a lawyer, I chanced to meet Julia Scott. Over lunch one day I mentioned my interest in Renaissance Art, an interest that Julia shares. She expressed the wish to read the novella. I was reluctant at first, but she persuaded me to give her a copy. The day after I sent it to her, she telephoned me. The enthusiasm of her reaction both to the story and to my writing was overwhelming. Over a period of two years Julia repeatedly urged me to turn my attention to writing the entire story that I told her about and, eventually, in July 2005, I was unable to resist her entreaties any longer. Without Julia's encouragement, it is questionable whether I would ever have turned my dream of this novel into the reality of the printed page. My gratitude to her is unbounded.

Once I dusted off the outline I realised that I needed to undertake a significant amount of research in order to fully understand the period and to properly set the story. I devoured a whole host of books but those that I particularly enjoyed and found useful included: 'The Medici: Godfathers of the Renaissance' by Paul Strathearn published by Pimlico; 'Leo X' by William Roscoe (Bohn); 'Gender and Society in Renaissance Italy' edited by Judith C. Brown and Robert C. Davis (Longman); 'Nuns' Chronicles and Convent Culture in Renaissance and Counter-Reformation Italy' by K. J. P. Lowe (Cambridge University Press); 'Marriage in Italy 1300-1650' edited by Trevor Dean and K. J. P. Lowe (Cambridge University Press); 'The Prince' by Niccolo Machiavelli (Penguin Classics); 'Machiavelli' by Quentin Skinner (Oxford University Press); 'Italian Renaissance Painting' by Sara Elliott (Phaidon); 'Sandro Botticelli' by Barbara Deimling (Taschen); 'The High Renaissance and Mannerism; Italy, the North and Spain 1500-1600' by Linda Murray (Thames and Hudson); 'The Rough Guide to Italy' by Ros Belford, Martin Dunford and Celia Woolfrey (Rough Guides); and, 'Eyewitness Travel Guide' to Italy edited by Francesca Machiavelli, Sophie Martin, Helen Townsend and Nicky Tyrell (Dorling Kindersley). A three-part Radio 4 documentary series 'Amongst the Medici' written and presented by Bettany Hughes was also a useful reference source.

In researching the musical aspects of the sixteenth century story I listened to much contemporary Renaissance music, most of it on the thirty-odd compact discs that I bought at different times during the period when I was working on the book. Amongst those that I particularly enjoyed and that I would recommend are 'The Cradle of the Renaissance: Italian music from the time of Leonardo da Vinci' by Sirinu; 'Trionfo d'Amore e della Morte: Florentine music for a Medici procession' by Piffaro and The Concord Ensemble; 'Canzoni e Danze' by Piffaro - The Renaissance Band; 'Barzallette: Frottole Italiane del Cinquecento' by Retrover, Markus Tapio, director; 'Canzonetta: 16th century canzoni & instrumental dances' by The King's Noyse, David Douglass, director, Paul O'Dette, lute; 'Alla Venetiana: Early 16th Century Venetian Lute Music' by Paul O'Dette; 'Lautenmusik der Renaissance' by Ricardo Correa and Hans Michael Koch and 'Tracce della tradizione orale in manoscritti italiani del XIV, XV sec. by Patrizia Bovi and Gilberte Casabianca.

My research began to assume the dimensions of an end in itself. Constantly failing to actually write anything and fending off regular enquiries from Julia as to how I was getting on and when she might be able to read something, I took a traditional route. I decided to get out of London for a week and to rent a cottage that was small and quiet and bereft of modern communications. I needed to test myself, ascertain whether or not I had a full-length novel in me.

In early November 2005 I made the first of three visits to Cricket Cottage in Ebrington, close to the edge of the Vale of Evesham in Gloucestershire. Starting off by adapting the opening chapter of the novella into the first chapter of the novel, by the end of the week I returned home with handwritten drafts of what are now Chapters I-V. By Christmas I had typed it out and waited nervously for the readers' verdicts. They were incredibly positive and wanted more – and quickly! Thus during the first half of 2006 I completed the first draft, much of it written in two concentrated stints at Cricket Cottage for the use of which I must thank Julia Fortescue, a most gracious and welcoming host.

I would also like to thank Nina Grun, astrologer extraordinaire and Tarot reader, who assisted me with the reading that appears in Chapter V – Portents. Julia Scott was always on hand to discuss Maria's motivations particularly in relation to the New Testament. Gabriella Somerville and Helena Hughes were frequently generous in sharing with me their knowledge of the scriptures. Carys Lincoln, my long-suffering assistant with whom I share an office, cheerfully put up with my undoubtedly wearing commentaries about how it was going and was one of those whose enthusiasm for the early chapters was hugely encouraging.

Lastly, but by no means least, my heartfelt thanks go to Ros who has been a wonderful support throughout every aspect of the process. Had she not suggested and organised our Tuscan holiday in 1999, I might never have had the idea for this novel. She has always been there to talk to me, to encourage me and to spend time making her insightful comments on my writing. Her critique of the first complete draft of the novel was invaluable and led me to revise a number of important sections at various points of the story. As if it is contagious, at about the time I set out to write this novel, Ros started working on a non-fiction book that, at press time, was, itself, well on the way to completion. It is already shaping up to be an unusual, original and interesting work.

Anthony David Morris
Hampstead, London
September, 2006

Acknowledgments

The cover incorporates the subjects of two paintings 'Portrait of the Musician Francesco dell'Aiolle' (c.1518) and 'Portrait of Maria Salviati' (1543), both by Jacopo Pontormo (1494-1557) © Galleria degli Uffizi, Florence, Italy / The Bridgeman Art Library and have been used under licence from the copyright owner.

The author also gratefully acknowledges permission to use the following copyright works being the English translations of the original song lyrics quoted in the text:

'Non e tempo' written by Marchetto Cara (Chapter II: Dream and Chapter 8: Awakening) translated by Sara Stowe and Jon Banks © 1995 and included on the album 'The Cradle of the Renaissance: Italian music from the time of Leonardo da Vinci' by Sirinu (Hyperion CDA66814).

'Ecco'l Messia' Anonymous (Chapter IV: Harmony) and 'Ben venga maggio' Anonymous (Chapter XII: Ambition) both translated by Piffaro the Renaissance Band © 2003 and included on the album 'Trionfo d'Amore e della Morte: Florentine music for a Medici procession' by Piffaro and The Concord Ensemble (Dorian DOR-90312)

'Tu dormi, io veglia' by Serafino dall'Aquila (Chapter XVI: Rescue) and 'Crudel et despietata' Anonymous (Chapter XVII: Betrayal) both translated by Avril Bardoni © 1999 and included on the album 'Barzallette: Frottole Italiane del Cinquecento' by Retrover, Markus Tapio, director (Opus OPS 30-243).

All other lyrics included in the text are © Anthony David Morris 2006

* * * * * * *

I

Arrival

Florence. June 1515

When the musician arrived at the Palazzo Salcoiati, evening had begun to wrap itself around the city like the folds of a favourite cloak. He jumped down from his seat beside the vintner, walked to the back of the wagon and unhitched the tailgate. From the shadows of the wine casks he removed two bags – one of tough leather panels sewn with gut, the other of red velvet.

"Vale, good Master Teruzzo," he said, slinging the leather bag over his shoulder.

"And may the angels sing your songs for God in Heaven," came the response.

The vintner clacked his tongue. The two horses began to pull the creaking wagon towards the oily darkness of the Arno River.

A liveried servant stood at the main gate to the palazzo. A low slung lantern painted his pockmarked face with streaks of blond light. A patch of worn hide covered his left eye.

"Palazzo Salcoiati?" enquired the musician.

"It is."

"Then I am expected."

"And you are?"

"Ragaci. Giacomo Ragaci."

The servant stared at him. Anticipating the questions that would inevitably be asked, he took in every detail of the visitor's appearance. The musician's long, oval face framed deep, brown intelligent eyes, an aquiline nose and lips that constantly failed to fight a smile that was anything but shallow. Ragaci's slim, yet muscular, build was disguised by a thick jacket that looked to be several sizes too large. The sleeves billowed formlessly. The cuffs cut away to reveal hands that commanded attention, extraordinary hands – broad, sculpted with long tapering fingers that summoned a thousand unwritten melodies from the mystery of the half-light.

"Wait here," said the servant, curtly and he disappeared behind a small door cut from the left hand side of the gate.

Though the evening was warm, there was more than a hint of an impending storm in the air and he was tired and dusty after his journey. He reflected on the events which had conspired to bring him to the city of the Medici.

Not two months earlier he was cultivating olive trees, tending sheep and milking cows on his family's modest farm outside of San Gimignano. Once or twice a week he went into the town to play his lute in a small taverna. Giacomo Ragaci was a virtuoso on the instrument. He would mix local favourites with some of his own compositions – ricercari and dance tunes and stirring frottole that he sang in a rich baritone. His original and unusual ballads, punctuated with delicate instrumental passages, captured the spirit of all that he knew and breathed and loved. Music was his first and best friend, his passion and his lifeblood.

Bartolo Storioni, the taverner's son, asked Ragaci for a new composition dedicated to his bride. The ode to love was premiered at a party that they threw to celebrate their marriage. The young musician farmer gave the performance of his life. It was heard by an uncle of the bride, a certain Mosciano Vannozzi, who lived in Florence and who was the manager of the Salcoiati Bank.

A scholarly-looking type, with a high, domed forehead framed by lank greying hair that belied an expression of youthful intelligence, Vannozzi was the Family Salcoiati's most trusted adviser. In his early sixties, he had a habit of squinting and bending his head forward when he wanted to make a point. He started working for Massimo Salcoiati's father, Ammanato, when the enterprise consisted of not much more than a trestle table in the Orsanmichele from which small loans were made to local traders. He was involved in every important discussion and his counsel was sought on every significant decision, not only those that involved commerce but also those others that involved the advancement by the Salcoiati of their personal status. It was Vannozzi who knew that his employer was intending to engage a musician and composer. When his niece's marriage party eventually broke up, he made a few discreet enquiries about Ragaci, the young baritone and lutanist with a marvellous ear for an original melody and an elegant turn of phrase, and recommended him to his employer.

One Friday evening in the spring of 1515, two well-dressed Florentine gentlemen arrived, unannounced, at Taverna Storioni. They were transfixed by the bravura performance given by the young Ragaci. They had not heard anything quite like it before, not even the recital that had been given in Florence the previous year by the visiting virtuoso, Joan Ambrosio Dalza. After a seemingly endless series of encores, Ragaci retired to a corner table to drink with friends. The evening wore on. Ragaci and his friends finished several bottles of wine. Vannozzi chose his moment carefully to cross the crowded room and to introduce Salcoiati to the young musician. He left the two of them to talk alone.

Although Ragaci agreed to sleep on Salcoiati's proposition, in truth, the decision was made without hesitation. The opportunity to earn his keep by writing and playing his music and to live in the great city of Florence was too good to turn down. A couple of weeks later Vannozzi returned to finalise the arrangements and a date was set.

In the days that preceded his departure, Ragaci's family firstly questioned and latterly berated the tempestuousness of his actions. If he went to Florence and did not return, there could be many profound consequences. It would be impossible for him to manage the farm and, therefore, unfair if he was to inherit it, even though his brother, Cesare, was younger. Then there was the question of the union that had been promoted by Gianbullari, the neighbouring farmer. His wife had produced five stillborn sons and but one child who had survived, a daughter for whom he sought a husband. That opportunity, too, could fall to Cesare. Giacomo listened to what his father had to say. He told his father that he would think it over though, in truth, he would give it little in the way of serious consideration.

And so, amidst the recriminations of his father, the tears of his mother and the carefully constrained hopes of his brother, Ragaci packed two cambric shirts, a second pair of breeches, a silk waistcoat, undergarments, a nightshirt and a few personal items into the leather bag and his lute into the velvet bag. His last evening was spent at the taverna, one final performance that was at once affected by melancholia and nostalgia and inspired by optimism and ambition.

The early morning crowing of cocks and the rustling of trees were the only accompaniment to the valedictions of his family. As the heavy wooden wagon wound its way through the tranquility of the Tuscan hillside, his new life lay in wait. His were dreams that demanded to come true. The choice had been offered and made, it only remained for destiny to allow the parts to be played in harmonies that would ultimately need no earthly expression of their perfection.

Ragaci looked up at the facade of the palazzo. Above street level he counted no less than three additional stories. The frontage of the building stretched for maybe eighty braccia[1]. This was clearly the home of a rich and powerful family. The pale glow of glittering candles seeped through gaps in the shutters. Somewhere, from an upper floor, he heard the opening of a window. He peered upwards. He thought he could see a young woman spying down at him. Then again, he may have been mistaken. His reverie was disturbed by the return of the servant who beckoned Ragaci to follow him into the palazzo.

"The master begs you to enter." Despite the warmth of his words, the servant's tone was abrasive, his manner abrupt and unnerving. Ragaci was to learn that Gottifredi the Miserable, as the servant was known, had lost his left eye in combat at the point of a sword. He had fought for the Florentine Militia in its defeat by the Spanish at Prato three years earlier, a defeat that had paved the way for the return of the Medici.

---

[1] *braccio (pl. braccia)*: a unit of measurement, the precise length of which varied from one city to another. In Florence a braccio was equal to 58.36 centimetres or slightly less than two feet

Ragaci was conducted along a passageway to a series of staircases that ascended the rear of the palazzo. Most of the household servants and retainers had small rooms or quarters on the top floor. Ragaci's room was modest in size. At least it would provide him with solitude, essential to the process by which he created the music that was the seed of his soul. He put his bags down on the bed and turned to thank Gottifredi, but all that he saw was the closing of the door.

A short while later, Ragaci was sitting on the end of his bed picking out a tune on his lute, when a young pageboy knocked at the door. He invited Ragaci to join the rest of the household retinue for supper. Hungry after the journey, Ragaci needed no persuasion. He put away the lute then followed the pageboy down to the basement of the palazzo.

The kitchen was dominated by an enormous fireplace in which, during the colder months, logs of pine and oak would burn vigorously. In the centre was a long table around which sat a dozen or more others – maids and footmen, houseboys and cleaners, a gardener, a handyman and a laundry mistress. Ragaci found a place close to one end where a voluminous woman with cheeks like overripe beetroots ladled stewed meat and vegetables onto earthenware plates. A cheerless footman stood beside her, pouring water from a wooden jug and passing cups around the table.

"So you're the musician?" enquired an ascetic looking man. He had a lazy eye and a large mole below his lower lip that gave the appearance of an insouciant beard. Bertuccio was Salcoiati's steward and head of the household retinue and one from whom his peers took a lead.

Ragaci nodded, his mouth full of food.

"Then after supper you will play for us?"

"And not for my patron and his family?"

"Tonight, the master and his wife are attending a dinner at the palazzo of Signor Ignazio Tolosini."

Ragaci acknowledged the remark as he tucked into another spoonful of meat. Before he could ask who Ignazio Tolosini was, Bertuccio continued, "so you will play for us, then?"

Framed in the form of a question, the words nevertheless assumed the dimension of a command. Even though the journey had tired him, Ragaci was keen to please the crowd of hopeful faces. He nodded again.

The stew was followed by a selection of sweetmeats and cakes. They were left over from a banquet for the Arte del Cambio, the Guild of Bankers, thrown the previous evening by Massimo Salcoiati. Unfazed by the ever-changing Florentine political landscape, the Salcoiati – God-fearing, conservative and self-contained – had not, in the early days of their enterprise, sought to curry favours from anyone. However, once their discretion and integrity were established, first Ammanato and, subsequently, Massimo served terms as a Consul of the Arte del Cambio.

By the time the meal was finished, the young pageboy had been despatched to fetch Ragaci's lute. The air of expectancy that filled the room was heightened as the musician carefully removed the instrument from the velvet bag.

The lute had originally belonged to an uncle. Following the uncle's death, Ragaci's mother gave it to him as a plaything. She could not have anticipated how quickly he would extract much more than a simple tune from the depths of its pear-shaped belly. A teacher was then engaged. It did not take long before the then thirteen-year-old Giacomo was more expert in the intricacies of the instrument than the teacher. Now, at twenty, he was well-versed in the new finger picking technique that had evolved as players experimented without using a plectrum. Ragaci was able to perform with a dazzling level of dexterity.

Moving his chair a little way back from the table, Ragaci took the lute and plucked each of its strings in turn. The single notes of music resonated. The hum of servant chatter died down. The only background accompaniment to the tuning process was the crackle of the cooking stove. Then, almost without warning, the single notes coalesced into a prelude of Ragaci's own composition. The piece was delicate yet imbued with a power that elevated and enticed, enchanted and entertained the enraptured audience. It was followed by a brace of dance movements – the first an up tempo piva, the second a lively saltarello. The tunes were both well known to his audience who clapped their hands and tapped their feet in time. He then progressed to a few popular frottole that some sang along with him.

Before the finale, Ragaci paused to make minor adjustments to a couple or so of the strings. While doing this he talked about each of the pieces. His words were as carefully chosen as each of the notes that he played.

"… and to conclude, I will play one of my own compositions. It's a ballad about love, duty and loyalty. It tells of the obligations of a warrior to his people, his love for a lady of noble birth and a crusade of liberation. Though the love is pure and true and vested with an intensity of spirit, it's a love that is not fulfilled during the warrior's lifetime and must therefore wait beyond the grave for the intervention of the divine."

Ragaci played the melody of the introduction. He closed his eyes and lifted his head upwards. The tale was elegantly told and poignantly accompanied. Each of its many verses added a layer of intrigue to the narrative or another dimension to the characters of the protagonists. The phrasing and carefully chosen lyrics were perfect for his voice which was strong and clear and full of feeling.

Ragaci stood and bowed to acknowledge the generous applause that greeted the end of the ballad. A couple of the men shook him vigorously by the hand and slapped him on the back. The women confined themselves to a polite yet effusive clapping of hands. The hubbub of enthusiasm subsided. He became aware of a young woman standing inside the door at the far end of the room who was watching him intently. She looked to be a little younger than him but there was an air of wisdom about her that far exceeded what might have been expected of someone of her age. He was instantly struck by the serenity and contentment that radiated from her. She would not have been cast as attractive in an obvious way, though her eyes of an unusual shade of green, delicate nose and full lips combined to define a beauty of which intelligence was the hallmark and to which sensuality was an unwilling but permanent conspirator. A few itinerant thick copper-brown curls strayed from her hair that was bound to her head with a plain white silk benda. Her clothes were graceful though not extravagant.

Realising that the visitor was Maria, their master's only daughter, the servants immediately stood. The men bowed their heads and the women curtsied. She took a couple of paces into the kitchen and acknowledged them. It was almost unheard of for a member of the family to enter the kitchen, though the servants were acquainted with Maria's love of music. It was hardly surprising, therefore, that she had been lured by the exquisite sound of Ragaci's impromptu first, albeit unofficial, recital in the Palazzo Salcoiati.

Unable to move a muscle, Ragaci could only stare at Maria. She intended merely to express her appreciation of the performance, yet the force that propelled her towards Ragaci was one she could not resist. She stopped a couple of feet in front of him.

"Signor Ragaci, welcome to my father's palazzo. Welcome to our home." Her voice was soft and mellifluous and sparkled as if polished with musical notes.

She extended her right hand towards him. He fell to one knee, took her hand in his and kissed the gold signet ring she wore on her third finger. He let the brush of his lips lay on the softness of her skin for a second or two longer than might have been considered acceptable. He believed that he detected the slightest of trembling. He withdrew his hand.

"This music of yours is beyond compare. The ballad of the warrior and the noble lady is truly charming. The melody is an invitation to explore the beauty that is abundant in your characters. Tell me, is this history based on a series of real episodes or is it one of your own design?"

"Signorina, the story was solely born from my own imaginings. Yet I believe that its themes and the experience that it relates are similar to those that have been shared by many."

"And are you one of those who have shared in such an experience?"

"No, signorina. No. At least not as yet."

She thought about his remark. "Rise, Signor Ragaci, rise," she said. "We do not stand on ceremony in this house. Our only ceremony is reserved for the Almighty."

He obeyed her request and waited for her to continue.

"I am told that you are a prolific composer of new works."

His response was informed by an awareness of what was expected of him as much as his characteristic modesty. "I am constantly practising additions to my repertoire. Whenever possible I like some of those additions to be original work."

"I greatly look forward to hearing something new and especially written for our great house."

For a silent moment he contemplated the request. "Yes, signorina and one of these I will dedicate to you." The musician and Maria Salcoiati stared at each other intently, each absorbing details of the other missed at first sight. Their silent communion did not escape the notice of some of the more perspicacious of the others. "Should the content concern the doings of this great house?"

"The theme may go to wherever your imagination may take you."

"And I will endeavour to make that a place which the signorina might want to investigate for herself."

"Very well then." She removed her gaze from him, nevertheless conscious that he was still looking closely at her, inhaling her scent, absorbing the very essence of her being. She turned away from him and addressed the servants. "And now," she said, "the rest of you may continue with your duties."

She walked back towards the door and paused. Thinking the better of turning to gesture goodnight, she continued out of the room. She closed the door behind her. The click of the latch acted as a signal to the servants. Some stood up to clear the table, others began ambling out of the kitchen to start work on their final chores of the day before retiring.

Ragaci took a soft cloth from the velvet bag and began to clean the lute. Only Bertuccio remained with him. His elbows were on the table and his chin rested lightly on his hands that were knitted together.

"A fine performance, Giacomo," he said.

The musician nodded at Bertuccio contentedly, slid the cloth behind the strings and wiped the fretboard.

Bertuccio continued, "my master's daughter, the Signorina Maria Chiara, is quite the lover of music."

Ragaci continued to work on the lute, polishing the front with round even strokes. "And tell me, does the signorina sing or play an instrument herself?"

"The signorina sings, mostly hymns and psalms. She is a young woman of deep religious conviction, a woman with absolute trust in God."

Ragaci finished polishing the instrument, picked up the velvet bag and put the lute away.

He looked at Bertuccio and said, "no instruments?"

"She has been known to play the recorder and for a while studied the viol."

"Then perhaps I might teach her the lute?"

"Perhaps. But before you enquire further you might remember that she is of noble birth and …"

"And?"

"And you, you are in her father's employ."

"That this is so ought not to prevent her from further developing her knowledge of music."

Bertuccio inclined his head to one side and grunted non-committally.

"A fine voice and an ability to play a musical instrument or two are an advantage to the wife of any man."

"Maybe so, Giacamo, but the signorina will not be permitted to become closely acquainted with just any man."

Ragaci feigned puzzlement.

"No, the signorina will only be permitted to become close to a man chosen for her by her father and to whom she will be married."

Ragaci thought for a moment then added, "and with such deep convictions, that can only mean a match made above by the will of God."

Bertuccio's expression was at once both blank and full of comprehension. He said nothing more, realising that whatever he did say could be seized upon and construed by Ragaci to his advantage.

"All is well then, good Bertuccio, for I too put my trust in God's will."

Ragaci stood up, slung the velvet bag over his shoulder and bade Bertuccio and the others a goodnight.

II

Dream

Florence. September 1515

For many nights after his arrival Ragaci found it hard to sleep. In between lengthy periods of staring at the ceiling, he dozed fitfully. Sometimes he found it hard to distinguish between his dreams and the floods of creativity unleashed by the stimuli of his new environment. Time and again he would be half asleep and half awake, his lute across his knee, working out a melody, a harmony or a rhyme. Scribbled snippets of lyrics and music in a parchment folio book were the only evidence that these episodes were no dreams. But the dreams were always there, shimmering in the shallows of his conscious mind. One sequence in particular replayed itself again and again.

There was a wide, circular chamber of infinite height with windowless walls of white marble. In the centre of the floor, to one side of an altar carved from a dense, white wood, there stood an angel. She wore a full-length robe of white silk. In her hands she held a lute, a magnificent instrument cast entirely from pure silver. Although she held the instrument correctly, she did not know how to use the fretboard to create different notes. After plucking each of the strings in even time, she began to sing – bright wordless tunes in a crystal clear soprano.

A doorway appeared opposite the front of the altar. Ragaci walked slowly into the chamber. The door closed behind him. The lute reflected the brightness that shined from above. The angel plucked the last string and moved her hand to play the sequence of notes again. Ragaci was momentarily blinded. He peered through the unfiltered luminescence of the chamber and looked at the angel's face. He recognised her, but the details of her features were dowsed in the brilliance of the light and partially hidden by a mass of thick, copper-brown hair. He became mesmerised by the sound of the single notes that echoed around him and entranced by the truth of the beauty that emanated from her. He resolved to mount the altar so that he could speak to her. He might even be permitted to show her how to play a simple theme. But, before he could haul himself up to where she sat, a rumbling sound began and the floor began to shake. The dazzling radiance redoubled in its intensity and, by the time he was able to see again, the altar had disappeared and so had the angel. He looked up, shielded his eyes and squinted in order to focus better. All that he saw was the circular wall rising inexorably towards the heavens.

And then the dream faded.

When he woke he did his best to hold on to the remnants of the dream. He tried to identify the angel, but never succeeded. Perhaps the creature he saw was not an angel but, rather, one of the muses sent from above to inspire him. However, he understood that the power the angel projected, though divinely conceived, was altogether more earthly in its intended effect.

He spent much time trying to make sense of the bastard creations of the night, fashioning them into finished verses and ballads and dance tunes. He worked for hours at a time, passionately, purposefully. Some of the fragments would not fit together. They remained uncovered in the debris of his mind, waiting to become part of the piece for which they were intended.

When he tired, he stared out of the window from which he had a clear view of the Arno River. He saw longboats floating cargo back and forth, ornate gondolas ferrying men of affairs to their villas a few kilometeres beyond the walls of the city and the swathe of butchers' stalls stretching the length of the Ponte Vecchio. Often in the afternoon he left the palazzo and took labrynthine walks through the city. As he became familiar with his adopted home, so he became acquainted with some of the characters who populated its teeming streets.

Anything he saw, or heard, could find its way into his songs. Even the air he inhaled, air once breathed by Fra Lippi and Botticelli, infused the torrent of creativity that poured forth from his soul. It mattered not to him that Rome had become the new centre of the Arts, the ancient streets on which he walked were not yet too dead for dreaming, far from it. The rhythm of the city was a rhythm that beat within him. He learned it so that he could anticipate when the number of beats in the bar would change. His senses would quicken at times of excitement and celebration. He slowed down and breathed more deeply when sombre news was posted - the passing of someone who mattered, a battle lost by an ally in parts afar remote.

Following their defeat at Novarro a year earlier and the death of the old King, Louis XII, there was talk of a renewed threat by the French towards the Florentine Republic. Less than three years since the return of the Medici had prevented an invasion by the Spanish, once again the shadow of war began to lengthen towards the walls of the city. Daily life was played out against a background of events over which no-one had control, about which everyone had an opinion and with an attitude of fatalism that did not prevent anyone from going about their business.

Now Ragaci was strolling along the Borgo Ognissante and turned up towards the Santa Maria Novello. The new Saint Maria. Maria. Maria Chiara Salcoiati. The only Maria for whom he cared was his patron's daughter. It did not take very much to connect his thoughts to her. Whether or not she would ever be canonised was, he guessed, very unlikely. It would matter not to him, she was more than a saint in his eyes and adored within his heart.

Very shortly after his arrival he had succeeded in arranging to give her music lessons, one or two a week to start with, then three or even four. Massimo Salcoiati had not needed much persuasion of the benefit, especially when the idea apparently came from Vannozzi. Vannozzi had taken it upon himself to keep an eye on Ragaci, knowing only too well from personal experience how daunting it could be for a country boy to find his feet in the city. He need not have worried. Ragaci was thriving and, even allowing for every other piece of good fortune by which he had been affected, the best of all was spending time alone with Maria and being required to do so as part of his work.

At seventeen, Maria was past the age when her formal education had been completed with the family tutor who had also taught her brothers. Nevertheless, as with girls from other wealthy families, Maria spent some time at a local convent learning to spin and to weave. Music had not then been prominently on the agenda beyond the formal singing of devotional material as part of services. This was an opportunity that she felt unable to refuse.

For the first couple of sessions, her mother, the Signora Aulina Salcoiati, sat in with them. On the occasion of the third, Aulina was affected by a bad cold and confined to her bed. Fuzzy headed and breathing uneasily, she quite forgot to delegate another to sit in her place and Maria chose not to make anything of her mother's absence. After her recovery, Signora Aulina stopped attending the lessons. The decision was partly informed by the decorous manner in which she had observed Ragaci taking Maria through her scales and confining the musical content of the sessions to hymns and psalms, and partly as a result of the entreaties of her daughter. Never one to express extreme views on any subject, Maria was unusually firm when advising her mother how much easier she found it working alone with the young musician. It did not need more than the merest raising of an eyebrow for Maria to realise the nature of her mother's concerns. "As I said, mother, it is quite the done thing for a young woman to be educated in all aspects of our culture. Music, dancing and singing are qualities that any husband will value. I will be as single-minded about my studies with Signor Ragaci as I have been in the past with all others, both those who taught me temporal subjects and those who taught me secular ones."

Maria Chiara Salcoiati was possessed of a distinctive soprano voice. She could wrap it around the densest of lyrics and turn them into crystal clear droplets of pure joy. There was nothing she liked more than to sing together with Ragaci. He explained to her notions of harmony and spent time creating arrangements of songs they could sing together. When he felt comfortable doing so, he extended the range of her repertoire to include frottole – some of his own composition and some by others. There was one song, in particular, she asked him to sing with her more often than any other. She never ceased to be amazed at the infinite variations that Ragaci's sensuous playing could extract from the improvised passages he inserted between verses. The song in question, 'Non e tempo d'aspectare', was written by Marceleto Cara, a composer who Ragaci held in the highest respect and some of whose songs he first learned from a travelling musician who once passed through his native San Gimignano.

Non e tempo d'aspectare	*There's no time to wait*
Quando se ha bonaza o vento,	*Whether it's calm or windy,*
Che se vede in un momento	*For you see in a moment*
Ogni cosa variare.	*Everything changing.*
Non e tempo ...	*There's no time ...*
Se tu sali fa pur presto.	*If you are going to act, do it quickly.*
Lassa dire chi dir vole.	*Let speak, who wants to speak.*
Che non duran le viole	*That violets don't last*
E la neve al caldo sole	*And the snow in the hot sun*
Sole in aqua ritornare.	*Returns to water.*
Non e tempo ...	*There's no time ...*
Quando se ha firmato el piede	*When you've stopped moving your feet*
Et in tutto intorno visto	*And looked around thoroughly*
Muta por fortuna sede	*Silent fortune still sits*
Che non val contra al provisto	*And doesn't go against what's meant to be*
Che gli e ben da pocho e tristo	*That to him is good from want and sadness*
Chi no sa col tempo andare.	*That doesn't know what time to go.*
Non e tempo ...	*There's no time ...*
Non aspecti a volti questa vota stabilita	*Don't expect from faces this longed for stability*
Molti sono stati accolti nel condur della lor vita.	*Many caught in sleep have not led out their lives.*
Non e tempo ...	*There's no time ...*

She last sang it with him eleven days earlier. Eleven days. He counted them and every hour, too, of each of those eleven days. There had been no more music lessons since then. Maria had been away. On the morning after their previous lesson, without warning and with a degree of unseemly haste, Maria accompanied her mother on a journey away from the city. Bertuccio let Ragaci know that they were visiting Signora Aulina's sisters who still lived in their native Arezzo, a distance of close to seventy-five kilometres. The trip had not been planned and the suddenness of Maria's absence sharply disrupted the gentle rhythms of Ragaci's existence. Not only did the break from their music lessons rip a gaping rent in the fabric of his days, but the physical removal of Maria from the palazzo sucked the colour out of his soul.

As the weeks had passed, so their relationship had deepened, even if an open acknowledgment of intimacy eluded it. It was not only the dictates of convention and the constraints of his position that inhibited Ragaci from telling Maria what he wanted to say. He could perform his music for an audience of strangers, but shyness, even diffidence consistently laid an ambush at the confluence of his senses. The lines were composed, but they never reached his tongue. Fear overcame desire every time the two emotions went into combat. It was a fear that was in no way assuaged by the belief that his conflict was one that was mirrored inside Maria herself.

Although she tried to conceal the secrets of her heart from Ragaci's view, Maria knew there were certain things that would always be visible to a man of his sensitivity. When she looked into his eyes what she revealed to him was something she had never previously needed to try to hide. When she took the lute and held it and he showed her how to press down the strings and their fingers touched, the rush of excitement that coursed through each of them was something that neither had felt before. Each time they were together his emotions intensified and at the time of the last lesson he came as close as he could to unburdening the weight of his feelings. He replayed the conversation in his head as he stopped for a moment to once again admire the beguiling patterns of the marble façade of the Santa Maria Novella.

"I think that 'Non e tempo d'aspectare' is your favourite," he remarked.

"I don't remember saying so," she replied coyly.

Ragaci did not want to contradict her, but giving it a moment's thought he concluded that she was probably right. She did not need to say it for him to know that it was so.

"You certainly enjoy singing it a great deal."

"I do?" she said mischievously.

Ragaci smiled, "is it the vibrancy of the melody or the sentiment of the lyrics that you find so seductive?"

"Seductive?"

"Yes," Ragaci simply repeated the word, enunciating every syllable, "se-duc-tive".

It was not the song she found seductive, but she could not possibly begin to admit that to him. "I've always believed that seduction had something to do with the way a man revealed to a woman the thoughts that he had about her, yet at the same time was still able to conceal his true feelings." Maria immediately regretted making the remark but tried hard not to show it.

Ragaci felt himself blushing. Maria sensed that she had gained the upper hand in the parley, though was not convinced that it was what she had truly intended. She wanted to let him know what she felt about him, to yield to him, but duty and her position made that impossible.

Ragaci carefully embarked on his mission. "Dearest signorina," the words came slowly, she listened intently, "if a man revealed his inner thoughts to a woman he would have no difficulty in revealing his feelings at the same time. Thus there would be no need for him to conceal anything, for that would be love. And love, well, as it has been said by another 'love is stronger than anything. You would give your life for it'."

"The Song of Solomon," she replied. Her heart was as much ablaze as was his, but the reality of her situation hung over her like a pregnant rain cloud. It made her grab for the nearest something to dowse the flames. "The Song of Solomon also tells us 'do not arouse or awaken love until it so desires'."

"But what if the time for that is now, Maria? The song tells us 'non e tempo d'aspectare' – there's no time to wait."

She was certain that his thoughts were in perfect harmony with her own. Almost without thinking about it she plucked a line from the song in response, "Indeed, 'se tu sali fa pur presto' – if you are going to act, do it quickly."

Then, suddenly, she became confused. Emotions that she had never previously experienced were taking hold of her senses and carrying her far away from the sanctuary of her expectations. She was convinced that the unusual but warming moistness that she felt between her legs was connected to the uncontrollable palpitations of her heart. Hypnotised by the love in his eyes, she sensed that he was about to reach out his hand towards her, to take her hand in his. But the duty that weighed so heavily upon her would not permit this to happen and crushed her moment of freedom. She turned her head away and looked past him towards the door. Instinctively he tried to see what had caught her attention and, as he did, she stood up.

"Thank you for the wonderful lesson."

Shocked into silence, Ragaci watched her walk towards the door. There was an irregularity about her movement, an almost imperceptible shakiness of her stride that exposed the conflict that was combusting inside her. When she reached the door it was all that she could do to stop herself from turning around to look at him. He found the words that he needed, " 'quando se ha firmato el piede et in tutto intorno visto' – when you've stopped moving your feet and looked around thoroughly …". He waited for her response.

Pausing at the door, she turned her head slightly towards him and replied as he hoped she might, " 'muta por fortuna sede che non val contra al provisto' – silent fortune still sits and doesn't go against what's meant to be".

"And what, Maria, is meant to be?"

"That is for each of us to discover in our own way."

When she left the room the door remained ajar. The echo of her footsteps was all that he could hear – a muted percussive coda to a serenade that the human voice alone could not sing.

Though the opportunity was lost, the moment was not wasted. Inspired by what he inferred as her meaning, he finally found a lyric to accompany the poignant melody he had saved to dedicate to her since the evening of their first meeting. The poetry he wrote to articulate what he had found so hard to say to her face came effortlessly.

The days passed, but by now he reckoned that she would have returned. Later that evening he would perform the piece, slipping it into his repertoire as unobtrusively as possible, so that only Maria would know that it was intended for her. Afterwards, when they next spent time alone together he would declare his love for her – openly, without condition and so that what was meant to be could then be.

While he replayed these thoughts and imaginings in his head for the thousandth time he continued walking. He passed on through the Piazza Santa Maria Novella and continued into the Piazza Santa Maria Maggiore that emerged by the Baptistry. On the far side of the Duomo, in the middle of a maze of tiny streets was the welcoming hum of the Taverna del Cielo.

When not required to sing, and play, for his supper at the Palazzo Salcoiati, which was once or twice a week, Ragaci would sometimes play for change by day in one or other of the city's markets or stand up at the Taverna del Cielo and try out new compositions in front of an audience that was anything but indulgent.

There was still some time before the evening meal and the warmth of the September afternoon had worked up his thirst. He made his way to the taverna, pushed open the creaky door and was instantly greeted by a melange of smells that reminded him of the Taverna Storioni back in San Gimignano – casked wine, stale air, overcooked food, sweat and the odour of men who needed to take a bath. Before he could reach the bar, Bruno Nurchi, the aging taverner, poured him a drink.

"Thank you, Bruno." Ragaci took the cup and raised it in a toast to Nurchi. He took a couple of swallows of the dry, fruity wine and cast his eyes around the taverna.

The main drinking area was contained within a great square room with a high ceiling. On the opposite side to the street door a weathered wooden bar ran most of the length of the room. The whitewashed walls, reduced by time to a lacklustre shade of shabby cream, were stained by the blemishes of forgotten arguments and causeless brawling and the slops of a thousand spilt drinks. On either side of a wide aisle there were a few long tables at each of which were benches that could hold four or five people and even six at a squeeze. There were no more than a half a dozen or so customers scattered about the place. Most sat alone but for a group of three gnarly types, unshaven and wearing porters' aprons, huddled together in a corner, talking in hushed tones. Ragaci imagined that they might be planning to steal a bale of their employers' goods.

"And of what is the talk today, Bruno?" enquired Ragaci, half-hoping to catch the attention of at least one of the other customers. Previous conversations with Nurchi usually devolved into a one-way tirade against anyone in power and everyone who aspired to exercise it within the Republic. Still, if there was any news, it somehow reached Taverna del Cielo before anywhere else that was accessible to the musician. Even if the banditori made a proclamation in the Piazza Signoria about an event, details would be omitted or a misleading slant put on the official version of the story that Ragaci would only appreciate once he had heard more from those with whom he regularly drank at the taverna.

Nurchi leaned across the bar as though about to share a great confidence. Only in his early fifties, years of poor diet, long hours and sharing the drinking habits of those for whom drinking was a way of life had left him looking much older. Reddened veins in his cheeks and bloodshot eyes were surface marks of the ravages of too much sampling of his own merchandise. What was left of his hair flew out to the sides in eccentric white wisps.

"Today it's the French." Nurchi's voice sounded as though he gargled with gravel. "King Francis I has organised a great army of one hundred thousand men and even now they are marching through the Alps towards Italy."

"It's Milan that they want, not Florence," replied Ragaci.

"Was it ever thus," added Gianluca Cavaliere, a goldsmith who had befriended Ragaci the first time he wandered into the taverna, a day or two after his arrival in Florence. Cavaliere walked across to join them at the bar from where he was sitting on the far side of the room. He was a good looking man in his forties, tall and broad shouldered, olive skinned, clean shaven, with dark brown eyes that blazed and shoulder-length coal-black hair that was parted in the middle.

"This time they say it is the whole of Italy and our city in particular on which the new French king has set his sights," said Nurchi. The articulation of this thought brought him the realisation that his own cup was empty. Instinctively, he reached for a bottle and poured himself another.

"The pope won't stand back and watch Florence perish," said Ragaci.

"You'll be lucky if the pope stands at all," boomed Nurchi.

A chorus of laughter greeted the waggish remark that referred to the pontiff's ungainly physique. Much of what Nurchi said had the ring of a punchline to a joke.

"And watch?" added Nurchi. "He'll look but see little or nothing," another barb, this time aimed at the pope's short-sight and the eye-glass that he habitually employed.

"He'll do no more and no less than when the French invaded three years ago," said Cavaliere.

"This time things are different," said Ragaci in between deep swallows of wine.

"Things are always different, every time," replied Cavaliere sagely. "Yet whoever it may be – Neopolitans, French, Spanish, Milanese – certain things will remain constant."

"And what are they?" asked Nurchi sceptically.

"One is that you can't trust any of them." Cavaliere paused and pushed his hands through his luxuriant hair. "The other is that many fine men will lose their lives, many good women will become widows and many young children will be left without fathers."

Cavaliere had gone into battle with his brother in defence of the Florentine Republic against the French when they had invaded in 1494. Though his brother had died at the hands of the enemy, Cavaliere had escaped with his life and had long resolved to avoid armed conflict if ever he could. He traded the cold steel of sword and pike head for the smelting and fashioning of pure gold into ornament and decoration. His initial contact with Ragaci was to take him to task over the lyrics to a song that he had written and sung of the glory of the universal soldier.

"The pope has made an alliance with the Spanish and with the Holy Roman Emperor," said Ragaci. "Together they will repel the French."

"They will do what!" Cavaliere laughed, a roaring bellow that attracted the attention of those in the bar who had hitherto been otherwise absorbed. "And who told you this? Your patron, Massimo Salcoiati?"

"Salcoiati," said Nurchi sagely, "now there's a man who should watch out for his own neck.

"Why so?" asked Ragaci.

"Salcoiati is a man with enemies."

Ragaci looked surprised. He had never before heard that said about Salcoiati. In fact he had never heard anything negative about either Massimo or his family, even during the course of his regular visits to Taverna del Cielo. To Ragaci's provincial way of looking at things, Massimo Salcoiati was a religious and upstanding citizen and as much a part of the fabric of the city as the Duomo, or the city walls, or even the pavements on which he walked. Doubting the seriousness of the taverner and knowing him well enough that the remark could have been intended ironically, he turned to Cavaliere. "Do you know anything of this Gianluca?"

Cavaliere was nonplussed. "Salcoaiti may have the look of a staid and honest banker and, well, I suppose he may be. But, you can't be so prominent a figure in this city for so many years and expect to be everybody's friend."

"Prominent? In terms of commerce, yes, I agree. But from what I have been given to understand my patron keeps his own counsel on matters of politics. I know not where he stands on the issues of the day."

Cavaliere continued, "he's been financing the militia since it was established by Soderini and Machiavelli."

"A little more than ten years ago, or thereabouts," added Nurchi.

"His involvement with the affairs of the state was brokered by Feduccio Castellani."

"Feduccio Castellani?"

"Castellani was an important member of the Signoria and a close confidant of Soderini. Salcoiati made good money from his connection with Castellani and lots of it. For a while Castellani was his best friend." Cavaliere paused to sip from his cup. "Not long before the Medici's return, Salcoiati promised his daughter's hand in marriage to Castellani's eldest son. They started to make arrangements."

"Was this made public?" asked Ragaci, shocked that a marriage for Maria had once been contemplated about which he previously knew nothing.

"No."

"How do you know about it?"

"Castellani commissioned me to make a salver as a present for Salcoiati which was to be engraved with a suitable message."

"So what happened?" asked Ragaci in a tone of concern. Then he quickly drained his cup.

"What happened?" Cavaliere snorted. "What happened is that the Medici returned. The Castellani have been in opposition to the Medici for generations. Castellani's position was inextricably tied to that of Soderini. Soderini fled across the sea to Ragusa and into in exile. The Medici then threw Castellani out of the Signoria with the rest of Soderini's men. Once Castellani lost his position of influence, a union with Salcoiati's daughter … Maria …?"

Ragaci nodded. The merest mention of her name was enough to set his heart racing.

"… such a union was of no advantage. It would not have done for Salcoiati to have been seen scuffling around with yesterday's men, especially with all that money tied up in the City's finances. Castellani had enabled Salcoiati to charge and receive a healthy rate of interest."

"A very healthy rate of interest, I wager," added Nurchi.

"And what of Castellani?" asked Ragaci, "… and his son?" he added, pretending it was an afterthought.

"Nowadays Castellani spends most of his time outside of the city looking after his farm. It's just the other side of Marignolle," said Cavaliere.

"And counting his money, too," added Nurchi.

"Probably," agreed Cavaliere. "It's often been said that he's the richest man in the Republic."

"And not even a swingeing tax bill made much difference to that."

"That's part of his gripe with Salcoiati."

"How so?" asked Ragaci.

"When the Medici returned to Florence, three years ago, as you know, they used Il Magnificente's old trick of investigating the affairs of those whose coffers might most easily be used to swell those of the exchequer," said Cavaliere.

"And lining their own at the same time, no doubt," added Nurchi.

"It is said that Salcoiati helped the investigation in return for immunity against an enquiry into his own dealings, particularly those with the State. At the same time he reached an understanding with the new Medici government that he would benefit from a mutually rewarding relationship with the regime."

Ragaci thought about what he had been told as they each drank. "If Castellani is so successful, why didn't the Medici try and bring him into their fold rather than drive him out?"

"There never has been any love lost between the Castellani and the Medici. Their mutual hatred goes back many generations," said Cavaliere. "There was never any chance of that changing."

"Some say that Castellani and even some of the others of Soderini's followers would support the French if they were to come here," said Nurchi.

"Somehow I doubt that," replied Cavaliere. "Let's not forget that Soderini is now in Rome and has apparently buried his differences with the Holy Father. Though one thing's for certain."

"Which is what?" asked Ragaci.

"That Castellani will seek revenge against Salcoiati whenever the opportunity arises and will do so in the nastiest way possible. And to rub salt into the wounds, Castellani will be even less happy if Salcoiati does what the rumour says he will do when it comes to the marriage of his daughter."

It was said that Florence was a city in which it was impossible to keep a secret. Even so, Ragaci never ceased to be surprised at how much Cavaliere, and indeed others with whom he was acquainted, knew about the inner doings not only of the Signoria, but also, as it would seem, the normally discreet Salcoiati household. He was not aware that any match was being proposed for Maria. The thought alone distressed him.

"And what are those rumours?"

"Nothing has been announced as yet, as you will know yourself. However, Salcoaiti has been getting increasingly close to Ignazio Tolosini."

That much was known to Ragaci. Tolosini was a prominent member of the Signoria whose fortunes had sharply improved under the Medici. Tolosini's father had been a great friend of Lorenzo Il Magnificente. The elder Tolosini had benefited materially from the part he played in bringing to justice the Pazzi conspirators who failed in their plot to assassinate Il Magnificente himself, but who had succeeded in murdering his younger brother, Giuliano de Medici. Following the death in 1492 of Il Magnificente and the exile of the Medici, Florence had fallen under the spell of the religious zealot, Girolamo Savonarola, who had preached piety and humility in all things. Like many others, the Tolosini had been forced to watch many of their treasured possessions burn on Savonarola's bonfire of the vanities – a pyre sixty feet high on which was piled everything from wigs and pots of rouge and perfume, 'pagan books' such as the works of Ovid and others of the greats, drawings and paintings of profane subjects, sculptures of naked women and even musical instruments. The fire had burned for many hours and the embers smouldered for many days. It lay to rest the splendour of the previous century and the era of Il Magnificente.

In 1502, Piero Soderini, a long time opponent of the Medici, consolidated his own position as the head of Florence's republican government with his appointment as gonfaloniere for life. While Soderini held sway over the city, the Tolosini left to take up residence in Rome where they had considerably expanded their own fortune. Ignazio Tolosini and his family returned with the Medici and presently had a hand in every aspect of the affairs of the State. In addition he wielded significant influence over many leading members of the guilds who were only too willing to ingratiate themselves with him and thus obtain favours from the Signoria for pecuniary or other consideration.

The Tolosini had been dinner guests at the Palazzo Salcoiati on a number of occasions, most recently a few days prior to the departure of Maria and her mother for Arezzo. Ragaci remembered that Maria had looked unwell that evening and retired early, even before the meal was complete. Niccolo, Ignazio Tolosini's eldest son, accompanied his parents that evening. Ragaci suffered as Niccolo boorishly insisted on talking loudly through the performance of a piece that Massimo had particularly requested for the company that evening. The rest had listened and applauded generously. Ragaci was horrified that his patron would even consider offering his daughter to such an oaf.

"You don't mean Niccolo Tolosini, do you?" Ragaci could not hide his revulsion at the prospect.

Cavaliere nodded. "But I stress that it is but a rumour."

"Often what comes to your ears as rumour later emerges as the truth," said Nurchi.

"This rumour visibly troubles you, doesn't it?"

"My patron's daughter is pure and kind and cultured. She is devout in her belief in the Almighty and of a gentle disposition. It's hard to believe that her father would condemn her to spend the rest of her life with that lout and, worse, to bear his children."

"What makes you say that he is a lout?"

"I have witnessed it with my own eyes."

Ragaci then recounted in detail the events of the previous visit to Palazzo Salcoiati of Tolosini and his family. After the meal, Massimo and Ignazio retired to play chess in the library and their wives took their needlework and hot milk into the salon. Niccolo continued drinking wine with Tommaso and Tedice, Salcoiati's two eldest sons, who were then called in to speak with their father at the conclusion of the chess game. Niccolo, by then very drunk, tried to have his way with one of the maids on a divan. The maid was rescued with her honour intact but with some of her clothes partly removed. Two burly servants assisted the salacious Niccolo into his carriage where he remained in a drunken stupor until his parents were ready to leave.

"When it comes to the doings of men nothing is hard to believe," said Cavaliere. "It is the doings of those beyond this earth that most test our credulity."

Ragaci was not sure to what Cavaliere referred, but he

was too upset to cross-examine him further. He quickly finished his drink, left payment with Nurchi and hurried back to the Palazzo Salcoiati.

III

Vows

Florence. September 1515

Ragaci barely had time to change his clothes before he was due to perform for the family as they dined.

The dining hall was situated on the first floor above street level. The central panel of the high, vaulted ceiling was decorated with a painting of the sky. From its clouds, cherubs looked down on the room and its grand formal dining table that could seat as many as forty at once.

On the wall above the great fireplace there was an iconic painting, 'Feast of the Adoration of the Magi', that Massimo had commissioned from a Florentine artist by the name of Pier Paolo Forzetti. Massimo belonged to the Compagnia dei Magi, a brotherhood that, amongst other good deeds, performed services for the poor and for the sick – activities that were encouraged by his ascetic wife, Aulina. The painting, like many other similarly titled works, portrayed the grandiose procession that wound its way through the streets of Florence every fifth year on Epiphany, the feast day of the Magi. The magnificence and pomp of the occasion was apparent from the bejewelled robes and flamboyant headgear worn by the participants. Massimo agreed to the artist's suggestion that the members of the Salcoiati family be prominently represented in the painting.

Signora Aulina Salcoiati, whose motivation to support the Compagnia was solely for religious and ethical considerations, eschewed any display of ostentation. She was saddened that her husband's association with an organisation such as the Compagnia could be used as a pretext for self-aggrandisement, especially in the form of a painting that she felt was close to blasphemy. She made little secret of her distaste for the extravagance that her husband lavished on patronage of the arts, most especially the appointment of Ragaci. She did not accept the premise, a form of self-justification first offered by Cosimo Medici a century earlier. It was said that making money by charging interest on money was contrary to God's natural law and an offence in his eyes. Massimo knew well enough that usurers were to be found in the seventh and innermost circle of Dante's Inferno, along with blasphemers and sodomists. To make amends and secure the soul, those who made money in this way needed to be seen to use part of their wealth to confer benefits upon the public. Patronage of the Arts was one way in which this was done, bestowing gifts to charity was another. Of late, Aulina's stance had ameliorated as her daughter was so clearly benefiting from her musical studies. However, that apart, the extent of her condemnation of her husband's fripperies, and, more particularly, the Humanist philosophy that underlined them, went further. Though she had never been publicly identified as such, it was often thought that Signora Salcoiati had been sympathetic to the views of Savonarola and that she had given thanks for the Bonfire of the Vanities.

Aulina declined to sit for the painting, though Forzetti had cheekily included her at the side of the picture, in profile, bending down to attend to a child. She wore a large hat festooned with feathers and was therefore not readily recognisable. The image caught her short but unmistakably maternal figure and her hands that were placed on the child's shoulders; concealed from view were her features – deep brown eyes, impish upturned nose, narrow mouth and strong chin all of which had been inherited by her three eldest sons but not by Maria nor by her twin, Leonardo.

The rest of the family were easily identifiable in the painting. Massimo, short, portly, clear-skinned and grey eyes that displayed no emotion, balding yet wearing what was left of his hair brushing his shoulders, was in the centre of the picture, portrayed as one of the Magi. Maria, in the guise of an angel, watched the proceedings from an upper storey window, a beatific smile the focus of an expression of ethereal radiance. Her four brothers were all positioned in the foreground of the work. This was but one of a number of larger canvasses by Forzetti that were prominently hung around the palazzo. Massimo's fondness for some of the younger and more recently established artists was only partly dictated by economics. He was excited by their reaction to the classic idealism of the higher art which had otherwise prevailed since the turn of the century. He enjoyed their obsession with style and the way in which they pushed exaggeration and contrast to the limit. He encouraged their cultivation of elegance and their technical ability.

Ragaci arrived in the dining hall a few minutes before the family was due to appear. The table was set for nine. No last minute guests meant that he might be able to relax, at least a little. Unexpected additions to the table were not unusual. Accomodating the whims of someone whose taste was unknown could play havoc with his planned repertoire.

To one side of the fireplace there was a small dais on which were placed a simple wooden stool, a footrest and a decorated stand for his music. Ragaci was already taking advantage of what Salcoiati's patronage made available to him. In addition to the alto lute that he had brought with him from San Gimignano, at his request, Salcoiati had acquired an altogether more sonorous tenor lute. Ragaci would use it to play those pieces that required intricate improvisation and that showed his instrumental virtuosity at its best. Always keen to explore what his contemporaries were doing, Ragaci had Salcoiati procure from Venice copies of the first books of music for the solo lute ever printed, Intabolatura de lauto, Libro primo and Libro secondo by Francesco Spinacino. Though Ragaci tended not to perform many works of others, on this occasion he brought the Libro primo as a prompt lest the enervation of his mood affected his capacity to play. He opened the book at a frottola that had been carefully intabulated and which he had regularly practised, then placed his old alto lute on the floor. He sat down and prepared to play. A rising hubbub of voices from the corridor indicated the imminent arrival of the family.

As was the case with many other lutanists, Ragaci would generally start a performance by improvising a few short ricercari – preludes – and 'tastar de corde' – chord sequences. This would enable him to warm up his fingers, establish an ambience and lay down a path for the pieces that would follow. Striking the strings of the tenor lute, he quickly seized upon a new theme on which he had started to work the previous day. Its opening scale passage greeted his audience.

First through the door were Tommaso and Tedice, the two eldest sons and their wives. Tommaso worked at the Salcoiati Bank and was being groomed so that, one day, he might take over the running of it himself. Tedice was similarly learning to manage the family's trading interests and was involving himself with the activities of the commercial guilds. Tommaso's wife, Aldoese, had only recently given birth to their first child. Tedice's wife, Phillipa, was in the latter stages of her first pregnancy. They were followed by Maria and her twin, Leonardo, who was destined for the Church, albeit somewhat reluctantly, and with whom Ragaci had formed a nascent bond of friendship. Leonardo made a point of smiling at Ragaci and nodded his head a few times to the rhythm of the music. Lastly, the third son, Josephus accompanied his parents. Josephus was resplendent in the red uniform of the Florentine Militia, complete with white cap and waistcoat and red-and-white socks, while his father and brothers all wore dark coloured trunk-hose and jackets. The weather was still warm and so none of them had yet added the ankle-length gowns that would be demanded by a more formal occasion and the cooler autumn evenings that were not far away. Maria, her mother and sisters-in-law wore plain dark dresses over fine linen chemises.

Salcoiati's sons had each inherited their father's stocky build, though both Leonardo and Josephus were taller than the others. All but Leonardo had dark brown eyes and shiny black hair. Leonardo's eyes, like those of his twin, were imbued with an ambiguous shade of green, his hair the same swirling mass of copper-coloured curls. Once seated, Massimo motioned Ragaci to stop playing and led the family in grace.

Maria's seat directly faced the dais, but Ragaci's view of her was obscured by the back of her sister-in-law, Aldoese, a tall and ungainly woman who dyed her hair blonde. Trying not to be too obvious, as grace concluded, surreptitiously, he altered the position of his stool so that he gained a direct line of sight towards Maria. She seemed to be deliberately trying not to look at him. He was sure that this was a ruse to avoid attracting the attention of the rest of the family. Satisfied with this explanation he resumed playing as the first course was served and polite conversation hummed around the table.

While the family ate and talked, he played and occasionally sang. In truth, for much of the time he was going through the motions, waiting for the moment when it was right for him to perform the new song that he had written especially for Maria. Before he did, however, he wanted to be sure that she would be paying her undivided attention to him.

* * * * * * *

Ragaci had been surprised at the suddenness of the departure of Maria and her mother. If a family member planned a trip it would usually be known for days, or even weeks, ahead as preparations were made. Signora Aulina's decision to travel to her native Arezzo was one that was made with uncharacteristic haste. That she was devoted to her sisters was not in doubt, but her occasional visits were usually organised in advance. What prompted the sudden decision was not something that would become known to anyone, not even Massimo, for a little while afterwards. As it was, Massimo was then away in Lucca for a couple of days attending to matters of commerce. All that any of the servants knew was that the signora had engaged in a conversation with Maria that had quite upset her equilibrium after which orders were given to Bertuccio to have everything necessary made ready.

Immediately after the last lesson, Maria shut herself in her room. Whatever duty might demand of her, whether it was the commands of her father or the requirements of her devotion to God, nothing had prepared her for the sense of helplessness that engulfed her. Her need to be held by the man she knew she loved was all-consuming. Her spirit was alive as if for the first time. She had never before felt so much energy coursing through her body and so intimately in touch with her very essence. But her emotions were at war with her thoughts. Her desires were not compatible with what was expected of her. There was talk of a betrothal, another betrothal. She was not certain who was being proposed, but she had a good idea. Her father had said nothing to her. He seldom did. Anything that she needed to know was generally passed on by her mother or sometimes by Tommaso, her eldest brother. On this occasion the information had been shared with her by Leonardo, not an hour before the lesson with Ragaci.

Leonardo could not be sure, but he thought there was talk of a marriage being arranged with one of the Tolosini. There was, of course, more than one possibility. Apart from Niccolo, there was another brother, Piero, though he was partially crippled and there was concern as to his ability to father an heir. Tolosini also took a close interest in two young nieces, the eldest of whom was not yet sixteen, They were daughters of his deceased brother whose widowed wife was of inadequate means. Though not unusual for a match to be sealed at such an age, neither Leonardo nor their brother, Jospehus, were likely to be the subject of discussion with the Tolosini. With the possibility of a bloody war with the French increasing by the day, Jospehus' predictable lifespan was rapidly reducing and with Leonardo seemingly destined for the priesthood that only left Maria and, inevitably, Niccolo.

"Discover what you can, dear brother, for I will be the last to know what others may decide for me," she implored him and, of course, he said he would. But as much as she trusted Leonardo, she knew that he would be kept in the dark as much as her. There was only one thing for it. She would have to speak with her mother, but how was she to raise the subject? Her mother was capable of being no more forthcoming than her father and the views that she would share with Maria were predictably narrow and universally informed by the scriptures. Whether her mother would be persuaded to share any information or simply resort to making abstract points with reference to the Testaments would probably depend on her mood.

As Maria lay on her bed, the thumping of her heart accelerated and the noise of the voices inside her head were raised to the point that it pained her. She began to cry. Attracted by the sound of her sobbing, one of the maids gingerly knocked on her door.

"Are you all right, signorina?" she called.

Alarmed that her consternation might import the unwanted attentions of others, she said, "I'm fine, thank you," but the gushing of her tears and her state of agitation choked the words so they were not heard clearly.

"Very well mistress, I'll fetch the signora."

Maria calmed herself down as best she could, dried her eyes and collected her thoughts. A few minutes later her mother came into the room followed by the maid. Maria was seated at her dressing table brushing her hair.

Life had been generous to Signora Aulina. The devotion that she shared between her family, her church and her God blessed her with a sense of self-contentment that no amount of material comforts could improve, nor from which any of the bloody conflicts of the age in which they lived could detract. Though she treated all of her children equally, there was no doubting the special place she held in her heart for Maria. It was not solely for the fact that she was the only girl. In Maria she recognised a level of spirituality of a special and intimate kind that needed both respecting and nurturing. Always keen to ensure that her daughter was enabled to do the 'right thing', she nevertheless made allowances for Maria's innate ability to comprehend the world and her place in it on levels that were hidden to all but a few.

"Mother!" There was sufficient an element of surprise in her voice that Aulina guessed she may have been summoned on a false mission. She turned to the maid and indicated that she should leave.

"I was told you were in a state of some distress."

Maria put down the brush and turned to face her mother, "does it look so?"

Aulina walked across the room and out her hands on Maria's shoulders, "there's something that's bothering you, isn't there?"

"What makes you say that?"

Aulina was not fooled by her daughter's bravado. "Because the red around your eyes speaks of tears recently shed."

Maria turned again to look at herself in the mirror and saw the reflection of her mother's stern but now kindly countenance over her shoulder.

"You can't hide these things from me."
"Nor can I tell you an untruth."
"Nor should you tell an untruth to anyone else."
"No, mother. I wouldn't."
"What is it then?"

Maria was vexed. She genuinely did not know how to begin to explain herself. She could not remember the last occasion on which she had shed tears. "It's hard to begin." She swivelled around to face her mother who sat down on the corner of her daughter's bed and waited patiently.

Maria found her starting point. "In a way it has something to do with what we have been saying."

"Yes?"

"How you said that we should never tell an untruth to anyone."

Aulina nodded.

"Mother, does 'anyone' mean oneself, that you should never tell an untruth to yourself?"

"Of course. Being honest to yourself in all things is as important as being honest to others."

"So if you are asked to take a vow and it is a vow that you don't want to take because you do not believe in the worth of the one to whom you will give that vow, would that be a dishonest thing to do?"

Aulina pondered the question. Though put in general terms it was obvious that her daughter had something specific, something very specific in mind. Aulina knew she would need to tread warily. "It might depend on who it was that asked you to take the vow in the first place," she said, measuring every word carefully, correctly anticipating that whatever she said, Maria would be ready with an incisive and intelligent response.

"If it were God then, of course, it would matter not because God is above everything. In such a circumstance I would not question his request that I should take a vow, any vow. No-one would question that. But I am thinking of a mortal man."

"I can quite see the distinction that you draw, but perhaps you should be more exact?" Aulina's expression of inquisition was genuine. She waited while Maria carefully composed her next comment.

"I speak of the possibility of pledging vows of marriage to a husband who is of no moral worth."

"If the question of moral worth is one that can be objectively judged then you would hopefully be able to trust your father to make that judgment correctly."

"Suppose he didn't, or suppose that father was blinded to the moral worth of my potential husband by the importance of his family, or even the amount of money they might deposit with my father's bank. In such circumstances would you be able to persuade father to take a course other than one that he'd set for himself?"

Aulina, too, was unable to speak untruthfully and so kept her own counsel. Her silence was Maria's answer but she wanted her mother to be under no misapprehension as to her feelings.

"Put another way, what is to happen if I am required to marry someone, but there is another for whom my heart is intended?"

"The only destination for your heart is the one that is chosen for it by your father."

"My father once chose another when I was too young to know or feel anything different. How often may such an important destination change in one lifetime?"

"As often as your father may decide, until, of course, the destination is reached."

"And what if my heart has reached a destination ahead of my father's choosing?"

"Then that would not be its final destination, it would be but a temporary resting place that you will inevitably have to leave behind when it comes time to move on."

"Suppose I'm required to move on and I follow the course my father sets for me and yet my heart remains anchored in the place that I chose for myself? In that case I would be required to make a vow to a mortal man to whom I would not, in good conscience, be able to give my heart and to whom I would resent giving my body."

Though her daughter's logic was sound, the sentiment behind it was alien to Aulina's upbringing and outlook. Maria spoke as if under the influence of Humanist philosophising that had no place in her life nor, as far as she was concerned, in the lives of any of her children. She, too, was party to a marriage that had been arranged. At the time of her betrothal to Massimo she was already past the age at which her elder sister, Bartolomea, had been married and Aulina was yearning for children. Chosen by her father, Massimo was steady and respectable and God fearing. All of that was and remained enough for her.

"And so your heart has found a harbour in which it is anchored?"

Maria thought carefully before answering, "yes, mother, it has and the chains that hold it steady will never be broken, not for all eternity."

It was not hard for Aulina to guess the identity of the object of her daughter's affections. She did not need to name him. Both Maria and she knew very well that, however strong the bond of love, it would be impossible to defy her father and marry a mere musician.

"Whatever you may think or believe, I can promise you that as of this moment your father has not pledged your hand to anyone."

"What of Tolosini?"

"And what do you know of Tolosini?" Aulina failed to hide the defensiveness of her tone by endeavouring to assume an expression of innocence that only came over as one of disingenuousness.

"I know only what snippets my brother Leonardo has picked up and passed onto me."

"And that is all that there is."

"Truly?"

"At this time."

"At this time? What do you mean, 'at this time'?"

"Apparently there has been an approach made by Tolosini but your father has neither intimated agreement nor engaged intermediaries to start discussions."

"And when will I be told about any discussions that there may be?"

"I know little more than you. What I do know is that this is an enterprise on which your father will not embark lightly, not after what happened with the Castellani. There are many details to discuss, details that affect your father's business and position. It will take some days and even weeks to resolve."

"What about me? What about my position?" Maria seldom demonstrated anger but was finding it hard to suppress her emotions.

"Suppose your father told you that he did intend to give your hand in marriage to Niccolo Tolosini and had agreed terms with Ignazio?"

"Give me to him? I would rather give myself to God and be done with it."

Aulina looked at her daughter thoughtfully, "I'm sorry that I am unable to change the way you think about such things."

"And I'm sorry that you're unable to change the way my father thinks about such things."

Then Aulina thought that perhaps there was a way. "Let me see what I might accomplish."

Hardly reassured, Maria nodded philosophically, turned back to face the mirror and continued brushing her hair, while her mother left the room looking thoughtful.

* * * * * * *

Ragaci had an unfailingly astute sense of how to programme the sequence of pieces that he would play on any given occasion. With a second course on the table he knew he would find it difficult to compete with the food and conversation for the attention of his audience. While they ate, he stayed with instrumentals, although from what he could see, Maria was eating very little. Once the plates were cleared, he picked up the aging alto lute and strummed three strident chords that drew the attention of even those who sat with their backs to him. The chords then progressed into a gentle repeated pattern. After a couple of bars of improvisation based on the chords an exquisite melody emerged over which he half sang and half recited:

Though the summer is all but gone
And shadows of autumn begin to fall
The warmth of the sun
Is ever in my heart
And will never set
For all that I am
All that I can ever be
Is but one part
Of a single spirit
The rest is her
Our souls collide
Singing in harmony
Though our mortal flesh
May not be joined
Till journey's end
Other bodies
Another time
Another life

The lyric was subsumed once again by the melody. He opened his eyes and observed the company. At one end of the table Massimo and his two eldest sons were talking in whispers. The rest listened to him with varying degrees of attention. Leonardo gave him a knowing look and pretended to clap his hands in an understatement of appreciation. Ragaci promptly turned his gaze away and was surprised to note that Aulina was watching him intensely, as if able to penetrate the thoughts in his head. Then he focused his attention on Maria who did her best to ignore him. Conscious that he was watching her, she stood and wished her family goodnight, excusing herself for being tired after her long journey.

Observing how hard she tried not to look him in the eye was enough for him to know that she had fully understood what he had shared with her. The conversation that had started between their souls was one that could never be interrupted.

IV

Harmony

Florence. September 1515

The following day news reached Florence of a great battle in the north, not far from Milan. On the thirteenth and fourteenth of the month the invading French army of one hundred thousand men had been confronted at Marignano by the forces of the Papal Alliance. Following the accession of Francis I to the French throne on the first of the year, the pope ignored advice proffered by some, including prominent members of the Florentine Signoria, to sign a treaty with France. It was thought by those who favoured it that such a treaty would deter Francis from invading not only the Papal Territories but also the Florentine Republic. The supporters of the proposed treaty believed that French ambitions were limited to restating their claim to Milan and to Naples. However, the pope was convinced that the young king's intentions were broader and that ideally he wanted to subjugate the entire Italian Peninsula to French rule. Accordingly, the pope concluded that the better option was to enter into an alliance with Spain and the Holy Roman Emperor to oppose the French.

The initial result of the pope's gamble could not have been worse. Led by Francis himself, the battle was decided by the French artillery and a cavalry charge that completely overwhelmed the Papal troops. Even as the news reached Rome, the French were preparing to move south, with Florence in their sights.

When the news began to circulate around the city, Massimo and Tommaso Salcoiati were conducting commerce from their chambers above the main trading floor of the Salcoiati Bank. Shortly after the death of Ammanato Salcoiati, his father, Massimo acquired a derelict building on the Via di Giove, not far from the Orsanmichele. It had once housed the offices of one of the guilds. He gutted the building and spared little expense in refurbishing it to provide a grand setting from which the Salcoiati could run their enterprises.

The top two storeys contained a number of modest apartments occupied by a few of the bank's employees. The Salcoiati's private chambers were located on a mezzanine floor above ground level. They were reached through a series of ante-rooms. The first three were occupied by a number of secretaries and clerks, the last, a somewhat larger room, was Vannozzi's personal office. A short, windowless corridor led to a grand high-ceilinged room. At one end, furthest from the imposing double-doors, each of Massimo and Tommaso had a large desk, individually carved from oak, and incorporating much in the way of gilt-edged decoration. Wooden cabinets and a few functional pieces of furniture were scattered around the room. A number of chairs were arranged in a semi-circle in front of Massimo's desk and next to a wide window where guests would be invited to sit for meetings. The walls were decorated with a series of large canvasses depicting scenes from Boccaccio's Decameron. Behind an unusual tapestry with an oriental theme, a panel disguised the door to a hidden stairway that led to a secret entrance to the rear of the building.

Massimo and Tommaso were deep in discussions with some merchants from Perugia seeking to finance an expedition to the Americas. Interrupted by a messenger bearing the news that they shared with their clients, Massimo brought the meeting to a premature and inconclusive end. The Perugians indicated that they would remain in Florence for a few days longer and await the turn of events.

After concluding the formalities, Massimo asked Tommaso to show the visitors out. When he returned to the room, he found his father sitting behind his desk and staring towards the window. At times of contemplation, Massimo would slide his gold signet ring off his finger and fiddle with it abstractedly. Tommaso knew not to interrupt his father's train of thought, so said nothing and waited to be addressed.

A couple of minutes passed before Massimo acknowledged Tommaso's return and said, "well, son, what thoughts do you have?" Not yet twenty-seven, Tommaso was possessed of a maturity that belied his age. The responsibilities his father encouraged him to assume were already beginning to line his face and fleck his hair with grey. Short like his father, Tommaso's stocky frame was marked by the round shoulders of one who spent too much time poring over a desk. Red eyed and hollow-cheeked, he looked permanently tired, an expression of careworn worry never masked, even at moments of celebration or triumph.

"The House of Salcoiati that your father established and which you've built up over the past twenty years has survived Savonarola, prospered under Soderini and flourished further under the Medici. There is no reason why it should not remain thus, even were the tentacles of the French king to stretch towards our republic and attempt to seize our city."

Massimo responded to the remark with what could have been something approximating a smile. "Our task is to ensure that our continued prosperity will be the outcome, regardless of who holds power in the Republic. But first we must know what the Signoria proposes."

"The Signoria will propose what the Holy Father decrees."

"The Holy Father?"

"Yes, I believe so." As he spoke, Tommaso walked across the room to the wide window that overlooked the street and that had so recently occupied Massimo's attention.

"That a Medici maybe holy is of itself somewhat ironic, don't you think?" Massimo permitted himself the rare indulgence of a discreet chuckle. Before his appointment as Pope Leo X there had often been discussions at home in which the fitness of Giovanni de Medici for the office was decried by virtue of the Humanist education that he had received. Most often it was Aulina Salcoiati who had queried the suitability of a son of Lorenzo Il Magnificente to become leader of the church, her church. Tommaso was not sure whether it was less polite to join in or to pretend not to understand the comment and to ignore it. He thought about it and put his hands above his head and rested them against the frame of the window and looked out at onto the street below.

"And what of the Salcoiati, father, where shall we stand?"

"The Salcoiati will stand with those whose opinions and decisions will matter most."

"And who now means more than the pope? His brother is the Captain General of the Republic and his cousin a cardinal and until recently the Archbishop of Florence. Once again the Medici are taking the lead in bringing to our city the magnificence that had latterly deserted it."

"Just as the Medici fell before, so may they fall again."

Tommaso turned around and looked at his father pointedly. "It cannot be in the interest of the French king to challenge the power or even the position of the pope."

"You may be right but we must be prepared for every eventuality."

"It has previously been said that the Holy Father may make an overture of peace towards Francis."

Massimo raised his head and screwed up his eyes. "The pope has neither the wit nor the charm of his late father. I fear that if such an overture is made it will be one that is costly, not only to the office of the pope himself, but also to our Republic and thus to ourselves."

"Irrespective of that, father, it is inconceivable that the pope will not emerge from this episode with his authority intact." Tommaso crossed back across the room and took a chair and sat down opposite his father.

"It is our task not to show too much favour to those who might be replaced, especially at the expense of those who could replace them."

"It would also be a mistake to show too much favour to those whose present actions may be based solely on hope with little or no expectation of success."

Massimo nodded in agreement. Finally the signet ring found its way back onto his finger. "I think you should seek out Tolosini. Find out what is the news from the Signoria. Even though he has been a good friend to us, it might be useful for us to put a little distance between ourselves and him, at least until such time that we may know the way that events will turn."

"Will that be necessary?"

"Is my meaning not plain enough?"

"We have an appointment set with Tolosini for the hour of nine tomorrow morning. There is already much on the agenda for discussion, not the least of which is the proposal for the betrothal of our sister to Niccolo Tolosini."

Massimo acknowledged his son's comments and thought for a moment.

"Tell him that with this present news abroad we should postpone our appointment on matters of personal business, at least pro tem, as there are urgent matters of commerce that have suddenly arisen to which we must direct our attention."

"From the way that his aide spoke at the time we arranged to meet, it appears that Tolosini has already nominated an intermediary to negotiate the dowry."

Massimo betrayed little surprise at hearing this. Tolosini's impatience was well-known as was his displeasure when failing to get his own way. "Tolosini's primary, if not only, interest in this matter is the dowry negotiations and how he might use the discussions about them to his own advantage."

"Clearly father, nevertheless, I imagine that he will be expecting us to advise him of our nominee for this task."

"He can expect what he likes. With sons and no daughters he will never have to consider raising a dowry."

"There are nieces for whom he has taken responsibility."

"But they are not daughters and if it suits him at the time, in my judgment, he would think nothing of sending them to a nunnery. Our position is as I have stated."

"Very well, father." Tommaso stood and made ready to leave.

"Tell him one more thing. Tell, Tolosini that the Salcoiati Bank is open to listen to any further requisitions for assistance that may be made by the Republic to address the problems abroad."

Tommaso left the room. Massimo slid the signet ring off his finger and, once again, abstractedly started to play with it.

* * * * * * *

That evening Leonardo Salcoiati kept Ragaci playing and talking in one of the smaller salons that was often the venue for Maria's music lessons. It was long after the rest of the family had retired to bed. If his father had done nothing else that was positive for Leonardo, at least he had instilled in him a love of art. From an early age he demonstrated a fascination for drawing and painting that Massimo was prepared to indulge for as long as it suited him not to do otherwise. For some time, Leonardo had been studying with Strufa Gambaloto, an elderly portraitist. Gambaloto was the first artist to be commissioned by the Salcoiati. In the time of Il Magnificente, he painted a portrait of Leonardo's grandfather, Ammanato, which held pride of place among other family portraits that hung in the library of the Palazzo Salcoiati.

Leonardo was not possessed of the business acumen of his two eldest brothers, Tommaso and Tedice, but was vested instead with a deep sense of aesthetics and refinement. He was totally in tune with the rhythm of the times that he was able to express on canvas with a talent that showed genuine promise. Quite apart from strong technique, Leonardo was blessed with a vivid imagination. He used it to best advantage in his depictions of fantasy scenes imbued with equal measures of religious imagery and covert iconoclasm. Whether or not he would be enabled to continue developing as an artist once he did his father's bidding and took the cloth at the age of eighteen was something that greatly troubled him.

"Fra Lippi was one of the great painters of recent times and he was a monk, wasn't he?" said Ragaci, laying his lute down on the floor and stretching his arms above his head.

"True enough," said Leonardo thoughtfully.

"Then you ought not concern yourself too much. I'm sure that your father might prevail upon those with whom he arranges your ordination to ensure that you can continue painting thereafter."

"Maybe so, but that wouldn't be all."

"It wouldn't?" Ragaci lowered his arms and put his hands on his thighs.

"You must understand my predicament. After all, you have run away from duty to pursue your dream."

"Duty?"

"To do your father's bidding," said Leonardo assuredly.

Ragaci had never considered his position in this way.

"You could have carried on playing music while farming your family's land, but would it have been enough for you?"

Ragaci shrugged his shoulders. "If that was all I had ever known then I suppose it would have been enough."

"That's my point, Giacomo!" Leonardo gesticulated with a wide sweep of his arms. "I have known and lived a life that has thus far been rich and full of beauty. How am I to adjust to one where service to the Church takes priority in all that I do, a life that will even deny me the opportunity to love a woman and to marry her? Such a life seems to me to be contrary to the very nature of God's own laws."

"Can you not reason with your father? Can you not persuade him of the importance to you of being able to live a life of your own choosing?"

"To my father the matter is one of honour."

"How so?"

"He promised my mother that one of us will serve the Church. It was a vow that he made to her at the time of their marriage and also made the subject of a public pronouncement at some point. He will not go back on that as to do so would be dishonourable."

"Why you?"

"From an early age he has always shown favour to Tommaso and Tedice who are now working in my father's enterprises and, of course, both are already married. Josephus is a soldier."

"An unwilling one I wager."

"Maybe so, but a soldier nonetheless and doing my father's bidding by becoming one."

"And was not the late Pope Julius a soldier before he became a man of the church?"

"But Jospehus will never be a man of the church."

Ragaci nodded. He was little acquainted with Josephus but knew enough about his grizzly temperament and aggressive sense of self to realise that he was wholly unsuited to the cloth. "And then there's Maria Chiara," said Ragaci wistfully.

"In whom you show much interest."

"She is my pupil," replied Ragaci scrambling for safety as deftly as he might.

"But your interest extends beyond that, doesn't it?" Leonardo squinted at Ragaci, as he did, failing to suppress the vestige of a conspiratorial grin.

Ragaci tried to sound convincing but realised that he may not have done. "I'm not sure what you mean."

Leonardo was sure that he did, but would not press the point. "Maria will not be permitted to do anything with her life other than marry the man my father chooses for her."

Hearing it from Leonardo churned his stomach even more than had the tittle-tattle of the Taverna del Cielo. "I suppose that's right," he said blandly, trying as best he could to disguise his true feelings on the matter. "Is there anybody in view?"

"Apparently so, but I don't know much about it. Whoever it is won't make much difference. I'm as stuck with my father's decision about me as will Maria be with the husband that is chosen for her."

Sensing that to enquire further about Maria would disclose too much and knowing that there was little he might say that would cure Leonardo's predicament, Ragaci picked up his lute. He started to strum the melody of a melancholy saltarello by Joan Ambrosio Dalza that he knew was one of Leonardo's favourites. While Ragaci played, Leonardo stared at the floor in front of his feet, contemplating his future with little in the way of equanimity. After the echo of the final note faded, Leonardo stood up and bade the musician good night.

"Goodnight, Leonardo, and fear not," replied Ragaci. "My feeling is that your desires will be rewarded by Providence."

"Oh that it will be so, Giacomo. Oh that it will be so."

After Leonardo had left him and, as was his custom, Ragaci went down to the kitchen where he took something to eat. Most of the household had retired too, so he ate alone. Inevitably Bertuccio stopped by on his final round. He sat down opposite Ragaci and poured himself half a cup of wine.

"All well then friend Giacomo?"

"Mm," nodded Ragaci with a mouthful of food.

"I have a message for you from Signorina Maria Chiara."

"Mm?" Ragaci was still chewing but raised his eyebrows and beckoned Bertuccio to continue.

"The signorina will not be taking a music lesson in the morning."

Ragaci swallowed what was in his mouth and tried not to show his disappointment. "For what reason?"

"She is still feeling quite exhausted after the exigencies of her trip to Arezzo."

"Still?"

"Yes."

Ragaci's suspicions were aroused. He assumed that on the day after her return Maria would have been tired. He had already prepared for the following morning when he felt certain that she would have been keen to spend time alone with him and when he might then make his declaration to her. This was an excuse not a reason. "And that is all?"

"That is all I have been asked to convey to you," replied Bertuccio.

"And what were the reasons that you have been asked not to convey to me?"

"None that were shared with me, though were I to speculate, I would guess that the cancellation of the lesson is the doing of Signora Aulina."

Ragaci betrayed no emotion in response as Bertuccio stood up, drained his cup, then bade him goodnight. Ragaci could eat no more and pushed his plate aside. He remained at the table and stared at the fading embers in the fireplace until long after the last of the maids had cleared away his plate and left him on his own in the kitchen.

Believing that she clearly understood the message he had sent to her in his song, he was turning over in his mind what he had to say to her and how he would phrase it. The only opportunity that he would ever have to do so would arise if they were alone together, with their music. Now even that was denied to him. He wondered whether there would subsequently be other reasons, or excuses, to curtail her musical education altogether. He cursed himself for having sung his declaration to her in front of everyone.

Eventually he summoned the energy to stand up and take himself to bed.

The dream of the angel in the circular chamber returned, though on this occasion it evolved in a peculiarly different way. Instead of playing a silver lute the angel only sang. Instead of Ragaci preparing to teach the angel to play, the angel herself gave Ragaci several sheets of manuscript and instructed him to sing along with her. The work was a sacramental cantata in a language with which Ragaci was not familiar. The symbols and icons in which the lyrics were written bore no relation to the alphabet. Saddened that the harmony she sought was not forthcoming, the angel stopped singing. Ragaci made to climb the altar to explain his problem with the piece but the rumbling sound began and the dream concluded as it had before.

* * * * * * *

After a fitful night he woke up late, but in time to join the rest of the household retinue for the morning meal that was taken at ten o'clock. His air of melancholy was noted around the table, but no-one felt able to enquire after its cause. He was therefore considerably surprised when the hitherto absent Bertuccio came into the kitchen, took him to one side and advised him that the signorina felt sufficiently refreshed after a good night's sleep that she wished to take a music lesson.

"And when would the signorina like me to meet her?"

"She asked if it would be possible for you to attend her immediately that I passed you her request."

Ragaci had not made much headway with the plate of food that had been set down before him and was happy to have a reason to leave it unfinished. "That would certainly be possible." Though trying to appear nonchalant, Bertuccio thought that the musician did a poor job of trying to contain his excitement. Ragaci's tone of voice was muted but was a little too deliberately matter of fact. There was no vestige of sobriety at all about the way that he clattered his spoon onto the plate and hurriedly pushed his chair away from the table to stand up.

"She is presently in the cappella, where she awaits you."

"The cappella?"

Ragaci had been in the small family chapel on a few occasions and then only briefly. He would attend church services as a congregant no more often than was decently acceptable. When he did, he had developed a preference for the Church of Santa Croce where he would go with Bertuccio and a couple of the other members of the household.

Bounding with energy, he stormed up the stairs to his room and grabbed his alto lute. Then he made his way back down to the courtyard at the back of the palazzo on the far side of which the cappella was situated. It was a simple stone building that had been designed in close consultation with Signora Aulina. Apart from a plain, white marble statue of the Virgin Mary that was placed outside its entrance, there were no external decorations. A couple of stained-glass windows in each of the flank walls portrayed Christ and some of the apostles. One side of the double door was open. Ragaci stopped at the entrance and peered inside the plain interior where a single candle threw Maria's shadow across the short aisle. She had her back to him and was kneeling in front of the altar where she prayed. He stood quite still and inhaled the moment, instantly intoxicated by its purity.

When she finished, she crossed herself, rose gracefully, then took a step back. She gazed at the image of St Andrew that was on the window nearest to her and smiled at it serenely. She turned to take a seat and saw Ragaci, where he still stood, motionless, in the doorway.

"Please come in, Giacomo."

There was so much he wanted to say that he did not know where to start. She beckoned him to sit beside her. They gazed at each other in the muted light, each waiting for the other to speak.

"What was the urgency of your journey?" enquired Ragaci.

"My mother needed to visit her sisters. She didn't want to travel alone."

"Was it an enjoyable trip?"

"My mother achieved her purpose. I am pleased that I was able to keep her company."

"Were your aunts in good health?"

She smiled again.

"And the rest of your mother's family?" he continued solicitously.

"All of those with whom we passed the time were in fine health."

"And what of you?"

She too had counted the days they had been apart but would never say what she knew he wanted to hear. No amount of small talk would lead her there. Nevertheless, her purpose in meeting him, alone, was the same as his. She wanted him to know her heart, but without her having to admit as much.

"Come Giacomo, let us sing! I have brought a hymn with me from Arezzo. It isn't new but I never heard it before. You may put down your lute. It will be enough if you listen to the tune and then join me after you hear the melody." She took a sheet of manuscript that she had put on the front pew, and held it up in front of him. He listened as she started to sing. He had heard her many times, but never quite like this. In the setting of the chapel, the passion and feeling in her voice coupled with the beauty of the words that she sang connected him directly to a force that was more powerful than anything he had previously imagined.

Ecco'l Messia, ecco'l Messia	*Behold the Messiah, behold the Messiah*
E la madre sua Maria.	*and his mother Maria.*
Venite alma celeste	*Come celestial souls,*
Su da gli eterni chori.	*in your eternal choirs.*
Venite, e fate feste	*Come and celebrate*
Al signore de signori,	*the Lord of Lords.*
Vengane et non dimori.	*Come and don't delay.*
La somma Gerarchia.	*The Supreme Hierarchy.*
Ecco'l Messia.	*Behold the Messiah.*

Venite angeli santi	*Come sacred angels,*
E venite sonando.	*come making joyous noise.*
Venite tuuti quanti	*Come one and all*
Giesu Christo lodando	*to worship Jesus Christ.*
Alla Gloria cantando	*Sing unto his Glory*
Con dolce melodia.	*with dulcet melody.*
Ecco'l Messia …	*Behold the Messia …*

The melody itself was simple enough and easily remembered. He joined in on the second verse, picking out a deep bass line that was ideally suited to the soaring melody that she sang with perfection. The overall effect was euphonious, as though one person was singing with two voices. When they finished, Maria put the manuscript on her lap and looked down at it. Ragaci half-turned towards her. For a full minute, perhaps even longer, nothing was said.

"When I first heard this hymn in Arezzo I could only imagine how it might sound if you and I were to sing it together. It was as if it had been composed with that single object in mind."

Ragaci understood her perfectly, he edged closer towards her. "Has there been any song we have sung together that does not seem so intentioned?"

"Only the song of life."

"Your meaning?" he said slowly, pretending not to understand her.

"There are songs on the printed page and some of those that you have written yourself that we may sing together, as one, for as long as we are enabled to do so. But the greater song of life is one that we must learn to sing in separate parts."

"When you and I sing together it is not only our voices that are in harmony, but our hearts too."

"A heart is but one element that forms part of our being. If a human heart seeks the beat of another, the rhythms may not match, however closely they may seem to."

Her intent was clear, but the words that she spoke came not from her, but from that of another. Now was the only opportunity he might ever have to say what he needed to say. "I know well that what I desire may be impossible to achieve and I know too that you must follow what is expected of you by others. But if it takes the rest of this life and a thousand others that follow, there is nothing that I would ever want other than that my heart would find the rhythm of yours and stay in time with it for ever after and in all eternity."

He finished speaking. She could no longer combat the logic that imprisoned her feelings. The surge of emotions that overwhelmed her was impossible to damn. She leaned towards him, rested her hands on his shoulders and kissed him lightly on the lips. He reached out his arms to embrace her. The chimes of the clock in the chapel tower struck the hour. She looked down then drew away from him.

"Maria …"

She stood up. He mirrored her movement and once again stretched out his arms towards her. She backed away into the aisle.

"I love you, Maria. I love you." He breathed life into the words that swirled around her as though they were part of the ancient stone from which the chapel had been built.

Her heart fought hard, but her head won the battle. Whatever power was released by the passion his words aroused within her, she had the fortitude to withstand it. "I think it would be better for everyone if we both immediately forgot that you ever said that to me."

Before Ragaci could reply, she stood up, turned and left him, alone, the echo of her words challenging him, daring him, defying him. He watched as she closed the door of the chapel behind her. He sat down on the pew and noticed that she had left her manuscript. He picked it up and held it. It was steeped in her scent. He inhaled deeply then stood, bowed his head towards the altar and crossed himself. He turned to leave and noticed two inscriptions on one of the walls

Wives submit yourselves to your husbands as unto the Lord. For the husband is the head of the wife, even as Christ is head of the Church: and he is saviour of the body. Therefore, as the church is subject upon Christ, so let the wives be to their own husbands in every thing.

Husbands, love your wives even as Christ also loved the Church, and gave himself for it; that he might sanctify and cleanse it with the washing of water by the word. That he might present it to himself a glorious Church not having any spot or wrinkle or any such thing; but that it should stand without blemish.

As much as anything, the valedictions of St Paul were a blueprint for the Salcoiati philosophy of family, of Church and of God. And yet, even if these philosophies contained a universal truth, would he not have Maria for his wife, then he would have no-one.

— V —

Portents

Florence. October 1515

"I have important news to share with you!" The great booming voice announced the arrival of Ignazio Tolosini.

Massimo walked around to the front of his desk where he was running through loan calculations with Mosciano Vannozzi. He indicated with a subtle move of his hand to Vannozzi that he should stay with them. Massimo greeted Tolosini who was accompanied by his consigliari, Cibaldo Rimbotti and then followed into the chamber by Tommaso Salcoiati. Tolosini stooped to embrace Massimo. He was a big man in every sense of the word, a full head and shoulders taller than Salcoiati, broad-chested and with an immense stomach that attested to an appetite for which the word greed was an inadequate description. Several chins competed for prominence beneath strangely delicate features that looked to be out of proportion for the size of his head.

"From the smile that you cannot suppress, I surmise that the news is not only important but good as well?" replied Massimo as he sought to find a polite way to disengage from the suffocating swathe of Tolosini's arms. He did not need that degree of physical intimacy to understand Tolosini's desire to maintain the impetus of their relationship. The postponement of discussions concerning the suggested match between Niccolo and Maria had not unduly concerned Tolosini. Not for the first time his personal interests were forced to take a back seat to the affairs of state. The suggestion, or at least the notion, for the union originally came from Tolosini himself. Nevertheless, in conversation, he was happy to add credibility to the other view, that it was Massimo who had originally fostered the idea.

"Good, Massimo? No news can be good when there are troops on the march, particularly when one hundred thousand of them are French and encamped not one hundred and fifty kilometres from this very spot."

Rimbotti nodded prodigiously. Rimbotti was short and sprightly. Heavily lidded eyes, narrow nose and protruding front teeth gave him a rodentine look that was easily lampooned. Enthusiastic and loyal he was nevertheless malleable and his intellect was no match for that of his opposite number, Vannozzi. He contributed little to the meetings that he attended with Tolosini and, when he did, he spoke in a voice that had the texture of warm custard.

Following the French success at Marignano, the pope despatched the Duke of Savoy and his envoy, Ludovico Caniossa, to negotiate an alliance with Francis I. By the time they met, Francis' troops were already constructing a bridge over the River Po in order to attack Parma and Piacenza that were both within the borders of the Papal States. The king wanted to exact a heavy price for peace. In return for his agreement to protect Florence and the Medici, Francis required the pope to surrender both Parma and

Piacenza. Caniossa agreed the terms but the pope would not ratify them. For the previous few weeks, the Florentines had waited uneasily as Francis made ready to attack the Papal Dominions in Lombardy and threatened to send troops into Tuscany.

The period was one of great activity. As efforts were made to bolster the strength of the Florentine Militia, Tolosini was delegated by the Signoria to negotiate additional loans from the Salcoiati Bank and others. Massimo detached himself from the concerns of the politicians and made judgments based solely on what would be best for the Salcoiati. It was clear to him that the Florentine Militia could not withstand the might of the French Army, whether or not it was provided with additional resources. The potential for the Militia to have been wiped out was great; the risk of Salcoiati incurring the disfavour of the Signoria for failing to make the loan was greater.

Using the barometer of events as a measure, Massimo not only set a higher than average rate of interest but required a guaranteed seat on the Signoria within a year for Tedice, his second son. As much as Massimo was wary of the true motivation of the needy, he was even less comfortable in the embrace of what he perceived as bonhomie that was not merely forced but calculated. He grabbed at the sides of Tolosini's robe and gave himself enough leverage to break the embrace.

Permitting himself a smile that was polite and functional if not warm, he asked, "why the good humour?" Massimo always maintained the level of gravitas that he believed to be essential to his position. Business, for Massimo, was a serious matter and the affairs of state more so.

"Because, if not good, the news is at least positive," replied Tolosini.

"Is there such a thing as positive news that isn't good as well?" enquired Tommaso.

Tolosini roared with laughter. "But of course. If it's good for one side, it is not necessarily so for the other!" Before Tommaso could qualify his point, Tolosini continued, "were I to tell you that there were one hundred thousand Frenchmen lying dead on the road between Piacenza and Milano, that would be positive news that would be good for us, but not so good for one hundred thousand French mothers, would it?" He laughed again.

Massimo was accustomed to the man's bombast. It was not a quality that he would have chosen to be at the top of the list when selecting an ally. Nevertheless, Tolosini had proven himself to be both constant and reliable. For his part Tolosini acted as though he regarded Massimo as a true friend. Massimo believed that it was no more than an act, that Tolosini's goodwill was conditioned by the regular consideration that he was paid by Massimo to ensure the favours of the Signoria. Irrespective of that, what was important was that Tolosini was an intimate confidante of Giuliano Medici, the Captain General of the Florentine Republic who, in turn, was brother to the pope. It was also rumoured that Tolosini was in line to become gonfaloniere. The joke on the streets was that the appointment would be blocked for budgetary reasons. People doubted that the state treasury could afford to kit him out in the required livery: the long loose crimson velvet coat lined with ermine and embroidered with golden stars and the cap turned with ermine and trimmed with gold, lace, pearls and silver embroidery of a size to accommodate the gargantuan Tolosini.

"Tell us, Ignazio, what is this news of yours that is both important and positive?" asked Massimo endeavouring to suppress the testiness that Tolosini was generally able to engender within him.

"Patience, dear Massimo. Haven't you forgotten something?"

Massimo nodded and motioned Tommaso towards the door. "Please do continue and please do take a seat," he added motioning towards the chairs that were ranged in front of his desk. Tolosini and Rimbotti each selected a suitable chair and twisted them to face Massimo who rested his elbows on the desk, knitted his fingers and pouted at Tolosini expectantly.

"The pope has sent word to the French that he would like to meet them. He wants to lay the foundation for a lasting alliance. The king has agreed. The pope is making ready to leave Rome to meet him."

Tolosini spoke as though orating to a crowd in the Piazza della Signoria. He waited for an indication that they would share the view that this was, indeed, positive. From his previous dealings with them he should have known better. Massimo and Mosciano Vannozzi looked at each other, neither of them giving the slightest indication of either approval or disapproval. Without thinking about it, Massimo slipped off his signet ring and started to play with it.

"It could be a trap," said Vannozzi being deliberately provocative.

"One thing of which you may be sure is that the king dare not hurt one hair on the head of the Holy Father," said Tolosini dismissively.

"That would cast the whole of Europe into a war in

which the French would be at the mercy of every other Christian nation," ventured Rimbotti, quite certain that the comment would have the total backing of his employer.

"Where will this meeting take place?" asked Vannozzi.

"I was coming to that, but it would appear that there is a somewhat more pressing item on the agenda." Tolosini nodded towards the door of the chamber.

Tommaso was followed back into the room by a young maid carrying a tray of wine and cakes. She placed the tray on a sideboard then poured wine into silver cups, handed around the cakes and then withdrew.

"Salute!" They raised their cups and drank.

"So, Ignazio, the location for the meeting," continued Massimo.

"The pope thinks it would be imprudent to admit Francis to Rome or even Florence, and so …" Tolosini grabbed another piece of cake, held it up to his face and gazed at it gluttonously.

"And so?" prompted Vannozzi.

"Bologna. The pope is making ready to leave for Bologna, Massimo, and what is more …" He paused to push the piece of cake into his mouth whole. He masticated and swallowed and washed it down with hearty slugs of wine.

"Good cake! Good wine, too!" Ignazio's rounded off his compliments by belching loudly.

"And the additional point of interest?" said Massimo with a degree of irritation that was noticeable.

"En route the pope will stop in Florence," said Tolosini triumphantly, anticipating at least a gasp of enthusiasm from his host that, in the event, was not forthcoming.

"That's a positive?" enquired Vannozzi.

Tolosini looked aghast, his jowls hanging in disbelief, "is that a serious question?"

"Of course it's a positive," said Rimbotti. "It will be Florence's first opportunity to welcome home its first native pope."

"Precisely," added Tolosini. "The Signoria met today and agreed that festivities should be organised greater than anything that the city has ever previously seen. It will be an occasion of great celebration, perhaps not known since the time of Il Magnificente."

"Even greater than when the news of the pope's election was brought to us some two years ago?" asked Vannozzi innocently.

"Even greater!"

"Those celebrations lasted many days," mused Massimo with a marked lack of conviction.

"Nevertheless, what is contemplated will have to go some way to equal the experiences under Il Magnificente," observed Vannozzi.

"It will not equal those," Tolosini paused for effect, "it will exceed them."

"And who's going to pay for all of this?" enquired Massimo leaning back in his chair and putting his short arms up in the air then bringing his hands behind him and resting his head in his palms.

"Who will pay?" Tolosini saved his most raucous laugh that resonated around the chamber. "Why, the grateful citizens of Florence will, of course."

"Do the grateful citizens of Florence have the necessary funds immediately available?" Massimo's tone was frosty.

"Well that depends," said Tolosini.

"Depends on what?"

"Depends on whether you are lending or borrowing."

Massimo rocked on his chair and looked benignly at Tolosini and then at Rimbotti, who twitched nervously and was thus at his most rodentine.

"Have you yet made an estimate of the required cost?" interjected Vannozzi, picking up a pen from the desk and dipping it into a bottle of ink.

"As we speak the Exchequer is working on it." Before Massimo could seek clarification, Tolosini continued, "to answer your next question, yes of course there is the matter of finance. In addition to a special tax that will be levied, I am tasked with sourcing an increase in our loan from you."

"How much?" enquired Vannozzi, turning to a fresh page in the ledger that contained the figures he had been discussing earlier with Massimo.

Tolosini shifted in his seat. He knew that Salcoiati might not want nor even be able to advance the entire amount required. He also knew that the Salcoiati would not be keen to lend money for a celebration when an additional loan may be required shortly thereafter to further underwrite the more important purpose of defending the city. "The amount that will ultimately be required will not be known until the Exchequer has completed its work which may take another few days or so." Tolosini tried not to sound too evasive. He reached across to the flask and poured himself a second cup of wine. "However, our initial reckoning is a minimum of fifty thousand florins."

Massimo looked at each of Tommaso and Vannozzi in turn. Tommaso shifted in his seat. Vannozzi's eyebrows travelled imperceptibly towards his domed forehead and then wrote the figure down.

"Ignazio, you know that the Republic has a loan account

with us that currently runs at close to seven hundred thousand florins," observed Massimo.

"And twice, twice in the last six months you have been forced to renegotiate the terms of that loan. How much more of a burden can you impose on our fellow citizens?" asked Vannozzi.

Tolosini was never one to dwell too long on the negatives. "No burden can be too great for our citizens to show their love and affection for the leader of Christ's mission on earth, particularly when he is one of their own."

Massimo looked at Vannozzi and then at his son. Again, the signet ring moved up and down his finger. "I think we should review a complete budget for this extravaganza and consider the proposed taxes and levies before we can answer any request."

Tolosini had been down this path with the Salcoiati before. He reckoned he knew how to ensure that the requisite loan would be forthcoming. "I will let you have whatever you need as quickly as I can, though there is not much time to lose as I understand that his Holiness will be starting his journey within a few days. There is much to do and artists and craftsmen are already engaged in preparations."

They let the matter rest and moved on to small talk. Tolosini managed another couple of slices of cake and two more generously filled cups of wine before readying to leave. "There is but one other matter that remains open on our agenda."

Massimo guessed what was coming but, nevertheless, endeavoured to appear intrigued. "There is? And what is that?"

"The proposed marriage of our children."

"In good time," said Massimo impassively.

"And when might that time be?"

"When it is good for me and for my family then will it also be good for you and yours. But do not worry. The door is unlocked, Ignazio. Pushing it open, however, will not gain you entry. You will be admitted when I choose the time."

Tolosini wanted to observe protocol, but the wine was strong and made him feel light-headed. There were reasons why he did not want to delay formalising what he believed was an understanding reached in principle. He respected the Salcoiati and guessed why they were prevaricating, but the alcohol got the better of his inhibitions. "I am looking forward to it, Massimo, but there are occasions when you may unlock the door and find that there are some for whom there is a limit to how long they are prepared to wait before it's opened." He tried to sound matter-of-fact but the words came out sounding like a threat.

Tolosini hauled himself to his feet, his many chins quivering with the movement. Massimo stood to bid Tolosini good day. Tommaso escorted Tolosini and Rimbotti to the door of the chamber and then out to their waiting carriage. He rejoined Vannozzi and his father who were hunched over the ledger that Tommaso recognised as that in which the Salcoiati Bank's dealings with the Signoria were recorded. He remained standing and waited for them to acknowledge his return to the room.

"Yes? What is it?" said Massimo, looking up.

"Father, is it not time for the match between my sister, Maria, and Niccolo Tolosini to move forward?"

"What's he been saying to you," enquired Massimo sternly.

"Nothing," said Tommaso truthfully.

"Or did he have that thug, Tazzi, threaten you?" Vannozzi

referred to Adamo Tazzi, one of Tolosini's aides who Massimo had long forbidden from entering the inner sanctum of his chambers. Tazzi's contributions had never been cerebral and his menacing presence was not welcome in meetings. Massimo insisted he remain outside during meetings.

"Tazzi wasn't with them today, not even outside."

"Before we can entertain this any further we must be quite certain of the outcome of the pope's talks with the French," asserted Massimo.

"Irrespective, father, the Medici are firmly re-established in our city. They have the Signoria in their pocket and there is no more important member of the Signoria than Ignazio. Whatever the outcome of the talks in Bologna, we should not lose the opportunities offered by a marriage with a Tolosini." Although the remark was addressed to his father, Tommaso ensured that Vannozzi was clear on the point as he looked from one to the other.

"The stability of the House of Salcoiati is inextricably linked with the stability of our State," replied Massimo. "We must be certain that events abroad do not undermine the present Medici rule in Florence."

Vannozzi twisted around to half-face Tommaso and picked up the theme, "many great artists and sculptors have made their names and homes in Rome and have stayed there in spite of the Medici's return to their native city. The Medici Bank has relocated its head office to Rome and has yet to re-establish a major part in the commerce of Florence. And remember, the bank was the original source of their power and influence. The Medici were quick to seize the opportunity to regain influence over the destiny of our Republic when it was offered. However, they have not yet been back long enough to prove unassailable."

"That is not relevant to the matter in hand," said Tommaso. "The king has no option but to make an accommodation with the pope." He pulled up the chair that had latterly been occupied by Rimbotti and sat down.

"But if the king does not accept the ministries of the Holy Father, there is no guarantee that the present regime will survive in our Republic. If that was to happen the Medici could be gone for good," added Vannozzi.

"And if that is the way that events unfold then you can be sure that Ignazio Tolosini will be amongst the first to be removed from the Signoria, thereby rendering him completely useless to us," said Massimo. "We must be very careful when pledging the security of our most valuable assets."

"You talk of my sister as though she were but an entry in a ledger." Tommaso's remark was almost disdainful, though it would have been dishonest of him to deny that he had ever regarded Maria in such a way himself.

"Your sister may prove to be of considerable assistance to the future prosperity of this family. All great families make sacrifices. The sacrifices to be made by those who aspire to be great may need to be of correspondingly greater proportions."

"Exactly, father. I could not have put that better myself. However, consider this," Tommaso paused to ensure maximum attention from his father and Vannozzi. "Quite apart from his influence with the Signoria, Ignazio's merchant enterprises are the largest and most profitable in the Republic. At this very time he has several ships on the high seas between here and the Americas. It is inconceivable were the Medici to fall again that he will not retain his influence."

"His position will inevitably depend on the political complexion of any new order. That could be an order imposed by the French or the Spanish or even the Holy

Roman Emperor and each of them is capable of changing the colour of their coats," said Vannozzi.

"The king will not seek to disturb the balance of the pope's influence in places where the French have no business" contended Tommaso, "and the French have no business in Florence, especially at a time when the pope is a Medici."

In the silence that followed Massimo looked to the far wall upon which hung a dramatic painting that depicted the defeat of the Guelphs at the Battle of Montaperti in 1260.

"It is inconceivable that the king will push on against Florence, even if he maintains his claims on Parma and Piacenza," continued Tommaso.

Massimo looked at Vannozzi who raised an eyebrow.

"Even if you're right," mused Vannozzi, "now would not be a good time to consider commencing discussions about a marriage."

"Indeed," added Massimo, "even were we to put this matter at the top of our agenda, Tolosini will be pre-occupied for the next few weeks or so with preparations for the arrival of His Holiness."

"The opposite is true, father," said Tommaso excitedly.

"It is?"

"Of course. Has it not always been your greatest concern that Ignazio's avarice would make the price of our sister's hand a heavy one? For the next few weeks his attention will be concentrated on the Papal visit. He will be endeavouring to endear himself to the Medici to seek further personal advantage. To make the celebrations a success, a facility with the Salcoiati Bank will be essential. There is no other house in Florence that is presently able to make sufficient funds available at the level required. Now, more than ever, Ignazio needs the goodwill of the Salcoiati."

"Therefore you suggest that now is the most perfect of opportunities for us to negotiate the terms of a dowry."

"The terms of an agreement could be in place before the pope's visit ceases to be a distraction," continued Tommaso, beginning to believe that he was influencing his father's opinion sufficiently that it would accord with his own.

"Then there would be pressure to arrange the date for the public meeting between our kin and those of the Tolosini at which the terms of the dowry are notarised and the match becomes legally binding," said Massimo.

Tommaso had already considered the point. "I suggest that having reached an agreement, we might easily defer the public meeting until the outcome of the discussions between the pope and the king is known. After all, it will take some weeks for the terms to be concluded."

"We will need that time. It's going to be some weeks before the pope will arrive in Bologna." Vannozzi's tone suggested that he needed no more convincing of Tommaso's views.

Tommaso looked to his father and then to Vannozzi, his expression demanding them to defy his logic.

"You have analysed the situation well," said Massimo approvingly. "Take word to Ignazio that negotiations for a dowry should begin … in early course."

"Who shall I say is appointed as intermediary?"

Massimo looked towards Vannozzi who nodded.

"Inevitably Mosciano shall be my nominee in this enterprise. And you, Tommaso, you shall be his second. And now gentlemen, we have other matters to attend to."

* * * * * * *

Maria Chiara's musical tuition continued, albeit in a somewhat different vein. Her mother insisted on attending every lesson and the content was strictly limited to religious material. In the main, selections were made by Aulina Salcoiati. She would meet Ragaci before each lesson to discuss its content. She was polite towards him but, once Maria joined them, she would immediately squash any attempt that Ragaci made to lead the conversation to matters that related to anything other than the music. "I think you were at verse two," she would say; or "perhaps Maria would be happier singing that hymn in a higher key?" He would take the cue and return his concentration to the piece on which they were working.

When he saw her for the first time after their meeting in the cappella, he knew more than ever that what he felt about her was real and not imagined. Nothing that she said, or rather refrained from saying, led him to believe that she felt any different about him. With no other means of contact, their emotions could only be shared through their music. Music was the language of their souls and it was a language in which each was able to comprehend the other perfectly.

The atmosphere of the lessons changed. It mattered less to him that he was unable to hold or to kiss her or even to speak about anything that mattered. There was an understanding, a belief, a bond that was sealed and unbreakable.

When he was alone, it hurt Ragaci to know that he would go through his life without once making love with Maria. It hurt more when he imagined her being made to submit to another man, particularly when that man was Niccolo Tolosini. But whenever these thoughts possessed him, the images fractured and then vanished as quickly as he had summoned them. There was always something there to persuade him that, perhaps, things could turn out otherwise. His status as a musician and his background from a family of farmers were, of themselves, enough to thwart any chance that Maria would ever be permitted to have any kind of relationship with him. Nevertheless, there were occasions when he would permit his fantasies to overcome the reality.

With the spectre of invasion hovering over the Republic, Maria perceived that, of late, she occupied even less of a place in her father's thoughts and concerns than was usual. Though she knew that her father was spending time with members of the Signoria, there had been no recent visits to the Palazzo Salcoiati either by Ignazio Tolosini or by any of his family.

Maria redoubled the intensity of her devotion to all things spiritual and spent hours each day in the cappella deep in meditation and in prayer. The situation then changed as suddenly as it had when her father had withdrawn from the discussions with Feduccio Castellani.

"They've started talking about the dowry," announced Leonardo one afternoon as he pushed open the door to her bedroom. She had been fasting since daybreak and sat reading the scriptures, her heart's desire for Ragaci suppressed, her attention focused on her faith. She raised her eyes from the page of the book and beckoned Leonardo to come and sit beside her.

"How do you know this?"

"I overheard Tommaso talking about it in the library with Vannozzi. It seems as though they have been appointed as the intermediaries and have met at least once with those of your intended."

"And for whom am I intended?"

Leonardo laid his hands on his sister's shoulders, "Tolosini. Niccolo Tolosini."

Maria stared at him impassively. She remained quite still. Whatever entreaties her mother may have employed to try and influence her father had been ignored. It was as she expected.

"You are resigned to your fate?" he asked sympathetically.

"As all of us should be."

"Such is the nature of life's journey."

"And I will thank God for giving me the inspiration to continue with mine."

"And where will this journey take you?"

"To a place where I can fulfil the purpose for which he has sent me to this earth."

"And may I hazard a guess as to what that might be?"

Leonardo expected that her response would at the very least reveal the extent of the despair he was sure she felt. However, her demeanour throughout the exchange did not alter. She neither smiled nor frowned at him. Her voice, though emphasising every syllable, revealed nothing but a stoic calm. She considered each word carefully before allowing him to hear it.

"My purpose is to enable the purest and truest love to be shared by those for whom it is intended."

"The love between a man and a woman who destiny blesses with matrimony is such a love. Their bringing of children into this world fulfils God's purpose for all mankind."

"And so it does," she responded, "but that is only one way of doing his will. Your example omits one important element."

"It does?" he said.

This time she did smile. It was a smile that was informed by wisdom and compassion and knowledge. "It omits the element of choice. All of us have the ability to make a choice."

Before Ragaci came into her life there was only one path and it was a path that had been mapped out for her by others. Now she believed that no-one should be made to live a life in any way other than one that made sense to her. The conflict within her threatened to rage out of control. Once there had been no choice and now there were many. Once she would not need to have considered 'what if', now she could not stop. The only time she felt alive, in touch with her inner spirit, was when she was with him and yet, all she could do to let him know, to reassure him that she felt about him the way she knew he felt about her, was to sing. When they sang together it was everything, though she knew that they could not sing together forever and, when it came, the interruption would be permanent. Some of the choices that suggested themselves to her were more imagined than real and she discounted them. However, what was real was within her grasp. Making the final decision would be testing but would yet prove less cathartic than its fulfilment.

"The only choice that you have is the one that our father makes for you," said Leonardo solemnly.

As much as she wanted to, she could not let Leonardo be party to the choices that she saw facing her and the decision that she had to make between them. "That may be true but there are also choices with which we are presented by God."

Leonardo looked puzzled.

"Either you may choose to do God's will and to obey his commandments or to ignore him," she said assuredly.

"Nothing you say prevents you from obeying our father.

Don't the commandments tell us to honour our father and our mother that our days may be long upon the Earth?"

"But at the same time God wants everyone to seek a destination of his choosing and that is also a destination that I must seek."

"Which is where?"

"Which is where I must go!"

"Is this place nearby?"

Maria giggled, something that she rarely permitted herself to do.

"Well, sister?"

"Of course it is nearby, but ..."

"But what?"

"But it is everywhere."

"Everywhere? What do you mean?"

"Just that. Everywhere."

Leonardo pushed his hands through his hair and then shook his head in frustration. "Was there ever a time that you didn't speak to me in riddles?" he asked playfully.

"Was there ever!" and as the words left her mouth she clearly saw the path that she would choose to take. It opened up before her and it was a path that was illuminated by the truth. Despite her equivocation it had been there all along. The period during which the negotiations for her dowry had been postponed had pushed the choices to the back of her mind. Now there was no doubt, no doubt at all.

"I must go to seek the truth and the truth is nearby. But yes, although it is within my grasp and within yours too, the truth is also everywhere."

* * * * * * *

The normally vibrant city streets were even more highly energised by the news of the pope's impending visit. Barely troubling themselves with the thought of the French army encamped a few days march away, the people of Florence were in party mode. Not since the days of Il Magnificente had there been so much fervent planning for a celebration. Once the event was announced, a route for the pope's passage into the city was planned. The finest artists and architects, sculptors and builders were engaged to design and construct a series of fifteen triumphal arches to mark the route. A number of other ornate and magnificent structures were to be erected in some of the larger piazzas. Progress was continually interrupted by interludes of drab wet weather.

One afternoon, after the rain had stopped, Ragaci escaped from his room where he had been working on some new canzoni and found himself in the bustling market of the Via di Montepulciano. On Tuesdays and Fridays the narrow street that wound its way for a few blocks east from the Via de Tornabuoni was lined with colourful stalls that sold every kind of fish, fruit, vegetable, bread and biscuit, cake and confectionery, wine and ale, leather and jewellery and knick-knacks, tools and utensils, clothing and headgear and material from which some would make their own. On street corners or in gaps between the stalls, where gaps were to be found, acrobats and jugglers, conjurors and musicians gave impromptu performances. They diverted attention from the goods on sale and spare change from the pockets of the stallholders. Some of the traders actively competed with the entertainers for the attention of their audience, hawking their wares in rhyming couplets and bantering loudly with anyone who answered back.

From time to time, Ragaci would take his lute, find a pitch in the market and play and earn himself a few florins. After singing with Maria Chiara, he was mellower of mood and less likely to want to perform for a rowdy audience. On those occasions it was enough to lose himself in the hum of the crowd. The city embraced him fondly and comforted him as his heart reached out in vain to the woman he loved.

Ragaci repaired to the Taverna del Cielo which was busier than normal. A combination of the market, the unexpected break in the weather and the general excitement that was in the air had brought people out. He bought himself a cup of wine and leaned against the bar next to Gianluca Cavaliere. Inevitably the conversation focused on the pope's impending visit. Cavaliere spoke in the general direction of Nurchi whose attention was focused on a barrel behind the bar.

"I can't see what the fuss is about. Whatever happens when the pope meets the French, those on the streets and those who toil for the owners of the palazzi will remain on the streets and continue to toil for the owners of the palazzi. The only difference this time is that the Militia will need to expand. Some of those who would otherwise be toiling for the bastards will be pressed into fighting to protect the owners of the palazzi and will die in the process."

"And some of those in the palazzi may enjoy an outing on the strappado and then execution!" exclaimed Nurchi from the nether regions of the bar.

"That's stretching a point don't you think?"

Raucous laughter from around the bar greeted the comment. "Better in exile than on the strappado," whistled Turrichio, a toothless, wizened old man from across the room.

"Better in Florence than in exile," said Nurchi.

"If the Pope can keep the French away from me then I will doff my cap to him," said Turrichio, removing his hat from his head and bowing in exaggerated fashion.

"What makes you think that the French would be interested in you, Turrichio?"

More laughter.

"The French king seeks only one thing," said Cavaliere, sagely.

"And what's that?" asked Turrichio.

"Self-aggrandisement and additions to the territory of France. It is no more and no less than what French kings have always wanted. On this occasion he has the might to achieve it. There is not a force to be mustered in all of Italy that could successfully oppose him on the battlefield. The best the pope can do is to make an alliance with the Spanish and the Holy Roman Emperor and that's not going to be enough to stand up to the French."

"Even so, there are not enough Frenchmen in the whole of France to maintain control of every state in the Italian peninsula," contributed Nurchi.

"Aye," nodded Cavaliere, "that would be an enterprise too great and too fraught for anyone to achieve."

"Even an Italian," joked Nurchi, his comment nevertheless well founded. The Italian peninsula was continually affected by internecine strife while its city states constantly squabbled amongst themselves. "You mark my words, an accommodation will be reached. Francis has proved his point. The pope will not want to test him any further."

"In truth, I do not much care about the rest of Italy, so long as Florence is preserved," added Turrichio.

"Hear, hear," echoed a few voices from around the taverna.

"I'll drink to that," said Cavaliere, raising his cup.

Ragaci stood and listened, taking the occasional swig from his cup.

"What ails you, Giacomo?" enquired Nurchi, solicitously. He was finished fiddling with the barrel and stood facing Ragaci with his hands on the bar.

"That's no ailment," observed Cavaliere. "That's the countenance of a man whose heart is deeply affected by the charms of a woman."

Ragaci acknowledged the observation with a slight shrug of the shoulders, but said nothing.

"If you ask me, it's about time that his prick was affected by the charms of a woman." The author of this observation was Angelica Margherita Gondi, a buxom fruitseller, whose low cut bodices left as little to the male imagination as was acceptable and who proclaimed the virtues of the produce she sold in metaphors garnished with bawdy double entendres. Hardly in the first bloom of youth, her main interest in life lay in trying to attract the attention of strong young men to satisfy her bountiful libido. Ragaci met her specification, though he had never shown the slightest interest in her enticements. Defying the convention that generally kept lone women, even widows, away from public places, Angelica was a regular customer of the Taverna del Cielo.

"We didn't," said Cavaliere.

"Didn't what?" asked Angelica Margherita.

"Ask you. And we wouldn't have done being well able to predict the likely nature of your response."

"Is there not one hard cock amongst you?" she blared.

"Not one that would be wasted on a trollop like you who would know no more of one than any other," added Nurchi, a remark that was greeted with roars of approval by several of the men who were spread around the taverna.

"Come, gentlemen, whatever you may think, Signora Angelica is a lady," suggested Turrichio. "She may need to wash out her mouth with soap, but that's no reason to insult her."

"Why should we change the practice of a lifetime?" enquired Nurchi. "She certainly won't change hers."

More laughter.

"Tell us, Giacomo, who is the woman that affects you so?" asked Cavaliere.

Ragaci remained silent. The straitjacket that imprisoned his emotions made it as impossible for him to tell anyone who the woman was as did the reality of her status.

"Not merely an affectation then, but love?" continued Cavaliere.

Ragaci smiled weakly. "There's little point in telling you. She's not attainable."

"Oh yes!" exclaimed Angelica Margherita. "The sly fox has his eye on a married woman. Let me tell you that when I was with my husband, God rest his soul, it never stopped me having fun."

"Then your soul and those with whom you dallied and who were also married will perish in hell," said the God-fearing Turrichio assuredly.

Ragaci pretended not to hear her. Sometimes, he was known to humour her with a tart response. Presently his mood was not tuned into her vulgarity. She moved close to him, slid her arm around his waist and pulled him close. "Don't worry, there's plenty of others out there. The sickness that presently affects you will go. Your time will come."

"You think so?" asked Ragaci, unconvinced.

"Why don't you ask Zotti?" She pointed to a small table where a dark-skinned man with deeply-hollowed brown eyes and silver hair sat quietly reading a book. Ragaci had never seen him before.

"And what can he tell me?"

"He will read your Tarot, tell you what lies ahead."

"Isn't that pure superstition?"

"Give him a chance. See what he says."

Without thinking too much about it, he allowed Angelica to lead him over to the corner of the taverna.

Zotti motioned Ragaci to sit down. Angelica returned to the group that was gathered at the bar. Zotti wore a dark indigo velvet gown on which various astrological and mystical symbols were embroidered in a rainbow of colours. He reached across the table to a small wooden box from which he removed a deck of hand-painted Tarot cards wrapped in a piece of black silk. Carefully, he unfurled the silk and squared the cards by tapping them on the table. He split the cards into two uneven stacks and handed the smaller one to Ragaci.

"You are?"

"Ragaci. Giacomo Ragaci."

"Very well, Giacomo Ragaci, take the cards and shuffle them." He spoke slowly in a deep voice with an accent that was exotic and unknown to Ragaci.

As Ragaci began to shuffle, a drunk stumbled into the taverna and caused a minor commotion at the bar. He calmed down when Nurchi poured him a cup of wine.

"While you shuffle," continued Zotti, "concentrate on the cards and only on the cards. Shut yourself off from the room and ignore those around us. You are alone with the cards and with your mind."

Ragaci ignored the shenanigans and noisy banter that came from the bar and did as Zotti had asked him.

"These are the cards of the Major Arcana, the cards of life," Zotti explained.

Ragaci finished shuffling.

"Cut the cards from right to left, then select the lower deck and pass them to me."

Zotti then asked Ragaci to take the top card and place it in the middle of the table. "This is the Significator. This is you. The King of Cups. The Lover."

Zotti then took the next three cards and lined them up across the top of the King of Cups. The first, the Wheel of Fortune, in the centre, the second, the Lovers, was to the left and the third, Death, to the right. He then reassembled the smaller stack of cards and put them to one side. He had Ragaci shuffle the second and larger stack, the cards of the Minor Arcana, and repeated the process. This time Zotti laid out nine cards in three rows of three immediately below the King of Cups. Ragaci watched Zotti's long, dark hardened fingers handle the cards deftly and precisely.

"You're interested in affairs of the heart?"

It was more of a statement than a question. Ragaci nodded.

Zotti spent a couple of minutes studying the spread of the cards. He furrowed his brow. Sporadically he would point to a card and nod to himself, though the expression on his face revealed nothing.

"The Lovers represent you and the one you love and who also loves you. This love is central to your existence – present and future. In this position the Wheel of Fortune represents your life as it unfolds. Death next to the Wheel of Fortune suggests that your life is subject to many changes so that what you embark upon will not always be accomplished."

Zotti paused and started scanning and pointing at the three rows of cards beneath the King of Cups. Ragaci did not know whether he should say anything. Before he could, Zotti continued. "Here," he said indicating the first two cards on the first row, the Two of Cups on the left and the Ten of Cups reversed immediately below the King. "The Two of Cups comes immediately after Death, the two lovers come together … hmm … but then the Ten is reversed … hmm … but wait a minute … then …"

The Tarot reader's focus was drawn to the final row of cards to which he pointed. His features remained fixed in concentration yet to Ragaci they suggested a degree of concern. Zotti looked up from the table and into his eyes. Before he could speak the drunk had lurched across from the bar to where they sat, crashed into the table, knocked it over and sent the cards flying. The drunk followed the table and landed in a heap at Ragaci's feet.

"I'm sorry," the drunk slurred, somewhat dazed.

"Don't worry, it was an accident," said Ragaci who stood and helped the drunk back to his feet, sorting out limbs from cards and the table which he replaced. The drunk said little else that was intelligible and hobbled back towards the bar.

Zotti was crouched on the floor picking up the cards. Ragaci began to help him and asked, "can you remember which card was where?"

Zotti kneeled up and replied, "it matters not. Even if I could remember them all, I wouldn't be able to reveal to you what they told me."

"Why not?"

"Because what happened was not an accident?"

"No?"

"It was Fate intervening to deny you present knowledge of what is to come."

Ragaci looked puzzled.

"What the cards revealed was both profound and improbable and perhaps only properly understood at a higher level."

"Do you remember which card was where? I certainly remember a good many of them myself."

"A good many is not all and not all is not enough. Each and every card and its precise position has an important bearing on the part in the story played by every other."

"From the expression on your face at the point of the interruption, you had construed at least some part of what the cards showed."

Zotti thought for a minute then kneeled down to pick up the rest of the cards. Ragaci helped him to his feet and looked at him expectantly. "All I can say is that a woman may do as her father desires, though she will not always take the path he requires."

"The woman I love?"

"The woman, Giacomo? A woman, it was a woman, that is all I observed."

Ragaci considered this. He waited but knew there would be nothing more. He reached towards his purse.

Zotti shook his head. "The reading was incomplete. I may not receive payment."

"Let me at least buy you a drink."

"Thank you but I am due elsewhere." Zotti carefully wrapped the cards in the silk, put them back in the box, placed it and his book in a leather bag that he slung over his shoulder. Ragaci watched him walk towards the street door.

"May we do this again, sometime?"

Zotti turned at the door and smiled then said, "perhaps, but perhaps it would be best if we did not."

"Why?"

"For some, it is better to experience and to accept than to hear and then to anticipate; for anticipation is an occupation that time forgets. Experience and the memory of it is what makes up a life."

Zotti pushed the door open and disappeared into the street. Ragaci stood for a moment and stared at the door.

Angelica Margherita had been keeping an eye on what was happening. "Never mind, Giacomo, what will be, will be. You won't be able to change things anyway. If I were you I'd try and forget her. There's plenty of others available and you don't have to look very far."

"Leave him alone, Angelica," implored Cavaliere. "There are other things to talk about."

"Like what?"

"Like the impending arrival of the pope."

"I know what you mean," sighed Nurchi, taking the cue to change the subject. "I need to decide how I'm going to play my part in the celebrations."

"You?" laughed Angelica. "Play a part? It will be no different than any other party. Your customers will come in here and get roaring drunk. At about two in the morning, when the whores have finished working their way through the out-of-towners on the streets, they'll descend on this tavern like vermin."

Nurchi's face lit up, "do you think so?"

"They'll promise you everything for free drinks, which you'll give them. Then, when one of them has you in a corner with your hose around your ankles and your cock hardening in her hand, she will take you for whatever she can."

Laughter erupted around the tavern.

"If that's what you reckon, I'll make damn sure that I give her a good seeing to."

A few of the men emitted cries of encouragement. Angelica was not to be discouraged. "If you get that far, all you'll need is a cloth to wipe her hand."

The laughter rushed through the taverna like an incoming tide. There was no stopping it.

Like several of the others, Nurchi was used to being made the butt of Angelica's humour. The absence of an immediate riposte meant that it was best if he tried to ignore it. "I was referring to what I might organise to mark the event apart from having the place redecorated."

"That you are affected by these events is a surprise to me," observed Cavaliere.

"It is impossible for it not to be so. Besides, the place needs brightening up. It was something I planned to do anyway."

"You have been planning it constantly since Michaelangelo was commissioned to decorate the walls of the Palazzo Vecchia and that was at least ten years ago."

"Aye," replied Nurchi, "these things do take time, don't they."

"I suppose it will be a good time for you too, Giacomo," said Cavaliere. "Times of celebration are never complete without music and, for music, there is a need for musicians!"

"And there's none better in Florence than you," said Angelica flirtatiously.

"You flatter me. There are many better and more established musicians in Florence than me."

"The rumour is that you are to be directly involved," said Cavaliere confidently.

Ragaci blushed but said nothing.

"Is this true?" asked Nurchi set a cup down on the bar and poured wine for Ragaci.

"I suppose so," Ragaci responded coyly.

"You'll be playing for his Holiness?" pressed Cavaliere. Ragaci nodded.

"Tell all!" said Angelica excitedly, thrusting her bosom forward.

"Yes go on," added Nurchi.

"My patron, Signor Salcoiati, has arranged for the Signoria to commission me to write a ballad especially for the occasion. I am then to perform it at a banquet that will take place in the Palazzo Vecchio. The pope has been invited to attend and it is expected that he will accept."

"Do you yet know what you are going to write about?" enquired Nurchi eagerly.

"In truth not. It is a far from easy commission. I have not yet made up my mind."

"I'm sure that something will come to you."

"I'm sure it will," he answered, less than convincingly. But his mind was elsewhere. Zotti's words were pounding inside his brain, 'what the cards revealed was both profound and improbable to the point of being almost frightening and perhaps only properly understood at a higher level' and 'a woman may do as her father desires, though she will not always take the path he requires'. What events did these words portend?

He worked his way through the evening, a performance for the family and some guests followed by a meal in the kitchen with a few others of the household retinue.

Eventually, he retired and went to bed and spent much of the night trying to figure out what Zotti meant in his reading. He would discover in due course, but the time was not yet right, not yet.

VI

Departure

London. July 1983

Matt Dayton sprinted through the departure lounge. He barely had time to catch his breath before a disembodied Tannoy voice requested those in rows twenty and upwards to board the flight to Pisa. His mother had missed the exit from the motorway and heavy traffic had waylaid them on the slip road into the airport. By the time he reached the check-in desk there was little choice of seats. He hated sitting next to the aisle and an aisle was all that was left. He expected to be stuck with the least prepossessing passenger on the plane. Not for him one of the interesting female students who would no doubt be following the same trail of Art and Culture as him; not even one of the beautifully-dressed, but wholly unattainable, cosmopolitan Italian women who looked as though they had walked straight from the set of a Fellini movie. But was that not always the way?

He watched the throng shuffle towards the departure gate. He laid odds with himself on one of two: a large middle-aged man with a mass of greasy hair snowing a shelf of dandruff across the back of his blazer or, perhaps, an old dear festooned with plastic shopping bags from

Oxford Street stores. He mentally played out alternative fly time scenarios: one, flicking away stray white flakes whilst he ate miniscule bags of roasted peanuts, the other, admiring the best bargains that Selfridges had to offer.

Virtually the last to board, Matt lunged awkwardly through the economy cabin. He ran the gauntlet of solicitous flight attendants with pre-arranged smiles that thinly disguised gritted teeth. Protruding backsides of passengers fighting with overhead lockers barred his progress. Gradually, the way to 21C cleared. The locker was full. He slumped into his seat and placed his leather duffle bag under the seat in front. Fastening his belt he noted that neither dandruff nor shopping bags were in evidence. For the first time in his limited experience of international air travel he had got lucky.

She was petite but well-proportioned, pretty – very pretty – and Mediterranean-looking. Thick black hair brushed the top of her shoulders, large brown eyes betrayed a vitality that was at once both playful and serious. Full sensuous lips pouted as she pored over a well-thumbed and weighty volume. She wore an opaque white cotton blouse and a classic skirt cut fashionably short. She looked to be about his own age – twenty, maybe twenty-one. As the aircraft doors were sealed, he diverted his attention from the enticements of her hemline. He began to compose an ice-breaking opening line that would combine both wit and sophistication.

The concentration with which she read suggested that a cerebral approach could reap dividends. He analysed the situation. Maybe she was Italian and would not speak English. He quickly dismissed that notion. She was flying out of London and was undoubtedly the cosmopolitan European who could switch from one language to another on cue. He was reassured by the fact that the book was in English. He strained to see what it was, but she was turned towards the window and the print was small. He guessed that a deep-rooted love of Renaissance culture drew her to Tuscany. That much they would have in common. A woman with an appreciation of the Arts might be interested in his knowledge and insight on the subject. He tried to guess who her favourite artist might be. Michaelangelo? Too obvious. Giotto? Too religious. Botticelli? Too much obscure symbolism. Maybe she was more of a pragmatist. Shit. This was going to be tougher than he thought.

"Bertrand Russell."

His ruminations were interrupted. The roar of the engines and a sudden burst of acceleration meant take-off. But, he thought he heard a confident female voice say 'Bertrand Russell'.

He continued gazing at the book but, as he switched back to what was going on around him, he could not help but notice the irresistible rise of her hemline and the tanned flesh of her thighs.

"A History of Western Philosophy," she added.

"Right." He tried to take control. The sound of her voice and the direct manner in which she spoke disarmed him. He tried to think of something to say but could only come out with, "right".

She flipped the cover of the book and showed it to him. "I'm majoring in History, but I'm taking a Philosophy foundation."

"Right," he said it again. It was all a little too much too quickly. She had spoken to him first. The accent? American, definitely American.

"And you?" she enquired.

A sudden sense of relief overtook him. A feedline. He was primed and ready with the right response. "Botticelli," he said. "Botticelli for sure."

"Botticelli? You're majoring in Botticelli?"

"No. Not really. I'm taking the Cambridge Tripos. Two years of English Lit, one of Fine Art. I'm spending a couple of months in Italy rooting around the museums and churches and so on. Florence is my first stop."

"And Botticelli is your favourite artist, right?"

"Right. Of course." He sorted out the questions and the answers in the right order. His face reddened. He started working on what to say next. He didn't need to. She extended her hand towards him.

"Olivia. Olivia Giorgianni."

"Oh right. Matt. Matt Dayton." He took her hand and shook it, not too hard but firmly. A newly-grown, student-spec beard did little to cover his blushes. She was touched by that. He was rather attractive too, she thought. Blue eyes, throbbing with intelligence, searched her face for clues. The handsome symmetry of his features was displaced by the break in his nose suffered when he fell off a rope in the gym at school. Dark, wavy hair was swept back and across from his forehead. His body was slim and wiry and was swamped by an oversized t-shirt and jeans that were generous in their cut.

"Where are you from?" he heard himself say.

"New York City. But I go to school at Williams College in Massachusetts."

"So this is a holiday?"

"My father's family come from Pisa. I'm visiting some relatives for a couple of weeks. Travelling around. Then going back home. Fall Semester starts right after Labor Day."

Another awkward silence threatened but he was happy to let her take control.

"So why Botticelli?"

Now he was on home turf. This was easy. He began to relax. "I love the way he emphasises line over mass. There's an innate simplicity about his style, even though there's also tons of symbolism to unravel. I particularly love the mythological stuff."

"And which painting would you choose to hang at home?"

"Well it would have to be the Venus. The Birth of Venus, I mean. That is if I had the wall space."

They shared the moment with a smile.

"Hmm. Mr Romantic then. A man whose favourite painting is an allegory for the creation of beauty. Cool. Very cool."

He blushed again. "Well, may be, but you have to remember that the source for the inspiration for the painting is a pretty grisly myth."

"It is?"

"Oh yes. The story is that Uranus was castrated by Cronus, one of the Titans. His severed genitals floated on the sea producing a mass of white sperm. Venus emerged from the sea after it had been impregnated. Beauty was therefore created through the mingling of the heavens with the physical world. In mythology, Uranus was the personification of heaven. The physical world is represented in the story by the sea."

There was a pause while Olivia racked her brains for more detail of the half-remembered myth that she thought Matt had omitted. It came back to her. "Yes, but don't forget that it was Gaea, the Earth, who'd first given birth to Uranus."

"Meaning?"

"Meaning that beauty is a wholly earthly concept.

Heaven is, and always has been a myth created to explain the inexplicable. Even in the times of the ancients."

"So you don't believe in heaven, or an afterlife?"

"No-one proved it to me yet."

"Or divine intervention?"

"Certainly not that!"

"And what proof do you want?"

"You really are too much. You really believe in all that stuff?"

"Well, ancient mythology is just that, mythology. But in order to explain the inexplicable, faith in something beyond this earth and this life is something in which I do believe."

"And does your belief extend to include a notion that this 'something' exercises control over our lives?"

"If you are talking about destiny, yes, I believe that we are all affected by destiny. Nevertheless, we each have the ability to make a free choice. On our journey through life we reach many forks in the road. Sometimes we will take the left and sometimes the right. The consequences will depend on the choice that has been made. But it is always our destiny that leads us to the point at which the ways diverge. And it is our destiny which makes available the alternatives we are given to choose from."

She listened intently but did not respond. She generally shied away from guys of her own age group. Her last steady boyfriend was four years older than her. They dated for three months before Olivia realised that the direction in which he was intending to lead her involved a permanent commitment. That did not bear serious thought and she brought the liaison to an immediate close. Since then she occasionally indulged a repeated request, but never a one-off invitation from the boys at college. The movie or the meal would be fine, but the expectations of what was to follow were never on her agenda. However, there was something about Matt that intrigued her, something fascinating. It was not only the way he spoke about subjects in which she shared an interest. There was something much more intangible, something almost, dare she say it, ethereal about Matt. She quickly pushed these thoughts away.

"We must agree to differ on that," she replied.

"You mean you have complete control over what you do and when and how you do it?"

"Right. Subject of course to the extent to which I may be directly affected by outside events."

He permitted himself a grin. "Right!" he remarked.

She figured that little purpose would be served by further attempting to articulate the differences in their stated views. A flight attendant interrupted them with an offer of drinks signalling a natural break in the conversation. Olivia took a Perrier, Matt a can of beer. They filled the rest of the flight with autobiographical details and shared their thoughts and their hopes and their ambitions.

The plane began its descent towards Pisa through layers of cumulo-nimbus. It occurred to Matt that the view of the tops of the clouds was one that had been denied to Renaissance man. They crossed the line that divided the crowded Riviera beaches from the inviting blueness of the Mediterranean. "Will you be coming to Florence at all?" asked Matt.

"Maybe. Maybe."

"Will I get to see you then?"

That question made her uncomfortable. "Who knows?" She began to fight the notion that she might actually want to go out of her way to hook up with this guy at some point.

Besides was it not always the way that the guys she sat next to on aeroplanes had only one thing in mind? Even allowing for his intellectual façade, she could not believe that Matt would be any different.

"Let me take your address and then I can at least send you a postcard," he said.

"OK." There did not seem much harm in that. She would give him the address of her school dorm. If he was that determined to stay in touch it would not take more than a call to directory enquiries to ascertain the whereabouts of her college. He already knew the department in which she was studying. He did not strike her as the type who would turn into a stalker. Besides he lived three and a half thousand miles away from her and was hardly likely to turn up on her doorstep unannounced. He reached down into his bag then handed her a notebook and a pen. He looked at what she had written and was visibly satisfied. He turned the page and wrote down his college address and telephone number as well as those of his parents, where he usually spent at least part of the University vacations. He also included the details of the pensioni where he would be staying in Florence. Then he ripped out the page and gave it to her.

After landing, Matt helped Olivia with her overhead baggage and carried it to the immigration line for her. He passed through the EEC gate and waited for her while she showed her passport to the officer and exchanged pleasantries in Italian. Again he waited. Her bag emerged some minutes after his. It was an awkward shape and very heavy. He manhandled it onto her trolley and walked through customs with her.

Once through customs she spotted her cousins who had arrived en masse to meet her. Matt stood and watched as she pushed on ahead to collect a full perm of hugs and kisses. Eventually she turned around and walked back to where he was standing.

"Thanks for helping with the luggage."

"That's fine." He looked deeply into her eyes. He wished he could spend more time with her, to get to know her better; to open himself up to her unconditionally. He wanted to find out everything that there was to know about her: what she had been like as a child, what she enjoyed eating, where she bought her clothes, her mother's maiden name, whether she had attended religion school.

"Goodbye then and stay in touch," he said.

"Yes, of course." She knew she did not sound convincing. "Arrivederci, Matt." She waved at him

The cousins picked up Olivia's bags and motioned her towards the exit. She took a couple of paces towards them then went back to where Matt was standing – transfixed, silent, still. She took his hand in hers and held it tightly. As their flesh touched, she was instantly consumed by an indefinable burst of energy. She tried hard to ignore it but it consumed her. He remained motionless, waiting for her to say something. She put her other hand on his shoulder and gave him a peck on the cheek. "Arrivederci, Matt," she repeated. "Maybe …" she paused. She loosened her grip. The energy dissipated. She reined herself back from saying anything that might be construed as suggesting any kind of commitment, however slight.

"No. Definitely," he said. "Definitely." He returned the modest embrace and then watched her follow her family out of the Terminal exit and into the hot August sunshine.

VII

Guidance

Florence. July 1983

Without warning, the dreams that lay in wait for him were ambushed. Impressions of Florence that for so long had filled his mind with their enticements became little more than the backdrop to a staccato newsreel continually playing in his thoughts. Images of Olivia constantly distracted Matt. The brush of her lips was the last thing he sensed before he went to sleep. When the half-light of dawn squeezed through the shutters, he made believe that she was lying next to him and looking at him with an expression that fused intelligence with sensuality. So much did he want to share it all with her that, during the time he spent in the presence of strangers, he allowed himself to make believe that she was with him.

Beauty surrounded him in every corner of every building and in every piazza. Walls whispered their secrets and told tales of a thousand trysts that had simmered in their shadows. Even the air was seeded with the sound of poetry and the intoxicating breath of enlightenment. The essence of his spirit was released in an outpouring of frenzied passion.

Rushing blindly from one gallery to another museum, between each awe-inspiring church and the next magnificent palazzo, he saw little and took in nothing. He hurried past the stoic countenances of statues and portraits that gazed down at him. They frowned at his failure to acknowledge them, yet were benevolent enough to pity his impatience.

After two days of unscripted wandering, he found himself in the Church of the Ognissanti, a block north of the Arno River. One of the frescoes attracted his attention. It was by Domenico Ghirlandaio and portrayed the Vespucci Family under the protection of the Madonna. Squeezed between the Madonna herself and a mysterious figure shrouded in a voluminous cloak, the hopeful face of a young man demanded Matt's attention. He considered the demand and then, involuntarily, and for the first time since he began his erratic assault on the city's treasures, he opened his guidebook. Officially, the identity of the young man was unknown but was believed to be Amerigo Vespucci. Born in 1454, Vespucci benefited from a Humanist education before joining the Medici Bank. In 1491 he was sent to Seville where the Medici owned a business that financed the fitting out of ships. Vespucci collaborated in the preparations for each of Columbus' second and third voyages across the Atlantic. In 1499, as dawn was about to break on a new century, he joined the movement of conquest westwards. Vespucci became a navigator and embarked on the first of a series of voyages of discovery. His eternal legacy was the name given to the New World – America.

Matt looked again at the unusual grouping in the fresco, then he reread the short sparse sentences that spattered snippets of information across the page. One by one the stated facts about Vespucci's life sounded a series of notes that ascended a major scale. Played together in sequences of chords, they convinced him to take hold of his mortal failings, to engage his processes of reason and, whatever his quest might be, to pursue it in an orderly manner.

He sought to gauge the emotions that his meeting with Olivia had exposed. His feelings seemed real enough. The truth was that they might never see each other again. Nevertheless, he continued to hope that perhaps he might run into her in the Piazza Signoria or at the entrance to the Duomo, that once again he might look into her dark brown eyes that had promised so much, but of which she had revealed so little. Hope could be eternal and hope was not all bad.

Focusing on what had brought him to the city in the first place, Matt decided to retrace the steps he had taken in manic strides over the previous days. He sat in a pew beneath the fresco and reminded himself of the itinerary he had planned before leaving England. He referred to the notebook that he always carried in his leather bag and nodded soberly. One by one he would pay homage to selected icons in their carefully lit shrines and honour them with the dignity they each deserved. Losing himself in the detail of his plan, he was interrupted by a robed figure indicating that the church was to be locked up for the day.

* * * * * * *

Pensioni Ghibellina was a few blocks north of San Lorenzo and was believed to originally have been built in the early sixteenth century as a house and studio for an artist by the name of Pier Paulo Forzetti, about whom Matt knew very little. From the street it looked to be an unremarkable building in a city of remarkable buildings. Its narrow frontage was crammed between two unlikely neighbours.

To the left was a grocery store packed with pungent cheeses, spiced salamis and wines of local vintage. Three generations of the Baldoni lived in the apartment over the store. The family had made its living from selling food to the locals for more than a hundred years.

The rundown edifice that flanked the right side of the pensioni was silent during daylight but came alive as darkness swallowed the silence of the street. From early evening and throughout the night, a disjunctive procession of men crept up to the battered front door and furtively waited for it to open. Hastily concluded bargaining was followed by sultry sessions of emotionless intercourse. From time to time, one or other of the bordello residents would sit out on the second floor balcony overlooking the street. Matt stared upwards as he walked towards the pensioni. A wink from heavily made-up eyes, a shuffle of unfettered breasts and the exhalation of cigarette smoke from brightly-painted lips elicited a grin. It was the only response he could summon – involuntary, abstracted but not repulsed.

Matt went to his room and took a shower. The antidiluvian plumbing rendered the experience consistently unpredictable. Sometimes sharp jets of scalding water burned layers of skin with unrestrained energy. Today, the best on offer was something akin to an old man with a prostate problem. Then he went to the kitchen. He was permitted to keep a few cold beers in the chest-like fridge. He took two with him into the courtyard together with a day old copy of the Guardian, the price of which had been negotiated long and hard with a street vendor near the Ponte alla Carraia.

The three-storied pensioni opened up so that its rear was almost twice the width of its frontage. Behind it was a square yard that occupied the entire centre of the city block of which the pensioni, the grocery store and the bordello formed the northern flank. One half was covered by a tangle of unkempt shrubbery and ageing bushes. The other was a paved rectangle occupied by two wooden benches at right angles to each other and separated by half of a large barrel in which there was a cherry tree. Matt was not alone.

He had exchanged a few words previously with Anni Tizot. Breakfast was served communally at two refectory tables, so that it was hard to avoid a passing acquaintance with the other guests, many of whom stayed for two or three weeks at a time.

Anni was no more than five foot three. What had once inclined towards curvaceous had given up the fight to stay firm and would comfortably be termed voluptuous. Her hair flamed red in her younger days. Now it was faded auburn and waved in wild and straggling curls. The style was idiosyncratic and yet not so far from the rubescent tresses that adorned Botticelli's heroines of which Matt was so enamoured. Sometimes appearing green and sometimes blue, the colour of her eyes depended not so much on the tones and the shades by which she was illuminated, but switched according to her mood – green when mellow, blue when excited. They were eyes that had seen much and knew even more. Anni possessed a wisdom that was innately female, timeless, earthy, a mind that was sharp yet subtle and a charm that was beguiling yet adventurous. She looked to be in her middle fifties but could have been older.

Her name sounded French, though her accent betrayed elements of something more guttural and indeterminately mittel-European. When asked about her background she would chuckle elusively and come out with something along the lines of 'I am a bit of this and a bit of that, though I have always believed that there is something of the gipsy in me'. In addition to French and Italian and English, Matt had heard Anni conversing in German and a Slavic language that he thought might have been Polish. She switched from one to the other with the practised ease of a racing driver shifting gears around a hairpin bend.

Anni sat on the bench that faced west. The sun was on the verge of disappearing behind the roofs of the buildings opposite. She wore a white cotton chemise and a full-length cream linen pleated skirt. She was reading a paperback in French. It was Andre Gide's 'La porte etroite'.

Matt sat down at the farthest end of the other bench. He opened his Guardian at the Arts page, then took a couple of pulls from the first bottle of Moretti. Pretending not to notice him, Anni nevertheless watched Matt over the top of large-framed tortoiseshell spectacles that perched on the end of her freckled nose. She removed them and addressed him before he could put the bottle down and concentrate on what the reviewers had to say on the subject of the current cinema releases.

"Today you have calmed down a little, I think. No?"

Somewhat taken aback, Matt failed to respond.

"Since you arrived here something has been on your mind, but you are beginning to be comfortable with it?"

The mish-mash accent and the certainty with which she

spoke was disarming. His natural tendency was to dodge uncomfortable truths. Put in the form of a question, however, her words nevertheless constituted a statement with which he was unable to disagree.

"Well, sort of."

"Well, sort of!" she mimicked him, then giggled again, mischievously. "You are so English."

"I am?"

"Reserved."

"You hardly know me."

"You say much by the way you act. The way you walk. The expression on your face. I notice these things."

"How so?"

"It's my job to notice things."

"Your job?"

She looked at him with eyes deepening blue and nodded abstractedly.

"You're a psychologist?"

"You could say that, but not really. I do a number of things but at the moment I am a writer."

"Really?" Matt sounded impressed.

"Well sort of." Once again she mimicked him.

"What do you write?"

"Nothing profound," she said flapping the book in her right hand. "Travel guides. I write travel guides. 'Les Guides Aesthetiques'. In fact even that isn't quite right. I make contributions to the guides and also edit some of them."

Matt was familiar with Les Guides Aesthetiques, though his 'A' level French was not sophisticated enough to grapple with some of the detailed analysis of the art, philosophy and history with which the series of books enlightened and educated as much as guided and informed its readers.

"I help others to discover places and to learn about them."

"In French?"

She smiled elusively. "Language is just a code. Intelligence and observation are the language of the mind, no matter which tongue may be used to communicate them. The mind reflects upon the things that the eyes see and which the brain then analyses. Sometimes the mind responds to these things consciously. More often than not it is the unconscious responses that are the important ones, the ones that lead to the brain making decisions once it has made its discoveries." Anni chose her words carefully and constructed her sentences as if engaged in a translation exercise as part of an important examination.

"And I suppose you are in the course of discovering Florence for your readers."

"You might say that. What is important is that the discoveries you may make in the physical world will only assume real meaning when they have an application to the inner self, to what you believe in."

"I think I understand what you mean," said Matt, taking a swig of beer. "It's all about where you're going in life."

"If you like. You have a destination?"

"For the next few weeks it's studying the paintings and art here in Florence and then in the rest of Italy."

"And that will lead you where?"

"To my degree."

"That is only short term. Longer term there is a greater place for you to be at, somewhere you aim to stay for a while."

"I guess that I would like to have some kind of a career that involves using my knowledge of art and what that means."

"That is tangible, Matt. But where is your spirit taking you? In part it is already written, there is destiny after all, but there are still choices offered to you and decisions for you to make."

"You believe in that?"

She smiled at him knowingly, careful not to give away too much of what she knew herself, keen to ensure that he could appreciate whatever truths she felt confident enough to share with him. She made her position clear, "without a belief in destiny, it can be frustrating for some to navigate the course of life."

"Do you think that as part of life that we are each destined to meet our perfect match, our ideal partner?"

She said nothing and waited for him to continue.

"And even having met, the two may then not be destined to spend the rest of their lives together?"

"You have met someone?"

"I didn't say so."

"Of course not, but my guess is that that's so."

Matt was not in the habit of baring his emotions to strangers, but there was something about Anni Tizot that he trusted. Stripping away layers of reserve, he decided that it might do him some good to unburden his feelings and share them with her and even to seek her advice.

"I met this girl on the way over to Italy. And. Well, she seems to be everything I think I ever wanted. Bright, interesting, pretty. But there was more than that."

"More than that?"

"There was like a spiritual connection; it's like we were supposed to meet and be together."

"She is in Florence?"

"Pisa. Staying with family."

"Italian?"

"American actually. Italian family. I haven't stopped thinking about her since we said goodbye at the airport. The fact is that I may never see her again."

"If you are destined to meet, then you will."

"But when?"

"So impatient, youth. Destiny will take its course. Often it pays little attention to what may be perceived as the immediate needs of the human mind and body."

"But I know, at least I think I know, that maybe, maybe, this is the woman I'm supposed to be with, if that makes any sense."

"It does."

"Is it possible that something like this can happen after only one meeting?"

"From what you say, it has, but remember, destiny is as much about coming to terms with the past as it is fulfilling what may yet come to pass."

"Meaning?"

"Meaning just that."

"I don't understand."

"You mean that you're not yet ready to understand.

"And when will I be ready?"

"You'll know when you are."

He thought her answer to be imbued with sophistry and sophistry had never attracted him as a system of thought. He decided not to pursue the subject any further. After exchanging some pleasantries about their respective stays in Florence, Matt asked Anni about her background. Her tale featured a once landed family fallen on hard times, a derelict chateau in the Loire Valley and an Austrian playboy. He had seduced her widowed grandmother after the First World War then proceeded to gamble away her fortune and lose her future at the tables in Monte Carlo. Her description of childhood in the small village of Chenonceau was interrupted by the owner of the pensioni who called her to the phone.

* * * * * * *

The following morning Matt went back to the beginning of the itinerary that his uncharacteristic behaviour of the previous days had led him to abandon. First there was the shrine. Like all good disciples he must worship at the shrine. Walking into the Uffizi, he knew that he had been there a couple of days before. A ticket stub in the back pocket of his Levis was incontrovertible evidence of the fact.

He intended to view all of what the gallery had on display in the course of two or three visits. With so much else to take in and armed with a list of additional and lesser known 'must-see' places provided by Anni Tizot, he feared he may not have enough time.

He began to work his way methodically through the galleries of the East Corridor, particularly enjoying Giotto's Ognissante Madonna and Piero della Francesca's portraits of the Duke and Duchess of Urbino. Even though he was prepared to be patient, there was one part of the gallery for which he was not prepared to wait any longer. Further along the East Corridor were his favourite Botticellis. Sandro Botticelli, a mesmeriser, a creator of obscure tableaux for which no completely satisfactory interpretations had yet been found in five hundred years of trying; an idealist and possibly a romantic but whose later work had been badly affected by the falsity of the fanatic

Savonarola. Savonarola whose extremism had polluted the perfume with ugliness masquerading in words that praised God. 'Thou shalt not take the name of the Lord thy God in vain' ran the words of the third commandment; Savonarola had and others had taken notice of him including Sandro Botticelli, who had even thrown some of his own works onto the Bonfire of the Vanities.

Matt found it hard to believe that he had already stood in the Botticelli room and taken in nothing. The events of the previous two days were a blur from which the only clear image to emerge was that of Olivia Giorgianni. He suddenly felt that she was with him, looking over his shoulder. The place she occupied was not centre stage but in the background, somewhere from which she was able to keeping an eye on what was happening,

If the Birth of Venus had been Matt's favourite Botticelli before his visit, its supremacy was to be put to numerous challenges. Viewing the piece close-up was an experience that was light years away from the flatness of photographs in books and the posters that adorned the walls of classrooms and student bed-sits.

The story of a myth was contained in a single panel; Venus, the embodiment of beauty, a being divinely conceived but who was nevertheless born on earth. The more he looked at it the more he saw. The more he saw the more there was to see. He took his notebook out of his bag and began to jot down a few thoughts, reducing an experience that approached religious dimensions to a few savvy comments he might include in answering an exam question the following year. 'Botticelli's symbolism was an allegory for the awakening of the spirit of mankind following the chaos of the Dark Ages; discuss with reference to the imagery employed in his known major works between 1480 and 1500.' 'To what extent was the decline in Botticelli's art a direct result of the assumption of power in Florence by Savonarola in 1494?' It irked him to think that the magnificence of the man, the soul of an artist might be trivialised in such a way.

From the Venus he turned to La Primavera, the Spring, with its bucolic images and its symbols of rebirth. Then there was a painting to which he had not previously paid much attention, Pallas and the Centaur. To the left, the Centaur, half man, half beast, wild, lawless and inhospitable; a slave to animal passions. To the right, the goddess Pallas, better known as Athena, city protectress, Goddess of War and practical reason, essentially urban and civilised. The right hand of the Goddess grabbed the forelock of the Centaur whose pained facial expression was somewhere between horror and fright; horror at the thought of falling into the power of what was good and pure; fright at the prospect that in this confrontation his unrestrained and his freedom would be curtailed.

Said by some to symbolise the triumph of reason over instinct, Matt did not accept such a simplistic and obvious view as being the sole intent of the artist. Had it been so, surely Botticelli would not have bothered to litter the piece with as many symbols as there were: the imposing wall with waves of foliage that spilled along its summit; the Centaur's bow finger arched as though preparing to shoot, an attempt to assert his independence in the face of the predicament in which he now found himself; the curious red thong that fell across his shoulder; Pallas Athena's axe, upright, steady but the point of which was seemingly occupied by a turret: a tower of power, a symbol of steady government and not a weapon of imposition; Pallas' clothing decorated with the symbol of the Medici, the three interlocking rings – Botticelli's tribute to Lorenzo Il Magnifico by whom it was thought the piece had been commissioned.

Matt did not see the theme of the painting as a confrontation with a winner and a loser, but rather the beginning of a series of events that would lead to a reconciliation between the opposing forces that governed the human spirit. Botticelli's earlier work had been influenced by Marsilo Ficino, a Humanist philosopher much favoured by Lorenzo de'Medici. Ficino referred both to platonic ideas and to Christian ideology. He believed that the nature of love was a combination of earthly desires on the one hand and a spiritual longing towards God on the other. He considered that these forces were opposites and that the conflict was experienced in human terms when physical sensuality on the one hand clashed with the intellect and the spirit.

Matt saw something of himself in the Centaur, though not perhaps as unbridled in the extent of the excesses of its lawless passions, and something of Olivia in Athena. Perhaps the hand that grabbed the Centaur's forelock was a hand that kept him at a distance, until it was time for them to be together, the small ship in the background a symbol of the journey that one or other of them would need to take if destiny decreed that they should be together.

He wanted to savour the magnificence of the Botticellis, so decided to leave and return to view the rest of the Uffizi the following day. In the meantime there were plenty of other things to see and he decided to walk along the river to the underrated Museo di Storia della Scienza.

Leaving the Uffizi was like plunging through a time warp. After spending the day in the company of the spirits of the greatest artists in history it was enervating to find himself disgorged onto the hot dusty streets teeming with tourists. There those who came to see, those who had come because they thought that they should and even those who did not know why they were there at all: noisy students from Paris and Pittsburgh and all points in between who chewed gum and whose main concern was to smoke cannabis and make believe that their experience would thereby be enhanced; pot-bellied Germans whose idea of a holiday meant passing time and space between regular meals of impossibly large proportions; pale-skinned housewives from Surbiton and Solihull with novels by Catherine Cookson and Joanna Trollope sticking out of straw bags, ticking off monuments like items on a grocery list.

That night the serenity of his day was violently swept aside by the frenzied turbulence of his dreams. One followed another in quick succession. He could only hang onto images from the last of them. He was in the dining room of the pensioni. The doors onto the courtyard were open. The brightness of a summer's day traced sharp-edged shadows over carpets of an iridescent hue. Olivia was with him. They were sitting on mismatched antique wooden chairs. Set a little apart, their heads were turned slightly in the direction of each other. Olivia was holding an open book in her left hand. A larger book lay across Matt's lap. Its pages were covered in geometrical patterns and symbols that looked to be derived from an ancient language that no-one could remember how to read. A bow-legged man with a thick beard wearing overalls smudged with paint and whose face was in shadow stood in front of them and repeatedly urged them to move their chairs together. Outside, the sky began to cloud over. An ambient breeze that was cooling them down suddenly assumed the force of a hurricane wind. There was no time to shut the doors.

Matt and Olivia stood up and left their books on the chairs. They turned and walked to the doorway to watch the clouds thickening and to feel the rush of cold air. As they stood there, holding hands, bewitched by what was happening in the sky, each of them, in turn, was grabbed from behind, separated from the other very roughly, then thrown forcibly into the storm by two anonymous beings. Matt's abductor was decidedly female. Faceless and sly, she was wearing a red dress. Olivia was taken by an altogether more foreboding creature that proclaimed the glory of God and whose features had been entirely replaced by the sign of the cross painted over its face in blood. The forces that drove their abductors were omnipotent and neither Matt nor Olivia was in any way able to resist them

The wind blasted into the empty room with tremendous power. It swept everything in its path out through the open doors into the sky and beyond the visible horizon. After Nature had finished having its say, the room was stripped bare. The bow-legged man was now naked and sat cross-legged on the bare floorboards. All that was left of the paraphernalia that had previously filled the room were the two books. Both were now closed and face down on the floor, so that whatever may have been printed on their front covers was invisible. The naked man was saying something under his breath. It sounded like 'previty', though it was a term with which Matt was not familiar.

The next morning he went down and found Anni alone in the dining room. He was relieved to note that everything was in its place.

"Come and take your breakfast with me," she said.

He went to the buffet that was laid out in a small anteroom and loaded his plate with fruit and cheese and some cold meat. He sat down opposite her.

"Your night was disturbed," she said with a degree of certainty.

"How do you know that?"

She raised her eyebrows. "Intuition."

He described the dream to her, or at least as many of the details that he could remember.

"What do you think of that, Anni?"

"It was your dream, what do you think?"

"Somehow I thought it linked me to events in the past, events in which I may have played a part, but events of which I know nothing." He paused and her silent anticipation encouraged him to continue. "These events were, or should I say are, a part of a cycle that isn't yet complete. Although the dream had an ending, it was as if the whole experience was merely the beginning of something else, perhaps another cycle of events."

"Have you had such a dream before?"

"Not that I remember. But, even though it is my first visit to Florence, it was as if I had been here before, but I was forced to leave, as if what happened in the dream was something that happened a long time ago, but at the same time is part of something that has yet to happen."

Anni sipped her coffee thoughtfully. "Part of your destiny in this life is to resolve outstanding issues from a previous life. Somehow I think that you have a karmic score to settle."

"Whatever that means."

"Sometimes it's hard to be sure about anything. But

clearly your spirit has been unsettled by something while you have been here."

Matt looked at her a little sceptically.

"For days you were physically affected. Now your psyche has been unbalanced. You remember this dream in great detail and you have said yourself that you believe it relates to past events. Once you solve the conundrum suggested by this dream, you will find your balance again."

"I wonder how I would do that," Matt said, half to himself and not too sure what to make of her observation.

"Look around you. Draw on everything with which you come into contact. Life is everywhere around you. Though you should realise that there may be no instant solution. It may take time, even years, many years."

"Is there anything you think I should know that might help me?"

"There is much to know about life, sadly there is not enough time for most of us to learn as much as we would like to."

"Up until now I always believed that everything I needed to know about life might be found in great art," said Matt.

"Everything?"

"Art in the broadest sense. The Arts. All human emotion is there".

"But that is not the only thing that you will find in great art," she responded. "And I also think that you will find that much of what you ought to know about life will be found elsewhere."

"That I ought to know or that I need to know?"

She smiled a knowing smile and gazed at Matt with the look of someone who knew more than he did and certainly more than she was presently minded to let on.

"Matt, you are an intelligent man but there is still much for you to learn and then to understand about yourself. It will be revealed to you gradually. Knowledge will be derived from many people and from many places. One of them is the experience of life itself, another is your own soul. Reach into your soul and you will find the source from which everything else in your life flows – the immutability of the spirit, beauty, romance and also the truth of love."

"If I manage to learn about even one of those in my lifetime I will count myself a lucky man."

"There you are," exclaimed Anni gleefully. "You are already reaching into your soul and beginning to understand!"

* * * * * * *

That day Matt visited the Accademia and the Bargello, the latter reviving some of the more extreme images of his dream and its sense of previty. It was nothing to do with the sumptuous collection of statues that included Michaelangelo's seductive Bacchus and Donatello's ambiguous David. It was a sense, a feeling that he picked up from the building itself and the chill he felt when he stood alone in the courtyard, suddenly overwhelmed by a sense of spiritual emptiness.

He was keen to discuss it with Anni but when he returned to the pensioni he was told that she had checked out unexpectedly and travelled on somewhere else.

VIII

Declaration

Tuscany. July 1983

After the seemingly endless meal that they ate outside on the patio, Olivia's aunt and uncle kept her talking until very late. Even Magdalena, Olivia's cousin, began to flag. Olivia's spoken Italian was passable and certainly more fluent than her Uncle Paulo's faltering English. By midnight, she was beginning to feel the strain. Uncle Paulo's main concern was for his younger brother's marriage. It was a topic that Olivia refused to discuss on his terms, as to do so would be disloyal to her mother. She side-stepped his direct questions, ignored his pronouncements on the subject, then deferred to Magdalena when she could convincingly pretend that she had failed to pick up a grammatical nuance or a colloquialism.

Eventually Magdalena interceded on her behalf and accompanied her upstairs. A fold-down bed was set up for Olivia in Magdalena's bedroom. Magdalena perched on the end of it while Olivia changed in to her pyjamas.

Tall and thin, Magdalena Giorgianni's most endearing feature was a broad, dimpled grin that was never slow to emerge. Her nut brown eyes and full lips were almost identical to Olivia's. She wore her hair cut short in an asymmetric bob that was both quirky and attractive.

It was more than a year since they had seen each other, when Magdalena had visited New York. Nevertheless, Magdalena exchanged frequent letters and cards with Olivia and they never failed to phone on each other's birthday and at Christmas. At fourteen, Magdalena spent six months with Olivia's family while her mother successfully fought a debilitating illness. She learned to speak English and developed a close bond of kinship with Olivia. As an only child, Olivia revelled in the company of her cousin who was eighteen months older than her. By contrast, Magdalena was the youngest of six, the only daughter and had been doted on all her life as the baby of her family. Magdalena's arrival brought an unexpected bonus, it signalled the beginning of a cease-fire between Olivia's constantly warring parents. Sadly, the peace was fragile and unravelled as soon as Magdalena returned home to Italy.

Magdalena's home had always been filled with exuberance and fun, Olivia's with arguments and rancour. They each carried their respective backgrounds in their personalities like badges of allegiance. Magdalena wore hers proudly, Olivia tried to shut her eyes and to pretend she came from a place that was altogether more tranquil than it was.

"Who was the guy?" Magdalena had been itching to ask since the moment Olivia stepped through the arrival gate some hours earlier.

"Someone I met on the plane."

"What's his name?"

"Does it matter?"

"Of course it matters," replied Magdalena making mild mischief.

Olivia sighed. "Matt," she said as if pronouncing the name alone would explain everything. It did not.

"Matt seemed as interested in you as you were in him."

"Who said I was interested in him?"

"You closed your eyes when you kissed him!"

"You're imagining things!" Olivia's attempted denial was unconvincing. "Or perhaps you've been watching too much television."

"And after you kissed him goodbye, he stood quite still. He didn't take his eyes off you while you walked over to join us."

Olivia had finished sorting herself out. She went over to the bed and sat down cross-legged on the pillows. Magdalena had not yet concluded her cross-examination.

"Do you think you'll see him again?"

"Unlikely. He's at Cambridge University in England. I don't think he's got any plans to come to the States and I don't reckon on going to England."

"Do you have a boyfriend back home?"

"Not at the moment. I gave them up for Lent and haven't got back into the habit since. How about you?"

Magdalena slid off the end of the bed and went to her dressing table. She picked up a framed photograph of a handsome young man in his mid-twenties. He was sitting at a table in a street café with a cup of coffee in front of him. He wore a short-sleeved shirt that was open at the neck to reveal a simple, gold crucifix nestling on a thick mat of dark hair.

"This is Aldo."

"Known him long?" asked Olivia, taking the photograph in her hand and making a show of admiring it.

"A very long time. Since I was maybe fourteen. His family knows mine well, though we only started to date recently."

"Is it serious?"

"About as serious as you can get."

"And you didn't write and tell me?"

"I wanted to tell you about him face-to-face."

"That's serious. Did you sleep with him yet?" Olivia handed back the photograph. Magdalena replaced it on the dressing-table.

"Olivia! Really!" Magdalena's tone of offence was genuine. "I sleep with no-one until my wedding night."

"Still following that good old Catholic religion?"

"It's very important to me and it's very important to Aldo too. How would you like it if I asked you whether you'd slept with someone?"

"I'd tell you that I have. "

"Was he special?"

"Not very. Just persuasive. And before you ask, no, it didn't do much for me."

"If he'd been special it would have been different. Still, you can wait for someone special to come along and marry him. Then it will be good for you."

"Married? You're kidding. That's the last thing I want."

"Don't say such things. Everyone should want to get married."

"Try telling that to my parents. The state of their relationship tells me that some people should be legally prevented from getting married. Every day one of them phones me to complain about the other. I don't understand why they don't call it quits and get a divorce."

"It's that good old Catholic religion I expect," said Magdalena without a tinge of irony. "Divorce is a very bad thing."

"That's what they both say to me, but I figure that if they hate each other as much as they keep telling me they do, then there's no point in them staying together."

"So you're not sure about marriage and you didn't enjoy sex. Maybe you should become a nun," said Magdalena deadpan.

"Ha, ha! Who would want to become a nun? All that self-pity and humiliation, not to mention the cold rooms and bad food. Feh! I know what I want to do with my life."

"Which is?"

"Finish my degree. Take a Masters. Teach undergraduates. Maybe take a PhD and hopefully write books on history."

"That simple?"

"I'll be doing something I enjoy, making enough to live on and I won't be dependent on anyone."

"None of that would stop you being married."

"You're right. It wouldn't. But unless the right guy comes along, I can promise you that I won't go out of my way to find him."

"Maybe you don't need to. Maybe this Matt is the one for you."

"Magadalena, enough! I'm tired. I'm going to sleep."

* * * * * * *

A couple of days later, after Olivia had met every cousin that Magdalena's parents could unearth, they took the train into Florence. Olivia had not been there since she was too young to appreciate anything of its culture and its beauty. From the station they made their way to the Duomo and then to the Uffizzi.

They began by working through the galleries of the East Corridor. They entered the Botticelli gallery and Olivia stopped to read what her guidebook had to say about its content. Magdalena stood by her side, looking around, then suddenly grabbed her cousin's arm.

"Over there! Look!"

"What is it?"

"Isn't that your Matt?" Magdalena pointed towards the young man who stood in front of Pallas and the Centaur with his back to them and who was putting a notebook into a leather shoulder bag. Olivia froze.

"Let's go over and surprise him," said Magdalena enthusiastically.

"No. I don't want to."

"What do you mean, you don't want to? If we don't hurry he'll be gone. Look he's leaving."

"Let him," said Olivia resolutely.

"You stay there and I'll catch up with him." Magdalena made to do so.

"Don't. Please don't"

"Why not?"

Olivia rapidly reviewed numerous possible scenarios and mentally calculated the possible outcomes of renewing her contact with Matt. She refused to loosen her grip on her emotions. She could see nothing positive coming from it. "Because I'm with you. We're enjoying ourselves and I don't want to talk to him, or anyone else for that matter. There's no point. Come on and let's look at these amazing paintings."

Magdalena knew not to push it further, but was at a loss to understand the vehemence of Olivia's stated position.

Once they started to study the Botticellis – La Primavera, The Birth of Venus and Pallas and the Centaur – thoughts of anything else were forgotten. Magdalena never tired of any of any of them. Olivia thought back to her conversation with Matt on the subject of the 'Venus'. She recalled that he had referred to it as 'the mingling of the heavens with the physical world' and murmured the words half to herself. She was yet to be convinced about the existence of heaven.

"What was that?" asked Magdalena.

"Nothing. What do you make of 'Pallas and the Centaur'?" said Olivia, pointing towards the piece.

"I'm not sure that I can guess."

Olivia read from her guidebook, "it says here that Athena is a guardian and the centaur has forced his way into an area from which he is forbidden. Apparently, the centaurs were hurtful creatures who liked to hunt innocent nymphs. On this occasion, Athena has foiled the centaur's plans. The picture represents the supremacy of chastity over lust. How apposite!"

"You can mention it to Aldo when you next see him," joked Magdalena.

Later on, they made their way over to the Palazzo Vecchia. They were soon in the vast Salone di Cinquecento, originally built as a council assembly hall. When Olivia reached the middle of the room, she stopped to view Vasari's frescoes, but suddenly became very queasy.

"What's the matter?" asked Magadalena solicitously.

"I don't know. Let me sit for a moment. It'll pass."

She made her way over to one of a number of rows of

plastic chairs that were laid out for a presentation of some sort. She flopped down into one.

"Water?" Olivia nodded. Magadalena reached into her bag and produced a small bottle of aqua minerale. She unscrewed the lid. Olivia took it gratefully and sipped at it slowly. She handed back the bottle then leaned her elbows on her thighs and supported her forehead with the palms of her hands. She closed her eyes and, for a few moments, she was still and silent. Then she started to speak in a weak voice that barely sounded like her own. It was cracked and nasal and high. "It's probably something to do with all these crowds of people."

"Crowds?"

"In here. There's so many people in here and they're all talking at once. And the smell of that food."

"Olivia, there's hardly anyone in here, no-one's making a noise and there's no smell." Olivia's curious remarks coupled with her sudden physical infirmity began to worry Magdalena.

"I can smell something very pungent. It's like roasting meat."

"You're imagining it. Open your eyes and see for yourself."

"Give me a minute, please," croaked Olivia.

The brouhaha of the crowd began to diminish until all was quiet, save for the echo of footfall on the floor and the muted conversation of admiring tourists. She began to breathe more easily, but before she could open her eyes, she began to hear music. It was the sound of a lute and the tune was one with which she thought she was familiar.

"Olivia, what is the matter?" Magdalena sat down and put her arm around her cousin's shoulder.

"That tune. I recognise it."

"What tune?"

"The one that the lute is playing."

Magdalena shook Olivia very gently. "Come on, look. There's no-one playing any lute."

Olivia opened her eyes and, as she did, the sound of the music faded away. She could see for herself that there was no-one playing a lute. The smell of roasting meat had dispersed and, as Magdalena had stated, there were very few people in the Salone. Olivia was quite pale. She made to stand up, but her knees wobbled and she sat down again. She took a few deep breaths and her head began to clear. With Magdalena's assistance, she stood up and started walking gingerly towards the exit.

"Maybe we should take a cab and head back to the station," suggested Magdalena.

Olivia agreed and they picked their way down the stairs and out onto the Piazza Signoria. Olivia was fully recovered and walking normally. They headed across the Piazza in the general direction of the Stazione Santa Maria Novella. Groups of tourists were scattered around the grand piazza in even clusters. Some were ensconced with their guides, others gathered around a couple of street performers.

Close to the corner of Via del Calzaiuoli, Magdalena noticed a taxi pulling in and about to disgorge its passengers onto the piazza. Before she could say anything, Olivia's attention was caught by something happening in the opposite direction. The unmistakeable sound of a lute began to ring across towards them. Olivia stopped dead and watch the musician who had begun to play. A young man wearing a period costume, perhaps intended to be of Renaissance vintage, was standing on a wooden box playing a lute. The instrument's case was on the ground and open in front of him and in which he had strategically placed a few coins.

"That was it," exclaimed Olivia. She started to walk towards the performance.

The taxi was about to be commandeered by a Japanese family wearing identical baseball caps and carrying vast amounts of camera equipment. Magdalena gave up the idea of sprinting for it and craned her neck to see what had attracted Olivia's interest. Magdalena scuttled after her cousin and caught up with her. "That was what?" she asked.

"The tune I heard in the palazzo."

"You mean the tune you thought you heard."

"I heard it alright. I know it, too. I'm sure I've heard it before."

They joined the audience that had gathered around the lutanist. They listened politely. At the end of the piece they applauded dutifully and some of the tourists threw coins of modest denominations into the instrument case. The musician beamed at them gratefully and made some adjustments with the tuning pegs.

"Signor, excuse me," said Olivia. "Can you tell me the name of the piece that you just played?"

"It doesn't have a name."

Olivia looked puzzled.

"It's a piva by a composer called Ragaci. A piva was a type of dance popular in the Renaissance era."

"It has a great melody and I've always enjoyed it when I've heard it."

It was the musician's turn to look puzzled. "Signorina, I don't think that you could have heard this particular piva before."

"I'm fairly sure that I have. It is very distinctive."

"Indeed, and you're right about that. However, it has only recently been discovered in a book of intabolatura that has been lost for more than a hundred years. I came across it in the archive of the University where I am studying for my masters degree in Renaissance music. I'm certain that there are no other copies of the book that survive and that no performance of this piece has yet been recorded."

Although she was prepared to accept what he said, Olivia knew she recognised the unnamed piva and maybe even the name 'Ragaci'. "Maybe it was something similar," she said speculatively.

"Of course, signorina."

Olivia reached into her bag for her purse and added a five hundred lire note to the musician's haul. He started to play another piece.

Magdalena put her bag down on the ground, folded her arms and started to listen, but Olivia's mind was still on the previous piece. The melancholy mood of what the musician was playing fragmented her concentration and swept away the memories that she was earnestly trying to piece together. Oblivious to Magdalena and, indeed everything else that surrounded her, Olivia began to stroll in the direction of the Santa Maria Novella.

* * * * * * *

The day before Matt Dayton left Florence, he sent Olivia a postcard. On the back of a reproduction of Botticelli's Venus he scribbled, "nothing mythological about this!"

It was only once his train to Rome pulled out of the station that he accepted he would not run into Olivia again during the course of his Italian visit. He sent her another card from Rome. The text he inscribed to accompany a picture of the Trevi Fountain was "… and yes, I will come back. Will you?"

On returning home he was disappointed not to have received anything from her. Neither was there anything waiting for him when he arrived at college for the start of the new academic year. He explained this to himself by assuming she had lost his address. After all it had been written on a loose piece of paper and she had been rushing off with her family. She could easily have misplaced it. So he set about writing a letter to her. In between elaborate descriptions of Renaissance architecture and appreciation of galleries and museums, he told her how much he'd enjoyed meeting her, hoping that one day they might meet again. After much thought he signed it 'love, Matt' though decided against adding an 'x'.

Waiting for a reply was agonising. He calculated the turnaround time between the date upon which he had posted the letter to her, the time she would take to compose and mail her response and the time it would take to reach him. He guessed two weeks at the shortest and perhaps four at the longest. Each morning's deliveries were keenly awaited, inspected as soon as they were sorted and greeted with disappointment.

Had it not been for the exhortations of her room-mates, Olivia would probably not have bothered to reply, though Matt was not to have known that. Eventually she did. As much as the persuasion of others, something told her that she ought not to ignore the nagging suspicion she had that maybe there genuinely was something important about her connection with Matt. No matter how tenuous, she would hold onto it, at least for the time being.

Nearly six weeks down the line, when Matt was on the verge of giving up hope, her letter arrived. He read it and reread it again and again. It was a relatively brief account of her trip to Italy and a description of her college schedule for the new academic year. It was simply signed 'yours, Olivia'.

He searched for the nuance of something more than mere friendship, but failed to find it. He seized upon a reference she made to her study of Plato to discuss the concept of love. His language was carefully chosen, the expression of his ideas rooted in academia and laced with appropriate references. Nevertheless the spark was lit and it prompted a speedier reply than its predecessor. From then on the correspondence flourished, though it seldom strayed from a path that was littered with intellectualism, guided by summaries of their studies and supplemented with euphemistic notes about their social lives. Conspicuous by their absence were any mentions of any relationship that either may have had with a member of the opposite sex.

Of course Matt had girlfriends. Some lasted for a few weeks, a couple even for months, others were one-night stands. Then there were weeks at a time when he would not bother or struck out and became depressed. There were those he liked who chose not to like him and those who liked him but for whom he did not care. There were blue-eyed blondes from the Home Counties who had attended minor public schools and rode horses and self-confident girls with regional accents who were strident and earthy and independent. He was hung up for a while on a beautiful Asian girl whose family had been thrown out of Uganda by Idi Amin. But the interminable demands of her studies to become a lawyer sounded the death knell of their relationship sooner than he would have wanted. All of it was terribly normal. But there were always the letters from Olivia and his conviction that buried between the lines of her incisive prose were messages of affection, perhaps longing and possibly even desire.

Matt planned a trip to the States for the following summer. He was disappointed to learn that Olivia was scheduled to take an Oriental cruise with a group from college. He thought about going to the Far East so that he might hook up with her in Hong Kong or Singapore or Bangkok. But that part of the globe held little interest for him, the flights were expensive and the opportunities to spend time with her alone would be limited. Besides, he remembered that all great movements of conquest moved westward. So instead he decided to take a break and head south for Morocco with a group of friends and resolved to make it to the States when the outlook seemed more favourable.

IX

Preparations

Florence. November 1515

"Still not finished," said Tommaso Salcoiati as the carriage passed the triumphal arch that had been erected in the Piazza di Santa Trinita. "Leoni X laborum victori," he added, reading the legend inscribed across the top of the arch. Though by no means the most extravagant of the city's decorations, it was constructed in the shape of a circular building with the features of a castle that covered the piazza and was surrounded by twenty-two square pillars between which hung a series of magnificent tapestries.

"Nevertheless it's all looking splendid," observed Tedice. He pointed towards a large bust of Romulus and then to a number of other beautiful statues that had been transported from various corners of the city and sited around the piazza.

The buzz of activity that a dry day engendered in the Santa Trinita was mirrored along the entirety of the route that had been mapped out to mark the pope's triumphal procession. It would start at the city gates and finish at the Piazza di Santa Maria Novella. Everywhere, Florentines were preparing for the party to end all parties and working frenetically to finish the decorations. So badly had the weather affected progress that, the previous day, the pope was politely turned away and invited to return when preparations were complete.

The other occupants of the carriage were less concerned with what was happening on the streets than they were with the business in hand. Massimo Salcoiati and Mosciano Vannozzi were reviewing the principal conditions of what was proposed for Maria Chiara's dowry. They were deeply engrossed in their deliberations as the carriage pulled off the piazza and turned down a side street that would lead them towards the Borgo Ognissante and the Palazzo Tolosini.

"Barring one or two points of detail, your estimates have proved correct," Massimo said to Tommaso. "You and Mosciano have done a fine job in these negotiations. We have an arrangement that is more than pleasing."

"The problem will be persuading the Tolosini to delay notarising the terms and making the formal public announcement without seeming insincere," added Vannozzi.

"Indeed," added Tommaso.

"The delay in the pope's progress has hardly helped us," observed Massimo.

"If we are forced into agreeing an early date, I still believe that we will not be disadvantaged," said Tommaso confidently.

"The problem, however, is that such points of detail as remain unresolved are of less importance to us than the postponement of the public announcement," replied Massimo.

"To concede on the details will not be seen as a sensible quid pro quo with which to seek the delay; to argue over them interminably will seem petty and unreasonable," said Tommaso, summarising the dilemma.

"Once the details are agreed, Tolosini will want to push ahead with haste," added Vannozzi thoughtfully. "And that won't be limited to the public meeting and the notarisation of the terms."

"You mean he will be pushing to fix a date for the ring day too?" queried Massimo.

"As well as a date for the transfer of our sister to the Palazzo Tolosini," added Tommaso, almost matter of fact.

"That would be consistent with his usual way of doing things," said Tedice who had become involved as the dowry negotiations opened the way for a broad-ranging discussion on a number of matters of mutual commercial interest. Expansion of the Salcoiati banking operation with the establishment of a branch in Rome left Massimo with less time to focus on his trading interests. Employing his natural flair for commerce and enormous appetite for hard work, Tedice had persuaded his father to leave him in charge of the trading operations with little supervision and was proving to be a great success.

Not much more than a year younger than Tommaso, Tedice revered and respected his older brother, quite apart from regarding him as his closest friend. It was Tommaso who played the key role in the dowry negotiations that preceded Tedice's marriage to Philippa Malaghigna. During a crucial period when Vannozzi was required to travel, another potential suitor for Philippa came onto the scene. Knowing how much Tedice wanted to be with Philippa and notwithstanding his relative youth and inexperience,

Tommaso took it upon himself to keep the discussions alive, clearing obstacles from the path of agreement.

Like Tommaso, Tedice had inherited their father's demeanour and their mother's features. A little taller than Tommaso, Tedice was more robustly built, broad-chested and had an altogether healthier pallor. Unlike Tommaso, Tedice did not allow the burden of his responsibilities to prevent him from enjoying some of the good things that life had to offer. Together, they shared a sense of how important it was for each generation to play its part in shaping the destiny of a great family and, even more so, that of one aspiring to greatness

"There is nothing in the posturing of the French that will affect our trading adventures with the Tolosini," asserted Tommaso. "To allow this marriage to slip from our grasp would have greater repercussions than the mere failure to secure a husband for our sister."

Vannozzi nodded in silent agreement. Massimo observed Tedice, anticipating his inevitable endorsement of Tommaso's view.

"The discussions have enabled us to explore avenues of enterprise of which we previously knew nothing," added Tedice. "The connections of the Tolosini reach well beyond the Medici and extend outside of Italy. The commercial possibilities that this marriage will open up for our interests are limitless. In my judgment we, too, should proceed with all due haste and show that we mean to do so."

Massimo looked at his sons thoughtfully. "Oh were it as simple as that."

"And why is it not so?" asked Tommaso.

"There is but one matter that has been brought to my attention that I have not shared with any of you," said Massimo.

"So it's not the threat of invasion that is troubling you?" asked Tedice.

"No. Your arguments on that subject are persuasive. Your views are those that are shared by many others."

"So what is it, father?" asked Tommaso.

Confidently predicting the protests that would greet his observations, almost reluctantly, Massimo relieved himself of the burden that was weighing on his conscience. "The character of Niccolo himself, your intended brother-in-law," was all he said.

There was a pause as Massimo looked from one of his sons to the other. This was something they had previously considered between themselves.

"And what of it?" enquired Tedice solicitously.

"He has a reputation that is sullied by drink and brawling and fornication. It has been said that he has even scaled the walls of the Convent of Le Murate and had his way on a number of occasions with a novice."

"Niccolo is but one of Tolosini's sons and the other, Piero, in spite of his physical infirmity, is being groomed by Ignazio much as you have groomed us, father. Piero is a man whose mind is much like those of Tedice and myself. Where Niccolo may fail, Piero will succeed. Ignazio is shrewd enough to ensure that no damage will be inflicted on future generations of Tolosini by any requirement to pay lip service to rules of primogeniture."

"You speak with conviction, Tommaso," said Massimo.

"He speaks with knowledge also, father," added Tedice. "We have made it our business to spend time with Piero and to make him our friend. Great dynasties grow together. There is more to this match than merely the marriage of our sister."

"Though the marriage must necessarily take place," added Tommaso, "and soon."

The carriage came to a halt at the gates to the Palazzo Tolosini. In the latter part of the previous century Ignazio's grandfather had demolished a dozen townhouses to make space for the imposing stone monolith. Everything about the building was brash on a scale that was unnecessarily extravagant and crassly ostentatious, from the battlement-topped walls to the crudely phallic and largely redundant campanile. The driver negotiated entry and the great wooden gates began to open.

"What else troubles you, father?" enquired Tommaso.

"Nothing that should concern you," said Massimo.

Tommaso was not convinced. He noticed that his father had started to play with his signet ring, sliding it off and on his finger. "Nothing that should concern us, or nothing that should concern the Family Salcoiati?"

"Your father is concerned for your sister's happiness and her peace of mind," interjected Vannozzi, who, though having remained silent during the previous exchange, was privy to his employer's most private thoughts.

Tommaso looked puzzled. "Surely our sister's happiness and peace of mind are best served by her playing a part in bringing happiness to our family. Thereby she will contribute to the peace of mind of us all. Her role is to do our father's bidding. Our father bids her to marry into one of the Republic's greatest families so that advantage may benefit not only all of us, but our children and their children and grandchildren as well."

"Has it ever been thus in all great families," added Tedice.

"As you yourself said, father, all great families make sacrifices. The sacrifices to be made by those who aspire to be great may be of correspondingly greater proportions," added Tommaso, without a tinge of irony.

"Besides, how great a sacrifice is Maria being asked to make? She will live in one of the greatest palazzi in Florence," Tedice waved his hands around the courtyard where they had drawn to a stop. "She'll want for nothing and give birth to another generation who will be brought up to know and understand the best of everything."

"It's not her material well-being that concerns her," said Massimo, "it's her soul."

"What has that to do with her marriage?" enquired Tommaso.

"Of late your sister's devotion has increased."

"That is well noted," said Tommaso. "My brother Leonardo relates that she spends many hours in the cappella, fasts as often as one or even two days in each week and is constantly to be found immersed in the scriptures."

"She believes that the vow of marriage pledged to a man she cannot respect constitutes dishonesty and that such dishonesty will bring punishment to her soul," explained Massimo.

"That's pure sophistry, father, heresy even!" exclaimed Tedice. "The only earthly vow that should be of importance to Maria is her obligation to do as you require and, thus, the best for her family. You should not let what my sister chooses to characterise as the troubling of her conscience trouble yours. You are merely carrying out what destiny has decreed you must do, and Maria should do likewise."

Massimo was happy that his sons were convinced of the correctness of their enterprise. It helped him to assuage the doubts that he had allowed to enter his mind at the bidding of Aulina. He had listened to his wife's observations on the issue of Maria's beliefs on two separate occasions. He reminded her of the natural order of things. Nevertheless Aulina's words continued to resonate and there was also a dream that had recurred that continued to disturb him.

In the dream there was an angel sent by God himself. The angel was disguised as a peddler. In pursuing his trade, the peddler ensured that all those with whom he came into contact were treated to a lesson from the Gospels. He spoke in rapturous tones of love and the redemption that could be achieved by a man selflessly devoting his life to fulfilling everything his wife and family might expect of him. Unsettled by the effect the peddler had on their womenfolk, a group of men set a trap for him. Beating the human body to a pulp, they witnessed the return of the angel's spirit to Heaven. The men were then punished by the consequent infertility of their own wives.

Massimo was unable to reconcile the contradictory message of the dream with his own reality. He tried to peer through time to see his destiny and that of the generations to follow. He looked into the eyes of his sons and in their resolve he saw the future. That was enough to convince him of the correctness of what he was doing. Breaking the silence during which they had each been contemplating the dynamics of the play in hand Massimo said, "you both make your father a very proud man."

The carriage was greeted by a liveried footman who showed them into the palazzo. He took their cloaks then led them through to a grand salon that was known as the Salone d'Oro. The ceiling was high and divided into nine panelled sections. Each was framed in gold and individually decorated with a painting of one of the muses that included figurative representations of the art or science that she inspired. Scattered around the room were a series of exquisitely upholstered settees and chairs, many with details embroidered in gold thread. On the walls there were paintings by Andrea Mantegna, Bellini, Ghirlandaio and Botticelli and even one by Fra Lippi. At either end of the room hung a pair of immense tapestries depicting scenes from Florentine history and in each corner stood a series of four statues representing the four seasons. Winter had been carved by Michaelangelo and Spring by Donatello.

Before they could sit down, Ignazio Tolosini's booming tones echoed around the room. "Your arrival is timely."

He was accompanied by two others, his rodentine consigliari, Cibaldo Rimbotti, and Adamo Tazzi. The ban that Massimo had imposed on Tazzi's presence within the private chambers of the Salcoiati Bank did not extend elsewhere. Tazzi had only very recently been taken into Tolosini's employ. The Salcoiati knew little about him save that he came from somewhere in Lombardy and had a military background of indeterminate allegiance. Gruff and thickset, his face was marked by a jagged scar that ran from the corner of his left eye to his chin. He barely spoke and, when he did, he demonstrated a distinct preference for monosyllables. The Salcoiati assumed that his function was largely physical and not cerebral, though Ignazio did not describe it as such.

Greetings were exchanged and two servants distributed refreshments. After they withdrew, the gathering was joined by Ignazio's younger son Piero. Though both modest and polite and possessed of a keen wit he had not been blessed with a pleasing appearance. A childhood affliction had left him with a disfiguring limp. From the less prepossessing of his mother's forebears he had inherited pug-like features, a sickly complexion and a constitution that was hardly robust. Piero bowed towards the Salcoiati, smiling broadly at both Tommaso and Tedice. He then went across and whispered something in his father's ear. Ignazio's change of expression displayed a suggestion of irritation before he forced a smile and proposed a toast.

"It seems that we will not be joined by Niccolo who is apparently detained elsewhere on a matter of commerce. Never mind, let's drink. To Fortune and to Honour and to Destiny! Salute!"

"To Fortune, to Honour and to Destiny! Salute!" the others repeated, with the exception of Tazzi who simply waited a moment, looked at the faces of the Salcoiati then poured down his drink in one great swilling motion.

"No delay here friends! Your journey was not as fraught as that of the Holy Father to our city!" joked Ignazio.

"Indeed not," said Massimo. "I understand that even before he was turned away yesterday, that the Holy Father was refused hospitality in Sienna."

"Sienna is on the verge of bankruptcy. It was unable to accommodate his train of followers and companions which is apparently of some considerable size," said Rimbotti knowingly.

"Twenty cardinals and attendants, prelates and officers of the Papal Court, coachmen, pageboys and servants. Over a hundred and fifty in total," added Ignazio with a flourish of his drinking cup.

"You are well informed," said Vannozzi.

"A deputation of six was sent by the Signoria to pay homage when he was in Cortona but a few days ago. Giulio

Passerini made the pope welcome there before the entourage then made its way to Arezzo."

"Arezzo?" Massimo's tone was one of surprise. "My wife's sister has come from Arezzo to see the pope here. She could have saved herself the journey."

"I thought that your wife's sister was enclosed?" said Ignazio.

"Her youngest sister is a nun, but not enclosed. The sister who has joined us in anticipation of the Holy Father's visit is devout but not a nun. But tell me, where is the pope at this time?"

"He has withdrawn to Marignolle where he is staying at the villa of Jacopo Gianfiliazzi," said Rimbotti.

"Marignolle?" asked Massimo thoughtfully.

"Yes, Marignolle, also the seat of our former friend and ally, Feduccio Castellani," said Vannozzi.

"I'm sure that Castellani will welcome the Holy Father with open arms," scoffed Ignazio sarcastically.

"Stranger things have happened," said Vannozzi.

"But not many!" Ignazio drained his cup and greedily poured himself another.

"The proximity of Castellani may suit the pope," said Vannozzi.

"How so?" asked Ignazio.

"As you well know, it is said that Leo has destroyed the finances of the papacy with lavish entertainments and patronage and by adding extravagantly to the cost of running the papal household. The papal exchequer has been pillaged and has been without funds since the Spring. It is partly for these reasons that the pope is so keen to make an accommodation with the French. The papacy simply cannot afford to fund a conflict," said Vannozzi.

"And you think that the pope would even consider seeking a loan from Castellani?" Ignazio roared with laughter. "A Medici will never go cap in hand to a Castellani."

"And even if he did, the amount that Castellani could lend would be insufficient," added Rimbotti. "Besides, the papacy's condition is such that even a banker would find it difficult to expect the pope to repay a loan and Castellani is no banker."

"Ironic though isn't it," continued Ignazio in a raucous bellow. "For a hundred years or more the Medici salve their consciences for making money from usury by paying for good works and charity. Their bank is then decimated but, as though by way of divine compensation, they are then bestowed with the papacy. And yet their account with God must still be in debit for there has been insufficient dry weather to enable the papal procession to take place on time."

Tolosini roared with laughter at his own wit that prompted a few smiles from the others. References to the possible damning consequences of usury always made Massimo feel uncomfortable, that perhaps he did not do enough to even up the balance of his own celestial account.

"You're not looking happy, Massimo. Does the impecuniosity of the church upset you? You could always help out."

Massimo looked interested, " how in particular?"

"By spending a few thousand florins with the pope to buy a cardinal's hat for your son Leonardo."

Once again Ignazio was amused by his own joke.

"Even though your words are spoken in jest, please be assured that the Salcoiati would never do anything as vulgar as to buy favours from the Holy Church in that manner," said Vannozzi."

"Shall we address the business of the day?" suggested Tommaso, anxious not to permit the atmosphere to become sullied by irrelevant controversy. "As we have not yet finalised the terms, it is unusual that you should invite the male kin to be present at this point in the negotiations."

"Unusual, yes," agreed Ignazio, "but not unwarranted. When Cibaldo told me what was left in the argument I determined that such small details should no longer stand as an impediment. In front of all these men good and true, Massimo, I accept your proposal and I stand once again to drink; this time to future generations. Salute!"

Once again they all stood and joined in the toast. "Future generations! Salute!"

"Now dear friends, we must name the day on which the announcement may be publicly made and the terms of the dowry notarised so that the commitment may become legally binding on both parties."

"We must clearly give some thought to that," said Massimo

"Thought, Massimo? There's nothing to think about. No purpose will be served by any delay."

"Completely agreed," said Tommaso eagerly.

"Indeed," said Vannozzi, "but we should obviously wait until the pope has been and gone." The comment was a throwaway and said in such a low-key way that it was unquestionably rhetorical.

"That will be soon enough. The Signoria expects the pope to arrive on Friday and to stay no longer than three nights," said Ignazio.

"Towards the end of next week then, that's settled," said Tommaso. "Let's say Thursday. The sixth of December."

"That's fine by me," said Ignazio. "Though why not let's

get on to make an arrangement for the ring day and what lies ahead thereafter?"

Massimo remained silent.

"Doesn't this suit you, Massimo? You are happy with the terms?"

"Yes, of course I am," said Massimo in a tone that was hardly convincing.

"Then let's brook no delay. I'll trust that you'll not treat us as you did the Castellani when you withdrew the hand of Maria from a union with his son."

"Those were entirely different circumstances," said Massimo. "The misgivings that I had were subsequently proved to be well-founded and, besides, no terms were ever finalised, no announcement ever made public and no deed ever notarised."

"Then you will have no misgivings this time?"

As Ignazio spoke the doors to the Salone d'Oro were flung open and Niccolo Tolosini crashed into the room. His clothes looked as though they had been slept in. His lank mousy-brown hair was greasy and unkempt and he stank of drink and of a whore's cheap perfume. As tall as his father, time and even the extent of his own gluttonous idolatry had yet to vest him with a similar girth. His piggy eyes peered through fatigue that was accentuated by wrinkled shadows of puckered skin.

"Apologies for my tardiness, gentlemen," said Niccolo, slurring his words. Before he could fall into a heap, Tazzi stepped across and helped him into an empty chair. "I was delayed on a matter of commerce."

Refusing to be embarrassed, Ignazio welcomed his son and handed him a cup of wine.

"Your timing is perfect, Niccolo," said Tommaso. "Next

Thursday the betrothal will be publicly announced and the terms of the dowry notarised."

"Next Thursday it is, gentlemen … brothers." Niccolo raised his cup towards Tommaso and Tedice and then towards Massimo. "And to you too, father."

Massimo solemnly raised his cup to his lips. As he drank he closed his eyes and prayed.

* * * * * * *

While Florentines busied themselves in readiness for the pope's arrival the following morning, Ragaci wandered the streets. He despaired that Maria would soon find herself in a loveless marriage with the libidinous Niccolo Tolosini, her spirit marooned on an island of indifference. Leonardo had told him that within a week the betrothal would be publicly announced and become legally binding. Even though he could not be with her, she was constantly in his heart. Sometimes it hurt so badly that he had to cry out loud.

Surprisingly, the pain that ripped his emotions to tatters far from stultifying his creativity stimulated it. The compositions that he was writing demonstrated a lyrical maturity and a melodic sophistication that may otherwise have needed to await the further passage of time.

Trying to lose himself in the hive of activity that was beginning to reach fever pitch, he wandered through the quarter of the Bischeri. The sixth in the series of triumphal arches, designed by Rosso Rossi, was still in the process of being decorated with a great variety of ornaments and figures and inscriptions in honour of the Pope. Rossi himself stood at the base of the arch pointing this way and that as an army of helpers, perched precariously on ladders and hastily erected platforms, did his bidding.

Hypnotised by all that was happening, Ragaci returned to his other preoccupation. With precious little time left before his first major public recital, he had still to decide which of his new works to premiere for the occasion. Nothing he had yet completed properly articulated what he wanted to say when the city would gather its thoughts and sit and listen to his recital. A triumphal ballad celebrating the city's patronage of the arts was possessed of a powerful melody, but the lyrics, though laced with witty wordplay, lacked substance. He was pleased with a cycle of divisions based on some well-known frottole, but wanted his tribute to include a vocal. There were others, but most were unsuitable for one reason or another. In his deliberations, he gained little assistance from those around the kitchen table in the basement of the Palazzo Salcoiati. Some were so enamoured with his music that they accepted anything he played uncritically. Others enjoyed what he played and how he sang, but felt ill at ease when he asked them a direct question about it and so were unable to express anything approaching a considered view.

He had thought about asking Maria, but an attempt to discuss anything other than the hymns and psalms suggested by Aulina would have resulted in immediate censure.

Following the route that would be taken by the Papal procession, Ragaci reached the final arch that was next to the Church of Santa Maria del Fiore. Jacopo Sansovino had created a temporary façade for the church that was decorated with statues. The work was also enriched by a host of pencil-drawn carnival subjects in chiaroscuro contributed by Andrea del Sarto. One was a panel on which Romulus and Remus were suckled by the wolf. He took in the carefully created detail of the image. The expressions of concentration and contentment on the faces of the two infants were in semi-profile, while the impassive countenance of the wolf stared back at Ragaci. He glanced up at the other panels but his attention was repeatedly drawn back to the face of the wolf. From the melange of background sounds he heard the marching boots of a small detachment of Militia. The rhythm of their footfall played in his head after they had passed him. The confluence of these stimuli was all he needed and an idea for a ballad began to take shape in his mind. He turned around and headed back to the Palazzo Salcoiati.

Not a hundred braccia from the gate to the palazzo he encountered Leonardo who was returning home after spending the day at the studio of his teacher, Strufa Gambaloto.

"Giacomo. How has your day been?"

"Stimulating, as ever, and I would ask you the same question."

"This week is proving to be something of a special one for me."

"How so?"

"There's been a great deal of progress for me with the landscape that I'm working on."

"I'm pleased for you," said Ragaci with genuine warmth. "You look happy."

"Thank you Giacomo. Within but a short time I believe that I will be able to take many steps forward. But tell me, have you decided what you'll be playing at the banquet?"

"I'm not yet certain, but I have a lyric in mind for a new piece that I might be able to complete in time for tomorrow evening."

They walked through the outer gates, across the courtyard and then into the palazzo. In the main entrance hall, carefully balanced on a table and leaning against the wall, was the most exquisite portrait that Ragaci had ever seen. It was of Maria Chiara Salcoiati and painted by Piero Paolo Forzetti, an artist with whom Massimo Salcoiati was quite taken and who, for a while, had studied with Raphael in Rome.

Against a plain dark background, Maria was posed wearing a black dress and a white mantilla. Her left arm was parallel to the ground and held in front of her stomach. Her right arm was in shadow. In her left hand there was a prayer book and the string of a rosary. Forzetti had captured the look of one who was trying to resist doubts that were eroding what, only a short time before, had been certainties, but one, nevertheless, whose faith was unshakeable.

Ragaci could not take his eyes off the picture.

"I didn't know …" he began.

"My father commissioned the work some weeks ago. I had quite forgotten about it."

Ragaci moved closer and admired the brushwork and technique of the artist. "Oh that I might own a portrait like this; do you yet know where your father will hang it?"

"In the library, I imagine," said Leonardo. "As you know yourself, that's where the rest of the family portraits are to be found."

"You may be sure that I will become a more frequent reader than I have been in the past." Although Ragaci made the comment half to himself, there was little doubt that Leonardo had picked it up.

"And the painting will have to do on its own once Maria becomes Niccolo's new wife and moves to the Palazzo Tolosini, said Leonardo mischievously."

Ragaci tried to show no emotion and listened for more.

"I could never believe that my father would consider that a seat on the Signoria and a fleet of merchant vessels on the high seas would match the ability to play and sing the finest and the wittiest of frottole," said Leonardo impishly.

Ragaci furrowed his brow, feigning puzzlement. "I don't know what you mean," he said.

Leonardo knew that he did but would not press the point. No matter what, Ragaci would never confess his love for Maria to another, not to Leonardo, not to anyone.

"No-one can change anything," continued Leonardo. "The marriage is so important to all of them, especially to my brothers Tommaso and Tedice. My guess is that they are already counting the additional fortune that they see as coming to them with the increase in commerce that an alliance with the Tolosini will bring. They are as much, if not more, exercised about it than even my father or Vannozzi."

"And yet Vannozzi is a good man!"

"So you say, Giacomo, so you say."

"I do. Now I must get up to my room and start work. I have a new piece to write and there's precious little time for rehearsal as it is."

"If there were ten thousand people standing in the Piazza della Signoria and you were given but a minute's notice in which to prepare a recital, you would be note perfect and perform magnificently."

"I thank you for your belief in me."

They embraced each other. Ragaci paused to take another look at the portrait of Maria then strode through to the rear stairs of the palazzo.

When Ragaci reached his room, he picked up a lute and started working furiously on the new piece that he would play for the pope. The tune was one that was already complete. It was an elegiac melody to which he would set a story about devotion to God in the context of temporal love. The lyrics were easy for him to conceive but hard to fit to the unusual metre that awaited them. Yet his determination to finish the piece required that he continue uninterrupted until he was totally satisfied with the result. By the time the closing stanza had been rewritten for the fifth and final time, a crescent moon reflected in the rippling wash of the river. He lay down in his clothes and slept till well past noon the following day.

* * * * * * *

Knowing there was nothing that could stop the relentless progress of an immutable force, Feduccio Castellani reviewed his position in the light of ever-changing circumstances. For the first few months of his retirement that began after the return of the Medici, he busied himself on his estate. He ordered the construction of new buildings, bought new equipment and hired additional hands as he sought to boost the fecundity of his farmland. He soon tired of it. He missed the adrenalin of power and the intoxication of its exercise. At night he restlessly paced the salon of his villa thinking, planning, plotting, determined somehow to make a return.

He was tall, very tall, yet slightly built, wiry limbed and of angular posture. Dark brown eyes above the hollows of his high cheekbones smouldered and narrowed to fissures when he spoke. His nose was bent to one side, testament to an assault at the entrance to the Palazzo Vecchia by a disgruntled merchant who accused him of cheating on a business deal. Castellani's bodyguards quickly disposed of the accuser.

For three generations his family had opposed the Medici and for three generations the ambitions of the Castellani were thwarted and their influence periodically reduced. His grandfather, Claudio Castellani, was amongst those who became discontented with the rule of Cosimo Medici and who, in 1464, opposed the succession of Piero the Gouty, Cosimo's son. Feduccio's father, Gualento Castellani, particularly suffered when, following Cosimo's death, the Medici Bank called in several large debts. Faced with bankruptcy, Gualento joined the factions of the Pitti and later the Soderini who were consistent in their opposition to the Medici rule. Employing a mixture of stealth, bribery, cunning and damned hard work Gualento built up a substantial fortune that Feduccio, his only son, subsequently multiplied.

Feduccio Castellani acquired power and exercised considerable influence in ruling circles, being appointed to the Signoria in 1499. During his years in office he frequently took counsel from Niccolo Macchiavelli. Macchiavelli had been no great friend of the Medici and was even tortured on the strappado following their return to Florence in 1512. Ironically, following his accession to the papacy, Pope Leo sought Macchiavelli's views on how to deal with the French. Macchiavelli now made only occasional visits to Florence to take part in literary gatherings. He retired to his own small farm in Sant'Andrea where he was writing a series of books. Once again, it was to Macchiavelli that Castellani turned after reading one of these books entitled 'The Prince' that was published at the end of 1514.

In conversation, Machiavelli explained to Castellani the nature of the mistakes consistently made by many, if not most, of those in office who he had observed at close quarters. Those destined to fail would try and impose their personalities on what was happening in the hope that they could shape the times. This was a strategy that was nearly always ill-advised and likely to lead to defeat. Machiavelli believed that Castellani could be successful and regain his former position if he sought to align his person and his standing to the vicissitudes of the times. If that meant making an accommodation with the Medici, then, that was something that Castellani would have to contemplate and then address. The second lesson that Machiavelli preached was to be learned from those rulers who raised armies from amongst their own people instead of hiring mercenaries. The support and loyalty of a native force would never be doubted

For a time, the manner in which he might seek an accommodation with those who had taken over the government of the Republic eluded Castellani. The choice of a force to support him, however, was more easily made. It would include a few former allies still active in Florence that were close to him and upon whom he could rely, together with his children. There were only three children, their mother having died in labour with a fourth who did not survive to breathe even once.

Machiavelli had also spoken to him of Fortune. To achieve Fortune's two foremost gifts of glory and riches, Castellani was encouraged to seize opportunities and use them to his advantage.

Castellani concluded that the only way back for him was to engage directly with the Medici and not to oppose them.

Opposition had achieved nothing for his father or his grandfather. In order to engage with the Medici he would call his children to aid, but would first need Fortune to favour him with an opportunity.

He considered the parts that his children might best play. His elder son, Guido, who was twenty-five, had been sent to Venice not long after the beginning of Castellani's exile and the breakdown of the marriage negotiations with the Salcoiati. There he established a mercantile base in a location where Castellani's wealth was more easily invested. Guido's success materially exceeded his father's expectations.

His younger son, Rinuccio, was an altogether different proposition. Ascetic, cerebral, bookish, Rinuccio used the language of a scholar and possessed the manner and demeanour of a priest.

Then there was the moment, the moment when Fortune arrived in the shape and considerable bulk of the Pope himself. While his brother, Giuliano de Medici, the Captain General of the Florentine Republic, frantically urged his fellow citizens to complete the preparations to welcome him home, Pope Leo X was in Marignolle enjoying the hospitality of Castellani's neighbour, Jacopo Gianfiliazzi.

The glory and riches of Fortune arrived on Castellani's doorstep and he did not need to do much to acquire a cardinal's hat for Rinuccio. The Pope immediately took to the young man and needed no convincing of his aptitude for the role. The hat was provided immediately, the formal ceremony of appointment would wait. More tellingly, the amount of gold that Castellani deposited with the Holy Father's secretary was more than enough to bury any lingering memories the Pope may have held for the historical enmity between the Medici and the Castellani. Of course, there was more. Castellani could influence wealthy financiers all over Italy who would not only guarantee further assistance to the Papal exchequer but also to Florence. That guarantee alone would ensure his return to the Signoria at the first available opportunity.

And then there was Donatina, his middle child. She was a resource that he had yet to deploy. She had inherited the alluring beauty of her late mother and the sharp-witted intelligence of her father. She would yet be employed to attract a husband from one of the leading families, an alliance that would be of mutual benefit to both parties. Returning to the city and restored in the eyes of the establishment with the seal of Medici approval would improve his hand no end.

He was pleased that he had yet to conclude an alliance for any of his children, though one had been proposed shortly before his exile. Guido had been intended for Maria Chiara, daughter of Massimo Salcoiati, the banker and self-styled patron of the Arts. Within hours of the wind of change blowing through the Republic in the wake of the Medici's return, Salcoiati had abandoned his former friend and ally and pretended that the intended union between their respective children had never been seriously considered. Unctuous, mealy-mouthed and sly, it was Salcoiati that he blamed for the worst of the consequences of his forced removal from the city of his birth and of the birth of his father and grandfather. Maximising the benefits from the contacts that he, Feduccio Castellani, had originally introduced to Salcoiati, the duplicitous bastard had immediately made himself indispensable to those who would only bring harm to the Castellani.

Whenever he thought of Salcoiati his face twisted into a contemptuous sneer. Even were he not to have returned to Florence, he would have sought revenge. That he was once again restored to a position of influence and, in due course, power as well, opened up opportunities that he would soon seize to ensure that Salcoiati and his puny kin fully understood that his treachery was something that would be revisited a hundred times over.

X

Celebration

Florence. November 1515

Before the packed crowds massed along the streets could catch a glimpse of the Medici pope, they had to wait patiently whilst the important, the self-important and the not so important paraded ahead of him.

The procession assembled in the pale winter sunshine outside of the Porta san Gaggio at the southern end of the city. The French ambassador and the magistrates of Florence led off and were followed by the pope's personal guards. Next came the pope's nephew, Lorenzo de Medici, Duke of Urbino, with fifty of his followers and after them a host of scarlet clad cardinals and other senior churchmen, deacons, priests and bishops. One hundred young men of noble families uniformly and splendidly dressed, including Leonardo Salcoiaiti and Piero Tolosini, immediately preceded the pope himself, who was beneath a canopy held by the gonfaloniere, Pietro Ridolfi, and the chief magistrate. The pope was wearing dazzling white robes, bedecked with jewels and, on his head, a sparkling tiara. Beaming as he went, he waved at the crowds and stopped to admire the extravagant decorations at which he squinted through his eye-glass.

Following the pope were chamberlains, physicians, secretaries, other officers of the pope's household, including treasurers who distributed money amongst the crowd, a long procession of prelates and minor ecclesiatics and, bringing up the rear, the pope's horse guards.

From the Porta san Gaggio the procession wound its way to the San Felice in Piazza through an arch on which there was set a statue of Lorenzo Il Magnificente, the pope's father, and which was inscribed 'Hic est filius meus dilectus'. On seeing this, the pope was deeply affected and was seen to shed a tear. Continuing along the Via Maggio to Santa Trinita where the crowds were even thicker, they then proceeded through the Mercato Nuovo and on to the Piazza de Signori. There, an octangular temple had been erected on which was inscribed 'Leon X P Max propter merita' and which was overshadowed by a colossal figure of Hercules.

Amongst those who waited outside of the Church of the Santa Maria del Fiore to receive the Papal blessing was a group more frequently to be found at the Taverna del Cielo. Reckoning that until the procession was over there would be little in the way of custom, Bruno Nurchi locked the door of his newly whitewashed premises. He pushed his way through the heaving streets to where Cavaliere, Turrichio, Angelica Margherita and some others had secured a position from which they would have a clear view of proceedings.

"Have I missed anything?" enquired Nurchi breathlessly.

"No, the front of the procession is just arriving," said Cavaliere pointing towards the shining armour and double-bladed axes of the German troops who constituted the pope's personal guards.

"They waited till they knew you would be here," quipped Angelica Margherita. Even by the standards of her own immodesty, the depth of her cleavage that was presently on display left little to the imagination.

"Goodness, Angelica, have you no shame!" said Nurchi.

"None that I brought with me," she replied.

"But what if the pope comes in this direction?"

"I doubt that he will be interested but today there are others who will be," said Angelica Margherita confidently.

"Like the Duke of Urbino," suggested Cavaliere drolely. "He's looking your way."

"I don't mind if he does."

"Good God!" exclaimed Cavaliere.

"What's the matter?" asked Nurchi.

"Over there, see!" Cavaliere pointed towards a phalanx of cardinals whose robes were suddenly caught by a gust of wind.

"I see a group of cardinals wearing scarlet robes and silly hats!" exclaimed Nurchi.

"Exactly! And look who is among them!"

Nurchi and the others strained to see what Cavaliere had spotted. "I see no-one I recognise, none of my regulars! Just a bunch of cardinals."

"In the final row, nearest to us, if I'm not mistaken, that's Rinuccio Castellani!"

"Rinuccio Castellani," said Nurchi thoughtfully.

"Youngest son of Feduccio Castellani, former member of the Signoria and sworn enemy of the Medici. What could possibly have occurred to enable a Castellani to acquire a hat?"

"The pope came in from Marignolle did he not?" said Nurchi.

"Apparently so."

"That's where Castellani lives, isn't it?" said Nurchi.

"Yes, and I'll wager that the hat was not the only consideration with which the pontiff has parted for the sum of money he no doubt obtained in return from Castellani."

"And what else might that be?" asked Turrichio who was standing on tiptoe as he thought he could see the Papal group coming into view.

"It is well known that Leo has bankrupted the papacy with his acts of bounty to those of the Medici's lackeys that he has appointed to office. These days anyone with a few florins can buy whatever they want from the Church," said Cavaliere.

"Or from the Medici," added Nurchi.

"And Castellani isn't short of a few florins," observed Turrichio.

But his remark was drowned as the pope came into view. A huge sound of cheering went up as Leo waved towards the area where the taverna regulars stood and waved back. From the far side of the street they heard the sound of a trumpet fanfare. The pope headed towards the sound.

"Always the great lover of music," said Nurchi as the finale of the fanfare fractured then echoed from the top of the buildings behind them.

"I wonder if he will enjoy young Giacomo's performance at the banquet?" mused Cavaliere.

"That he will," said Nurchi. "Tis a pity we can't be there as well."

"It's always a pity when we can't be with Giacomo," said Angelica mischievously.

"You never give up, do you," said Nurchi.

Angelica smiled, "but for you, dear Bruno, I will always make an exception!"

After they received the blessing, they repaired to the taverna while the parade then edged towards the Santa Maria Novella. The crowds began to disperse from the procession route and the party got into full swing.

* * * * * * *

So many people teemed through the streets, it was as if every town and village in Tuscany had emptied its entire population into the centre of Florence. No soul alive could have failed to enjoy the festivities. Music and other entertainments were everywhere around them. However, for those who mattered and even for those who did not but thought they should, the highlight of the day was the grand banquet and pageant.

Il Magnificente's preferred way of doing things had been to mix the conventional with the unorthodox. Attention to detail was nevertheless encouraged by equal measures of the spontaneous and the unpredictable; and so it was for the pageant that was prepared for his holiness for which the venue selected was the Piazza della Signoria. The highlight was a young boy standing on a raised plinth who was covered in gold paint and who was intended to symbolize the start of a new golden age for the Medici and for the city of Florence. The irony of the underlying reason for the pope's visit and the real threat that pointed to the heart of Florence was not lost on some. Once the pageant concluded, somewhat poignantly, the gold-painted boy fell mysteriously ill and then died, presumed to have suffered poisoning from the paint or some allied cause.

Thereafter a gargantuan banquet was thrown in the grandiose Salone di Cinquecento in the Palazzo Vecchia. The most beautiful works of art were borrowed from the great palazzi. An extraordinary array of paintings lined the walls and a splendid selection of statues was scattered around the Salone. Running half the length of the Salone, the top table was raised on a dais. It was more lavishly appointed than the rest, resplendent with ornate silverware and oversized displays of flowers. The several hundred guests sat at dozens of long tables placed at right angles to the top table. Included amongst them were members of the Signoria, representatives of the guilds, the artists and sculptors who had contributed to the decoration of the city, leading merchants and bankers, musicians and poets, bishops and priests and even a few ordinary citizens selected to represent the various quarters of the city. Many of those invited were accompanied by their wives and some by their children as well. Yet taken together this was not the sumptuous splendour of Il Magnificente, this was ostentatious and contrived. Sadly, many of those who were present, particularly those not old enough to remember, were unable to tell the difference.

The ringing of a bell signalled the company to be silent and to stand for the entry of the pope and his retinue. One by one they filed into the Salone and took their places along one side of the top table. The Salcoiati and the Tolosini sat opposite each other immediately below the centre of the top table and therefore but a few braccia from the gaze of the pontiff.

Grace was recited by Cardinal Giulio Medici, the pope's cousin. The gonfaloniere then made a short but rousing speech of welcome whereupon the banquet began.

A regiment of waiting staff had been hired for the occasion. They began serving a series of wonderful dishes. The culinary specifications had challenged the collective imagination of some of Florence's finest chefs. Exotic combinations of spiced fish and fowl were complemented by vegetables casseroled with cheese. Whole roast sucklings marinated in red wine and seasoned with aromatic spices were accompanied with individual puddings of suet and sage. In between and afterwards there were stuffed breads and pastries, sweetmeats and tarts, and limitless quantities of fine Tuscan wine.

Throughout the meal, the ebb and flow of conversation was punctuated by a parade of entertainers – magicians and acrobats, jugglers and jesters and musicians. Everything that was much admired by the pope was catered for.

"It is said that Nero fiddled while Rome burned," decreed Pier Paolo Forzetti expansively to anyone that might have been listening. The artist, whose work was much favoured by Massimo Salcoiati, was known not only for his sardonic wit but also his patronising cynicism. His barrel-chested torso was out of proportion to his short bow legs. Yet he carried himself with the grace and elegance of royalty and his hands were undoubtedly those of an artist, broad, long fingers, rough and stained with fading patches of paint. He was ruggedly handsome with brown eyes that sparkled with intelligence, a patrician nose and an unfashionable thick and shaggy beard.

Not much loved by his peers, they still treated Forzetti with respect and were accustomed to hearing him express his forthright opinions. More than a few of them fully appreciated the intent and the wit of his observation. Politeness and the proximity of the guest of honour dictated that they pretended not to have heard him. Conscious that he was being ignored by those who knew him, Forzetti turned to one who did not. Ragaci sat opposite him and one along.

"And what do you say on this subject?" asked Forzetti, gesturing with his cup.

"I've often wondered who is alleged to have made the remark," said Ragaci.

"What difference is it who made the remark?"

"From identifying the source one might then properly divine its meaning and intent."

"Who gives a fuck who said it. The man in question, Nero, was a bastard and cared not for anyone or anything but himself."

"That is what the author of the remark intended those like you to believe, whether or not it is true," said Ragaci assuredly.

"And you believe otherwise?"

"I believe the evidence of my own eyes and ears."

"And what do you see and hear?"

"Over there, a man who may enjoy the music of others but who will not see Rome, nor for that matter, Florence burn." Ragaci motioned discreetly towards the pope who was engrossed in conversation with the gonfaloniere who sat to his immediate right. "And directly opposite me the frustrated agitation of one who captures beauty and who perhaps resents those with whom he must share it, being those who pay for his art."

Forzetti laughed. "You have seen my work?"

"I live with your work."

"How so?"

"My patron is one of yours, Massimo Salcoiati."

"So you must be Giacomo Ragaci, the young musician that everybody is talking about."

"I know not this everybody, but yes, I am a musician."

"At this moment 'everybody' includes the Signorina

Maria Chiara Salcoiati, the most recent of the clan to sit for me. She spoke of you, your compositions, your recitals and the fact that you will be performing a new work for this company this evening."

Ragaci remained nonplussed. He was learning to contain his feelings for Maria. "She has been studying with me. I have been coaching her voice and teaching her to play the lute a little."

"And is that all?"

"I am not qualified to teach the scriptures and, from what I believe, that is the most significant of the Signorina's other interests. What else could there be?"

Forzetti looked Ragaci in the eye. His ability to find the truth that lay behind a person's expression and to paint it on canvas suggested that there was something else, but even his bluntness was sufficiently injuncted by the tone of the occasion and the imminence of Ragaci's performance. Applying a degree of subtlety that for him was unusual, Forzetti decided to say nothing more. His attention was suddenly caught by a minor commotion that erupted a few tables away, where the Salcoiati and the Tolosini sat.

"Our patron would appear to have been joined by a latecomer," observed Forzetti.

Ragaci turned around to look but he did not have a clear view. "And who is it?" he asked.

"That to me looks like Niccolo Tolosini. I suspect that the nearest whorehouse would give him no further credit then invited him to leave. And so he finds himself at the banquet sooner than he would have wished."

Political controversy had not enticed the participation of others in Forzetti's conversation with Ragaci, muck-raking gossip did.

"And last seen sober when he was about fourteen years old," chimed in Francesco Granaci who sat next to Ragaci. Granaci was an architect who had designed triumphal arch that stood near the Palazzo del Potesta. He added "you'd think he should behave better than that in front of his future in-laws."

"In-laws?" enquired Forzetti. "Did you know anything of this, Giacomo?"

"I only know rumour," said Ragaci, trying not too become involved in a subject that he found uncomfortable to discuss.

"As do I," said Granaci, "but it is a rumour that gains credibility when the two families are sitting in such close proximity on an occasion such as this."

"And when the principals spend so much time licking each other's arses," added Forzetti.

"And all of it happening right in front of the Castellani, too," said Granaci.

"Castellani? Who's in charge of this beanfeast?" snapped Forzetti. "God's messenger on earth or Lucifer himself? Castellani! Where is he?" Granaci stood and pointed across the Salone towards Castellani and his family. "What's he doing here?" continued Forzetti, visibly irritated "That bastard has owed me money since he was run out of the city three years ago!"

"I suggest you don't ask him for it now, though you may soon get ample opportunity to do so."

"How so?"

"Apparently he has bought favour with the pope and will be reinstated in the Signoria as soon as an opportunity arises."

"I suppose that will mean another poisoning, then" said Forzetti sarcastically.

Indifferent about adding to this part of the conversation, Ragaci chewed his food thoughtfully and joined in again as other topics surfaced. After the first round of desserts had been served one of the secretaries to the Signoria tapped him on the shoulder and indicated that the time had come for him to perform.

On his way to the dais that had been set up at the end of the Salone he passed his patron and his family. He returned Massimo's smile and looked along the row of familiar faces. Maria Chiara was placed between her mother and Leonardo. She had sat serenely throughout the evening, saying little, eating modestly and drinking only water. She barely noticed the disturbance when Niccolo Tolosini had arrived. He had not sought to greet her, an omission to which she was oblivious. She contemplated her future with equanimity. The material splendour of her father's successes could never match the reward to which she aspired. The temporal life of comfort and grace that were hers would not bring her the redemption for which she could only pray she was worthy. The marriage that she knew was to be formally announced did not trouble her. The love in her heart was reserved for Ragaci but she was not permitted to share it with him. Trust in her father was something that she would try not to question too closely, but her faith in the future and in her own destiny was absolute.

When Leonardo acknowledged Ragaci's smile he nudged Maria to do likewise. She pretended not to notice, bowed her head, laced her fingers together and placed her hands on the table.

Pietro Ridolfi, the gonfaloniere rose and made a short announcement, "Holy Father, reverend cardinals, honourable bishops, Captain General of the Republic, members of the

Signoria, my lord of Urbino, gentlemen, ladies, with thanks to the patronage of Signor Massimo Salcoiati I wish to present to you a wonderful musician who has been in Florence for but half a year. For his first official performance outside of the Palazzo Salcoiati please welcome and show appreciation for Signor Giacomo Ragaci."

While the gonfaloniere spoke, Maria watched as Ragaci organised himself for the performance. Breathing deeply as he started to play she became lost in the sound of the music and spiritually seduced by the rich dark tone of his voice as it began to fill the room.

He started with a short devotional piece with which he assumed the pope would be familiar. He was and visibly enjoyed it. Two instrumental pieces followed, one of Ragaci's original compositions and one by Heinrich Isaac, the first flowing naturally into the second with consummate musical excellence, as if the two pieces had been written as one. To conclude, Ragaci performed the epic ballad on which he had worked so feverishly the previous evening and through the night.

He recalled the angel from the circular chamber of his recurrent dream and sang of her. As the instrumental introduction fused into the melody of the verse, the angel opened the door at the foot of the chamber to find herself in bucolic, undulating Tuscan countryside. Assuming human form as an extraordinarily beautiful young virgin, she sat on the verdant bank of a slow-moving river, playing her silver lute and begun to sing. Her crystal clear voice attracted the attention of a handsome and virtuous young shepherd who listened to her for a while before resuming the herding of his flock. The angel followed the shepherd and his flock for many days. At night they found beds of thick grass and lay on their backs singing love songs before falling asleep in each other's arms.

They eventually arrived at the edge of a thick forest that stretched as far as the eye could see. The angel refused to enter the forest, believing it to be too dangerous. Quite apart from packs of wild and aggressive wolves that were known to roam the footpaths, there were malevolent spirits who inhabited certain trees and who could emerge without warning to wreak horrors upon the unsuspecting. The shepherd tried to persuade the virgin to accompany him, and assured her that she would be safe with him. Although he wanted to stay with her, he knew that he could not delay too long as it was essential that his sheep reached the market on the far side of the forest as soon as possible. The virgin agreed to remain at the edge of the forest to await the shepherd's return.

After she watched him disappear into the forest, she was kneeling and praying for his safe return when a priest, who was passing, stopped to greet her. She told him her story and he blessed her before moving on. Later on, as the sun began to fade, the priest returned with two others. In front of the virgin's eyes they turned into wolves and attacked and killed her before returning into the heart of the forest. The next day the shepherd returned to find the corpse. So distraught, he was seized by madness and spent the rest of his short life berating himself for having left her alone before he died of a broken heart.

Although the emotional agitation of the religious elements in Ragaci's composition was disturbing, the spirituality that filled his performance was total. The inventive fantasy was accepted by some, though the indulgence in the bizarre proved too much for others.

He played the final notes of the coda to the piece that he wholly improvised. Some immediately clapped and cheered, others remained silent. The pope lay his eye-glass down on the table and applauded heartily, which was a cue for those who remained silent to join in. Ragaci stood and bowed to the pontiff and then to the rest of his audience. Some began to get to their feet, Pier Paolo Forzetti amongst them. Ragaci looked towards the table where the Salcoiati and the Tolosini sat.

Maria was standing but not joining in with the applause. One hand to her forehead she looked perturbed. Leonardo and Aulina stood up. Leonardo put his arm on Maria's shoulder and bent his head towards her. Aulina was supporting her daughter under her other arm.

Ragaci was desperate to go to them and to find out what was happening. Realising that there was nothing he could do he accepted that events would take their course. His return to his place at the table with the other artists and musicians was delayed as many stood up as he passed them to pat him on the back and shake his hand.

* * * * * * *

"Maria, what's the matter?" asked Aulina, evidently most concerned.

"I'm not feeling very well. Actually, I haven't been feeling too good all evening, but now I feel sick."

"Perhaps you should go home," said Aulina.

Maria thought for a moment. "Won't that be a bother? Everyone's enjoying themselves and I don't want to spoil the party for others."

"You shouldn't stay if you're going to be sick," continued Aulina.

Massimo leaned across to find out what was happening. Not wishing to show any irritation he nevertheless agreed that if Maria was not feeling well she should leave. "But I will not permit her to travel through the streets alone in a carriage, especially tonight. She must be accompanied."

"I'll go with her," said Aulina.

"You may accompany her, but you will need a man to act as your escort."

"The carriage driver will take care of us," said Aulina. "Besides, it isn't that far."

"That's irrelevant." Massimo looked towards Tommaso who could not quite hear what was going on.

"Don't worry, father," said Leonardo. "I'll be happy to escort my mother and my sister, then return with the carriage afterwards."

"Thank you. That's very kind of you and I bless you for it."

With the decision made, Aulina and Leonardo helped Maria walk gingerly through the great Salone.

Once out onto the Piazza della Signoria, Leonardo managed to locate one of the Salcoiati carriages. It then manoeuvred its way through the waiting ranks of others to a point at which it was convenient for Aulina and Maria to board. Leonardo gave instructions to the driver. They started to pick their way through the crowded streets that were packed with rowdy revellers, many of whom were very much the worse for wear.

South of the Ponte Vecchio, the throngs thinned out and the carriage picked up speed. A little way before the Palazzo Salcoiati, Leonardo leaned out of the window and ordered the coachman to stop.

"We will walk from here. My sister would like to take a little air and to stretch her legs. Wait here and when I return in a few minutes you can take me back to the Palazzo Vecchia."

"Very well, sir," said the coachman. Leonardo helped Aulina and then Maria out of the carriage. They started walking and turned at the first corner into a side street. It was deserted save for a waiting carriage with two horses. It was occupied by a single figure. They stopped at the carriage and Leonardo opened the door.

"I thought you were never coming," said the passenger. "I was beginning to give up hope and it's so cold this evening."

"Never mind, aunt," said Leonardo. "We're here now. Is the luggage all on board?"

"All packed and safely stowed away. Now, where's my travelling companion?"

Before Leonardo could help his sister up into the carriage, Aulina took her and held her close. "God speed, sweet Maria," she said, "God speed."

"Yes mother."

"And remember us in your prayers."

"Of course mother."

"I'll miss you at Christmas but I will come and visit as soon as I can afterwards."

"Yes, please. Thank you mother."

They exchanged kisses.

"And you too, dear Leonardo," she said, taking her twin brother into a warm embrace.

"I thank you for this sacrifice," he replied.

"This is no sacrifice, this is my chosen path, this is my freedom. The gratitude that I may receive will be that of God and of God alone."

She drew away from Leonardo who then helped her into the carriage. Final farewells were exchanged and then the carriage pulled away to start its journey to Arezzo.

Leonardo escorted his mother home before returning to the Palazzo Vecchia.

* * * * * * *

"Bene, multo bene, Giacomo," said Forzetti enthusiastically as Ragaci rejoined his table and sat down.

"That's a true compliment," said Granaci, "for Forzetti is the critic of all critics."

"Tell me, Giacomo, what was your inspiration for this truly unusual ballad?"

Ragaci smiled. "A dream. A dream, a thought, a longing of the heart and a belief."

"But you must be thirsty. Let me have your cup filled." Forzetti called over a servant. Others on the table began directing their conversation towards the young musician. As the evening wore on, they made Ragaci feel that he genuinely belonged to this exalted company of Florence's finest creative souls.

Not long after midnight, Ragaci was disturbed by a gaunt looking young man wearing the livery of a house with whom he was not acquainted.

"Excuse me, Signor Ragaci?"

"Yes."

"I am directed to you by my master."

"Yes," said Ragaci.

"And who is your master?"

"Feduccio Castellani."

Even Forzetti who was drunker than most of the rest of them was listening.

"And what does your master seek?" enquired Ragaci, familiar with the name but, in his current state of inebriation, quite unable to remember the context in which he had previously heard it.

"My master was most taken with your performance. He seeks to engage your services. He would like you to compose something to commemorate the appointment of his son as a cardinal. He would then like to select an appropriate occasion on which you might perform it."

Momentarily, the flattery of recognition threatened to take over Ragaci's intoxicated self, but he managed to stop himself from saying the wrong thing. "Please tell your master that I thank him for his attention but I regret that I am unable to respond to his request."

"Why so, sir?"

"Even if I was interested in his commission, and perhaps I could be, presently I am exclusively engaged by my patron, Massimo Salcoiati. It is to him that your master should direct his enquiry."

"Thank you sir. I will advise my master accordingly."

Castellani's footman bowed to Ragaci and disappeared into the bowels of the Salone.

"Time was when no-one around this table would have dreamed of turning down a commission from Castellani," said Granaci.

"And maybe that time is returning," added another voice.

"And maybe I can see about getting paid the money he owes me from three years back," said Forzetti.

"And maybe it's time for another drink," said Ragaci.

"Maybe," said Forzetti looking around and noting the absence of Maria from the ranks of the Salcoiati. For a full minute he framed the scene in his mind for future reference then picked up his cup and drained it once again.

XI

Christmas

Tuscany. December 1515

By the time Ragaci left Florence to spend Christmas with his family in San Gimignano, Maria's clandestine disappearance and the collapse of the marriage negotiations with the Tolosini were established fact. Leo X had met with Francis I in Bologna, reached an accommodation, then returned to Florence to spend Christmas with his family. With their exile at an end, the Castellani demonstrably and very quickly began to re-establish their power base.

Maria's absence from the Palazzo Salcoiati was not discovered by Massimo for more than a day. It was the first Sunday in Advent. Maria was not present at the morning mass which reminded Massimo of the apparent cause of her early departure from the Papal banquet. After mass was over he went to her room to see how she was and found it empty. He returned to find Aulina sitting in one of the smaller salons, alone, and making ready to start on some needlework.

"Aulina, what's happened to Maria. Where is she?"

Aulina did not look up as she spoke. She had selected a reel of vermillion thread from a basket at her feet and was busy looking for her box of needles. "She went to Arezzo with my sister Bartolomea who has delivered her to the Convent of St Perpetua and St Felicitia. It is a Benedictine Order where she has entered as a novice."

Seldom known to raise his voice, Massimo exploded. "What in God's name has she done? This was never countenanced. Why, this coming Thursday we are due to notarise the terms of her dowry that will legally certify her impending marriage to Niccolo Tolosini!"

"I wasn't aware of that until this very moment. Was it ever made known to Maria herself?" enquired Aulina. She briefly gazed at Massimo with a deadpan expression, then returned her attention to her needlework basket.

"What do you mean?"

"If no-one took the time to tell her what was happening, it's hardly surprising that she didn't know." She continued to rustle around in the basket. "You haven't seen my box of needles anywhere, have you?"

Massimo ignored the question, his normally pale complexion becoming increasingly puce with frustration. "But she has no legal right of which I am aware that entitles her to leave my home without my permission."

Aulina said nothing. She removed a number of items from the basket and put them one by one on the small table.

"I must have left them in the library," said Aulina, oblivious to her husband's ire.

"Maria. What about Maria?"

Aulina stood up and faced her husband. "Maria is a woman of principles and of the highest moral values." She spoke calmly and with an authority that defied challenge. "She has committed herself to the service of God and to his son, Our Lord Jesus Christ, to whom she is now betrothed.

No other earthly endeavour can be as worthy as the choice that she has made."

"Did you conspire with her to achieve this?"

Aulina looked at her husband and spoke in a tempered manner. "There was no conspiracy. Maria first expressed a desire to serve God when we were in Arezzo in September. While there we visited the convent where she now resides. Incidentally, it isn't the same convent as that where my youngest sister, Bonagratia, lives. The arrival of Bartolomea for the Papal celebration was a happy coincidence. Maria regretted that she could not discuss the matter with you, but you were otherwise occupied with matters of business. She decided that the opportunity to return to Arezzo with my sister was a good one and so she took it."

"She decided! The decision wasn't hers to take. Besides, how could she have paid a dowry to this convent."

"As you know, Bartolomea is childless. Her husband has no kin, so what would otherwise have been available for their own has been covenanted by him to the convent.

"Was Leonardo a party to this?"

"As you will recall, Leonardo escorted us back home then returned to the Palazzo Vecchia where he rejoined you at the banquet."

Aulina prayed in her heart that God would forgive her interpretation of the facts. The truth was that the entire subterfuge was meticulously planned and thought through in some detail: the manner in which they had seated themselves at the banquet; Maria's feigned illness; Leonardo volunteering to escort them then return, correctly predicting that in so doing his altruism would readily be indulged by his father and brothers. He rightly guessed that none of them would have wanted to miss even one minute of the great banquet. What was more, and though he had not yet said as much to Aulina, Leonardo hoped that with his sister committed to the service of the Lord, the threat to make him do likewise upon attaining his eighteenth birthday would abate.

"I won't accept this, not for one moment. I will send Tommaso to Arezzo immediately to bring her back!" stormed Massimo.

Aulina acknowledged the remark thoughtfully. "He may try and so may you, but my belief is that he will not even gain admittance to the convent buildings," she said.

The order to which Maria had pledged herself was not enclosed. She might meet with visitors once arrangements had been made with the Madonna Suora. That was irrelevant. Maria had requested that, save for Aulina herself and her Aunt Bartolomea, she would not see anyone for the first twelve months of her residence. Short of bringing a lawsuit or, failing that, engaging armed men to use brute force, there was little chance of Tommaso or Massimo or of anyone else for that matter being permitted entry through the front gates.

"That is ridiculous. She is my daughter and I will demand that she sees us."

"I fear that you are wrong about that."

"Wrong? What do you mean, wrong?"

"The truth is that she is no longer your daughter nor mine. She belongs to God."

Massimo stood rooted to the spot, smouldering with anger as Aulina went to fetch her needles. Much worse than the actions of his daughter would be the repercussions on his relationship with Tolosini. He might put off the date for the notarisation and public announcement once with a lame excuse, but doubted that he would be able to buy a second postponement similarly.

Aulina's prediction proved to be accurate. Neither Tommaso nor Tedice, who accompanied him, were even allowed through the gates of the Convent of St Perpetua and St Felicitia. Imploring their Aunt Bartolomea to escort them made no difference. Massimo was faced with having to explain the inexplicable. No, his daughter had not defied his wishes; that much was true in that Massimo had never actually made them plain to her. He attributed Maria's actions to an unpredictable act of madness, that the girl had simply lost her mind.

Ignazio Tolosini would have none of it. A week following the date originally set for the notarisation of the dowry terms and upon the failure of Tommaso's mission, Massimo, accompanied by Mosciano Vannozzi, was received at the Palazzo Tolosini. Rimbotti and the sinister Adamo Tazzi flanked Ignazio Tolosini as he marched into the Salone d'Oro. Formalities were dispensed with. Ignazio and his aides sat down opposite Massimo and Vannozzi. Ignazio went straight to the point.

"We came to an arrangement that was due to have been notarised more than two weeks ago. She should have been under lock and key and watched twenty-four hours a day if her moods were so susceptible to extreme change," barked Ignazio.

"That was never previously the case."

"You are a fool, Massimo. You have benefited from many favours that I have done for you and favours do not come cheaply."

"Don't forget that you have benefited from these arrangements also."

"And do you see them continuing, Massimo?"

"We have already engaged a lawyer to bring a lawsuit to secure her release. Her admission to the convent was obtained without my consent," said Massimo confidently. "That is quite as much against the law in Arezzo as it is in Florence."

"I have no time nor inclination to wait for or rely on a magistrate coming to a decision, especially one that sits in Arezzo."

"May I be permitted to add something," said Vannozzi. "Maria's actions were wholly incapable of being predicted and completely out of character. That she is removed from our firmament ought not to have any effect on our commercial relationship nor, indeed, our friendship"

"And if you believe that then you're as much of a fool as your employer. This isn't just about commerce or even friendship, it's also about honour. Surprising as it may seem, it was important for the Tolosini that the marriage took place. That the bride has been removed through no doing of ours makes the Tolosini into a laughing stock."

"But no formal announcement …"

"Formal announcement? Irrelevant. This is Florence at the end of the year of our Lord of 1515. Everyone knows when everyone else is going to shit even before they pull their pants down. What's more, this is the second time you have done this."

Massimo swallowed hard then quickly sought to disguise his action by coughing.

"Actions such as these have previously created one enemy for you. Now that Castellani has inveigled his way into the Medici fold, he is alive again and a danger to you and for certain others also."

"What are you implying?"

"I am implying nothing, Massimo. I tell you this so that you may consider your options carefully," said Tolosini pointedly.

"What options are you talking about?"

"Your options for the future."

"Is there a problem?"

"Castellani suffered not only exile but also financially at the time of the return of the Medici. It is well known that you co-operated with the investigation that resulted in his paying substantial amounts of tax."

Massimo would not dignify the remark with a response. In his role as a member of the Signoria, Ignazio himself had been a major protagonist in the persecution of Soderini's followers. In the mood that he found Tolosini, Massimo decided to keep his counsel on the subject. Vannozzi did not "it's the duty of every citizen to co-operate with the requirements of the state. Nothing that the House of the Salcoiati has ever done is anything other than what any upstanding and law abiding citizen would do, including you."

Ignazio ignored the innuendo of the remark. "Perhaps that isn't Castellani's perception."

"And what are you saying?" asked Vannozzi curtly.

"I'm not saying anything, merely making an observation."

"Based on surmise, no doubt."

"Based on intelligence."

"Intelligence or information?"

"Intelligence, Massimo, intelligence."

Vannozzi stood up as though to follow up his question, sensing that Tolosini knew and could say more. Tolosini was not interested in discussing the matter any further. He, too, rose out of his chair. "And now, gentlemen, if you don't mind, I have matters of importance to address." He started to walk towards the door and snapped his fingers at Tazzi and Rimbotti who followed his lead like tame puppies.

Vannozzi was determined to elicit an answer. "What intelligence, Ignazio?"

Ignazio paused briefly and looked over his shoulder, "I have made my position as clear as I can. I believe the meeting is concluded. Tazzi here will show you out." Ignazio stared at Vannozzi imperiously daring him to say more.

"If there is intelligence that concerns Castellani that affects our house then we will become party to it and address the matter in due time," said Massimo with dignity. He, too, stood up and added, "I thank you for your time."

He nodded at Vannozzi. They turned and walked towards the door, followed by the menacing form of Tazzi.

* * * * * * *

Christmas at the Palazzo Salcoiati was an unusually sombre affair.

Eating a Christmas Eve meal that was intentionally frugal, arriving in silence for Midnight Mass at the cappella, Aulina partook of communion with an intensity of passion that she had never previously felt. Her devotion established a pattern that was followed by the rest of the family. Her actions became its spiritual heartbeat. Aulina's inspiration had each of them open the door to their souls and enable them to welcome God inside. As the priest addressed them, they remembered that it was God who had sent them his son, Jesus Christ, to spread the word and who had given his life for their sins. For a day or two, concerns of matters temporal were banished from conversation. Christmas for the Salcoiati was as it should be, a time for reflection, a time for prayer and a time to contemplate what would yet unfold in the New Year that was almost upon them.

The atmosphere of serenity that the festival prescribed pervaded the palazzo. All that Aulina saw was good. She had no fears and was content. Though surface calm often covered turbulent undercurrents, Aulina's belief was that such undercurrents were unusually the product of ambition. She had no use for ambition. She only saw that it brought no lasting benefit either to those who chased it or to those who were affected by its pursuit. After the initial flush of self-fulfilment the only lasting products of ambition were disappointment and distress. Though she would not usually have considered it as a proper subject upon which to expound, on the day following Christmas she made her views known to the rest of the family.

Fleeing from her words as if in the face of an invading foe, each of them was able to justify a distinction of his individual position from the generalisations of Aulina's proposition, though none of them spoke anything of it aloud.

Massimo berated himself for his recent mistakes. They were, in his mind, entirely disconnected from any notion of ambition. He should have responded to Tolosini's proposal when it had first been made. The arrangements would have been finalised before the condition of madness had affected Maria. Tomasso and Tedice were right all along. There had been no danger from the French. The deal that had been struck with the king was hardly advantageous to the pope, but Florence was preserved and the advance of the French army halted. At Bologna, what was previously proposed to the pope's envoys in October was accepted. In addition, the pope ceded to the king the right to make all senior church appointments in France. The consequent loss of papal influence in France would be matched by a large loss of revenue.

There was also a suggestion that he should have sought to acquire a cardinal's hat for Leonardo. He had automatically retreated from it even without taking into account that Aulina would frown at the idea. But what did Aulina know of such things? Accessing the upper echelons of the Church would not only enable his son to achieve a closer relationship with God, but also empower the family to move in circles that had hitherto not been open to them. As soon as it was convenient and before the pope returned to Rome, he would arrange an audience and make his opening bid. The Salcoiati had established sufficient credibility with the Medici that he might yet match or even trump the card that had been played by Castellani.

Tommaso and Tedice had not yet conceded defeat in the endeavour to secure their sister's marriage to Niccolo Tolosini. Without the knowledge of either their father or of Vannozzi, lines of communication had been maintained with Rimbotti and with their friend, Piero Tolosini. They were considering how they might gain entry to the Convent of St Perpetua and St Felicitia and remove their sister, by force, if the lawsuit proposed by their father was to falter or fail.

With the peace accord concluded, Josephus' detachment of the Florentine Militia had returned from reconnaissance in the north and was garrisoned on the outskirts of the city.

Having recently viewed the might of the French army and its allies at close quarters, he expressed gratitude in his prayers that battle had not been joined. He had willingly committed himself to the service of the Republic, but was concerned to arrange an exit from the Militia as soon as he might, without affecting the honour of his family.

Leonardo was a Humanist at heart. He joined his family in prayer as he was expected to do, though was at best agnostic in his beliefs. It was not long before his eighteenth birthday when he would be sent to the priesthood. If God was listening, he hoped that his prayers would be answered and that he would be enabled to fulfil his desire to become an artist. He would happily spend part of the time creating works for the Church and painting religious scenes. That would surely be enough, would it not?

The days passed and the muted spirit that had cast its melancholy tones over the Salcoiati's Christmas subsided onto the horizon of the New Year that was fast approaching. As soon as he considered it convenient so to do, Massimo made contact with one of the Pope's secretaries to arrange an appointment with His Holiness before he returned to Rome. Tommaso and Tedice engaged a spy to go to Arezzo and to acquire intelligence about the routines and doings of the Convent of St Perpetua and St Felicitia. Josephus started to compose a letter to his father that attested to the horrors of armed conflict and how he might secure an honourable discharge from the Militia. Leonardo resumed attending the studio of Strufa Gambaloto and continued to paint.

* * * * * * *

After celebrating Midnight Mass at the church of Sant' Agostino, they emerged into the cold shadows of the town. An eccentric collection of towers watched over the centre of San Gimignano like a detachment of rectangular sentries. The Family Ragaci huddled together and sang hymns as a pair of farm horses pulled their wagon home through the misty air of the early hours of Christmas morning.

The comfy familiarity of the church and the welcoming tone of the priest reminded Giacomo that he was home. He felt at once both inspired by, yet detached from, the proceedings of the service. He joined in with the hymns and carols, singing with a lusty vigour. His voice soared to the lofty rafters of the old church and resonated with cadence before cascading over the heads of the congregation and in unison with them. However, kneeling for prayer and taking communion were both jarring and disjunctive experiences. Without anything in the way of tangible proof, he was prepared to accept that Jesus Christ had died for his sins and, if they liked, for those of the rest of the congregation. He would never have suggested otherwise. Analysing the words that the priest recited on the question of the individual's relationship to sin led him to question the need for him to confess to anything. The only act of which he was guilty was that of loving Maria Salcoiati.

Once she had been unattainable by virtue of status and family and latterly made more so by the vow of chastity she had taken upon entry to a convent. And this vow, what had been its portent? Was it the love she had for him, Ragaci, that she was unable to openly assert and to which she was unable to respond? Or did she feel the need to pay penance for the offence that she had committed against her father by disobeying him? Ragaci would never know the answer. If he could find it in himself to pray with his heart, it would be for reassurance that Maria's actions were at least partly designed to reciprocate his love for her. Absence of physical presence made no difference. He felt bound to her for all eternity.

While others bowed their heads and whispered words designed to comfort their souls, he gazed at the icons that adorned the Church. From one that included an image of the Virgin there appeared a vision of Maria Salcoiati, serene, ethereal and content. He closed his eyes and imagined her, in her convent, kneeling, black mantle, white wimple, black veil. Seeking redemption in the only way of which she felt certain, Maria had placed her faith in God.

On Christmas Day, the Ragaci were joined by relatives from nearby and their neighbours and close friends the Gianbullari. Dulce, Giacomo's mother, and Imiglia Gianbullari worked together to produce a splendid meal.

Giacomo spent much of the time observing his brother, Cesare, and Lucia Gianbullari for whom, originally, he had been intended. Shorter and even slimmer than Giacomo, Cesare was possessed of a certain taciturnity which contrasted with his brother's understated eloquence. Lucia was a delicate girl with the porcelain skin of her mother and the slightly sorrowful look that never seemed to be far from her father's countenance. Despite the apparent physical mismatch, the affection that Lucia and Cesare showed for each other was real and visible to all. No formal arrangement had yet been made as to a marriage. Tadeus Gianbullari was happy to open discussions at a moment's notice, but had been put off for some weeks by Bonaccio Ragaci. Ever the traditionalist, Bonaccio still nurtured hopes that Giacomo would come to his senses, that this foolishness in Florence would reach a conclusion, that he would return home to claim his birthright and a bride who could not be more perfect in every way.

"Do you like Lucia?" asked Cesare with a degree of trepidation. He and Giacomo were in the ramshackle cowshed a short distance behind the farmhouse where they were milking the cows that were part of the Ragaci stock.

"Yes, of course I do. She's a fine and pretty young woman."

"Our father still considers that she should be pledged to you."

"He does?" For a moment Giacomo stopped working the teats of the old brown cow and turned towards his brother.

"He believes you should come back from Florence and do as he wants you to."

"And is that what you think I should do?"

"That's not for me to say."

"But what do you feel, Cesare, what do you really feel about it?"

"What do I feel?" He hesitated before continuing. "I'm not sure."

"I think you are. I have observed you and Lucia."

"You have?" there was a tone of nervousness in his voice.

"Yes. The way you look at each other, the way you react when she comes close to you. Even the way you spooned vegetables onto her plate."

Cesare blushed a little. Giacomo finished his share of the task and put away his stool. He carefully covered the bucket of milk and placed it by the door of the cowshed. He walked towards Cesare, then stood to his side, resting his hand on the cow's haunch. "Do you love Lucia?"

Cesare was hesitant to respond. "I'm not sure what you mean."

"I meant what I ask. Do you love her? Do you feel as though you want to spend the rest of your life together with her? Do you want to inherit our father's farm and then enjoy Gianbullari's holding as part of Lucia's dowry? Is that what you want?"

Cesare had never heard his brother speak so openly. He guessed that it was something he had learned to do in Florence. Giacomo had become the sophisticated cosmopolitan. He was a humble farmer and it would not do for him to speak in such an open manner.

"It's not for me to say," said Cesare with complete certainty.

"Why not?"

"Because you are the older brother and what's yours is yours."

"Cesare, this may not make sense to you now, but I want you to think about it. Do you know the only thing that is worth having in this life?"

"The only thing worth having?" mused Cesare half to himself. He thought for a moment. "I'm not sure I do know."

"I'm sure you do. The only thing worth having in this life is love, it's true love. Lucia Gianbullari loves you not me. And you love her. That love is worth more than a thousand farms and a thousand farms are worth nothing to me. I love you for the brother that you are and when a love is true you will do anything for it."

Cesare thought he understood, but he wanted to be sure. "So you don't want to marry Lucia, then?"

"The match with Lucia will not be made between her father and ours, it is a match that has been decreed by a force much greater than that. It is not a match that depends on a dowry and an exchange of worldly goods."

"So you wouldn't mind if I married her then?"

"No, Cesare. I positively encourage it."

"But you still want the farm?"

"No. I don't want anything. I have set a course to work as a musician and a composer. I love the farm and I adore and respect our parents, but it is not my path to take what our father would give to me. Stay here and marry Lucia who will bear you many healthy children."

"And what of you? Who will you marry? What will you inherit?"

Giacomo looked at Cesare ruefully. "My heart is already accounted for but I will inherit nothing. I have my music and through that I am able to make a livelihood. My life is planned as much as yours."

"But you haven't answered my question?"

"The answer you heard is the only one I am able to give you."

Cesare pondered this for a moment. "You truly mean what you said though, about the farm and everything?"

"Of course, why else would I say it?"

"I don't know. I've never heard of such a thing before. I mean an elder brother being so generous."

"There is a precedent."

"Is there?"

"Esau exchanged his birthright with Jacob for a mess of pottage."

"And I'm not giving you even that."

"You don't have to. Knowing that you and Lucia will live a long and happy life together is enough for me."

"Then you will visit us to ensure that we do?"

"Whenever you invite me, yes, of course I will."

"You will need no invitation, brother." Cesare stood up from his milking stool and wiped his hands on the backs of his breeches. He raised his arms towards Giacomo and they embraced.

Cesare finished the milking and they returned to join the rest of the company.

* * * * * * *

Under the roof of his parents' house, where he had spent almost his entire life, Giacomo passed several sleepless nights. He always knew that Cesare and Lucia were intended for each other. Neither he nor anyone else could do anything to interfere with the force that decreed their union to be sanctified in the name of God. The destiny of the spirit was part of the divine will. He was destined to be with Maria, but circumstances had wrenched their earthly beings apart. Yet he believed that man made rules and requirements would not ultimately override the divine will.

From time to time images of Maria disturbed him. Whether those images came to him in dreams or during moments of semi-consciousness he could not always be sure. On each occasion her appearance was awash with garish, almost fluorescent, colours. Formless shapes surrounded her, elongated figures with sunken eyes and distorted physiques. Lurking in the background, they contrasted with Maria's grace and simple, but cultured, elegance. Each time he tried to dislodge her from his conscious thoughts she invaded them once again. The process was both exhausting and frustrating. Like Maria, he believed that the inspiration for his own journey was one that came from a higher force. And yet, if he was unable to join Maria at the place to which she had been directed, he queried the earthly whereabouts of the destination he should now seek for himself.

This uncertainty was shared by his father whose disappointment with Giacomo's decision sporadically turned to anger. "Is there nothing you can say to him that will make him change his mind?" he said to Dulce, his wife.

"Nothing that I know. Since the day I gave his uncle's lute to him you know he's been a musician at heart."

"And I wager that you regret giving it to him in the first place."

"Regret it? No. Even before that he was keen on singing. Remember how they used to give him solo pieces to sing in church when he was no more than six or seven years old?"

"I still find all this hard to accept."

"You can't crush the spirit of free will."

"Free will? Nonsense. There's no place for free will here and I'll say something more …" Bonaccio stared at Dulce in the hope that she might sense what he was going to add, thus making it unnecessary for him to articulate the thought that troubled him.

"What's that?"

"It's that … I am certain that no good will come of it."

Dulce did not share his view but it was clear that anything she might say would have no effect.

There were numerous further conversations on the subject. When it came time to return to Florence, Giacomo was reassured that his father understood there was to be no change of mind.

And so amidst the mutterings of his father, the tears of his mother and the unrestrained joy of Cesare, Ragaci made his way into San Gimignano. There he was due to meet Vannozzi who would then give him a ride back to Florence in his carriage. Upon arriving at the entrance to the Taverna Storioni, Giacomo was greeted excitedly by Bartolo, a gangly, awkward looking young man. His round even features broke into a huge smile.

"What news, Bartolo?" asked Ragaci as he embraced his friend.

"Cicilia is with child. I am to be a father!"

The news, though unexpected, could have been predicted, though not the timing of its announcement. Bartolo was the first of Ragaci's contemporaries to wed and he would be father to the first of a new generation.

It was not the fact of Bartolo's impending fatherhood that stopped Ragaci in his tracks, it was the sudden realisation that, by forfeiting the hand of Lucia Gianbullari and consciously abandoning any intention to love anyone other than Maria Salcoiati, he would deny to himself the possibility of procreation. He began to understand the need his father had to ensure his succession.

"It's an important moment when friends start to become fathers," said Ragaci coyly.

"You won't be far behind me, Giacomo. How long will it be before you come back from Florence to marry Lucia Gianbullari?"

"That will not be, Bartolo."

"Of course it will. That much is known to everybody."

"Lucia will marry my brother, Cesare. It is already agreed. And I will remain in Florence, at least for some time hence. Even after that I have no intention of returning to live here."

"What you say cannot be true!" Bartolo's expression was one of genuine surprise.

"As true as the news that you shared with me only moments ago."

"What will you do?"

"I will continue to pursue my calling as a musician."

"For the rest of your days?"

"Yes, for the rest of my days

"Without a wife, without children."

"That, Bartolo, is not in my hands but in the hands of destiny."

"You mean in the hands of the Almighty?"

"As you wish."

"As I pray."

"And I will pray for you too, Bartolo."

They were joined by Vannozzi who was ready to depart.

When the carriage pulled away from the Taverna Storioni, Giacomo looked back as though it was the last occasion on which he would gaze upon its ancient towers. For centuries they had watched over the doings of San Gimignano and its citizens and his thought turned to what they represented – stability, continuity, succession.

Two days before Christmas he had arrived, the eldest son of a local family pledged to the future, to continue its line, to inherit its wealth and to fulfil the role that had been determined for him at the moment of his birth. Now there was no turning back from the path that he had chosen for himself. It was but a few months before he would return to celebrate the marriage of his brother and the birth of Bartolo's first child. Nothing would prevent him from being part of either of those two events, nothing, but beyond them he could see no further and imagined the gates of the town closing behind him for the last time.

XII

Conflagration

Florence. January 1516

There was no telling how it started. Some said it was arson, that intruders broke through a window and used tapers to set fire to tapestries and other furnishings in the Great Hall and elsewhere. Others arriving on the scene soon after the flames became visible swore that they heard a series of explosions. They surmised that barrels of gunpowder had been secreted in various corners of the building and ignited. All believed that whoever was responsible, and it could not have been an accident, had been helped by someone on the inside, a servant who had betrayed the trust of his, or her, master. If that 'someone' survived then he, or she, was unlikely to be identified. Those who perished were no more than ashes. The traitor presumably fled before the conflagration took hold of the building and would probably be starting a new life elsewhere, the means provided by those who committed the deed. Then there was always the possibility that the guilty ones took the more straightforward option and simply murdered the traitor and buried the body.

Within minutes of the first onlookers arriving on the scene, the stained-glass windows of the Great Hall exploded, revealing a candescent wall of flame that was soon licking the ceiling and burning through to the bedrooms above that were already ablaze. It was not much longer before jagged fingers of fire clawed their way through the roof and scratched golden patterns onto the shiny darkness of the winter sky.

Those inside who woke to the malevolent cacophony of the conflagration immediately realised the peril that confronted them. A few managed to open windows but were either roasted alive if too afraid to jump or died on hitting the ground if they were not.

What a few hours previously had prescribed the orbit of forty or more lives, and was intended to do the same for those of a score or more future generations, was transformed into a spectacular funeral pyre. The majestic grandeur of the palazzo was rapidly devoured and, with it, the ambitions and aspirations of Massimo Salcoiati and his sons reduced to a pile of rubble.

The carriage bearing Giacomo Ragaci and Mosciano Vannozzi arrived at the palazzo a little before five in the afternoon on New Year's Day. By then, the intensity of the heat had diminished but flames still sputtered in various parts of the building. What remained was a burnt out shell, roofless, the outer walls blackened with soot. The immediate area was covered by an umbrella of smoke that shrouded the fading daylight. The crowd of people who had stood and stared throughout the day had diminished. A few Republican officers milled around in front of the main entrance and stopped anyone from intruding. Vannozzi and Ragaci stepped out of the carriage.

"How in God's name did this happen?" gasped Vannozzi, addressing the officer who appeared to be in charge.

"Nobody knows," he replied. "Some of those who live nearby say they heard explosions at around four o'clock this morning."

"Explosions?" asked Vannozzi.

The officer shrugged his shoulders. "That's what they said."

"Any survivors?" enquired Ragaci.

"None that we know of. Everyone was asleep and, so far as we are aware, they were all burned alive."

"Everyone?"

"Yes."

"That means the whole family and all of the household!" gasped Ragaci whose emotions began to get the better of him.

Vannozzi tried to stay calm, "though some, like us, were away."

"Not many and not the family." Ragaci was choking his words out through tears that he was no longer able to hold back.

"Apart from Maria Chiara," said Vannozzi.

"Though she will not learn of this for some days."

Vannozzi put his arm around Ragaci who put his hands either side of his face. The officer left them. They stood silently watching the remains of the blaze having its say. Their awestruck contemplation of the disintegrating palazzo was interrupted by the sound of crashing timbers from somewhere deep inside the building.

"Such can be the fate of the material manifestations of human endeavour," said Vannozzi.

"And of life itself," said Ragaci, "which is more disturbing. The inferno of which Dante wrote could not have been worse than this. If this was deliberate then whoever was responsible will surely burn in hell."

"And that is the only place they will burn."

"Why so?"

"I know so."

"You are sure that it was no accident?"

Vannozzi snorted. "If there were explosions then it could not have been an accident."

"Do you have suspicions?"

"I do, but that is all they are ever likely to be. Come, Giacomo, let's go and see if anything is left."

Persuading the officers of the authenticity of their connection to what remained of the palazzo, they drew their cloaks across their faces as protection from the smoke and carefully made their way through the main gate and into the courtyard. The cappella was more or less intact. The plain, white marble statue of the Virgin Mary that stood in front of it was covered in soot, her delicate features charred and saddened. They inched as close as they could to the rear entrance to the building, but it was impossible for them to enter. In spite of the insipid pallor of the day and the cold grey snap of the Winter twilight, the heat from the building made them sweat and the interior was thick with smoke and the sound of falling debris.

Emerging back onto the street, a carriage pulled up in front of the palazzo. A familiar figure emerged followed by three others.

"Leonardo!" exclaimed Ragaci. "You are safe! Alive!"

One of the others Ragaci recognised as Leonardo Salcoiati's friend, Amelio Delgamba, a second he assumed to be Amelio's father and the third, a servant. The Delgamba lived in Grassina, a short way out of the city. Ragaci assumed that Leonardo had spent the previous night there, celebrating the arrival of the New Year. Leonardo fell into Ragaci's arms and started sobbing. "My God, Giacomo, my God what's happened? What's happened?"

"Nobody knows, though there is talk of explosions. Apart from Giacomo and me and anyone else who may have been spending last night elsewhere, there are no other survivors," said Vannozzi gravely.

"And my sister, Maria," gasped Leonardo between sobs.

"Yes, of course."

"Who must be informed as soon as time permits," said Leonardo pulling himself away from Ragaci's embrace and trying to control himself.

Vannozzi counselled Leonardo against viewing the devastation. "There is nothing but smoke and ash, Master Leonardo. You cannot get beyond the courtyard. Maybe we should return in a day or two when the fire has burned itself out, the embers cooled and the smoke dissipated."

Leonardo stared at Vannozzi and then peered through the outer gates of the palazzo. He could see the corner of the cappella and the charred figure of the Virgin. The tears began again and he received Ragaci's embrace like a child seeking solace from its mother. For several minutes they stood together, a gesture of compassion that would forever define the brotherhood that each would henceforth share with the other.

As they pulled back from each other and wiped away their tears, Vannozzi offered both of them a place to stay at his apartment on the Via del Corso until such time as they could collect their thoughts and come to terms with what had happened. Bewildered and bereft, Leonardo readily accepted without question. Ragaci thought for a moment, then politely declined the offer.

"Will you return to San Gimignano, Giacomo?" asked Vannozzi.

Of course it would please his father no end if he was to return and play the role for which he was cast at birth. But, having already stated plainly that he would not exercise options that were safe, he could not change his mind.

"Mosciano, were it not for you I wouldn't have come to Florence. I wouldn't have been able to realise my ambition to earn my livelihood by composing and playing my music. You showed faith and belief in me when no-one else could have done. I can't turn my back on what you've helped me to realise thus far."

"So you will remain in Florence?"

"Florence is somewhere I only ever used to dream of visiting. I have lived and worked here these past six months and achieved more than I could ever have hoped or expected. I believe that it's my destiny to remain, so I'll find a way to do so."

"And where will you go? To a friend?" Vannozzi's tone was one of concern.

Ragaci nodded, a weak smile momentarily replacing his look of sorrow. "Presently, I will seek the company of artists and others who live and work to satisfy the lust of our city for beauty in all things. Even before this tragic event one of them offered me a place to stay if ever I needed it."

"And of whom do you speak, that I may know where you are headed?"

"Pier Paolo Forzetti."

Following the Papal banquet, Ragaci accepted a couple of invitations to visit Forzetti, whose brooding intellect he found invigorating. The company of the other artists and writers that Forzetti kept was a fertile ground for new ideas.

At the same time Ragaci would not describe Forzetti as a friend. No. Forzetti was altogether too bound up in the world of his own creations to have any friends. In fact, Forzetti, and those like him, never formed friendships, but rather they entered into a series of shifting alliances. These alliances lasted for as long as they proved mutually fruitful. Ragaci adjusted his provincial outlook, which respected the sanctity of true friendship, and adapted to the ways of the city. He had formed an alliance with Forzetti.

"He was much admired by my father," said Leonardo. "You may be sure of a warm welcome from him."

"And also time and space to mourn," said Ragaci.

Images of those who he had got to know and in whom he had learned to believe flashed through his mind. Massimo, the patriarch; Aulina, the conscience of the family and of the palazzo who had policed his contact with Maria, but who he always believed had understood and empathised with the impossibility of the situation in which her daughter found herself with him; Bertuccio, reliable, constant, a man he regarded as a good friend, a close ally and a loyal supporter, and a whole host of others who had welcomed him into their lives and with whom he had shared his music, his hopes and his aspirations.

During the few silent moments of community that followed, there was no doubt that Vannozzi and Leonardo were tuned into similar thoughts as they each put their arms around the others and shared their loss.

"Come," said Vannozzi. "Leonardo and I must have rest and find time to grieve before we address what must be addressed."

"I fear that time may be short," said Leonardo, failing to hold back the tears that once again started to flow.

"I fear you may be right," said Vannozzi, "but we'll deal with each obstacle as it falls across our path. Come, get into the carriage. We'll take Giacomo to Forzetti's house. It isn't far from where I live."

Leonardo said goodbye to those who had accompanied him from Grassina who told him that they would find lodging in the city for the night. They indicated that they would stop by Vannozzi's house in the morning in the event that there was anything they might do to assist before returning to Grassina. They followed Vannozzi's carriage as it started off along the Lungarno Terrigiani and headed towards the Ponte Rubaconte.

* * * * * * *

Forzetti lived in a four-storey townhouse house located a few blocks north of San Lorenzo. The house opened up so that its rear was almost twice the width of its narrow frontage. Ragaci received the warmest of welcomes. Forzetti offered him a modest but comfortable room on the second floor. Declining the opportunity of resting, Ragaci accepted something to eat and drink before settling down to talk with his host in the large bright room that served as a studio and that opened onto a square courtyard at the back of the house.

Earlier in the day Forzetti had heard about the fire and went to watch the blaze when it was at its most intense. Rumour and gossip about its cause was already gripping the city.

"Doesn't anybody know how the fire started?" asked Ragaci.

"Only God."

"No human hand played a part?"

"All earthly events are consequences of human endeavour."

"And the Art?"

"Gone. All gone."

Ragaci made a mental list of the lost treasures, works by some who had been at the banquet and by others who had not. There were two magnificent canvasses by Domenico Beccafumi depicting scenes from Ancient Rome, a dramatic representation of 'Balshazzar's Feast' by Raphael and a work called 'Autumn' by the late Sandro Botticelli and which Salcoiati had acquired in settlement of a business debt. Then there was a whole host of family portraits, some by Forzetti, others by Perugino, Gamabaloto and Pontormo. The list continued. There were sketches by the great Michaelangelo and many more by other artists, some of wide repute and others not. All were destroyed. The effect of what had happened began to sink in.

"All of it?"

"Every single piece."

"There were many of your own works there, Pier Paulo."

"There were."

"How do you feel about that?"

Forzetti thought for a moment. "What's gone is gone. It can't be replaced. I won't mourn the loss."

"But a painting contains something of the spirit of the artist as well as those whose images are reproduced."

"A painting lives as a separate entity and then only while it is there to be seen. Once destroyed it lives only in the memories of those who have seen it. When they are gone so is the image."

"You do not care that your art survives and remains as your earthly testament?"

"I care not for what I can never know. And for you, Giacomo. How does the loss of your music affect you?"

"Fortunately I had my manuscripts and my instruments with me, so there was no loss."

Ragaci stood up and walked around the studio. He looked at a couple of works in progress. "Who are these people?" he enquired.

"Ghiraldo Lamberti, a merchant from Pistoia and his wife, Veronica. The merchant is an odious little man with an opinion of himself as large as the Duomo. He insists that his face appears as smooth as silk, yet it bears the residue of many festering sores. His wife is lively and not at all unappealing. She detests her husband but will not admit it. She may be on edge when he is near her, but I warrant that if she attends her next sitting alone she will willingly bed me and I will not resist the temptation."

Ragaci tended to ignore the libidinous side of Forzetti's character. The artist's reputation as a philanderer was well-established. He did not need to boast about his conquests, though often did. Ragaci studied the canvasses carefully.

Forzetti had an unusual ability to expose the inner workings of his subjects. Emotion was heightened by the use of brilliant hues. His work was consciously stylised and the unpleasantness of the merchant was only thinly disguised. His wife's suppressed notion of romance was also apparent – not only in the expression on her face, but also in the pose that Forzetti had contrived for her. In front of a flat background of indeterminate dimensions she sat demurely but wearing a silk dress in a pale, neutral shade that showed her shapely bosom to its best advantage. The angle at which her hands were placed emphasised movement. Forzetti had exaggerated her smile that brought out her innate sensuality. The composition was infused with an infectious vibrancy.

Continuing to browse, Ragaci noticed that the portrait of Maria Salcoiati was leaning against the wall, half hidden by a pile of materials. He assumed the work to have been destroyed along with the rest of the family collection. The vivid realism of the painting was magnetic.

"That one did not perish, dear Giacomo. By good fortune it was saved. Salcoiati asked me to repair some small damage to the edge of the picture shortly before Christmas."

"I wonder how the good lady will bear the loss of her family."

"You should go and see her in the convent and find out. After all she is the woman with whom you are in love."

Ragaci was startled to hear these words spoken aloud. "I beg your pardon!" he exclaimed, challenging the controversy of the statement.

"It's obvious, even from the way you look at her image in oils."

Ragaci had still not admitted to anyone else that it was love that he felt for Maria and love that he hoped she felt for him. In the context of the moment he decided that he could discuss the matter in the abstract with his new ally.

"Even were it so," sighed Ragaci, "speaking theoretically, this earthly life is no place for unrequited love."

"Two questions. The first; how would you know that a love is unrequited and may never be made whole? The second, if not this earth, then where?"

"And what makes you suggest that a love that is unrequited can be made whole?"

"The demeanour of the woman and, in this particular case, the discussions that I had with her when she was sitting for me."

Ragaci's heart began to pound. "What did she say?"

"It's not what she did say but rather what she did not."

"Meaning?"

"I am an observer of people. Maria Chiara is graceful, yet complex. The words she used about her devotion to achieving the divine purpose implied references for a love that may only exist between a man and a woman in this life. The man of whom she spoke was undoubtedly you."

"She identified me?"

"No, but I am quite certain that the references she made were to you."

"And what were these words?"

"There were several. The conversations took place over a number of sittings. It was as though she wished to unburden all of her temporal thoughts before retreating to do His will."

Ragaci sat down again. He picked at a dish of sweetmeats that Forzetti had offered as a dessert.

Forzetti continued. "It didn't surprise me to learn of the way in which she left under the cover of the night to take her vows."

"No?"

"No. Even so, she recognised that while love for God was the ultimate to which she might aspire, she did not deny the importance of the love of a man and a woman for each other." Ragaci carried on chewing while listening intently. Forzetti continued. "Nevertheless, she said that artificial rules and conventions that may prevent a man and a woman from achieving their ideal in this world could not interfere with the process by which she, a Christian, should dedicate her life to serve the will of the Almighty."

"These conventions included the notion of an arranged union?"

"That much was obvious. She also spoke in the abstract."

"Of what?"

"Of the power of the united spirit with a perfect balance of its male and female halves."

"What did she see as the nature of this power?"

"That the power must be harnessed and then accepted by both partners before the spirit may progress on its path to realise the divine purpose."

"And did she suggest what that purpose might be?"

"She did not. My guess is that it is a purpose at which we may only guess and which is not to be revealed during the earthly passage of the spirit."

"And what if the two halves of the spirit are prevented from uniting in this life?"

Forzetti shrugged his shoulders, "Of this she did not speak. It's clear to me that the path Maria Chiara has chosen is irrevocable and so it would be of no relevance to her."

"And what path for me?" he said, half under his breath.

"You will learn to love another, for you ought not to be alone."

Ragaci listened impassively, his expression remaining completely neutral. "And you?" he asked Forzetti, genuinely interested in what the response would be.

"I cannot abide the thought of being tied to but one. It's against my nature."

"And if I am unwilling or unable to learn how to love another?"

"That goes for no man. You will."

"How can you be sure?"

"Experience tells me so. Even if you can't be with the one that you love, there will be those who you will be with and with whom you will want to share the pleasures of the flesh, if not romance."

"That's not my destiny."

"Love and destiny are not mutually exclusive. With or without love it is clear that your destiny lies in the gift that you have to make music. Your music touches people. You write songs that teach people about their lives and their place in the world. Your compositions will always be your progeny."

Ragaci mused about Bartolo Storioni's pregnant wife and related the idea of the birth of a child to his own creativity. The birth of a child enabled a spirit to take human form. The songs that he wrote were no more than musical expressions of thoughts and emotions. It alarmed him that someone such as Forzetti had glimpsed a part of Maria's soul to which even he had not been privy. Yet for all of the artist's insight and perception, Ragaci had not openly admitted anything directly of what he truly felt for Maria.

* * * * * * *

In the weeks that followed, Ragaci set about finding ways to continue working as a composer and musician. His first hope was that Leonardo Salcoiati might rebuild the palazzo and pick up where his father had left off. The stipend that Massimo had paid him, though modest, had been sufficient. It was, however, more of a hope than an expectation.

After a period of mourning that was as short as he had predicted, Leonardo resolved to do what he could to preserve the family assets. On the occasions when he met with Ragaci all he would say was that his affairs were beset with problems, that Vannozzi was doing his best to resolve those problems and that it would all take time. As much he would have liked to engage Ragaci, resources were not then available for patronage of the arts.

In addition to his impromptu performances at street markets and at the Taverna del Cielo, Ragaci started to play at various events around the city and energetically wrote new material. He earned enough to pay Forzetti for his keep, though the durability of their alliance could not be indefinite.

A little while after the musician's arrival, Forzetti decided that he wanted to paint his portrait. Ragaci was naturally flattered.

"But how will I afford to pay you?"

"Don't worry, it's more important that Florence's leading musical talent be recognised in oils on canvas. One day you will pay me."

Ragaci brought his lute into the studio. He wore a fine black tunic, black leggings and a black velvet four-cornered cap. It was the costume that he wore for performances. He found a place in the best-lit part of the studio, where he knew that Forzetti liked to place his subjects, and arranged himself into a pose.

"I don't think you should pose with the lute."

"And why not?"

"Your playing and your skills as a musician may be forgotten, but the music which you write may live on. I know that you care that your work might 'survive and remain as your earthly testament'!"

Ragaci smiled. "Touché."

Forzetti posed the musician on an elegant wooden chair. He held a book of music manuscripts open on his lap. The cover of the book and the back of the chair were subtle tones of red, the only suggestions of colour that the artist used in an otherwise monochrome composition. The background was plain and sombre. Ragaci had resolved not to look at his portrait until it was finished, though from time to time he made clandestine forays into the studio to gaze at the portrait of Maria.

It was a few weeks before Forzetti found time to complete the work. Ragaci was out, playing at a banquet at the Palazzo di Parte Guelfa. Though not yet dry, Forzetti placed the portrait of the musician next to that of Maria Salcoiati. Ragaci was to the left and Maria Salcoiati was to the right. The face of each was inclined a little towards the other. Forzetti waited for Ragaci to return and solemnly ushered him into the studio. The atmosphere in the candlelight was one of suffused gentleness.

He could not have prepared himself for the emotions that started to drown him. Temporarily overwhelmed he looked from one picture to another and then at Forzetti.

"Your work is magnificent."

"Take them to your room."

"Them?"

"Your portrait you can pay for as we discussed. The one of Maria Salcoiati you can keep."

"Surely it now belongs to Leonardo?"

"And I am sure that I can come to some arrangement with him. I am owed some money by the estate of his father"

"If you can that would be fine, and yes, I would like to

keep it. But do that first and let me pay you for my portrait and then I will take them to my room."

"The happy couple together at last."

"You have a vivid imagination."

"And so may it secretly begin!"

Ragaci drew closer to his portrait and inspected it closely. "Exquisite, just exquisite. It's hard to believe that you can create such work. But you have yet to sign your name."

"In good time, Giacomo. In good time."

XIII

Devotion

Arezzo. January 1516

The dull tone of the bell that called the sisters to Vespers imbued the Winter twilight with tints of sorrow. Maria Chiara Salcoiati, having eschewed convention by not choosing another name and now simply Suora Maria, knelt, hands clasped, head bowed. What began as silent prayer inevitably meandered into lengthy bouts of contemplation and self-analysis. Those pillars of certainty upon which she had carefully constructed the foundations of her life had become deeply eroded with doubt. What was worse, the doubt itself ate into the very fundaments of the system of her beliefs.

'By night on my bed I sought him who only my soul loveth; I sought him, but I found him not'. The words that repeatedly drowned her conscious thoughts also confused her. She no longer knew who it was that her soul loved most that it should seek him above all others, whether it was God above or a mortal man who walked the earth.

Earlier that day the news of the destruction of the palazzo and the death of her parents and brothers and their families had been brought to her by Leonardo. The injunction by which she had forbidden contact with visitors, other than her mother and her Aunt Bartolomea, was lifted by the Madonna Suora as soon as the circumstances were made known. Leonardo was permitted to enter the Convent of St Perpetua and St Felicitia.

Following his uncle's directions that took him a short distance out of Arezzo, Leonardo soon found the convent perched on a rocky hill. It looked out of scale against a backdrop of snow-capped mountains. The unprepossessing main building squatted anonymously behind a high stone wall. There was little in the way of external decoration. Even the church was no more than a simple construction of plain blocks. The convent was designed and laid out in such a way that it shamelessly proclaimed the austerity of those who dedicated themselves to live and to pray within it. The only sign of extravagance was the grand campanile, recently restored to incorporate within its architecture a marble coat of arms of Julius II, the previous pope, who was born in Arezzo itself.

The Madonna Suora was probably no more than forty but looked younger. Had she chosen another path she would surely have commanded the attention of many male admirers. Piercing grey eyes beneath arched eyebrows and a bow-shaped mouth could have been the pride of a courtesan. Her features were obscured by the shadow of her mantle and often swallowed by the eremitical darkness of the mediaeval building. The tone of her voice was peaceful, its volume never raised much beyond a whisper. She exuded no deep sense of spirituality. She bore the demeanour of one who had been persuaded into a life that she accepted reluctantly, never admitting to herself that something better would have been available in the temporal world.

Leonardo was shown into the refectory where all visitors from the outside were received. Attached to one side of the cloisters, it was wide enough to accommodate the three rows of simple wooden tables that ran the length of the room. Brittle sunlight barely permeated the small square windows punched into the outer wall, some way above head height. As a concession, a couple of candles flickered restlessly on the mantelpiece above a large but muted fireplace.

Maria was waiting for him at the end of the room. She was bemused as to why she had been called away from her chores in the middle of the day and then astonished to see her twin brother walking towards her, unusually dressed entirely in black.

Heard only once, the description of the shell of the palazzo was enough. She said little in response, but allowed him to hold her close in a silent bond of kinship. The sadness in them both made her body tremble. She felt the sky tumbling down on top of her. Above the sky was heaven from which God could observe her, testing the strength of her faith. He would surely punish her for her doubts. She could not escape punishment whichever way she turned. For failing to do the will of her father, the God-fearing Massimo Salcoiati, she would suffer with guilt for the rest of her earthly life. That was something with which she would need to learn to live. She prayed that the further punishment that would inevitably be visited upon her beyond the grave would not be eternal damnation. Perhaps she might be required to live another life in this world and given a further opportunity to progress beyond it. That was a choice she would willingly make if offered to her.

And what of the musician, the charismatic Giacomo Ragaci? Whatever she might have felt, no human system of which she was aware would tolerate a union between the daughter of a well-to-do banker who moved in the upper echelons of society and an itinerant musician from a family of farmers. She wondered what he might be doing. Leonardo had spoke of those who perished. The name of Giacomo Ragaci was not amongst them.

"And what of the musician, Ragaci?"

Leonardo believed that there was more than innocent concern concealed behind the veil of her enquiry. "At the time of the fire he was with his family in San Gimignano. He returned with Vannozzi a short time before I arrived to witness the remains of the blaze."

"Where is he now?"

"He's lodging with Forzetti and is currently seeking another patron."

Maria received the information impassively. Her expression of sorrow was fixed. It occurred to Leonardo that now he was head of the family he could, if he so wished, arrange a marriage for Maria to someone of her own choosing. Though neither Maria nor Giacomo had ever made any open confession to him of any emotional attachment, whenever the subject of the other had arisen in conversation, their respective thoughts and feelings were transparent.

"You realise that as I am our father's heir I have become legally responsible for you," he said.

"In a manner of speaking," she replied.

"No, as a matter of law."

"I have been accepted by the sisterhood of this convent. My relationship with God and with my convent assumes priority over everything, even over my family."

"Sister, listen to me. If you decide to renounce the sisterhood, you may leave this place and return to Florence."

"For what purpose?"

"That you may resume the temporal life that you loved so well.

"Is that all?"

"That you may unveil your feelings for the one who you love."

"Those who I love are everywhere that I am, my God and his son, Our Lord Jesus Christ."

"There is also love in your heart for another, a mortal man."

Maria received the comment impassively. She considered her response carefully. "Were it so once, it cannot be now."

"You wear a habit but you are not veiled. Have you yet undergone the ceremony of profession?"

Maria hesitated before answering then lowered her eyes.

"You have not yet professed your vows, have you, Maria? It's not too late for you to turn back."

Maria placed the palms of her hands together, lifted them to her breast then bowed her head. Leonardo watched as she prayed in silence. After she finished and made the sign of the cross she observed, "it's true that I have not yet undergone the ceremonies of either profession or of consecration. I am not yet formally integrated into this holy community and I have yet to receive the veil. However, in my heart and in my mind I have already pledged my vows to God and betrothed myself to our Lord Jesus Christ. I cannot turn back."

Leonardo saw the resolution of his sister's expression, he also perceived her doubts. In good conscience he had to pursue his point. "The mortal man of whom I speak is Giacomo Ragaci. Though you have never admitted as much to me, it is he who I believe that you say you once loved and who you now pretend you didn't. I know not for a fact whether your love is reciprocated by him, but I believe it to be so. Return with me to Florence that once again you may each gaze one upon the other. If the love that I believe lies dormant is not immediately awakened, then I will bring you back to this place that you may spend the rest of your days as you have planned."

As much as she tried to suppress them, the doubts began to take control. She began to cry and, once again, she lowered her head into her hands. Leonardo put his arms around her and comforted her.

"You came to tell me of the tragedy that has befallen our family, one that will take me many months and perhaps longer to understand. Now you try and persuade me to abandon my faith with your speculation about a love that may not even exist. Do you think that I would contemplate leaving this holy place in such circumstances?"

Though her indignation was forced, her intent was real. He could broach the subject no further and turned to other matters. He shrugged his shoulders and waited for her to lead the conversation in another direction. She had many questions. Some he could answer and others not.

"I take it that you will continue with your studies as an artist?" asked Maria.

"That is my intention. As soon as the business matters have been settled I intend to pursue art as my calling."

"Is there much to settle?"

"There are many complications, some of which I confess that I do not truly understand, but Vannozzi is helping me."

"What complications?"

"There are problems with several large loans made to the

Republic. The Signoria is questioning their legality and have suspended making the repayments."

"For what reason?"

"As I say, there are complications that I do not fully understand."

Maria furrowed her brow, none the wiser but concerned nonetheless. "And what of the palazzo. Can it be rebuilt?"

"That's not something I'm sure that I want to do. It was always too grand for me. There's more than enough money to buy or even build a fine town house and I am in the process of doing just that."

"And what of our parents and brothers? Where will they be buried?"

"There can be no burial. All who were in the palazzo were burned to ash. There are no remains to bury."

Once again, Maria's emotions got the better of her outward display of stoicism. She fell into her brother's arms and sobbed onto his shoulder. Once she had calmed down, Leonardo took it as his cue to leave.

Maria saw him to the door of the refectory where they said their goodbyes. A veiled sister then escorted him to the Madonna Suora.

"Please look after her," Leonardo asked her.

"We look after all of our sisters." She emphasised the word 'all' as if it was vested with magical significance. "And you may visit again, but, please, not too frequently."

"Thank you Madonna. Perhaps I could attend the celebration of her profession. Is that possible?"

"It is possible, but not usual in our Convent."

Leonardo nodded.

"We are not enclosed but what takes place within these walls is our affair and our affair alone." The Madonna

Suora adopted a tone of admonishment that made Leonardo wonder what precisely did happen within the walls. He had asked Maria very little. It had not been the right moment. He would make amends on his next visit by which time he anticipated that Maria would be veiled. He bade the Madonna Suora farewell and rode back to meet those who had travelled with him. They would spend one more night in Arezzo before returning to Florence.

After Leonardo left her, Maria went into the church, lit a candle and knelt in prayer at the altar that was dedicated to St. Pulcheria. Failing to commune with God, her mind connected disparate thoughts. Leonardo. Home. Family. Servants. Household. Chapel. Music. Giacomo. The last she tried to push away, though she knew that his very being would always continue to play havoc with her subconscious mind. Wherever she turned and wherever she tried to hide herself he would always be inside her head, tempting her to share her life with him. She could not do so. She could not blame Giacomo for the turn of events that led her to her present situation, but, had the love in her heart for the musician not contributed to her decision to go against her father's wishes, would she not have perished in the palazzo with the rest of her family?

She was left alive to suffer with her conscience, as would Leonardo for assisting with her escape. She could not permit her guilty soul to return to the scene of the crime for which, for no logical reason, she felt responsible. She would not taunt the memories of those who had perished by doing what she knew they would have forbidden. As persuasive as Leonardo's suggestion may have been, she could not share her life with Giacomo. The vow she had made to God was made without knowledge of the fate of her family. Though it might be blasphemous to admit it, the consequences of that vow were part of the punishment that she would endure for the rest of her natural life.

She opened her eyes and looked again at the icon of St. Pulcheria. She redoubled her attempts to pray, but her mind was still flooded with the disjunctive thoughts that a few moments earlier she had tried to push away. Giacomo Ragaci. Music. The ballad that he had sung at the Papal Banquet. The virgin had not trusted the young shepherd to lead her through the forest. Though it was legendarily dangerous, the shepherd had successfully completed his mission of taking the sheep though the forest to market and come back safely. The virgin had put her trust in a priest who turned out to be a wolf in disguise and then murdered her. The imagery was chilling. She had heard the ballad only once but, even at the time of its performance, the story seemed familiar, as if she already knew its lurid outcome before Giacomo had sung the final verse. There was something else that had struck her about it. The tale was told in the language of prophecy. Previously she had not been troubled by that, but now she was.

The dull tone of the bell continued to sound. At the last chime she stood, surrounded by her sisters who had made their way into the church. The service began. She concentrated as hard as she could on the lesson. It came from the Gospel according to Mark:

Children, how hard it is to enter the kingdom of God! It is easier for a camel to go through the eye of a needle than for a rich man to enter the Kingdom of God."
The disciples were more amazed, and said to each other, "Who then can be saved?"

Jesus looked at them and said, 'With man this is impossible, but not with God, all things are possible with God'.

Her father had been a rich man. She prayed that at the moment of his death that he and the rest of her family had been at one with God and that they had safely entered the Kingdom of which the gospel spoke.

XIV

Adultery

Florence. March 1516

"Thank you so much for finishing it in time" said Ragaci. He held the gold goblet in his hand and admired the delicate design that was engraved upon it.

"Even for you it'll cost ten florins," replied Cavaliere.

"That's fair enough." Ragaci did his best to hide the tinge of disappointment in his voice, though he well knew that the price was a fair one. There was only so far that his advance would extend. That, together with what he had managed to save, was all but committed.

"If you can't pay me straightaway you may pay me as and when you can. I'll take whatever terms you offer, just leave me something on account."

Ragaci immediately smiled. "Gianluca, you're a real friend."

"We'll drink to it."

Cavaliere walked to the back of his small goldsmith's workshop. He took a jug of wine and a pair of cups from a shelf that was otherwise full of instruments that he used in his craft. He had taken over the workshop from the master goldsmith to whom he was indentured after fighting the

French in the war of 1494. Modest in size, there was enough room for three workbenches and a furnace. Cavaliere, his wife, their younger son and his family lived on the upper floors. The Taverna del Cielo was a few doors along the street.

If not practising the lute or composing in his room or out walking through the city, Ragaci had taken to stopping by the workshop. He would spend an hour or two and sometimes even longer watching Cavaliere and, at times, his part-time assistant at work. While he did, he would provide a musical accompaniment as he rehearsed new and old material. Ragaci was constantly fascinated to observe the molten gold heated to liquid in the furnace. Cavaliere would pour it carefully into a mould in which it would solidify before emerging as a finished object. He was content for Ragaci to stay for as long as he liked. Ragaci would sit at an empty workbench playing and singing and, on occasions, composing new pieces. He dedicated a song to his friend that he entitled 'Il Orificeria Gentile' – 'The Friendly Goldsmith'.

There was a suggestion of spring in the air and Cavaliere had opened up the front of the workshop. Periodically people would gather on the street outside to listen to the talented young musician who had played for the pope himself.

"Salute, Giacomo!"

"Salute, Gianluca." They clinked cups and drank.

"Why did you want me to make this goblet for Forzetti?"

"I have secured patronage and a lucrative patronage at that," said Ragaci excitedly. "I want to thank Pier Paolo for his hospitality and encouragement."

"So you'll be moving out?"

"To an apartment provided by my patron within his palazzo."

"Excellent."

"What is more, my terms are no longer exclusive."

"Which means?"

"Which means that as long as I meet my patron's requirements, I am free to accept commissions from others and to perform when and where I can."

"Even better. So who is your new patron?"

Before Ragaci could answer they were interrupted.

"Drinking on the job?" called Bruno Nurchi. He was passing by outside on his way back from the Porta Rossa and carrying a tray of fresh baked loaves in the direction of the Taverna del Cielo. He stopped and put his head round the door.

"You've made a career of it," quipped Cavaliere. "Come in. Join us and toast Giacomo's good fortune."

"I don't mind if I do. I've got a few minutes before I need to open up."

Nurchi came into the workshop and put the loaves down on the empty bench. Cavaliere poured another cup of wine and handed it to him.

"And what good fortune has befallen you, Giacomo?"

"Ignazio Tolosini has offered me patronage."

"Tolosini?" queried Cavaliere, frowning.

"Out of the fire and into the frying pan," said Nurchi before realising that the joke was hardly in good taste.

"Tolosini? Are you sure about accepting it?" asked Cavaliere dubiously.

"Of course I'm sure. Why not?"

"You've not heard the rumour, then?" Cavaliere clutched the cup to his chest between sips.

"Until he approached me, I had heard nothing about him since Signoria Maria Salcoiati made it impossible for his son Niccolo to wed her by removing herself to a convent in Arezzo."

"And if my memory serves me well, you were not much impressed with Niccolo's appreciation of your music," added Cavaliere.

"That is true," said Ragaci sheepishly. "But it is not Niccolo Tolosini by whom I have been engaged."

"That's hardly the point," replied Cavaliere.

"Tell me the rumour that you heard," asked Nurchi.

"I've heard it said that it was Ignazio Tolosini who had men place gunpowder in the Palazzo Salcoiati and blow it up," said Cavaliere.

"The rumour I heard," countered Nurchi, "was that it was Feduccio Castellani who was responsible."

"That can't be if what I heard but half an hour ago is true," continued Cavaliere, "which is that Castellani has today appointed a magistrate to conduct enquiries into a number of those who had dealings with Salcoiati and to the possible culpability for the destruction of the Palazzo Salcoiatio. "

"Castellani? Appoint a magistrate? How come?" enquired Nurchi.

"Castellani has been given a seat on the Signoria by the Medici."

"Really? The new Signoria has been in office only since the first of the year."

"A vacancy arose," said Castellani ruefully.

"Ah. So you mean that one of the incumbents suddenly died!"

Castellani nodded.

"Another poisoning, no doubt," smirked Nurchi.

"No doubt."

"The next we will hear is that Tolosini will appoint a magistrate to investigate Castellani likewise!" said Nurchi.

"And after that each magistrate will buy off the other magistrate who will each then conveniently find no evidence either way," said Castellani.

Ragaci listened with increasing incredulity. He responded with genuine disdain. "I can't believe that our Republic is governed in this way."

"You'd be as well to, because it is," said Nurchi.

"Has it ever been thus," said Cavaliere. "Even if it was neither Tolosini nor Castellani who was responsible for the extermination of the Salcoiati, then it was someone else and whoever it was will never be formally identified or brought to justice."

"Or put another way," said Nurchi, "no witness has yet come forward to suggest that in addition to paintings and sculptures, Massimo Salcoiati liked to collect barrels of gunpowder and secrete them in hidden corners of his palazzo."

"If there was gunpowder," said Ragaci.

"If … yes … and if the pope is a Medici and the Medici were able to manipulate the Signoria, then the Church and the Medici would run our lives," said Nurchi with a deadpan expression.

"But, the pope is a …" Ragaci stopped mid-sentence. The others laughed.

"Why Tolosini?" asked Cavaliere.

"He was the first to make me a proposal and it is an arrangement that is considerably more favourable to me than the one I had previously."

"Strange that he knew about you and yet waited nearly three months to make his approach," interjected Cavaliere.

"It has something to do with some business agreements that he had with the Salcoiati Bank. My indenture with the Salcoiati had some time to run. I thought that the fire brought it to an end. But, Leonardo – you know he's the youngest of the brothers and a good friend, too – discovered the deed in his father's chambers. He, Leonardo that is, considers that he is still bound by it. He has agreed to pay me what is owed to date but also to release me as part of whatever else it was that he was discussing with Tolosini. Something to do with some loans or something."

"Tolosini will yet have young Salcoiati's undergarments, I fear," said Nurchi.

"Meaning what?" asked Ragaci.

"Another rumour," continued Nurchi, "is that there's an unwritten conspiracy amongst some of those in power to fleece the Salcoiati legacy for whatever they can."

"Why so?"

"The Republic owes many hundreds of thousands of florins to the Salcoiati Bank."

"So does every merchant in Tuscany," added Cavaliere.

"The cost of the Papal celebrations only recently concluded was mostly borrowed from the Salcoiati. The total of that was eventually seventy thousand florins alone."

"Seventy thousand!" gasped Cavaliere. "And for nothing of permanence!"

"With the family virtually extinct, there is no-one but your friend Leonardo to collect the debts."

"Aye and the word on the street is that young Leonardo has not inherited his father's business acumen," observed Cavaliere.

"There's Vannozzi and others who work at the bank," said Ragaci.

"The others will be bought off and so will Vannozzi for that matter," continued Nurchi.

"Vannozzi isn't like that."

"Then he'll be poisoned too," said Nurchi. "He's been around long enough to understand how the game is played. They'll throw Leonardo enough scraps to keep him quiet. The rest'll be gone before he'll have time to count it."

Ragaci stared at Nurchi open-mouthed. He turned to Cavaliere incredulously.

Cavaliere nodded, drained the last of his wine then added, "accusations will be made about Salcoiati's dealings and there will be no-one, not even Vannozzi, to answer them."

"What accusations?" asked Ragaci.

"Does it matter?" said Cavaliere.

"Who will make them?"

"A magistrate."

"Appointed by the Signoria, I suppose?"

"Inevitably," said Nurchi who banged his cup down on the workbench as if to underline the point. "I should be going. Time to open up." Nurchi stood and picked up the tray of loaves and shuffled out of the workshop and down the street to his taverna.

Ragaci looked into his empty cup. "I should warn Leonardo."

"It'll do no good, Giacomo. If he makes trouble they'll take care of him too."

"God in Heaven."

"He's an artist, yes?"

"An aspiring artist, yes, and a very good one too."

"Then the best he can hope for is that some of those who can afford to will engage him to paint for them."

Cavaliere cleared away the cups and crossed to the other side of the workshop where he attended to the furnace. Ragaci packed his lute into its velvet bag that also accommodated the gold cup that was wrapped in a roll of cloth. He counted out some coins from his purse and placed them on the workbench. "Thank you Gianluca. I'm leaving you five now. I will pay off the rest just as soon as Leonardo pays me."

Cavaliere turned from the furnace. "Whenever, Giacomo, whenever. There's no hurry."

Ragaci picked up his bag and left in the direction of Forzetti's house.

* * * * * * *

"Easter is upon us," said Forzetti.

"You're observation is well founded." Veronica Lamberti was enjoying the experience of her second commission of the artist so very much more than the first. Posing as Venus, the Goddess of Love, she was naked and draped across a divan. Propped up on one arm, her ample breasts were exposed above a length of silk of burnished ochre that barely covered her labia. Later, Forzetti would add male figures representing two of the Goddess's many lovers. Aries would be on one knee by her feet in a pose of erotic supplication. Adonis would stand behind her, making as though to leave, with an expression of disdainful envy.

Forzetti knew not if her husband, the merchant Ghiraldo Lamberti, had approved the image. He had come to the conclusion that Lamberti would probably not give a stuff.

Progress, however, was slow and, given the amount that he had agreed for the commission, much slower than Forzetti would have preferred. His estimation that Veronica had been ripe for seduction was correct. On the first occasion he bedded her she responded like a pile of dry timber that needed the smallest of sparks to burst into flames. He feasted on her luscious body and filled her three times in succession. Forzetti was not the first lover she had taken during the course of her marriage, though he was the most accomplished by a long way. So long as she was discrete, Forzetti need have no fear of condemnation or recrimination. Her husband had only been interested in sex for the purpose of procreation and three children were enough for him. Ghiraldo's only passion lay in sodomising one or other of the string of handsome young stable boys that he would hire and then dismiss on a regular basis.

On the second occasion Veronica fucked Forzetti, she insisted that they employ each and every item of furniture there was by way of prop to vary and enhance the positions in which she achieved a series of climaxes of increasing intensity. As her visits to his studio became more frequent, so the rate of his productivity began to decline. By the time he finished Veronica's portrait he had begun to tire of her. He was also sexually involved with another, a pretty young serving girl who worked in a palazzo nearby. But termination of the arrangement was not on Veronica's agenda.

When she first suggested a second canvas many times the dimensions of the first, Forzetti was unable to resist the lucrative commission. Even more, he was excited by the challenge of painting a full-length, reclining, nude Venus in a scene of unrestrained eroticism. She did not hesitate to seize on his suggestion that she be immortalised in a pose that equated her image with one of the deities. What he did not realise was that the canvas was of secondary interest to her. She was obsessed by his ministrations to her desires and could not contemplate doing without them. When he eventually sought to ignore, then refuse, a request that he pleasure her, she made it clear that failure to do her bidding would result in a charge of rape. She knew the location of every blemish on his body and would not hold back from using that knowledge in evidence if he disobeyed her. She made clear what she wanted, when she wanted it and even how she wanted it. The only response that she would permit was his blind obedience. Faced with the threat of prosecution, probable conviction, a fine, perhaps a public flogging and the likely ruin of his career, Forzetti had no alternative but to do as he was told.

Veronica's obsession with Forzetti was not solely defined by carnal desire. She began to collect his work, seeking out portraits owned by others and picking up a number of the better pieces that were displayed around the studio and for which she would always have her husband pay generously.

"Easter means that I will be travelling to Mantua," said Forzetti.

"And what's in Mantua?" It was an hour since she had had him inside her and was starting to feel that it was time he did something to remedy the situation.

He was familiar with the signs of her hunger and carried on painting. He was making progress. The tones of the flesh of her thighs were exactly as he wanted. Her face was finished and he was working assiduously on some minor adjustments he needed to make to the line of her hair. Soon he could finish the canvas without her.

"A dear friend and the possibility of a major commission."

"Oh no, Pier Paolo, that will not do." She sat up and let the length of silk fall to the floor.

"Damn it woman, can't you stay still," he snapped.

"That wouldn't be much fun for either of us, would it now?" She opened her legs and placed the flat of her hand on her abdomen. Slowly, she slid her middle finger towards her clitoris, then began to stroke it.

"If you would keep still I could finish this damn canvas and get on with some real work."

"What's the hurry?" She stood up and faced him, her legs apart. The length of silk fell to the floor. She walked across to where he stood behind the canvas.

"There's something I need to tell you about Easter and I want you to listen very carefully." As she spoke she slipped her hand into the front of his breeches and closed them around his testicles. "Easter is when my delightful husband will be taking our three equally delightful children to see his even more delightful parents in Prato. It will be an ideal opportunity for you to come and visit me and to do some very hard work on planning your next canvas for me. Understand?" She started to exert pressure on his testicles, not enough to hurt but enough to threaten to do so.

He grabbed her wrist and put as much pressure on it as he could. She yelped and let go of him. He dragged her across the studio and threw her back on the divan. Sometimes they had played rough but she realised that this was not a prelude to a good hard fuck.

"Enough is enough. Easter I'm going to Mantua and not to Pistoia. Do you understand?"

"You bastard. You foolish bastard. Do you realise what you are saying?"

"Yes, I damn well do."

"Are you refusing me?"

"Yes, I am."

She leaned back on the divan, crooked one leg into an arch and swayed it gently as she spoke. "So if I tell you that I want you to fuck me again, now, will you refuse me?"

"Yes."

"Do you know what that means?"

"No, what does it mean?"

"It means that I will bring a charge against you for rape, as I threatened to. Understand?"

"And when did I rape you?"

"Not an hour ago. I will say that whilst I had my clothes off you forced yourself upon me. See, even now I am filled with you." She motioned towards her vagina as if to prove the point.

Forzetti kept his distance. "And what if I say there is evidence to support my story which is, of course, what actually did happen."

"Oh? And what do you say 'actually happened'." She spoke in a tone that was intended to both mock and to challenge.

"That whilst trying to do my work you kept opening your legs, that you got off the divan, that you crawled across the floor on your hands and knees, that you undid my breeches and took me in your mouth before demanding that I fuck you?"

"I'd say you were a liar!"

"And then you tried to blackmail me by making false accusations."

"I'd say you were a fool as well as a liar!"

"Very well." Forzetti raised his hands in front of him.

"Don't you dare hit me, you bastard," she snapped.

"Don't worry, I wouldn't dream of it."

Forzetti clapped his hands. Three men stepped out from behind curtains that hung from ceiling to floor and that divided the studio from a small anteroom where he kept his store of artist materials. Veronica, grabbed the length of silk and covered herself.

"What's going on? Who are these men? What are they doing here?"

Forzetti pointed to each in turn. "First may I present Signor Davide Cristofani an officer of the Court. Then there is Signor Stefano Stoldi a friend of mine, another artist and an honest citizen of the Republic. Lastly, there is Signor Graziano Nasi who is a notary. They have been here since before you arrived. Signor Stoldi has been watching everything through the gap in the curtains. He will swear a statement as to what happened between us that will then be notarised by Signor Nasi who will then pass it to Signor Cristofani who will file a charge of blackmail. The statement could also be passed to your husband should he wish to file a charge of adultery that would lead at the very least to your disinheritance. As you know, under the laws of Florence, where a man has been involved in a situation such as this, with a woman who is only too willing to be pleasured, I will not be penalised in any way at all."

The officer, the notary and Forzetti's friend stood silently in front of the curtain.

"You monster! You pervert! You …" Veronica's face was red, her features twisted with anger. Forzetti said nothing. "Tell them to get out!" She gestured wildly at the three interlopers. Forzetti motioned towards the door and waited till they were out of the room.

"You would do the things that you threatened?" Veronica

spat out the words as if they had made the inside of her mouth dirty.

"Your behaviour leaves me no choice."

"Then that is the end of our relationship?"

"It is."

"And what of the canvas?"

"You can take it."

"It's not finished."

"You can get someone else to do that."

"My husband has paid you for it. One hundred and fifty florins in advance with a promise of a like amount on completion."

"What of it?"

"If you won't complete the canvas then I will take the return of my money."

Forzetti had not reckoned on this. The amount of time he had spent on Veronica Lamberti meant that he had passed up other work. At one point he even reckoned on asking for a further advance, but he saw that that was impossible. Nevertheless, he was ruinously short of money.

"I'm not in a position to pay you right now. Give me a couple of weeks and I will do so."

"And I will cry thief. What will your friends in the next room say to that?"

Forzetti thought for a moment. Even were he to complete the Venus it would take time and he needed to start on other work, some portraits, that would give him some quick cash. Maybe she would take something else instead.

"How about taking another work, one of equivalent value?"

She stood up, secured the silk around her torso, pushed past him and looked at the Venus. Her vanity demanded the flattery that the commission had intended to satisfy. Now she decided that she would best be away from him and never return.

"Alright, but it had better be good."

"I thought you believed all of my work to be good?"

"Stop with your insufferable arrogance."

Forzetti went to the far corner of the room where there were a number of assorted canvasses stacked one behind the other. In truth they were not amongst his better works. Veronica looked at them one-by-one. She had seen them before. They pleased her no more than they had previously. She sneered and said, "you would have me take these immature doodlings instead of my Venus?" She looked around the studio. "What about those two over there?" she said, pointing at the portraits of Ragaci and of Maria Salcoiati.

"They're already sold. You can take any of the others, you can even take them all if you like, but not those two."

"Apart from the two portraits, the rest of them together aren't worth as much as one corner of the Venus and you know it. I will take those two portraits."

"You can't."

"Then you will finish the Venus and you can carry on now." Veronica walked back to the divan and began to arrange herself in her pose.

Forzetti strode towards her and through gritted teeth he said, "I will not have you in my studio and I'm not going to finish the Venus."

"Then you are a thief and I will file a charge."

"Then take the paintings in the corner."

"I wouldn't take them even to keep the fire alight in the middle of winter. Give me those portraits, the one of the musician and the one of the young woman. I will then get dressed and we need never see each other ever again."

Forzetti was flummoxed. At that moment the only thing he wanted was to be rid of Veronica Lamberti. He made a decision and would take the consequences in his stride. "You may have the portraits but get out and get out quickly."

"I will have my coachman come in and fetch them as soon as I walk out of here."

She went behind the screen where she had hung her clothes and began to dress before making ready to leave Forzetti's studio for the last time.

* * * * * * *

Not long after Veronica Lamberti left, Ragaci returned to Forzetti's home where he found the artist sitting at the table in his kitchen working on a sketch.

"Greetings, Pier Paolo. This is for you," he said, placing the small package on the table.

"What's this?" asked Forzetti, not showing much interest.

"Before I move to my apartment, I wanted to present you with a small gift to thank you for your hospitality and your friendship."

Forzetti unrolled the cloth and admired the goblet that had been handcrafted for him by Gianluca Cavaliere. "Thank you Giacomo. That's both gracious and very generous of you."

"There's also this." Ragaci put a small leather purse on the table. From the sound that it made, it obviously contained gold coins. "Twelve florins and fifteen soldi we agreed."

"Twelve florins and fifteen soldi? For what?"

Ragaci looked puzzled. "For the painting. My portrait. And now I'll feel happy about taking the portrait of Maria Salcoiati as well."

Forzetti thought for a moment and replied, "unfortunately those paintings are gone."

"Gone? What do you mean, gone?"

"They have already been sold and were taken away this afternoon."

"I don't understand."

"I was put in a position where I was forced to part with them."

"They weren't stolen?"

"No," said Forzetti tentatively, for a split second, afterwards thinking that it would have been smarter to say 'yes'. "No, they were not stolen."

"You had already accepted my offer."

"Yes, yes." Forzetti now seemed to be distracted.

"Another offer? More money?"

"It wasn't the money."

"What was it then?"

"It was life."

"Life?"

"Life sometimes means that you do things that you have to do and not because you want to do them."

"Doesn't friendship mean anything to you?"

Forzetti was beginning to collect his thoughts. How stupid he had been, even more so not to have rehearsed a script in his mind before Ragaci came home. "Not when placed next to love," he said, trying to anticipate the next question before Ragaci asked it.

"And what do you know of love?" demanded Ragaci.

Forzetti picked up the gold cup and started to twist it in his hand.

"You once told me that you had no time for love, that you didn't believe in it," said Ragaci. "That it didn't happen to work for any longer than the time during which you were in the company of a woman who sought gratification. That you had no more time for it than that."

"I wish I'd remembered that when it was important for me to have done so," said Forzetti abstractedly, now twisting the goblet in the opposite direction.

Ragaci looked at him contemptuously, but Forzetti was avoiding eye contact as he continued to gaze at the goblet while he played with it. Ragaci picked up the purse and left the room. Their alliance had reached its inevitable conclusion.

The following morning Ignazio Tolosini sent a carriage to collect Ragaci and to transport him and his belongings to the apartment that awaited him at the grand palazzo on the Borgo Ognissante. Easter was only a couple of weeks away and he had been asked to compose some sacred music to celebrate the festival. Before he started that, he needed to finish a ballad that told of the disappearance of a collection of valuable paintings. Its theme was a metaphor for the loss of innocence and the consequences that arise from the destruction of aesthetics and idealism.

From time to time Ragaci ran into Forzetti, but the bond was broken and could never be repaired and neither of them would ever again see the portraits of the Musician and Maria Salcoiati.

— XV —

Reunion

New England. October 1985

A cool breath of wind skimmed across the sparkling maroons and golds of the New England fall. The undulating calm of the Berkshire Mountains rested easily in the stillness of the autumn sunshine. Bucolic splendour was temporarily replaced by urban shabbiness. Routes 7 and 20 stuttered through the weary diffidence of downtown Pittsfield, Massachusetts.

Matt Dayton pulled the rented Chevy into a gas station. He still had close to half a tank, but he had been on the road for more than three hours since leaving his Manhattan hotel. He needed to take a break, drink something cold and mentally prepare. As exhilarating as it was, his first ever visit to New York had exhausted him. Three days locked in meetings in the air-conditioned claustrophobia of a Third Avenue skyscraper drained his energy and sapped his strength. Having justified the cause for the trip, he was free to concentrate on his main purpose.

After graduating from Cambridge, Matt had taken a job with an advertising agency. Greenbridge Delaney Fox McLaren gave him the opportunity to work as a creative and sufficient incentives to turn down the offer of continuing at University to study for a Masters. Fifteen months later, his talent and ideas were already winning recognition. His work on the copy for a new range of cosmetics made him indispensable to meetings at which its international launch was planned. Extending his stay for a long weekend had not been a problem.

For more than two years he had exchanged correspondence with Olivia Giorgianni, though the relentless pressure of his new career left him little opportunity to write letters and less mental space for her. Often he managed not much more than a page or two, briefly reviewing movies or plays that he had seen and restaurants where he had eaten. Yet the correspondence kept going. He believed that sooner or later they would meet again. When face to face with her, he might better know whether or not there was more to their relationship than a chance meeting on an aeroplane and a correspondence that, to him at least, always promised more than a muted, albeit sincere friendship.

Now he was only twenty miles away from her. Now he could start to live the dream. Now the reality of her existence began to consume him.

Matt got out of the car, stretched his arms and squeezed his eyes shut. His mind opened the picture that he always carried there. It captured the moment when they parted at the airport in Pisa. It was so much more vivid than the occasional snapshot that she had sent to him. He could still feel the grip of her hand, the touch of her lips and smell the scent of her hair.

"Good morning."

Matt opened his eyes. The gas station attendant was a portly man in his mid-sixties with a ruddy complexion, silver white hair and a walrus moustache. He wore a baseball cap and blue overalls on the breast pocket of which 'Tom' was embroidered.

"Fill her up?"

Matt nodded. He watched Tom click the pump onto auto, then start to wash the windscreen with a tattered sponge.

"Here on vacation?"

"Kind of. I've been in New York on business. I'm on my way to Williamstown to visit an old friend."

"Couldn't 've picked a better time."

"Right. Though I have left it two years."

"Hey, don't worry about that. It's always like this around now. If you miss out one time, there'll always be another." Tom dropped the sponge into a bucket and started to work with a squeegee. "Yup. Every year Fall comes round, the leaves are always … like that. Beautiful." He motioned towards the tree-covered hills at the edge of the town, a patchwork quilt of brilliant colours.

"How long does it stay like this for?"

"Till about the time the first storm comes in around the end of the month. First strong wind and they blow off pretty quick."

A flock of birds flew overhead, wheeling from the west to the south. They were watched by a solitary broad-winged hawk that sat on the roof of the gas station and started to caw.

"Someone's going to miss the mating season," mused Matt.

"Sure as hell is. He should have taken an earlier flight." Tom chuckled to himself and finished wiping the windscreen dry. "I reckon you'll be able to see a little clearer."

"Right. Thanks. I'm sure I will."

"That'll be eight dollars and forty-seven cents."

Matt followed Tom into the single-storey brick building. He took a can of cold Pepsi from a cavernous fridge and dithered over the confectionery counter. A childhood steeped in Cadbury's Dairy Milk meant that the appeal of the much vaunted Hershey's chocolate had passed him by. He toyed with the widely heralded Snickers, but with which he was unfamiliar. Eventually he went for a Mars bar, supposing there was not too much that could be done with the recipe to make it inedible. He settled up with Tom.

"If you're heading for Williamstown and you have the time, you might want to take a side trip up to Greylock," said Tom.

"Yuh? What's there?"

"Highest point in the county. Marvellous view on a day as clear as this."

"How do I get there?"

"Stay on 7. There's a road off to the right about ten miles down. It's posted. Shouldn't take you more than about fifteen, twenty minutes to get to the top."

"OK. Maybe I'll do that."

Matt returned to his car and pulled back on to the highway. Time was moving on and he did not need to be side-tracked. Perhaps Olivia would want to take a ride up there over the weekend. He imagined surveying the magnificence of the vista alone with her, their arms around each other, silently breathing in the clear mountain air. Approaching a signpost marked for Greylock, he slowed down and noted the surroundings for future reference. He put his foot on the gas and carried on north. He wound down the windows, turned up the radio and kept his speed at a law-defying seventy whenever he could. The effect of the drive was liberating.

A short while later he entered Williamstown, passing the sign at the town line indicating that it had been incorporated in 1765. After driving through dense woods the road opened out. The Williams Inn came into view. It was modernised but had the flavour of an old-style inn and exuded New England tradition. It was packed with city dwellers who had come to enjoy the luxuriance of the fall foliage.

During the two years since their first meeting they had never once spoken by phone. Calling her on arriving in New York to finalise their arrangements was a necessary thing to do, though he was almost relieved when she had not been there to speak to him.

In truth, Olivia deliberately did not pick up the phone. She monitored all of her calls with an answering machine and, on this occasion, she allowed the tape to record his message. She listened to his educated English tones and then, when replaying the message for a second time before deleting it, she detected a nervousness in his voice. It mirrored the trepidation that she felt about their meeting, though her reticence was for reasons that were very different to what she imagined his to be.

When returning his call she made a point not to get through to his room, but to leave a message with the front desk. Matt held the neatly-typed note in his hand. 'Olivia Giorgianni called and said that she would meet you for lunch in the lobby of the Williams Inn at 12.45 on Friday'.

The clock moved on to twelve forty-one and he was standing anxiously in that lobby. He browsed through tourist leaflets arranged neatly in a rack near the bell desk. Local tourist sites vied with arts and craft stores for attention. The clock behind the front desk tipped onto twelve forty-two. He was attracted by the movement of the second hand. There were one hundred and eighty seconds left for him to wait.

When Olivia walked through the front entrance, she saw him turn again to look at the leaflets. He picked up one that extolled the virtues of a museum in nearby Bennington, Vermont dedicated to the naïve artist Grandma Moses.

She stood looking at him. She hoped that he would not notice her. He was dangerous this one. Her heart may still have been open but her mind was not. Whatever she felt, her sense of self demanded that she should not divert from the course upon which she was already set. She would not let herself be prevented from reaching the frontiers of her ambition by a cold blast from the old world.

She maintained her equilibrium in spite of the forces that conspired against it. The perfectionist standards to which she aspired were continually tested by the expectations of her faculty. Her concentration was disrupted daily by phone calls from the battlefield on which her parents were fighting over the diminishing assets of their marriage, having finally decided that a divorce was the only civilised way in which they each might continue with their respective lives.

Olivia took a carefully calculated approach to her life. Her main precept was to avoid repeating the mistakes of those around her. Determined to achieve self-sufficiency and financial independence as soon as possible, her plan was simple but certain. She would graduate at the end of the following semester and start her Masters in History soon thereafter. A graduate scholarship and a part time job at an academic bookshop would be sufficient to enable her to live modestly but comfortably. She would take a position teaching undergraduates and possibly look to study for a doctorate. Then she would be free of the continual attempts of her parents to make her feel guilty. Sometimes they succeeded.

The path she intended to take was one in which her career would be the stabilising force. Though she preferred to get on without the distraction of a relationship, she had not completely ruled out the idea of marriage. At some point, a carefully considered marriage with an undemanding partner would at least keep the other guys at bay, those who constantly hit on her, whether they were academics in the faculty or those introduced to her by well-meaning friends. Sexual politics and the adolescent games that people played using the pursuit of love as a pretext held no interest for her. She suppressed any feelings she might have towards any particular man, including Matt Dayton. She found it hard to admit even to herself that he had been able to provoke in her something that no-one else yet had. All there had been was a two-hour plane ride and a correspondence that she had originally entertained almost reluctantly. She was almost embarrassed to admit to the jump her heart gave every time she saw a letter arriving in her mailbox with a British stamp in the corner and an English return address on the back. When the knowing nods and nudges of her room-mates demanded comment, she would pull herself back and explain, quite truthfully, that theirs was a purely intellectual correspondence and that there was no suggestion of any romantic attachment. That was the written word. Seeing him standing not more than a few yards away, she knew otherwise. The restrained content of her letters that was intended to preserve her isolation and independence was under attack from her emotions.

He sensed that she had arrived. Flipping the Grandma Moses leaflet back in the rack he turned again towards the main door. The suddenness of his movement took her by surprise. She blushed.

Immediately he saw her, he, too, knew that the emotions he had carefully kept under wraps for more than two years were real and waiting to unfold. She was even more beautiful than he remembered, natural good looks that needed little make up. A short leather jacket over a light-coloured cashmere sweater and narrow-cut slacks emphasised the trimness of her physique.

He walked over to greet her. He badly wanted to kiss her. Something prevented him – as though she projected an invisible force field borrowed from a low-budget sci-fi movie. He gently took her hand and shook it.

"You just got here?" he asked excitedly

"Actually I've been here for a couple of minutes," she said. Then she quickly added a white lie, though, on reflection, she did not know why she needed to justify herself. "I didn't realise it was you over there."

God, another two minutes wasted, he thought and said, "I'm so pleased to see you again."

"Likewise," she said, politely, but deliberately suppressing any emotion.

All of his carefully rehearsed lines disappeared. He fumbled for something to say. "It worked out well. Coming here now."

"Right. It's the best time of year, with the Fall and all of that."

"I mean that I was coming here for work and it wasn't far to come to see you."

She was listening carefully to everything he said. She would take evasive action if there was any possibility, no matter how remote, that he might lure her into saying anything she might subsequently regret. They looked at each other studiedly: Matt suddenly overwhelmed by the impact of the moment unable to articulate his thoughts and feelings; Olivia, stoic, withdrawn, afraid. Matt unable to take the conversation where he wanted it to go. Olivia unwilling to let him even try.

"Where do you suggest we eat?" asked Matt.

"I thought we'd go to one of the places on Water Street. We can walk from here. You'll get an idea of the town and I can point out some sights as we go"

He followed her out onto the street. They walked towards the campus that dominated the middle of the town in a manner that was both modest yet subtly impressive. She relaxed a little as she motioned towards this or the other building and topped up her gestures with information about the history of the town and the college.

They decided on a vegetarian deli with a quaint shopfront and ordered salads and fresh juice squeezed from organically grown fruit. Matt took an object from his leather bag.

"Here, this is for you."

He handed her a gift-wrapped package. She accepted it gracefully but with a look of surprised embarrassment. "I didn't get you anything."

"You didn't have to. Just you being here with me is enough."

She pretended not to hear what he said. "Thank you. Thank you very much. Shall I open it?"

Matt nodded and watched as she unwrapped her present. Inside a red velvet bag was a delicate olive wood music box. The lid was decorated with a reproduction of a Baroque painting.

The painting was called 'Time Overcome by Hope, Love and Beauty' by a seventeenth-century French artist, Simon Vouet. It depicted Time as an old man being attacked and defeated by Hope and Beauty, shown as two nubile women. Each of the assailants wielded vicious weapons and were visibly elated with the victory that was theirs. The old man's scythe had been beaten out of his right hand as he had used it to try and fend off his assailants. His hourglass lay sideways on the ground. The sand was static, unable to flow one way or another. Leaning over a bough in the centre of the picture and presiding over the proceedings was Cupid.

Olivia handled the box carefully, taking in the details of the painting. She flipped up the clasp and opened the lid. A quaint tune started to play. Inside the box was the key for the clockwork mechanism that played the music and a small leaflet. It included biographical details about the craftsman who had designed the box, a brief appreciation of the painting and some information about the music. The tune was from a ballad composed by an unknown musician, probably Italian, and believed to date from the first half of the sixteenth century. Apparently there were lyrics that were lost but were believed to tell the story of a shepherd and a virgin who is devoured by a demon wolf disguised as a priest. Olivia thought the piece sounded vaguely familiar, but she could not immediately place it.

Matt watched her carefully. Her body language gave away almost as little as her silences. She looked up at him briefly but averted his gaze by turning her attention to the leaflet which she read assiduously.

"You like it?"

"Yes, really," she said. "it's very beautiful."

"And the painting?"

"It's interesting. Is it one of your favourites by any chance?"

"How did you guess! I saw it in the Prado when I was in Madrid last year. It really blew me away."

"So you think that time can be made to stand still?"

"Not really. I see an interesting paradox in this picture. Time constantly moves forward and changes the physical world through which it flows. More to the point, time affects the lives of people and the way they live. And yet, there are other forces that are dynamic and eternal and exist outside and beyond the concept of time. These forces are the things that matter to a human life."

The look in Matt's eyes as he spoke told Olivia all that she needed to know. She found herself fighting her instincts and retreating behind her intellect.

"I think you're reading too much into it. It's just a sentimental view about romantic idealism."

"But don't you think that all idealism is, by its very nature, romantic?"

She thought for a moment.

"Put it another way," he continued, "what are you idealistic about?"

That was easy. "My work."

"Where will that lead you?"

"Somewhere I can achieve my ambitions."

"And what are they?"

"To do the best that I can in my undergrad and then my Masters. Maybe then a PhD. At the same time I want to teach and share what I learn with others. That's it." And then she added, "I really love my work."

"Love implies at least an element of romance!"

"Yes. And a whole lot more besides."

"Right. And the purest expression of love is that between a man and a woman who are totally dedicated to each other."

"Hey, Matt. That's just fairy tale stuff. That's a dream."

"Life is all about making dreams come true."

"There's something in that but I don't happen to share the dreams of an unreconstructed Renaissance man like you."

They were interrupted by a waitress bringing their food. They had not noticed that the music had come to a stop. Olivia carefully closed the lid and put the box back into its velvet bag.

She turned the conversation neutral. "What are your plans for the weekend?"

"To spend time with you. Anything else is a bonus. As long as I don't get in your way. I thought that maybe we could take a trip up to Greylock. I'm told that the view from the top at this time of year is outstanding."

She tried to hide a look of concern by being nonchalant. "Hmm. Well this afternoon I'm planning on finishing an assignment and tomorrow I'm invited to a wedding."

His face fell. He couldn't believe that after two years she would not have been able to organise things so that they could spend as much as possible of this precious weekend together.

"But there's a faculty party tonight. You're welcome to come along."

"Great." An intimate dinner at a quiet corner table in a candlelit restaurant was what he had in mind, but so long as he was with her he would accept what was already planned. Maybe the wedding would be finished by late afternoon so they could meet in the evening; and then he didn't have to leave on Sunday until after lunch.

"Yes. We can pick you up at your hotel at around seven. Is that OK?"

"Er … yes … OK."

Olivia could see that the reference to 'we' had fazed him. He tried hard to disguise the fact. Although he was itching to know who she meant by 'we', Matt was overwhelmed by a sudden bout of uncharacteristic Englishness and decided not to ask. She steered the conversation back to safer terrain. She let him ask her about what she had been like as a child, what she enjoyed eating, where she bought her clothes, her mother's maiden name. However, he forgot to ask if she'd ever attended religion school.

After lunch, they left the restaurant and wove their way through untidy scrums of tourists and shoppers. The colours of the day were fading and saddened by layers of cloud that began to fill the sky. They stopped at the top of Water Street. Before heading back to her studies, she directed him towards the Sterling and Francine Clarke Institute where he might enjoy a little-known collection of Impressionist paintings.

He bent forward to kiss her cheek. The gesture was subsumed by a fierce gust of wind that blew down the street, angrily rustling trees and momentarily silencing the early afternoon hum of the town. He watched her walk towards the heart of the College campus then he turned in the direction of South Street. The wind redoubled in its intensity and flying leaves began to fill the air. He bent his head, squinted into the wind and headed towards the Clarke.

* * * * * * *

If the afternoon had been anti-climactic, then the evening was positively cathartic. The other part of 'we' turned out to be Greg; tall, fair-haired, well-built, good-looking and with remarkably little to say for himself. As much as Matt discovered about him was as much as he needed to know. While attending a State University, Greg concentrated on playing basketball and on the doings of his fraternity. The degree that he achieved was of secondary importance to someone being groomed to take over the long-term administration of the family's substantial real estate holdings. Greg Worsley was not the sort of guy who made enemies. He greeted Matt politely and showed as much interest as was appropriate for a brief encounter with a passing acquaintance from another continent.

Matt could only feel envy for the man who, from time to time during the early part of the evening, put his arm around Olivia and drew her closer to his side. Early on and possibly later too, Matt did not hang around too long to find out. He did not think that Greg meant too much in the greater scheme of things. His was the nervous kind of physical contact with a woman, where the man is not too sure of how he is doing, and the woman fails to respond, deliberately. The gaps between relationships in Matt's curriculum vitae suggested that a woman's failure to acknowledge the contact either constituted a test, or, most often a complete lack of interest. Olivia remained unruffled throughout each repetition of the process, holding her glass in two hands and pretending not to notice. Nevertheless Matt found the situation hard to take.

In spite of the fact that his English accent and ostensibly trendy occupation had a bevy of young women buzzing around him, he gradually slipped onto automatic pilot, became irritated, then annoyed and then made his excuses and left.

* * * * * * *

The next morning he drove aimlessly out of town, east on Route 2. A few miles down the road there was a signpost for Greylock. This time he resolved to make it to the top. He followed the road as it switch-backed up the side of the mountain. He slowed as the gradient steepened. What looked to be overcast from the road was actually low cloud that covered the upper part of the mountain like a shroud. Doggedly he continued while realising that the much touted view would almost certainly be obliterated. Eventually he reached the summit. He stopped the car and got out. The raw cold and the dampness of the air bit through his sweater. Visibility was less than a dozen yards. The top of the observation tower could not be seen from its base. He resolved that one day he would return and reckoned that when did he would be able to see a little clearer. With the weekend faltering to a disappointing end he decided to cut his losses, head to JFK and fly back to London a day early.

On returning to the Williams Inn the receptionist handed him a package. It was a present from Olivia. He unwrapped a book of paintings from the collection of the Metropolitan Museum in New York. A page was flagged with an envelope addressed to him. The picture she marked was 'Pygmalion and Galatea' by Jean-Léon Gerôme. Matt recalled that the Pygmalion of Ovid's Metamorphosis was a sculptor who created an ivory statue portraying his ideal of womanhood. He fell in love with his own creation. Venus, the goddess of love then answered the hapless sculptor's prayers and brought the statue to life. In this particular painting, Pygmalion was embracing his love as her life emerged from solid mass. Galatea was viewed from the back. Her legs were white and static, segueing into flesh tones at the level of her buttocks. Her naked torso was bent towards the sculptor whose left arm was around her. She gripped Pygmalion's right hand with her left as though trying to pull it away from the region of her breast. Venus' bidding was done by Cupid who fired his bow from the top right hand corner of the frame. A number of other symbols littered the scene – dramatic masks, a warrior's shield, a fish at the feet of Galatea, the sculptor's discarded hammer, fragments of chipped ivory and a couple of completed statuettes on a shelf.

Matt opened the envelope. On a plain card Olivia had written: 'Sometimes when dreams come true they turn out not to be what was wished for'. The irony of the sentiment was too obvious. He stopped himself from jotting a quick note back to say so.

He went to his room and called Olivia. There was no reply and so he left a short message thanking her for the present and hoping that they might stay in touch. He hurriedly packed, checked out and was on the road and gone.

* * * * * * *

As soon as he was back in London, work took centre stage once again. Nevertheless, he continued to mentally replay the events of his relationship with Olivia, his own ivory statue. His sense of realism elbowed the notion of ideal love to one side. However, with an urge that he was unable to quell, he attempted to resume the correspondence. He went through several editions of a succinct note in which he endeavoured to explain what he felt about her. Yet, however hard he tried, the cleverly drafted double entendres too often came over like cheap come-ons and so he kept with meaningless nothings. The only response arrived a few weeks later in the form of a Christmas card inscribed with pithy sentiments. He sent one back and then heard nothing more. The following year they exchanged Christmas cards once again and, in the year after that, his card was returned marked 'Gone away. Return to sender'.

XVI

Ambition

Florence. April 1517

The patronage that Ragaci enjoyed under Ignazio Tolosini was altogether different to his previous experience with the Salcoiati. Summoned by his patron to play less frequently and with a more substantial budget at his disposal, Ragaci began to experiment with other musicians and to compose and arrange for larger ensembles. Left free to accept commissions and invitations to perform wherever he chose, his recitals became sought after events. Although the extended artistic freedom enabled him to adopt many styles of composition, he was most in demand for his hallmark ballads that were imbued with elements of mysticism, religious imagery and the pursuit of perfection in all things.

His self-effacing charisma and handsome looks found many female admirers. He could easily have become attached to some of them. He uniformly kept them at a distance. Mere attraction and physical desire were not the same as love. The love in his heart could only be shared with Maria Chiara and she would never be there to share it with him.

For all the increase in his popularity, Ragaci did not forget those he counted as friends. Once a week, and sometimes more often, he would stop by at the Taverna del Cielo. Never refusing a request, the rowdier elements that had once barracked and jeered if he performed something they did not enjoy were forced by the convention of the majority to applaud everything that he played and sung for them.

Leonardo Salcoiati moved to a house on the Via Benedetta, a short walk from the Palazzo Tolosini and Ragaci's apartment. Through partly his own efforts and with considerable help from Vannozzi, Leonardo realised enough to provide him with all that he needed and most of what he ever might need. Accepting advice and the realisation that he was not destined to be a man of commerce, he liquidated the family holdings. There were plenty of others left to scheme, to connive and to fight to fill the void in the world of finance that the death of his father and eldest brothers had left. He continued to develop as an artist and began to receive commissions of his own. Not long after the destruction of the Palazzo Salcoiati he was introduced to the daughter of a teacher at the University who was also a man of letters. Gianetta Centellini was a gentle and quietly spoken young woman who exuded a warmth that made Leonardo feel special from the moment he first saw her. Their marriage had taken place not long before Christmas 1516. Before he retired to his native San Gimignano, Vannozzi's last task for the Salcoiati had been to negotiate the terms of Gianetta's dowry.

Leonardo visited his sister but infrequently. The religion of her intellect had metamorphosed into a power of faith that came from within her soul. When she spoke it was with a depth of spirit that was ethereal. Her language was one of hope and of love. She did not need to quote from the scriptures to support her belief that, even beyond the moment of death, there was much to look forward in the afterlife. Soon after her veiling, Maria was appointed chronicler of the convent, though she was not permitted to show her writings to Leonardo nor to any other outsider for that matter. She had taken to adding miniature illustrations to her manuscrips that she enjoyed describing to him. One or two Leonardo was able to picture for himself and then endeavoured to recreate from his own imagination.

He showed all of his work to Ragaci. With money behind him, even the small part of the Salcoiati legacy that remained, he could indulge in painting larger canvasses without the usual prerequisite of a commission. His most recent work depicted two young nuns kneeling at the feet of a bishop. The bishop was viewed from behind. He held his hands above the nuns' heads and looked upwards. To this image that Maria had described to him, Leonardo added a backdrop of a building on fire. A number of ghostly figures ascended towards a large cloud hung from the sky over the edge of which appeared St. Peter and the Archangel Gabriel. In the middle distance a man wearing a long black cloak played a lute and appeared to be singing.

"You've given one of the nuns the features of your sister," said Ragaci. "And the musician, is that intended to be me?"

"You have a vivid imagination, Giacomo, but I fear there is a degree of contrivance about what you say," said Leonardo mischievously. "No resemblance to anyone close to me was intended."

"If you say so."

"People will see what they want to in any artist's work."

Ragaci looked at the canvas again. It was certainly an unusual scene. For all that the fire raged, the foreground was bathed in cool light. There was an elegance and an intimacy about the relationship of the priest to the nuns from which superfluous detail was eliminated.

"This is your best work yet," pronounced Ragaci. "I wonder what Maria would say about it."

"Nothing. She doesn't say too much about anything that relates to the palazzo, not even you."

"Why should she mention me anyway?"

"She doesn't have to," replied Leonardo knowingly. "If I mention you then Maria smiles, waits for me to add something. If I don't, she looks away altogether or brings up another subject of conversation."

Ragaci acknowledged the remark silently.

"What do you say to that?" enquired Leonardo playfully.

"Maria's only concern is to be true to God and to the words of his son, Jesus Christ."

"But not true to her heart nor to any man?"

" 'A woman may do as her father desires, though she will not always take the path he requires'," mused Ragaci.

"What was that?"

"Nothing important. Just something someone once said to me."

* * * * * * *

Feduccio Castellani looked back on the events of the previous year and a half with a degree of satisfaction. He thanked Fortune for the opportunities she had offered him and continued to remember the advice proffered to him by his good friend, Niccolo Machiavelli.

At the time of the pope's visit on his way to Bologna, he had reinstalled the family in his grand palazzo on the Via de Tornabuoni that had been left in the care of servants for more than three years. A few weeks later he was back in the Signoria. His need to make up for lost time was insatiable and he began to make an impact almost immediately.

Partly with a view to quashing the rumours that he was one of those culpable for the fire that had destroyed the Salcoiati and their palazzo, Castellani ensured the prompt appointment by the Signoria of a magistrate to conduct an investigation into the incident. Not more than a few weeks later the magistrate decided that there was no evidence to suggest any connection between Castellani and the blaze. As if to show that there were no hard feelings, he then approached Vannozzi and made a bid to acquire certain of the Salcoiati assets that were not then subject to claims by others. Vannozzi's initial reluctance to sell at what he considered was an undervalue was overruled by the entreaties of Leonardo Salcoiati who was principally concerned to ensure that he might have sufficient cash to at least provide himself with a home and enough to live on until such time as he might become self-sufficient as an artist.

Very soon after learning of the investiture of his brother, Rinuccio, as a cardinal, Guido Castellani returned from Venice, leaving a thriving house of commerce in the hands of trusted plenipotentiaries. In all matters of commerce Guido ably assisted his father, making strenuous efforts to recover the ground that had been lost during the three years of exile. Not long after returning to Florence, Guido was blessed with a wife, Santesa Moscadi, selected from amongst the closest of the Medici allies and who was expecting a baby within a few weeks.

Donatina, his only daughter was a resource that Castellani had yet to deploy. Short and slender and well proportioned, she had pale blue-grey eyes and a sensuous mouth that she had taken to painting a bright shade of red. Thick naturally fair-golden hair fell in wavy cascades to the middle of her back and shimmered as she walked. She was passionate and self-possessed and made no attempt to suppress her feminine wiles in order to get her own way. When she walked into a room there was never any man who could restrain himself from turning his attention towards her.

Quite apart from her many other qualities, Donatina had been indoctrinated by her father to be wholly committed to the cause of the Castellani. She was fully tutored in the role that she was expected to perform and waited patiently to perform it. Not yet twenty-one, Donatina was nevertheless beyond the average age of a woman for marriage. She was plagued by strong physical urges for which she craved satisfaction and that were no longer sufficiently fulfilled by the act of self-pleasure, an act in which she indulged with increasing regularity. Castellani saw how she acted around men and, of more concern, how they acted towards her. Following the family's return to Florence, he intensified the search for a suitable husband, only too conscious that, were she to lose her virginity, the worth of the match he might make would be considerably devalued. For such an exceptional young woman there needed to be an exceptional man. Progress was wearisome. Introductions were made by friends and acquaintances, intermediaries and even priests. After a while, the frequency of the introductions slowed then almost stopped completely. Those with whom he discussed the proposition thought the standards Castellani expected to be met by his future son-in-law were plainly ridiculous

In the autumn of 1516, Castellani was introduced to Bernardo Ambrogiano, the wealthy nephew of a high-ranking cardinal from Rome. Ambrogiano was amongst the inner circle of the pope's advisors and owned estates in both Romagna and Urbino. Donatina openly admitted to her father that she found Bernardo attractive and, more importantly, if this was the man that her father had chosen to marry her then she would do it without cavil. Intermediaries were engaged, negotiations for the dowry were opened but stalled soon afterwards and were then terminated by Ambrogiano's representatives. No reasons were given.

"There is news abroad on the subject of Ambrogiano," said Guido Castellani as the family sat around the dining table, eating the evening meal. Guido was as close in looks to his father as was Donatina to those of their late mother.

"And what might that be?" asked his father sullenly. The mere mention of Ambrogiano was enough to tie his stomach in knots.

"He is to marry Beruzza Tolosini."

Donatina was sitting at the other end of the table in conversation with her sister-in-law, Santesa. She had been half listening to what the men were saying and bristled at what she heard. "That fat, ugly frump! What possesses a man like Ambrogiano to accept such an unprepossessing tub of lard?"

"It can't be the dowry," surmised Guido, "Ambrogiano's got all the money he could ever want."

"You're right about that," replied his father, sagely. "No. I see the hand of Beruzza's uncle behind this, moving deliberately and with sinister intent."

"Ignazio Tolosini?"

"He's been a thorn in my side for twenty years. And before that his father and his grandfather actively opposed or interfered with whatever my father and grandfather sought to do."

"You mean that Tolosini has deliberately sabotaged our negotiations with Ambrogiano?" enquired Guido.

"Without proof I couldn't say for certain, but my suspicions and my experience say that it is likely."

"But father, who would have known of our contact with Signor Ambrogiano?" asked Donatina. "You told me that the discussions were secret."

"There were two sides to the discussions. I'm confident that those to whom I entrusted this endeavour held their peace. But wherever there's a secret there's someone for whom a few florins will be enough to betray it."

"Even for a great many florins I'm upset that Signor Ambrogiano would take the hand of such a gormless wench as Beruzza Tolosini," lamented Donatina. "What's wrong with me that you cannot find me a worthy husband?" she asked her father accusingly.

Feduccio stared at his daughter and did not reply. He had heard her outcries on numerous previous occasions and would not rise to the bait of an argument about the subject. The matter of her marriage was as important to him as it was to her. Debating the issue did not help.

"Am I not attractive enough? Do I not turn the heads of men? Would I not be able to satisfy a man's every need and desire?"

"Enough," snapped Feduccio. "I'm making every effort to do what I can."

"But it isn't enough. I'm a grown woman and beyond the age when many have already married and began to bear children. I have my needs and desires too. Here," she said pointing across the table, "Santesa will tell you."

"Donatina, I said enough." Feduccio shouted and banged his fist on the table. "Be very clear that I know what needs to be done. This news leaves us with two issues to address."

"Two?" she exclaimed.

"Firstly, the matter of a husband for you and secondly, and of no lesser importance to me, is the issue of the Tolosini."

Donatina exploded. "You put your concerns for the actions of a family of pumpkins on a par with the needs of your daughter?" she screamed.

"For the moment they are connected," interjected Guido, trying to be constructive and backing up his father.

"How dare you!" Donatina stood up, pushing her chair back, the violence of her movement knocking it flat. Her father also stood up. She flung her spoon down. It bounced off the table and clanged onto the floor.

"Donatina, I will not tolerate this behaviour at the table."

"You don't have to. I know where I'm not appreciated." She took the plate of food that was in front of her, flung it across the room, then stormed out.

"Sometimes she can be as insufferable as her mother was, God rest her soul," said Feduccio, watching the door slam behind her.

"She does have a point though, father," said Guido calmly.

"Which is?"

"That there is no obvious link between how we might address the problem of the Tolosini and the need to find her a husband."

"Anything that challenges us is a problem that we will use our intelligence and all of our resources to resolve. By the nature of the way in which we must approach their solution, all problems are necessarily linked. That's enough. Let's finish our food."

* * * * * * *

The following evening, Donatina was invited to attend a musical recital at the Palazzo Pitti. She was a guest of the Colesi family with whose younger daughter, Egidia, she was best friends.

Earlier in the day she rebuffed Guido's attempts to make peace between her and their father. This was not the first occasion on which the fraying of tempers had led to the breaking of china and the slamming of doors and which had then been followed by a rapid reconciliation. This time Donatina felt differently.

Family honour and personal pride demanded that she be found a husband. If the menfolk could not do it for her, then she would take matters into her own hands. 'Tell me who you marry and I'll tell you who you are'; so said the old proverb. At this time she was no-one other than Donatina Castellani. As much as she was proud to bear the Castellani name it had its disadvantages and, in her case, not only as an indication of her unwanted status as a spinster. Still, a name was not the only way to attract, or repel, a potential husband. Irrespective of the Castellani reputation and the status of her father, she was first and foremost a woman, some would say a beautiful woman, and a woman to whom men were attracted. Even if the man she decided to marry was not chosen by her father, one way or another she would ensure the match was acceptable. From now on she would rely on nothing but her own charm and feminine guile. There would be no better time for her to start than that very evening. These were the thoughts that ran through her mind as two maids helped her dress and prepare for the recital

Once the maids finished, she stood and admired herself in the mirror. She was wearing a bright red, full-skirted dress with white facing and decorated with hundreds of pearls and other small gemstones. There was powder on her face and rouge on her lips. Her hair was tied behind her and laced with red ribbons. She carried a tuft fan with a long handle carved from ivory that held ostrich and peacock feathers dyed in rich tones of red and blue.

Not long before seven, it was with a spring in her step and an expression of suffused seduction that Donatina Castellani entered the Sala Musica in the Palazzo Pitti. Arm in arm with Egidia Colesi and a step behind her parents, they were shown to seats in the front row. No taller than Donatina, Egidia was slightly built and wore her long dark hair tied back behind her head. Dimpled cheeks, retrousse nose and freckles suggested mischief, deep blue eyes danced with excitement and defined a sensuality that would find fulfillment in a matter of time.

Ornately decorated with exotic imagery and hung with magnificent tapestries, the Sala Musica looked out onto a wide terrace at the back of the Palazzo. Musicians and singers were beginning to assemble on the stage that was situated at one end of the room. The audience settled down and servants extinguished the lanterns. The only light emanated from two rows of flickering candles that ran the length of the stage. Shadows of the performers melted into each other on the wall behind them. Gradually they became still and the hum of the audience subsided.

The programme began with a series of canzoni composed by Francesco dell'Aiole who sat at a small pipe organ that he played on a few of the pieces and from which he conducted the ensemble. Six voices were backed by a group of musicians playing viols, shawms and a harp. Having satisfied herself that none of the men on stage were of any interest, Donatina spent the first few minutes turning her head as discreetly as she could to spy on the audience. It was too dark to make out much so she listened to dell'Aiole's performance as patiently as she was able.

During the interval, refreshments were served in an adjacent salon. Donatina and Egidia sipped cups of warm cider that they cradled in their hands. They gossiped in hushed tones about those they saw who they knew as well as those they did not. Donatina carefully positioned herself so that she might clearly take in all of the men on view, but she saw no-one to whom she was attracted.

After finishing their drinks, they turned and headed slowly back towards the Sala Musica. Donatina stopped in the doorway. Her attention was caught by a young musician who was organising another ensemble that was taking the place of dell'Aiole's group on stage. She was totally consumed by the elegance of his movements and the air of self-assurance that he exuded. While she stared at him, Donatina heard nothing of what Egidia was saying to her, something about a dress that she was having made for a ball. Egidia had a tendency to burble about the minutiae of things that were often of limited interest to others, flurried bursts of words that poured out like water from a broken jug. Conscious that she was being ignored, Egidia tugged at her friend's sleeve. "What now?" she asked Donatina. "You haven't stopped gawping at men since we got here!"

Donatina did not realise that she had been that obvious. "Whatever do you mean?" she said with feigned indignance. "That is truly not the case, but tell me, what do you know of that musician?"

"Which one?"

"The one who looks to be in charge."

"That is Giacomo Ragaci," said Egidia knowledgably. "Father says he is the finest composer in all of Italy and the greatest lutanist of our age."

"And what do you say?" Donatina was immediately concerned lest she might have competition for Ragaci's interest.

"I say that he has the most wonderful voice I have ever heard."

"And that's all?"

"Why? Whatever do you mean, Donatina?"

"I mean does your father know him?" she replied, obfuscating the true intent of her meaning.

"Know him? Why, yes. Signor Ragaci recently played at a recital that my parents organised for some of my father's relatives who visited from Lucca. Father had him compose a couple of frottole that he performed on the occasion. He was truly wonderful."

They moved slowly through the Sala Musica. Donatina could not take her eyes away from Ragaci. The anticipation of hearing his voice and his music took hold of her. They took their seats next to Egidia's parents. Ragaci stood immediately in front of them, at the edge of the stage and with his back to them. He was deep in discussion with a couple of the other musicians. Donatina strained to hear what they were saying, but caught only the occasional phrase that dealt with the technicalities of chord sequences and tunings.

"What are you doing, Donatina?" Egidia tugged at her sleeve.

"What do you mean?" Donatina was only half paying attention to her friend.

"It's so rude to eavesdrop on other people's conversations."

"Hardly," she said abstractedly.

"Then why are you are leaning forward like that?"

"I'm not."

Egidia saw no point in responding further. It was apparent that the music would start shortly as a quartet of male singers took to the stage. They wore identical long, dark green tunics over black leggings and ranged themselves to the left of the stage. Ragaci broke up the huddle and ushered the other musicians into their places. To one side of him was a second lutanist and to the other a guitarist. The three viol players who had accompanied dell'Aiole returned and took their places stage right.

Ragaci sat down, put his foot on the footrest and picked up his lute. He was no more than three braccia away from Donatina. She was sure that as he smiled at the audience, momentarily he looked into her eyes. The sweet torture of her virginity suddenly grabbed her soul and gripped it tightly, wringing any vestige of shame from her senses. Her heart was bared and it was bared for him. She felt her legs spread a little, subconsciously inviting him to enter her. She closed her eyes and imagined the ecstasy that she would share with him. She put her palms together and rested them on her thighs, a little below the warmth of her sex, and prayed. If she had sometimes failed to take God as seriously as her childhood lessons had taught her, here was living proof, if anything, that God had listened to her prayers. If Mercury was the messenger of the deities of myth, this musician, this Giacomo Ragaci, was the one who God had chosen to bring to her the message of love, the one who would release the chains that held her firm to the prison of her father's whims.

Her reverie was interrupted by the master of ceremonies, an elderly gentlemen by the name of Micucci, who walked with the aid of a stick. He shuffled onto the stage to welcome the audience to the second part of the recital. He introduced Ragaci and his ensemble in glowing terms. Donatina heard the words but paid them little attention. There was something about San Gimignano and the Palazzo Salcoiati. These were things past and she cared only for the 'now', the present and that she was sitting so close to a beautiful man who, she was convinced, had been sent for her.

Micucci left the stage to polite applause while Ragaci began to pick some bass notes from his lute. As ever, he began with some tastar de corde that seamlessly melted into the first of two ricercari on which he was joined by the guitarist and the second lutanist. Donatina watched intently, hypnotised by the spiritual embrace of Ragaci's music, transfixed by his facial expressions of concentration and of passion for his playing. When the melodies washed over his audience like the smooth rush of an incoming tide, Ragaci closed his eyes. When there was a switch in tempo or a cue for a passage of improvisation his eyes opened and focused on his hands. With virtuoso panache he navigated the uncharted twists and turns of the musical unknown, extracting every ounce of beauty from phrases not previously played, never written down but always hidden behind the melody, awaiting their discovery by him.

Ragaci struck the final chord with brio that was the spark for an explosion of applause. Donatina wanted to do more than merely clap. She had waited so long and so patiently but also needed her liberator to take control not only of her heart but of her body as well. Engaging her mind sufficiently to quell the anarchy of her emotions, she realised that she needed a plan and that there was little time in which to make it.

The applause died down. Ragaci thanked the audience and introduced the choir of voices and the next piece. "A poem by the late Angelo Poliziano, court poet of Lorenzo Il Magnificente, which I have arranged for these fine singers and set to a tune of my own composition. Though May is not yet here, Spring is opening up around us. It's a time for all who seek love to surrender to their hearts and to surrender them to the hearts of those for whom they are intended."

He placed the lute carefully on the floor, stood and turned to face the singers. He counted them in then turned once again towards the audience, adding his own voice as the fifth part of the harmony.

Ben venga maggio,	*Welcome May, welcome May*
ben venga maggio	
E'l gonfalon selvaggio	*and branching banner of the wood.*
Ben venga prima vera	*Welcome Spring*
che vuol l'uom s'innamori	*that causes men to fall in love*

E voi, donzelle, a schiera	and you, maidens lining up
con li vostri amadori,	with your lovers,
che di rose e di fiori	That with roses and with flowers
vi fate belle il maggio	May makes you beautiful
Ben venga maggio …	Welcome May …
Chi e giovane e bella	Who is young and beautiful
deh non sie punto acerba	knows no bitter branch
che non si rinnovella	that is not renewed
l'eta, come fa l'erba	in Summer, like these leaves.
Nessuna stia superba	No-one is more wonderful
all'amadore il maggio	than lovers in May
Ben venga maggio …	Welcome May …
Ciascuna balli e canti	Everyone dance and sing
di questa schiera nostra	in this procession of ours,
Ecco che i dolci amanti	behold that the sweet lovers
van per voi, belle, in giostra:	joust for you, beautiful ones:
qual dora a lor si mostra	such strength they show,
fara sfiorire il maggio	to pluck the flowers of May.
Ben venga maggio …	Welcome May …
Per prender le donzelle	To capture maidens,
si son gli amanti armati.	are these lovers armed.
Arrendetevi, belle,	Surrender, beautiful ones,
a'vostri innamatori;	to your lovers;
rendete e'cuor furati,	give in to our burning hearts,
non fate guerrail maggio	don't make war in May.
Ben venga maggio …	Welcome May …

After the third verse Ragaci sat down again and took up his lute to play an instrumental passage in counterpoint to the melody that the second lutanist repeated for a couple of choruses. The final verse, Ragaci sang alone. Donatina was convinced that he sang the refrain 'Surrender, beautiful ones, to your lovers,' especially for her. She had never previously been as touched by music as she was by Ragaci's sound and the message that he shared through his performance. She lost herself in the sensuality of the moment, then continued to bathe in the subtle colours of the rest that followed. Frottole, dance tunes and a few of Ragaci's idiosyncratic ballads, some new, some old, were all performed with supreme musicianship and vocal excellence. Every note of every melody captivated and entranced her, every word of every lyric enchanted her with its spell. Overwhelmed by a desire the vibrancy of which began to shorten her breath, she realised she needed to act. She tore her mind away from the music and concentrated. Donatina hatched her plan and, as the effervescence of the coda to the final piece melted into the applause of the audience, she executed it with ruthless efficiency. She leaned across Egidia and politely tapped her father on the arm. "Excuse me please, Signor Colesi, Egidia tells me that you are well-acquainted with Signor Ragaci. It's my father's birthday soon. Nothing would please him more than to be surprised with the gift of an original piece of music from the finest composer in all of Italy."

Before Manfredi Colesi could respond, Donatina continued, each word carefully rehearsed. "Could I prevail upon you to introduce me to Signor Ragaci so that I may invite him to compose such a piece?"

Unable to reply in any way other than positively, Manfredi Colesi said, "it will be my pleasure." He edged towards the side of the stage through a thicket of bodies that had congregated there and attracted Ragaci's attention. Once he was out of earshot, Egidia turned to Donatina and hissed, "I don't know how you can be so brazen!"

"I'm not sure what you mean." Whether or not Donatina believed in the innocence of her own remark that she might protest to Egidia did not matter. Ragaci was soon following Manfredi towards them.

"You certainly do," whispered Egidia forcefully.

"Egidia, you have been told before that it's very rude to whisper in company," said Euphemia, Egidia's mother, who generally showed an unhealthy interest in the doings of others herself. "If you have something to say then let me hear what it is as well." But she never got to find out what it was as they were rejoined by Manfredi who made the promised introduction.

Ragaci bowed towards each of the three women, taking their hands in turn and kissing them, first Euphemia, then Egidia and lastly Donatina. The touch of his lips on her fingers intensified the palpitations of her heart. She felt herself blushing and held up her fan below her eyes.

"Signor Colesi tells me that you may have a commission for some music for your father?" said Ragaci gracefully.

Donatina had rehearsed her lines and knew them by heart but could not find them. She clutched hold of the first choate thought that came into her head and decided to run with it. "Indeed, Signor Ragaci, but I fear that this is not the best situation in which to discuss it," she said breathlessly. She paused, then continued. "I also fear that it won't be possible for you to come to my home in case my father discovers my plan."

"Then by all means you may both meet at Palazzo Colesi where all may be settled."

Manfredi Colesi's offer was genuinely made and understood as such by both parties. Donatina assumed that Colesi had read her mind for it had been her intention to make the suggestion herself. Neutral territory with others present for her next meeting with Ragaci was what she had contemplated for the prelude. She had time to work out where they might have the privacy required for the next stage of her plan.

"I'm available to meet you tomorrow afternoon at three," said Ragaci.

Donatina nodded. Once again she raised her fan, this time to hide the smile of triumph. She looked deep into Ragaci's eyes, challenging him to reciprocate the declaration that she believed she was making perfectly clear. The kindness of his smile and his gentle manner were endearing, but not all that she had hoped for. Then again, she reasoned, that was a good sign. Clearly he was trying not to disclose his heart in front of others. Perhaps, that would not be the done thing. Not yet.

"Tomorrow at three it is then," beamed Manfredi.

Ragaci bowed towards each of them in turn then joined another huddle of people standing nearby, no doubt possible sources of commissions and requests to perform elsewhere.

Manfredi took Euphemia's arm and motioned Egidia and Donatina to follow them out of the Sala Musica to join the reception that was taking place elsewhere in the Palazzo. Once her parents were a few paces ahead, Egidia nudged Donatina hard in the ribs. This time Donatina did not hide her smile. "That's the man I'm, going to marry," she said assuredly.

Later that night, as Donatina lay in bed turning over the events of the evening, she was not sure whether she had actually said the words aloud or if they had merely echoed in her mind. Either way, Egidia had not replied. She just shook her head in disbelief and in secret admiration at her friend's boldness.

XVII

Conviction

Arezzo. March 1517

It had taken place one afternoon in the late summer, not long after the ceremony of her veiling. As far as Maria was concerned there was no argument. She did not contradict the Madonna Suora. She had not intended to utter a heresy. It was not as though others were present that they might have been influenced by what she said. She had read the words on the page many times and often thought of their significance. All she did was to share her convictions with the Madonna Suora, convictions derived from the words of the apostle, albeit an apostle whose appointment had not been made by Christ directly. The apostle's words validated the decisions she had made about her own life, those decisions she had made to turn away from the path laid out by her father and that had led her to the service of God, to betroth herself to his son, Jesus Christ, and to become part of a holy community.

Madonna Suora entered the small scriptorium where Maria was diligently at work on an illustration. It was part of an illuminated manuscript for a local landowner who had recently bestowed a large endowment on the Convent.

Maria was asked to pick a reading from the Bible, to copy it and to illustrate it as a gift of thanks from the Sisters.

On her desk the Bible lay open. The source for her work was one of her favourite texts, the Book of Galatians. In what Maria thought to be the greatest of his epistles, St Paul discussed important issues that penetrated the essence of his faith. He concluded that the heart of religion was inward experience and conviction and that the ritual and the law were of secondary importance. Maria construed his words even further.

"Indeed, Madonna Suora, Paul tells us 'that there is neither Jew nor Greek, there is neither bond nor free, there is neither male nor female: for you are all one in Jesus Christ'."

"Belief in the Lord by all will lead to their redemption. That's quite right Suora Maria."

"And of course it means more than that." Maria continued to draw in ink as she spoke.

"It does?" The Madonna Suora was very familiar with the text, but Maria's suggestion was puzzling. "How so?"

"Jesus gave his love to all persons equally."

"Yes, of course he did."

"Irrespective of their race or their creed and irrespective of whether or not they were men or women."

"Quite so."

"Which means that no person should be restricted by being who they are, from being as they wish to be."

The Madonna Suora looked puzzled. "I don't think I follow."

Maria put down the pen and looked up. "Whatever your race or creed and whether you are a man or a woman, Christ teaches that as we are all one within him, everyone should have equality of action and equality of entitlement in all aspects of this earthly life."

The Madonna Suora's look of puzzlement twisted into one of disdain. "You mean …?"

"That women should have the same freedom of choice and of action as a man in all things."

"All things?"

"Yes, Madonna, in all things. Everything."

"Even, for example, in the Church?" The Madonna Suora's tone was less interrogative than it was denunciatory.

Maria had thought about the matter specifically and considered the relevant pages in the scriptures in detail "Yes. There are many examples in the Bible of women being regarded as the equal of man."

"There are? Where?"

"In the Acts of the Apostles there is a reference to four young women who are prophetesses. In the Epistle to the Romans, St Paul tells us of Phoebe who is a minister of the Church at Cenchrea. Most important of all, in Corinthians it is said that 'if anyone is in Christ he is a new creation'. That can only mean that God regards all of us as equals, both men and women."

"And this is what you believe?"

"It's what is written in the Testament."

The Madonna Suora was horrified at what she had heard. "You clearly forget many other passages that clearly illustrate that what you have said is a heresy." She spoke forcefully, almost angrily. "'A woman should learn in quietness and in full submission. I do not permit a woman to teach or to have authority over a man. She must be silent.' 'Women are the weaker vessel.' That is what we are taught and that is what God has intended."

"I'm familiar with these passages too, however …"

"However, there is nothing more to be said on this subject," snapped the Madonna Suora. "I will not permit you to address me about it any further and you will at no time utter these heresies to anyone else. If I hear that you have then I will immediately take the matter to the bishop."

Maria gaped at the Madonna Suora open-mouthed. Before she could say anything the Madonna Suora continued, "you will go straight away to the Chapter House where you will be punished."

Maria immediately realised that protest or opposition would do her no good. The Madonna Suora stared at Maria sternly. She watched Maria stand up, bow her head then make the sign of the cross.

While Maria walked slowly out of the scriptorium and down the series of corridors that led out of the main building, she began to pray, fervently. She did not understand how a religious woman in a community of religious women could have taken offence to what she had said. The references were in the scriptures and, as far as Maria was concerned, they permitted no other meaning. There were of course many other passages that spoke similarly but about which she would keep her counsel, at least for the time being.

Before she reached the Chapter House she heard the chiming of a bell that was only ever employed to summon the sisters to gather together. In one corner of the Chapter House there was a small altar before which she kneeled and prayed, not only for herself, but also for Madonna Suora that her misunderstanding be forgiven.

Although she knew what to expect, the pain that she was to endure was nothing as compared to what He had suffered for her sins and for the sin of others. She could not help thinking that nothing had been learned by those who decided that a perceived wrong should merit such cruelty. As much as they might tear her flesh and spill her blood, they could not harm her soul and they would never change her ideas. Besides that, there was nothing they could do to change the language of the scriptures, even though they might continue to misunderstand them.

Curiously, the Madonna Suora did not go into any detail of the wrongs of which she had found Maria guilty. She did not even mention heresy. In her address to the sisters she merely advised them that Maria had used inappropriate language in a provocative manner. For a while afterwards there was some speculation as to what that might have meant. Within a couple of weeks it was forgotten when another miscreant was presented to the sisters to be punished for something equally arcane. Maria realised that it was not the degree of the perceived wrongdoing that merited the punishment. Fear of the whip was the primary instrument that guaranteed discipline in the Convent and strict adherence to what the Madonna Suora decreed as the requisite modus vivendi for all of the sisters. Periodically a punishment was handed down, sometimes for the most ridiculous and insignificant of infractions of the rules of the Convent. Punishment was a rubric, a tormentor, a reminder and an omnipotent threat that every sister endeavoured to avoid.

The entire community was obliged to attend and witness the ceremony of Maria's punishment. Stripped naked to the waist, she was forced to stand facing a blank wall. Her wrists were bound and tied above her head to a hook that was deeply embedded into a wooden lintel. The discipline, a dozen lashes with a whip of knotted cords, was administered to her bare back and shoulders. The nuns crossed themselves and lowered their eyelids in silent prayer as Suora Franchetta, a beefy woman with biceps the size of a blacksmith's thighs, laid into her task vigorously and with barely disguised pleasure.

The punishment was harsh, but Maria learned from it that she must accept the unquestioned authority of the Madonna Suora in all matters, both spiritual and temporal. Maria could not help observing an irony in the proceedings. The patron saints of the Convent, St Perpetua and St Felicitia, two young women, one having given birth not a few days earlier, had been made to stand side by side with men in the name of Christianity as wild beasts had devoured them in a Roman amphitheatre. Valiant and blessed martyrs, they were both elected to the glory of Christ in defending the faith.

The manner in which Maria accepted her punishment endeared her to those of her sisters who had previously given her little time or succour. The vast majority of them were either from Arezzo itself or from villages in its immediate vicinity. They were brought up to display a natural anathema to the Florentines, especially one who was said to be the daughter of a wealthy banker. Many of them had not chosen to become nuns, but had had the choice made for them by others. Some were the younger daughters of fathers whose resources were insufficient to underwrite the cost of a dowry. Others were from poor families where there was no future other than that offered to them by a life of dedication to the Church. They distinguished themselves from those, like Maria, who had made the choice on her own. They interpreted her preference for solitude as stand-offishness.

So badly did Maria bleed that even the most hardened of her sisters was moved to tears, not only by the pain from which she visibly suffered but also by the dignity with which she bore it. As soon as the stinging echo of the final lash had faded, Madonna Suora turned her back on her sisters and strode purposefully out of the Chapter House. A few of those who were standing closest to Maria released her bindings. They helped her to the infirmary where they dressed her wounds and where she then spent the night. Her sleep was fitful and continually broken by a rush of disconnected images and a series of dreams.

She dreamed of the Last Supper. In the place of the disciples, seated around the table were twelve women. They were women whose faces she recognised. They were her sisters, sisters of the Order of St Perpetua and St Felicitia and she was one of them. Jesus sat amongst them, wearing a hooded gown. They had finished eating and the company's heads were bowed in prayer. Following the grace that was traditionally recited at the end of a meal, Jesus went around the table and blessed each of the sisters in turn. He came to Maria last. As she looked up to him, he pulled back the hood. The munificent expression that gazed upon her was not that of Jesus, but that of Giacomo Ragaci.

"I am not Christ. I am not here to bless you. I am not the son of God who died for your sins. I am a simple mortal man who has been sent to love you, to unite my spirit and my body with yours that we may live this life together, and that we may thereafter be with each other in all eternity in the sight and under the protection of the Holy Trinity, the Father, the Son and the Holy Ghost."

He held his hands out and took hers. He led her away from the table where the rest of the sisters remained in a petrified tableau of silence. They left the Cenacle. She followed him down the stairs and to the door that opened onto the streets of Jerusalem. They stepped outside but they were no longer in the ancient Jerusalem of the Bible and of Herod. This was the New Jerusalem of prophecy a thousand times foretold – tall buildings made from shiny materials, wide thoroughfares lined with an infinite variety of trees and sleek wheel-less carriages that hovered above the level of the streets and that were propelled without the assistance of horses. Everywhere there were people and the people were of many different races and they were content. And Maria knew that all she saw before her was good.

After she woke and when she could no longer hang on to the images of the dream, all that was left was a sense of fulfilment, a sense that what she believed was right, that the Bible told her so and that Madonna Suora would be forgiven for her misunderstanding.

One of those who helped to dress Maria's wounds was Suora Graziella, a sixteen year old novice and one of those who Maria was teaching to read and write. She sat in a class with a few of the local girls who were in serbanza, a species of guardianship and who came to the convent during the day to be educated.

Graziella was the youngest of seven children, five of whom were girls. In order to save her from the streets where she would otherwise inevitably have ended up, a well-meaning relative secured her entry to the convent for which a small dowry was paid. She was quiet, even-tempered and polite. She possessed a humility of spirit that instantly made others warm to her and the aura of one from whom great things were expected. A permanent expression of purity and innocence was defined by plain, open features. At the time of her admission to the convent, Graziella had thick, shiny black hair that hung to her waist. When she took the veil, her hair was ceremonially cut very short. Maria found herself questioning the necessity of what, for her, constituted an act of barbarism against one so young. She thought twice before articulating her views on the subject to any of her sisters, let alone Madonna Suora.

Maria began to spend time alone with Graziella in the scriptorium, giving her extra help with her with her studies. Provided Graziella had no pressing chores, Maria would let her sit and watch while she worked on a manuscript or an ink illustration. Graziella marvelled at the strong even flow of Maria's pen and greatly admired her ability as an illustrator.

Sometimes, while she worked, Maria would sing. The perfectly pitched soprano that had once sung both spiritual and temporal pieces with Giacomo Ragaci was confined to the sanctification of the Lord and to the purely sacramental. Graziella marvelled at the purity of Maria's tone and secretly wished that perhaps, one day, she too might be able to sing as beautifully. As time passed Graziella began to memorise the words of the pieces that Maria sang most often. She encouraged Graziella to join in and discovered that she had a mellifluous voice of her own. Graziella was soon persuaded to sing the melody that gave free rein to Maria's soaring soprano to harmonise in performances of the devotions that filled the scriptorium with the sound of joy. The first piece that Graziella learned was the one that they enjoyed singing most often:

Ogn' om m'entenda divotamente,
lo pianto che fece Maria dolente,
del suo figliol tanto delicato.

O Jhesu Christo, bello, mio figlio
o Jhesu bello bianco e vermeglio,
odella trista madre el conseglio
su nella croce, su nella croce gia conficato.

Let everyone listen with devotion
to the lament of Mary, the sorrowful mother
as she grieves for her gentle son.

Oh Jesus Christ, oh my handsome son,
Oh, beautiful Jesus, white and crimson,
Oh the wisdom of a sad mother,
Nailed to the cross, already nailed to the cross

During the weeks that followed Christmas, Maria became concerned about Graziella. She seemed to be eating less than was healthy and her usual lightness of spirit was replaced by the worried look of a poverty stricken widow. It was in early March and on the eve of the celebration of the martyrdom of the Convent's patron saints that Graziella's appearance was so gaunt and her demeanour so dour that Maria decided to press the girl on it.

"You've not said much today," remarked Maria, taking a clean quill pen from her desk and dipping it into a pot of red ink. She started to colour in the outline of a small rectangle that formed part of the illustration in the book on which she was working.

Graziella said nothing in reply, but slumped her shoulders forward and raised her eyebrows.

Maria stopped and stared at Graziella. "Have you perhaps taken another set of vows that you don't want me to know about?"

There was something about the way that Graziella shook her head, something unconvincing, that began to worry Maria. The blank look in Graziella's eyes implied a hidden secret, the fear of exposing its truth foreshadowed ugly consequences that might follow in the wake of its revelation.

Maria put down her pen and laid her hands on Graziella's shoulders. "There's something bothering you, isn't there? Even though you may be afraid to say what it is, I'm not going to judge you."

Graziella remained silent.

"If it's something that I can help you with, then I promise that I will help. If it's something that I can't help with, then I will ask the Madonna Suroa."

Graziella shook her head vigorously at the mention of the words 'Madonna Suora'.

"It's something you don't want the Madonna Suora to know about?"

Graziella bent her head forward. Tears began to well in her eyes.

"What's the matter?" Maria pleaded, putting her arms around her and drawing her close. "You must tell me."

"I want to, but I can't," sobbed Graziella in the tiniest of voices.

"Why not?"

"Because they'll do something bad to me."

"Who will? What do you mean, something bad?"

"Madonna Suora and the bishop."

"Why, what have you done? What's happened?"

"It's what they made me do."

"Who? Madonna Suora and the bishop?"

Graziella sniffed, pulled away from Maria's embrace and looked at her intently. She nodded.

"What did they make you do?"

"Bad things."

"What kind of bad things? Tell me." Maria continued to speak softly, but there was steel in the tone of her exhortation.

Graziella pondered for a moment. "I … well … the bishop …" The words began to stutter out fitfully. She was beginning to pull her thoughts together when the chime of a bell sounded the call to the evening meal. She stopped, frozen in a moment of fear. Wide-eyed, she gasped, "they'll find out I told you and then they'll do even worse to me. They said as much."

"I promise I won't say a word to anyone," said Maria.

"I can't tell you now anyway, it's the bell. We have to go."

"Don't worry about that. We can be a little late."

"Are you sure?" she said hesitantly.

"Yes of course, especially if bad things are happening to you. They have to stop. Once I know what they are I'll see what I can do to stop them."

"Will you?"

"I'll try. At least let me know what the problem is?"

Graziella wanted to believe Maria and to trust her. Thus far in her sad and fragmented existence trust had seemed not much more than a commodity for which the price that was generally paid was disappointment. Her mother had died of illness when Graziella was no more than four years old, leaving her with nothing more than splintered memories of a kindly smile and the promise of maternal love, never wholly fulfilled. Her father, her dear brave and strong father with his simple beliefs and unswerving faith in Providence, had worked himself to death while doing all he could to provide for his family. Finally, she had been deceived by the sanctuary she had been persuaded to trust in order to avoid the worst of the squalid existence that had beckoned to consume her innocence.

"I know I can trust you. It's the others that I'm worried about."

"The others?"

"Can you trust the others?"

"Which others?"

"You won't be able to help me on your own."

"I won't?"

Graziella shook her head. She tried hard not to sob. "We're going to be late. We're going to be late."

"You'll suffer more by not revealing this secret to me than you will by missing grace before the evening meal."

Graziella thought for a moment. She saw kindness in Maria's eyes and acknowledged a spirit that she believed she could trust.

"Yes, you're right."

"So you'll tell me what it is then?"

"Yes." Graziella inhaled deeply and focused hard on the elaborate 'G' in 'God' on which Maria had been working.

"The bishop has been making me do bad things."

Maria waited expectantly for more and resolved to say nothing until she heard what happened from Graziella's own mouth.

"He makes me take off all my clothes."

Maria guessed what might be coming but wanted to hear it from Graziella directly.

"Then he touches me with his hands." Graziella looked up from 'God'. Energised by the force of truth and liberated by the power of confession, she blurted out the rest in a series of breathless sentences.

"It was in the room he uses when he stays here. In that little house at the end of the path that leads up to the mountains. He said he wanted to cleanse me from sin. He rubbed some oil on my body. Then he put his hand …" She pointed to her crotch. "Then he held his hand there … and … pushed his finger … inside … I started to feel … weak."

Graziella bowed her head and made the sign of the cross. Maria waited for her to continue.

"He made me lay down on the bed. He told me to close my eyes and to imagine the beauty of heaven. He said he would be a few minutes. That when he came back he would do something special for me that would make my picture of heaven even stronger. I guessed what might be going to happen but didn't believe that it would. I didn't think that a bishop would ever do … well … that to a girl. Especially a nun."

"Didn't you try to stop him?"

"How? I was locked in the room. He's a strong man."

"It's happened more than once?"

"Four times altogether."

"Why haven't you told Madonna Suora?"

"Because …" Graziella hesitated, suddenly paralysed by the potential consequences of her confession.

"Because?"

"She already knows about it."

Maria looked puzzled. "Why hasn't she done anything about it?"

"She knows about it because sometimes she comes to the little house and stays there while he does it. In case someone interrupts."

"Sweet Jesus." Maria dropped to her knees and prayed. Graziella joined her. When they finished Graziella was calm.

"Can you help stop it? Please Suora Maria, please?"

"I must do so. It's my duty. But I will need help."

"Who from?"

Maria thought for a moment. "Father Alessandro."

"Is he alright? I mean, can you trust him?"

"I think so."

"When will you see him."

"I'm not sure, but it will be soon."

"Do you know when the bishop is coming next?"

"I'm not sure of that either, but probably some time around Easter – either just before or just after. I think he is presently in Rome."

"I hope that you can help me before then. I mean, I'm not … you know … at least I'm fairly sure. But it could happen, couldn't it?"

"Yes child, it could."

Although she had been in the convent for not much more than a year, a sudden thought alarmed Maria. On two previous occasions she recalled young novices suddenly leaving the convent with little prior warning. In each case they were orphans and, knowing what she now knew, neither of the explanations proffered for their respective disappearances was convincing. One had certainly been confined for a week or two in the infirmary and was then apparently sent away to take the waters in Assissi. She had not returned since. The other had been sent on an errand to Arezzo and was reported to have been abducted on the highway. Maria surmised that they had each become pregnant and were shuffled away into service somewhere or perhaps to another convent. The babies, if they had survived, were presumably taken into the care of the Church, or perhaps fostered out to a suitable family. She wondered why Madonna Suora was covering up for the bishop.

"Suora Maria?"

"Yes."

"Are you alright?"

"I was just thinking about what I would say to Father Alessandro."

"Don't you think we should go and join the others now?"

Taking Graziella by the hand, Maria led her out of the scriptorium. Walking as fast as they respectably could, they hastened through the corridors that led to the refectory.

* * * * * * *

It was a day or so afterwards that Father Alessandro returned to the convent. His was a low-key approach to the business of confession. For Maria, confession was not the functional event that it was to many of her sisters, some of whom barely treated the ritual seriously. In the hours that preceded her visits to the confessional booth, she would cogitate about the events of her life since her previous confession and examine her conscience thoroughly. Anything she had said or done that constituted, or even might have constituted, a sin was considered, analysed and evaluated as material for confession. Once satisfied that peripheral matter could be eliminated, her carefully catalogued inventory of sin was revealed to the priest. Even so, the ritual seldom lasted more than a few minutes.

Gaunt and thin with pale grey eyes and a long nose, Father Alessandro had the bearing of a priest but the look of a man with something on his conscience of which he dare not speak. "You may go in peace, Suora Maria," he concluded from the other side of the confessional booth. More of an academic than a person who was at ease with other people, Father Alessandro was at his most relaxed when discussing the testaments and telling the stories of Christ's miracles. There had been a number of occasions on which Maria had spent time in his company with groups of her sisters in the acts of recitation and study. Father Alessandro had a lively mind that was as much informed by his observations of the doings of mortal man as it was by the revelations in the Bible.

Of the priests who regularly visited the convent, Father Alessandro was the only one who Maria could imagine being sensitive enough and possessed of sufficient strength of character to be able to take the matter to the ecclesiastical authorities and to have it resolved. Father Benedict was old and stupid; his only interest lay in eating all the food that he was able to fit on his plate, much of it scavenged from the plates of those who were prepared to indulge his gluttony. Father Nicodemo was weak and frail and suffered from a chest complaint that made him continually wheeze and cough. He was kind and gentle but on more than one occasion he had been seen to take fright in the face of the Madonna Suora's admonishments of a sister's wrongdoings.

Whenever any of the priests were at the convent, Madonna Suora's attitude was one of tolerant indifference, the extent of her welcome limited. She enabled the priest to take confession and to participate in such other rituals and routines as were prescribed by an authority higher than her own. Nevertheless, Maria had observed that Madonna Suora accorded Father Alessandro at least something that approximated respect.

Emerging from the confession booth into the cheerless gloom of the sanctuary, Maria embarked upon her mission.

"There is something else, Father."

He moved back towards the confession booth.

"No, it's not part of my confession, but a matter of some delicacy with which I need some help. I think that you're the one who may be able to help me."

Father Alessandro looked at her warily. In the three years during which he had been visiting the Convent of St. Perpetua and St. Felicitia he did not recall previously having been asked to do anything outside of the routine that had been prescribed by the bishop, a routine that he assumed had been first carefully discussed with and then approved by Madonna Suora.

Unsure as to whether he should be flattered or concerned, he was clearly bound to at least listen, even if the request was not one with which he was able to assist. Whatever it was, he assumed that it was unlikely to be whimsical. He knew Suora Maria to be a serious and genuinely religious soul. He also thought that she was not one who would seek the help of another unless it was a matter of some considerable moment.

"If I can, I will try. What is it?" He spoke tentatively, careful not to betray his true inclination which was that he would have preferred it if she was asking whatever it was to someone else.

She stepped as closely towards him as the decorum of their respective positions permitted, her expression equal measures of seriousness and hope.

"I speak of Suora Graziella," Maria paused long enough to give Father Alessandro enough opportunity to acknowledge whether or not he knew the subject of her entreaty without prompting.

"Ah yes," he said slowly. He nodded, but was careful not to imbue his response with anything that could convey the slightest semblance of over-familiarity.

"Her physical condition and her demeanour have lately deteriorated. I challenged her about it." Again Maria paused, this time to ascertain whether her observations had been shared by the priest. His silence suggested nothing either way.

"From what she tells me, she has attracted the attentions of the bishop." Maria lowered her voice. "With the connivance of the Madonna Suora, the bishop has been taking advantage of Suora Graziella."

Father Alessandro's continued silence suggested that he needed to know more before he would react.

"The bishop has been forcing Suora Graziella to have a carnal relationship with him. And though I have no evidence, my suspicions are that Suora Graziella is not the first young nun to have been the subject of such treatment."

The young priest looked at her thoughtfully. "And apart from the say-so of Suora Graziella, what proof do you have that what she says is true?"

"What do you mean?" asked Maria.

"I mean just that. How am I expected to address such a matter as this without proof?"

"The only proof I needed was the evidence of my own senses. Observing her these past few weeks, challenging her on what affected her and listening to her confession to me. And it was a confession that was elicited with not a little pain and some persuasion. Perhaps you could sit down with her yourself."

"Were it the case that Suora Graziella had engaged in carnal relations with the bishop then both would have committed a sin, irrespective of whether the bishop had forced her and of the part played, if any, by Madonna Suora. I have never yet been asked to hear the bishop's confession, but I have heard those of both Suora Graziella and Madonna Suora on more than one occasion in the recent past. At no time has either of them ever mentioned anything of such matters to me. It is hard to imagine that such an occurrence as being party to carnal relations with a man of the church, a senior man at that, within the walls of this holy place would not have been worthy of mention by either of them."

Maria was at a loss as to how to respond. Even within the boundaries of the discussion they were having, she was surprised that Father Alessandro would make any reference to what had or had not been said during the course of another's confession, a process that she had always believed to be totally confidential. What was more stark was his complete refusal to take anything of what she said at face value.

"Are you saying that you don't believe me, Father?"

Father Alessandro chose his words carefully.

"I'm not saying that I don't believe that you are truthfully relaying to me what Suora Graziella has told you. However, the circumstances of what you relate don't ring true. Further, to repeat such accusations about the bishop, even the role attributed to Madonna Suora, without any evidence but the word of a sixteen-year old girl is hardly sensible and possibly injurious to them both."

Maria was taken aback at the response, but determined to hold her ground. "Then perhaps it would be best if you were to speak to Suora Graziella directly, that you may assess the probity of her words from her own mouth."

"There would be little point in that, Suora Maria. All I will hear is the same tale that you have just told me, perhaps with an embellishment or two. None of it will prove the truth of what is alleged, certainly not to the point that I might make a representation about it to the ecclesiastical authorities."

"But, Father Alessandro, what proof do you want? Do you need to wait until she is with child ?"

"Suora Maria, I do not doubt your good faith," he begun to mollify the sternness of the tone in which he had previously addressed her, "but you do neither yourself nor Suora Graziella any good by repeating this story. Without proof, Suora Graziella's allegations are baseless. They will be regarded by others as nothing more than the unfounded accusations of a young girl who may have any number of reasons for making them. Your repetition of the story may, of itself, be nothing other than the repetition of a falsehood for which, if you like, we may return to the confessional to address."

Though there was a streak of cold logic that ran through what Father Alessandro had said, his response ignored one basic fact, Suora Graziella's distress that was clearly visible for anyone to see.

"Father, if it's proof that you want, then proof you shall have, even if I have to steal myself away and witness events with my own eyes." The comment was made as a reaction; as soon as she made it, she knew that she would have to make good its sentiment to convince others of Suora Graziella's plight.

He thought for a moment and looked around him. One of the few decorative concessions to the plain walls of the sanctuary was a small fresco depicting the story of the diseased woman who had touched the hem of Jesus' garment and had been healed. Jesus had told the woman that it was her faith had made her whole. Maria's faith in Jesus was her guiding light. She would pray that it was the same for Father Alessandro.

"Suora Maria, what may appear to be the truth may be an illusion, and what may seem fanciful, in fact, may be the truth. Sometimes it's hard to know what is right and what is wrong, but sometimes the truth may hurt more than any pain brought on by an illusion."

Maria was not sure that she comprehended his meaning. His intent was clearly to throw doubt on, or at least to question, the veracity of Suora Graziella's accusations. Maria was in no doubt of where the truth lay, but she saw that to engage in further discussion with Father Alessandro would lead nowhere.

"Thank you for your advice, Father. It has been helpful. Now I understand what I must do."

She bowed towards him, made the sign of the cross and turned to leave the sanctuary. A plan was forming in her mind, its execution would have to await the bishop's next visit that she knew would not take place until some time closer to Easter.

XVIII

Seduction

Florence. March 1517

"Father has asked me to pass on some good news," said Guido Castellani excitedly as he entered his sister's bedroom.

Still refusing to speak to her father, Donatina displayed little interest in what her brother had to say. From playing the role of dutiful daughter and supporter of the Castellani cause, Donatina took a revisionist approach to everything that her father had ever done. Their relationship had seldom been normal and fluctuated between extremes of devotion and disfunction. Feduccio's continual absences from home on matters of commerce scarred Donatina's largely motherless childhood. A series of weak governesses were never able to curb her temper and miserably failed to channel her energies in directions other than those of her own choosing. Feduccio's willingness to pay more than merely lip-service to her whims as compensation for the mother she had lost and who he was never prepared to replace, coupled with Donatina's stubbornness, fuelled the natural independence of her spirit.

Conscious of what her beauty alone would enable him to acquire as part of any marriage negotiations, Feduccio Castellani had long accepted that Donatina would ever remain the person his indulgence and complicity had let her become. His belief was that, when the time came, as it inevitably would, her strength of character would be usefully employed in taming her husband and thus influencing the family into which she would marry. That would only benefit the cause of the Castellani. He had learned to accept her mercurial temperament and to live with the extremes of her moods and behaviour.

"There's a possibility that our search may be over."

"Search? What search?" Donatina frowned and continued to brush her hair. She sat on a stool facing a mirror, talking to her brother's image that appeared over her left shoulder.

"For a husband for you."

The words connected. Neither their import nor their meaning did. It no longer mattered what her father proposed. She had vowed to find a husband for herself. She had succeeded in identifying the man she was certain would fulfil all of her criteria, even though he did not yet realise it for himself.

"He needn't have bothered," she said abstractedly. "It's too late."

"Pardon?"

Realising what she had said, she continued, "I meant, he needn't bother with me. I've lost interest. I'm thinking of becoming a nun."

"Very funny sister," he replied, assuming that she meant her remark as a joke. "Anyway, I thought you might want to know who it is."

Realizing that Guido might not have been there merely to placate her with meaningless platitudes, she stopped brushing her hair and turned to face him. "There is truth then in what you tell me?"

"Why else would I say such a thing?"

Donatina raised her eyebrows and smiled. "If I was to answer that question, you and our father would be embarrassed by the number of false alarms you have raised in my heart over these past three years."

"Sister," pleaded Guido.

"Sister yourself. Is anything yet concluded?"

Guido grimaced. "Not exactly."

"So quite plainly the search isn't over yet."

Guido tilted his head to one side and then to the other. The truth of the matter was that a target had been identified and, given the surprising circumstances, third parties sounded out as to the possibility of an approach succeeding. The initial feedback was very promising, though no formal proposal had as yet been made.

"Not really, but sort of."

"Either you can tell me about a husband or not. If there's nothing certain, then there's nothing at all. And if there's nothing at all and you think that by dangling possibilities in front of me you will temper my anger towards our father, then you're wrong. And to answer your next question, no, I will not dine with him this evening. I am invited to dine with Egidia at her parent's palazzo."

Donatina turned back towards the mirror and started brushing her hair again.

"How long will you keep up this battle? It's been nearly a week now."

"I've already told you. For as long as father refuses to

explain himself and to apologise for his comments and until such time as the matter of my marriage is settled."

"Father does understand how important it is to you that a husband is found. I promise you that something will be sorted out and perhaps a lot sooner than you may think."

Her brother did not realise how accurate he was. She knew not who this unidentified somebody was, nor did she much care. She had waited long enough while a whole host of somebodies had been identified, considered, pored over then rejected. Some of them she had known, others she met, wittingly or otherwise. None of it mattered now. She had found a man to love and who she believed would love her in return. Her wait would be over in a matter of hours.

The first part of her plan had been executed perfectly. She duly met with Giacomo Ragaci on the afternoon that followed the recital. Manfredi Colesi played host and Euphemia and Egidia were the chaperones. They sat around an open fire in the music room of the Palazzo Colesi as Donatina described her father and his tastes. The musician carefully reviewed the information. They settled on a frottola that would celebrate Feduccio's birthday and his return to the Signoria and agreed the price. Ragaci agreed to let her have something within the week and they agreed to meet once again at the Palazzo Colesi at three o'clock the following Friday.

Shortly afterwards, Donatina sent notes to both Manfredi Colesi and Ragaci claiming that she would be unable to attend at the appointed hour, citing a family commitment that she overlooked. She then sent a second note to Ragaci in which she proposed to visit him at his apartment at the Palazzo Tolosini a day later than originally planned when she hoped to hear his work, even if it was not yet then finished. Ragaci replied to her in all innocence, anticipating that she would be accompanied by at least one other.

* * * * * * *

Donatina's carriage was met at the gates of the Palazzo Tolosini by a servant who took her through to Adamo Tazzi. Tazzi's main responsibility was to protect the safety of Ignazio Tolosini and his family. He would often personally vet those who visited the palazzo, particularly those arriving for the first time. Satisfied as to the genuineness of her purpose, he motioned to the servant to show her the way to Ragaci's apartment.

When the servant announced her arrival, Ragaci was surprised to see her without a chaperone or a companion, but decided not to question it.

"You have a truly charming apartment," observed Donatina. She walked around the salon and peered through a door that led to the bedroom, though held back from entering it.

The apartment was one of several that had been laid out on the top floor of the east wing of the palazzo. Like many of the others it opened out onto terracing behind the battlements. The tenants were those who enjoyed the patronage of the Tolosini as well as a number of senior employees. Though self-contained, the apartments were connected by a series of corridors reached by an internal staircase that was located at the rear of the palazzo.

Ragaci's apartment was well-appointed. In addition to the furniture and rugs, wall-hangings and curtains provided by his patron, the room was festooned with musical instruments and music stands, manuscript books and pieces of parchment and pens and ink. His lutes were there as well as a small guitar that he had recently acquired, a harp, a viol, some pipes and tabors and even a shawm.

"Do you play all of these yourself?"

"Most, but not all proficiently."

"Not even all of the stringed instruments?"

"I can extract a tune from them all, but the lute is the only one that I would be confident to play in public."

Donatina tried to keep the opening exchanges to small talk, but the truth was that her heart was racing faster than her mind wanted to let it. She reined in her emotions long enough for Ragaci to offer to perform what he had written for her father. Before he sat down to play he poured her a cup of wine. While she watched him tune a lute and strum some tastar de corde, she gulped down half of the wine almost without thinking. It was red and thick and strong. It made her feel warm and light-headed and relaxed. She closed her eyes as Ragaci started to play the melody of the frottola. It was vibrant and upbeat and full of zest. There was a vase full of fresh flowers next to her. Their scent was robust and mingled enticingly with the nose of the wine that she still held in her hand. Her senses were drowning with stimulation.

Once he started to sing, she concentrated on the sound of his voice, paying little attention to the content of the lyrics. She caught the odd phrase – '*eventi del passato favoloso*' and '*pensiero saggi*', but most of it was subsumed by the earthy resonance of his baritone and the carnal response that it provoked within her.

When he came to the end of the piece, she remained quite still. Ragaci absorbed her pose of suffused ecstasy. It connected with emotions that he had suppressed for longer than he cared to remember. Uncertain as to whether he should disturb her reverie, he lay down his lute and waited patiently for her to open her eyes.

"That was wonderful," she said. "I'd like to hear more."

"The same frottola?"

The last thing that she wanted was to be reminded of her father, even if he had provided the pretext for her being there. "No. Something, more …"

"More what?"

"Romantic." She put her cup down next to the vase and leaned forward. "I would like you to sing me a song about love."

Ragaci had been quite taken by the presence of Donatina in his audience at the Palazzo Pitti recital. He could not have failed to notice the beautiful young woman in the front row who was enrapt throughout his performance and who then made an approach to commission him. He was surprised at himself when he realised that it was more than merely the promise of paid work that excited him at the prospect of meeting her again.

"Please, Signor Ragaci," she purred, "it doesn't have to be a long song."

Unable to rationalise either the seductive insistence of Donatina's plea or his own lack of resistance to it, Ragaci began to sing:

Embracing the beauty of your soul
Brings my heart to life
Hearing the velvet sound of your voice
Leads me gracefully to rest
In the warmth of your breast

When we are together
Every minute of every hour
Of your love
Makes me whole

It was a half-remembered piece that he had started to write with an idealised vision of Maria in mind, but which he never finished before her departure. He had completed the lyric of what was intended to be the first of three verses, but never composed a melody that he was now inspired to extemporise by the elixir of the moment.

This time Donatina watched him dreamily. She concentrated on every word and hung on to them all. Her expression was the window to her heart where she would guard the message of his lyric.

"That was so very beautiful, so very, very beautiful."

"Thank you," he said, putting the lute down on the floor, signalling his decision not to play more for her right then.

"The way you sang it, it could have been written for me."

"Do you think so?"

"Yes, I do. I think that … perhaps …" She did not know if she dare say aloud the words that were bursting inside her head. It was not quite what she had planned, but it felt right, felt as though he would understand.

"Perhaps what?"

"It's not perhaps, it is."

"It is what?"

Donatina rose from where she sat and stepped across to Ragaci. She rested her hands on his shoulders. "It is that … I love you, Giacomo. I love you very much and I want you, now and forever."

She leaned forward to kiss him. He felt his lips meet hers. It was a soft kiss, a sensual kiss, a kiss that connected more than just her lips with his and she believed that he understood that perfectly. His immediate reaction was one of paralysis.

There were questions that he had, too many to ask at once, but he did not know which one to ask first. The subject of each question broke down into words and the words swirled around in his head in a mist of befuddlement. One image emerged from his confusion with crystal clarity. Maria. He knew that she would never be his, but the commitment he had made to her in his heart was as strong as any formal vow of fidelity in a marriage.

"Take me, Giacomo, take me now." The breathless whisper was more in the nature of a command but was one he knew he should disobey. His vow to Maria was a silent vow but one that God had heard nonetheless. He would not dishonour the vow and could not betray the commitment he had made. He reached in his mind for the words to convey his response but, as he tried to speak, Donatina slid onto his lap and kissed him again, one hand on the back of his neck, the other on his cheek. He froze still and could not respond. As she kissed him she began to undulate very gently and the movement of her buttocks provoked an involuntary hardening of his penis.

"You're ready for me, aren't you?" she whispered.

Donatina misread his look of panic as one of caution.

"Don't worry, Giacomo. It's alright. Once I surrender myself to you, I will be your wife. No-one will be able to take me away from you. Not my father. Nobody. My virginity is a gift. I will choose who will have it. I have chosen you and you will be my husband."

He heard what she said but was incredulous that she could have meant it. He needed to point out that she was presumably mistaken, but she kissed him again. She took his hand and held it to her bosom. The bodice of her dress was cut low. His fingers felt the softness of her skin and, without realising that he had started to do so, he felt them start to stroke her breasts, then stopped. In a moment of lucidity he dropped his hands to his sides.

"Don't stop," she whispered, "you mustn't, you simply mustn't."

He had heard her tell him that he should not stop fondling her breasts, but his rational self knew that he must pull away from her. Whatever condition had affected her passions, he needed to resist it affecting his. Donatina Castellani was the daughter of Feduccio Castellani, whose reputation as a ruthless man of commerce and a recently reinstated strongman of the Signoria preceded him. Ragaci knew enough that, even his being alone with her, albeit in a situation that she had wholly engineered herself, was one that might not be good for his welfare. He realised that whatever fantasy she may have created in her own mind, there was no possibility of his ever becoming her husband, even if he wanted to.

He started to stand up so as to push her off his lap and, insodoing, slipped his arm around her back so as to prevent her falling. She misinterpreted the intent of his action of seeking separation as one of provoking increasing intimacy. She grabbed hold of him and kissed his cheek as she stood up. He put his hands against her shoulders, ready to push her away as gently as he might. She was nuzzling his neck and manoeuvring her thigh against his groin. Even through the layers of her clothing she could feel his erection becoming stronger. The sensation and its latent power excited her.

In spite of his physical arousal his sense of self was determined to regain control. He thought of what he might say without upsetting her. "Donatina, I think …" He stopped short as she slid her hand around the front of his breeches and began to stroke the outline of his penis. The firmness of her touch unleashed waves of pure sensuality that washed through his body, pent up energy that he had never previously released in the company of a woman.

"I need you, Giacomo. I want to make love with you," she said breathlessly.

He had intended to resist her, to deflect her and to politely ask her to leave, but he was beginning to realise that her needs and desires were becoming his as well.

"Come lie with me, Giacomo," she whispered, the rush of her breath into his ear sending a tingling sensation down his spine. She moved her lips close to his. This time he was powerless to resist her. He responded to her kisses with the force of passion a thousand times repressed. They held each other in a deep embrace. After a few minutes of silent communion, she felt that he had begun to relax. "Take me, Giacomo, take me."

"That cannot be," he replied, "that simply cannot be."

"Why not?"

Ragaci could not think how best to express his considered thoughts. The warmth of her lithe young body pressed against him, her breath on his neck and the look of lust that was in her eyes made it impossible for him to articulate what he wanted to say.

"There's no good reason, Giacomo, none at all. If you have to search for a reason it cannot be a good one. Now, come with me."

Fighting against his instincts, he was powerless to stop her from leading him by the hand into his bed-chamber. She launched herself at him, the suddenness of the movement knocking him off balance and backwards onto the bed. She pulled herself on top of him and this time he kissed her as willingly and as wantonly and with as little inhibition as she had him. She started to fumble with the fastenings of his breeches until they came unhitched. Before he could make any protestation, she turned around and was sitting astride him, with her back to his face. She hooked her thumbs into the top of his breeches and quickly slid them down to his ankles. He was ready for her. She rolled onto her back and lifted her skirts. She was wearing no undergarments. Feeling for his erection, she told him to get on top of her and to have her. Guided by her hand, he slowly entered her. As she felt his sex begin to pulsate, a myriad of sensations was released throughout her body. The sensations became explosions as she exhorted him to push deeper inside her, feeling her need for him ignite his for her. She started to meet the rhythm of his movements with her own as the naivety of her girlhood was shed and the wantonness of adulthood took control. Harder and faster, they moved as one until he reached the point at which he released the charge of life. The roar of his climax ignited the beginning of hers. She dug her finger nails deep into the soft flesh of his buttocks then seized the convulsions of his orgasm with her frantic movements to reach an exquisite climax of her own. Her scream of ecstasy finally released the bindings of her soul.

Serenely, they lay together for some while. Ragaci stayed on his back, Donatina was half draped across him, her left thigh pressed between his.

"You're mine, Giacomo, you're mine, my love, my husband," she murmured contentedly, the emotion subsumed by her moment of triumph.

It was the second time she had used that word, 'husband'. The confusion that had allowed her to get the better of his discretion began to lift. He realised that he had barely made any protest. He had submitted willingly to the charms of this young woman he barely knew and had tacitly accepted that she would be his wife. In permitting Donatina to lead him to coitus, he was committed to a marriage that an hour earlier had not even been within his contemplation. It was of no comfort that his actions amounted to nothing more than what Forzetti had predicted, that unable to be with the one he loved he would share physical pleasure with someone with whom he happened to spend time. He had forsworn his unfulfilled love for Maria and negated the vow of constancy for her that he had made to himself. "God protect me," he uttered.

"Pardon?" said Donatina.

Ragaci said nothing, though he reflected that it was by saying nothing that he found himself in his present predicament.

"You must come to my father's palazzo so that the formalities may be discussed. You will need to appoint someone to negotiate my dowry with my father. Tell me who that will be then come to the palazzo in a day or two. That will give me time to speak to my brother, Guido."

"Why?"

"My father is busy with the Signoria. Guido takes care of much of my father's business."

"Does he?" Ragaci was perplexed and not sure what he should say.

"But before that and before I must go, I want to feel you inside me once more."

The suggestion on its own was enough to startle Ragaci. He propped himself up on his elbow, "sadly there isn't time. I have an engagement to attend for which I am running very late."

"Please?" As she pleaded she moved her leg from him and started to run her hands along his groin.

"No, not now." He rested his hand on hers and gradually eased it away from him.

"Tomorrow?"

"I don't think that I can."

"Saturday then? The same time as today?"

He would not be able to delay meeting with her indefinitely. Two days would have to be enough. "Yes, then."

"I'll be here at three."

Ragaci moved off of the bed and hastily pulled up his breeches. He watched Donatina straighten her hair, smooth her clothes and make herself ready to leave.

At the door to his apartment, she threw her arm around him and kissed him again. He stood passively.

"Come on Giacomo? Do I not please you?"

He could not find the words with which to answer her, so he did his best to kiss her as passionately as he could. His heart was not in it. Donatina was too exhilarated with the apparent success of her mission that she did not notice his lack of conviction. She had not even remembered to finalise the arrangements for the commission.

"What of my performance of the frottola for your father?"

"We may discuss that on Saturday," she said.

"Will you not at least take the manuscript with you? I have written out this extra copy for you."

Graciously she accepted the rolled parchment that he proffered her

"On Saturday, then."

"Saturday," he said reluctantly.

"I love you , Giacomo, remember that. Remember that always."

* * * * * * *

On returning home, Donatina immediately sought out her brother. Guido was sitting in one of the smaller salons reading a book, while Santesa was working on a tapestry.

"Where have you been?" he asked.

"Arranging a gift for father's birthday," she said truthfully.

There was a lightness of mood that had been missing from her for more than a week.

"Peace at last!"

"Yes," she said.

"The timing couldn't be better!"

"Really?"

"Yes. I do have wonderful news for you."

"Oh and what's that?"

"A match has been made. Negotiations for your dowry will begin next week."

Santesa put down her tapestry. "I'll leave you two to talk it over." Santesa knew her sister-in-law well enough that she did not want to risk being caught up in the middle of another argument, if, as she predicted, the identity of Donatina's intended husband did not meet with her approval."

"No you don't," snapped Guido. "I want you to stay here."

Santesa looked meekly at Guido.

"Stay here, darling," he added, hurriedly infusing his tone with a degree of gentleness. "There are no secrets in this family."

"Who is it that father proposes that I marry?"

"A son of one of the most powerful and influential families in all of Florence, if not Italy."

"Who is?"

"Donatina, you're to be married to …"

She looked at him expectantly. Santesa quaked, waiting for the explosion. Guido beamed, anticipating a cry of delight. Donatina confounded them both. She took advantage of his pause to interrupt. "No, no wait. I won't hear it from you. I want to hear it directly from father."

"That pleases me."

"It does?"

"It means that you and father will be speaking to each other again."

"I said that I would like to hear the news from father. I didn't say anything about speaking to him."

"What do you mean?"

"If what he tells me doesn't please me then I'll say nothing other than to reject his choice of husband for me."

"How can you do that?"

"Easily. He may propose a husband and notarise a deed, but he can never force me to submit to a man I cannot love."

"What's that supposed to mean?"

"It means that I will only marry a man that I can love and if that's someone other than the man my father chooses, then that is the man I shall marry."

"Father will never countenance that."

"And I am no longer prepared to countenance a marriage without love. Father should have realised that when he permitted the discussions with Ambrogiano to fail."

Despite her show of bravado, Donatina realised that this unforeseen announcement required her to adjust the detail of the implementation of her plan. Perhaps she might have been better off to hear out her brother and to prepare for her father accordingly, but then again not. In the end it would make no real difference. She had already made the decision as to whom she would marry. The only slight change was that she would need to do whatever it would take to ensure that her father's intentions and those of the suitor her father proposed were swiftly neutralised.

XIX

Portrait

Florence. April 1517

"A little more to the left. Fine. The arm forward a touch. The right arm. Perfect."

"Are you sure this was how I was sitting last time?"

"Certain."

Leonardo Salcoiati had eventually persuaded Ragaci to sit for him. To begin with, Ragaci was put off by his experience with Forzetti. He was plagued by the sense that memorialising his image in oils was something with which destiny would interfere.

"So far, so good," said Ragaci. He briefly scanned the outline of the work. The preparatory sketches that were displayed on an easel in a corner of Leonardo's cluttered studio were encouraging. Leonardo agreed to compose the piece in Ragaci's preferred pose, holding a lute as if about to start playing. His left hand was on the fretboard, the right bent over the soundbox.

"In truth there's not much to look at yet," replied Leonardo as he picked up a palette and began to mix a flesh coloured tint. "It will need a few more sittings before there is."

Ragaci looked to be absorbed with a cerebral problem as Leonardo began to apply paint to the canvas. Ragaci gazed through the window that overlooked the yard at the back of the house where Gianetta, Leonardo's wife of a few months, was tending the shrubbery that covered the rear wall.

"Do you think you might stop jiggling your leg?"

"Was I?"

"Yes."

"Sorry."

Leonardo started to work on Ragaci's face.

"Can you relax your face muscles a little?"

"What do you mean?"

"Your expression. You look as though something is worrying you."

"Hardly."

"Something ails you Giacomo. What is it?"

"Nothing."

"Nothing?" Leonardo's tone revealed his scepticism.

Ragaci started jiggling his leg again. "Nothing you can help me with."

"Unless I know what it is, I clearly can't."

Ragaci thought for a moment. "It's hard to put into words." He wanted to share his problem with someone, but felt that by so doing he would expose himself to criticism and to the possibility of vilification. "Let's say it's a spiritual matter."

"Wouldn't you be better off talking to a priest then?"

Ragaci had already considered that option. "It's a spiritual problem, but set within an entirely temporal context to which no priest could relate. At least no priest that I know."

"And?"

"And, Leonardo. Tell me, do you believe in destiny, the destiny of the spirit?"

"The destiny of the spirit? I'm not sure what you mean." Leonardo was trying to concentrate on the region of Ragaci's chin and neck and the shadow of the one that fell upon the other. The subject matter of Ragaci's polemic made it impossible. He put down the brush and the palette and listened carefully.

"The destiny of the spirit, Leonardo, is part of the divine will. Man-made rules and conventions cannot override the divine will."

This was not something about which Leonardo had spent much, if any, time pondering. He operated within a somewhat different zone of contemplation, where art and beauty were his truth and to which all else was subject. He waited for Ragaci to continue.

"I believe that the uniting of the male and female spirits is a fundamental requirement for the soul to progress. At some point in its journey, a spirit will meet the one for whom it is intended. Obstacles may block the path and tests may be set. It is for the spirit to navigate its way through all of these and so reach its intended destination." Ragaci spoke anxiously, as if his knowledge and beliefs were a burden that weighed ever more heavily upon him, even as he began to share it.

"The way you speak about it suggests that you have an insight about your own destiny that may not be apparent to others," said Leonardo.

"My destiny is the love that I have for a woman."

"Is this a woman you've just met?"

"The woman of whom I speak was first in my life some time ago. There were obstacles that could not have been overcome. I abandoned any notion I then had that somehow I might be together with this woman. More recently I was set a test that I think I've failed. I've failed it badly. Very badly."

For a long time Leonardo had believed that his sister, Maria, was the woman who Ragaci loved and that his love was fully reciprocated. The obstacles to which Ragaci referred were easily identified. The test was something else, something new, something unknown, at least to Leonardo. "Let's assume that the identity of this love of yours is certain. What test were you set and how have you failed it?"

Ragaci prised open his soul and decided to share its secrets with Leonardo who was one of the few persons he felt able to trust. "A woman came to me, a young woman, a beautiful, unmarried young woman from a powerful and wealthy family. She wanted me to compose some music as a gift for her father. The commission was a ruse to attract my attention."

"And was it attracted?"

"It was, though I had not set out with that intention."

"You have become her lover?"

Ragaci hesitated before answering. "Yes and no."

"That sounds both good and bad."

Looking at the floor, Ragaci nodded ruefully. "Believe me, it's not good. Not at all."

"Didn't she please you?"

Ragaci looked at Leonardo, then picked out a point in the far wall and said, "it was as though I was not an active participant in the event, that I was a spectator. When it was over, all I felt was emptiness."

"Did you please her?"

"I don't know, but I think I so."

"How many times have you been with her?"

"She has returned to visit me at my apartment on two subsequent occasions during this past week."

Leonardo's tone changed from one of interrogation to one of concern. "She has? And did you …?"

"On her second visit I feigned illness and managed to fob off her physical desires."

"And then?"

"On the most recent occasion I contrived not to be alone before she turned up. Salvuccio, the guitarist, was rehearsing with me for a recital that we were giving later that day. She seemed happy enough to sit around and listen to our music."

"And she still wants more?" Leonardo moved from behind the canvas and stood directly in front of Ragaci

"She wants everything. From the very beginning she made it clear that by giving her virginity to me her intention was that we should be married."

Leonardo tried to hide his surprise. "A route to matrimony that is not the preferred one, but a route that is not unknown, nevertheless."

"Though not in the circles in which she moves."

"Lacking her virginity, her desirability in whatever circles she moves will decline and so will the worth of the man who would be prepared to marry her."

Ragaci nodded ruefully.

"Look on the bright side, Giacomo. It might please her father to save some money on the dowry and he will have you for a son-in-law into the bargain." Though well-intentioned, Leonardo's observation could have been construed as little other than flippant.

"I fear not."

"Why not?"

"Her father has other plans."

"Who are we talking about?"

Ragaci realised that having come thus far in his confession, there was no turning back. He put down the lute and stood up. He took a couple of paces towards Leonardo so that their physical closeness would emphasise the importance of the revelation that he was about to unfold. "Before I tell you, it's important you know that the woman of whom I first spoke is your sister, Maria Chiara. Maria is the one who I believe is my destiny but who circumstances prevent me from being with."

Leonardo nodded sympathetically.

"That you aren't surprised by what I have told you is no surprise to me."

"For a long time I have thought that you were enamoured of my sister. And I suppose that the test you think you failed is succumbing to the charms of this nameless, young hussy who seduced you and who wants you to marry her."

"I have failed the test and committed a sin, one that no amount of confession will cure," said Ragaci despondently.

"And when her father finds out that his valuable asset has been tampered with, you're worried that he's unlikely to welcome you into his family with open arms."

"And possibly worse."

"That may depend on who you are talking about"

Ragaci was almost embarrassed to continue. Leonardo made it clear from his knitted brow that it was essential that he knew.

"A member of the Signoria who is in the process of making arrangements for his daughter to marry the son of another member of the Signoria."

Leonardo put down the brush and the palette and folded his arms.

"You'll have to tell me who it is. I don't keep up-to-date with such doings."

"Nothing's yet been finally agreed and no deed has yet been notarised, but the woman I speak of is Donatina Castellani. Her father is Feduccio Castellani."

Leonardo gasped. "And the intended husband?"

"Donatina has been told by her father that he is in negotiations for her to marry Niccolo Tolosini."

"Niccolo Tolosini!"

"Yes. The son of my patron, which hardly makes things any easier."

"By the grace of God, Giacomo, you find yourself in the middle of a bear pit!"

"Somewhat."

"Does Castellani yet know of your position?"

"Donatina tells me not, but that she has already made it clear to her father that she will not be forced into a marriage with Tolosini."

"That a match might even have been contemplated between a Castellani and a Tolosini defies belief."

"Castellani has already engaged with the Medici themselves. He secured a cardinal's hat for his son and a return to the Signoria for himself. The Tolosini will be easy meat for him."

"But if the marriage is not made and it is the Castellani who withdraw, the Tolosini will not take rejection lightly."

"Nor, if it proceeds, that their new daughter is not intact. Even worse, that her virginity has been surrendered under their own roof to a man in their employ."

Leonardo nodded vigorously. "You assume that Castellani will ensure that Donatina accepts the marriage that has been planned."

"It's to be hoped that he will do."

"You say that you don't want to be her husband, but perhaps that would be the best solution?"

"She isn't the woman that I love. I have no wish to marry her. She doesn't engage my spirit, though by seducing my body she stole my will for long enough to condemn me to the path of a sinner. Now she seeks to possess my soul."

"And yet she doesn't soften your heart."

"My heart is with Maria."

"And hers with you," said Leonardo speculatively, but endeavouring to imbue his tone with a degree of certainty.

"Even now?"

"Even now."

"You're certain?"

There was a pause before Leonardo answered. "No Giacomo, I'm not certain, but there's only one way to find out."

"You'll ask her for me?"

"And you'll be there when I do so," he replied vigorously.

"I will?"

"I'm planning to visit Maria next week."

"For Easter?"

Leonardo nodded. "I last saw her at Christmas when all seemed well."

"I remember you telling me."

"Her most recent letter to me was delivered a few days ago. I detect a depression of her spirit."

"What's happened?"

"There's nothing explicit in the letter. I just know my sister well. Something's not right and she's not telling me what it is."

"Do you think that my being there will help?"

"More than that. It was always my father's plan to bring a lawsuit to secure Maria's release from the convent. He believed that what my aunt and her husband did by asserting they were Maria's 'next-of kin' was a deception that rendered Maria's acceptance by the convent illegal. Even without a lawsuit my sense is that my sister may be prepared to relinquish her vows. If you're willing to marry her that could influence her decision to come back home to Florence."

"Leonardo," said Ragaci, failing to suppress his excitement. "Do you think that's possible?"

"We can try."

"But what of Donatina?" asked Ragaci despairingly.

"Is she yet with child?"

"I doubt it."

"Then try and keep it that way."

"I will but what do I tell her?"

"Tell her the truth."

"I've told her that I can't see how I may become her husband while her father is discussing other arrangements for her."

"How did she respond?"

"She told me that she has made it clear to her father that she will not marry Niccolo Tolosini under any circumstances. That she will only marry a man that she loves and that she could never love Niccolo."

"And is her father aware of her desire for you?"

"Apparently not. Her intention is that I should go to the Palazzo Castellani and perform the frottola that I have written for him, whereafter she will make her announcement to him."

"And when is his birthday?"

"The week after Easter."

"Does Donatina yet know the destination of your heart?"

"No. I have kept my counsel on the matter."

"Then maybe now's the time to level with her as to where your heart belongs, before it's too late."

"You're right. I'll do it. I'll do it as soon as I can," said Ragaci. The tone of his voice was one of relief. It contrasted with the anxiety of his expression.

Leonardo moved back behind the canvas, picked up the palette and the brush and started to work with renewed vigour.

* * * * * * *

There was a chill in the early morning air, but by noon it was warm and an opaque sun illuminated the tops of the buildings. From his apartment Ragaci had a clear view of the grotesque campanile. Its bells were silenced during the time of Savonarola. The pious monk accused Ruberto Tolosini, Ignazio's father, of apostasy and ordered the bells to be removed. They had never since been replaced. Ragaci looked out of the window, across the battlement encrusted rooftop and up at the clouds that flecked the sky. He wondered how it would be to scale a mountain so high that he could look down and find out what the top of a cloud might look like. An angel could manage it without a mountain, but that was a feat no mortal man might contemplate.

Wearing a hooded cloak and inferior garments of cheap cloth, Donatina entered the Palazzo Tolosini as discretely as possible. She had made it her business to cultivate a relationship with Tazzi, the Tolosini's head of security. Tazzi had access to every part of the palazzo and keys to fit every lock in every door. She learned that Tazzi was in need of money to settle a family debt that was secured against the deeds to the house where his elderly mother lived. A silver coin or two here and there ensured her unchallenged passage to Ragaci's apartment. It took little more to persuade the normally reticent, but financially needy, Tazzi to keep her informed of progress of the dowry negotiation. She called a truce with her father. The dowry negotiations did not seem to her to be progressing quickly. It would not be long before she might make the declaration to her father that she believed would stop them in their tracks. Yet the truce was an uneasy one and her brother, Guido, said little that was not positive about the proposed marriage to Niccolo Tolosini. Tazzi, however, had another agenda. It was one that was not driven by money and one that he would not share with anyone, not even the lithe young rich woman who seemed so keen to ply him with money for his knowledge.

Tazzi had fought against the Medici and the Holy League in the war of 1512. He was at Prato when the militia threw down their arms in the face of the invading Spaniards who were led by Cardinal Medici, now Pope Leo X. The cowardice of those with whom he stood shoulder-to-shoulder denied him the possibility of avenging the death of his father and uncle, victims of Medici excesses of an earlier time. His quest to shed the blood of his enemies lured him to Florence where he secured a position with Tolosini using a stolen letter of introduction. Biding his time was something to which his temperament was not best suited. Patience was a virtue that he had been slow to learn and found hard to exercise. Having identified a number of potential targets to which his senior position amongst Tolosini's retinue gave him easy access, his problem was engineering the perfect getaway or, at worst, the perfect alibi. His self-prescribed mission demanded that no less than seven of the Medici or their equally godless followers be eliminated and it would not do for him to fall short by even one.

Tazzi worked stealthily and alone. He appreciated that the Castellani had but recently made peace with the Medici and discovered, too, the ancient enmity that defined the historic relationship of the Castellani and the Tolosini. However, he appreciated and understood the intent behind the marriage discussions that Feduccio Castellani had instigated. Ignazio Tolosini was initially dismissive and subsequently suspicious of the approach. However, after a couple of sessions, Feduccio managed to impress the genuineness of his desire to bury a century old hatchet and seal the peace with a pact that would benefit both families. Ignazio warmed to the idea and established that Niccolo thought Donatina to be a truly appetising prospect as a wife, though he doubted that even her charms would be enough to keep his idolatrous son away from the temptations of the city's bordellos. Tazzi was charged with keeping Niccolo out of the view of the Castellani and their followers until such time as a deed could be notarised. For all of that, the negotiations progressed in fits and starts and there were constant disagreements about one detail or another. While Tazzi played no active part in the discussions, he was required to attend all of the meetings with Cibaldo Rimbotti, Tolosini's consigliari. Introduced as a clerk, Tazzi's only real function was to protect Rimbotti in the event that the medium of debate threatened to move from the verbal to the physical.

If it was not for the money Donatina paid him, Tazzi would see no benefit in disclosing details of the marriage negotiations. Given the parlous state of the discussions, he had half an eye on their failure and to what openings that might lead him. In addition, though Donatina had not confided in him, he guessed that her interest in Ragaci may not have been entirely related to his music. Tazzi concluded that an alliance with Donatina, as unlikely as it might appear and as temporary as it might be, was something he was prepared to nurture, while at all times keeping her as much at arms length as he could. There was a commonality of interest in one thing above all others and that was a mutual loathing of Niccolo Tolosini; it was something that neither of them had, as yet, formally admitted to the other. What Donatina was given to understand from snippets of gossip that she picked up from others was that Niccolo was an unsavoury fornicator and worthless drunk whose only advantage was the wealth into which he had been born. Tazzi's experience was first hand and derived from numerous incidents of rescuing the dissolute Niccolo from brawls, disinterring him from brothels and settling his gambling and other debts under direction from Ignazio.

Donatina's commissioning of Ragaci to compose a frottola for her father assumed another dimension. She intended to announce her intentions to her father immediately after Ragaci played the piece for him. Feduccio would be at his most receptive and, in her estimation, unable to deny her wish. Before she set a time for the recital, she would need to be certain that her father could still withdraw from the dowry negotiations with the Tolosini. While there was not yet any certainty as to when an agreement might be reached, she could not gamble that the discussions would unravel completely.

As Tazzi conducted her up the stairs to Ragaci's apartment, he revealed that only the previous day compromise was reached on all outstanding issues. A date would shortly be set for the public announcement and the notarisation of a deed. That she had not yet been informed of this by either her father or Guido rankled with her. On the threshold of Ragaci's apartment she turned to thank Tazzi for escorting her through the palazzo, but he had vanished. She was not surprised, as the same thing had happened on other occasions when she had been with him. Though she found it disconcerting, Donatina was careful not to let Tazzi know how she felt.

Before she knocked on Ragaci's door she flipped back the hood and pulled her hair over her cloak, shaking it loose. Ragaci opened the door and she launched herself at him, one arm around his waist the other on the back of his neck, pulling his head towards her and lathering him with kisses. Ragaci did not respond. The feel of her lips on his did not create a brush of enticement. He remained motionless, his arms at his side, his eyes wide open.

Donatina was becoming used to his reticence towards her physical advances. She ministered to his inhibitions but, even by his standards, the greeting was corpse-like. "Is this a proper welcome for the woman who would be your wife?"

Ragaci said nothing. He stood back and waved her into the room.

"Are you unwell, my love?" she asked tenderly.

He chose his words carefully. "In a manner of speaking. Yes."

"What is the matter?"

"Come. Sit down. We can talk. Would you like something to drink?"

He pointed to a jug of wine that he had drawn from a cask in Tolosini's cellar earlier in the day and that he had brought up to fortify his resolve.

"If you are, then I will. Thank you"

Donatina sat down and watched him while he tidied manuscripts into a neat pile and shifted them to one end of the table where he usually wrote his music. He poured two cups and set them down opposite each other.

"Not there, Giacomo, come and sit next to me."

He moved his chair to the end of the table and twisted it to face her. Immediately she took his hands in his, kissed them and lowered them onto his thighs where she held them.

"Tell me everything."

For a moment he looked away as he composed himself. He needed to ignore her radiant beauty, the cascades of golden hair that hung around her shoulders, the soft curves of her firm young body whose secrets she would share with him and no one else. He did not know where to start.

"Giacomo," she whispered. "Tell me. What is it?"

"Donatina, you are a very beautiful woman."

She waited. He said nothing.

"I, too, have something to tell you," she said, imbuing the announcement with a tone of significance. "It's something very significant. Maybe it will be easier if I tell you that first?"

He nodded. She let go of his hands

"The discussions about my dowry have reached the point of agreement. There is likely to be a formal announcement very shortly. It's the perfect time for you to come to the palazzo and sing for my father. When you have finished and he expresses his pleasure, we will retire with him and tell him our news."

"Now?"

"Not now meaning today, but certainly tomorrow."

That was the cue Ragaci needed. "Tomorrow's impossible. I have something important to attend to."

"Whatever it is you have planned cannot possibly be more important than the matter of our marriage. The day after tomorrow is Good Friday and I would not want to broach this subject with my father on such a holy day. Equally, we should not wait beyond that point lest my father agrees the date for the public announcement of my marriage to the vile Tolosini."

"Early tomorrow I leave Florence for Arezzo where I will stay for a few days."

"Arezzo? Why Arezzo?"

"I'm going there with my friend Leonardo Salcoiati and his wife, Gianetta. I'm staying with his family there over Easter."

"You did not mention this before," she snapped

Ragaci shrugged his shoulders.

"There's still time for you to tell Leonardo that you can't join him."

"Time? Perhaps. Desire? No."

"What do you mean?" Donatina was trying hard to restrain her annoyance and frustration.

"I have a matter to attend to in Arezzo. A personal matter."

"What personal matter?"

Having accepted Leonardo's counsel that he should be open with Donatina, he found it impossible to put into words for her what he knew he ought to say. He decided to sidestep her interrogation.

"It's to do with Leonardo's family. His father was my patron before Tolosini. I'm still close to the Salcoiati, or at least what's left of them. I've pledged my help to Leonardo in a matter that concerns his family."

"How can anything take priority over your obligations to your future wife?" snapped Donatina.

Quite so, thought Ragaci, though he resisted the temptation to say as much.

"Well?"

"Donatina, I have never agreed to marry you."

"What do you mean?" said Donatina uncertainly, trying to mollify her tone. She knew he could not be serious, not after he had taken the gift of her virginity in full knowledge of what that meant and what she had told him beforehand.

"As I have said before, I can't see how your father will give his blessing to us," he said hesitantly. "You and me that is. I'm not wealthy. I have no possessions. Little money to speak of. My only home is this apartment that I am only permitted to live in as part of my patronage. I own no land and I have passed on my inheritance to my brother in San Gimignano."

His words touched her, his weakness did not. What he needed more than anything was her support, her encouragement and her strength. She already knew how much power and energy she had derived from their lovemaking and assumed that it was the same for him, though he had yet to say as much. She had enabled him to discover his manhood and would continue by ensuring that he overcame his diffidence towards her father and their plan to marry. With her encouragement and support she would ensure that he was able to accomplish the objective she had determined to be in his best interest.

"Giacomo, you need none of that. My father has wealth beyond calculation. I already know that the dowry his seconds have been negotiating with Tolosini would constitute more than enough to keep us living well, even before the earnings from your music are taken into account."

Ragaci had his own clear view of matters. "Wouldn't it be easier for everyone if you did the right thing?"

"Which is what?"

"Marry Niccolo Tolosini," said Ragaci speculatively.

"How many times do I have to tell you that there is no-one and nothing that will make me marry that festering pig of a man," she barked.

Ragaci did not need to hear from Donatina what he already knew about Niccolo. He had seen enough himself to appreciate her sentiments on the subject.

"I won't give my father even the slightest indication that I will go along with his proposal to give my hand in marriage to Tolosini. Do you hear me?" She was shouting loudly enough that it would be impossible for others on the top floor of the palazzo not to hear her. She stood up as if to emphasise the point, though the question was entirely rhetorical. Ragaci made no attempt to respond.

"So, you do understand," she continued. "Before I give myself to you, I want you to promise me that you will abandon this nonsensical idea of going to Arezzo tomorrow and come to the Palazzo Castellani and play the frottola that you have been paid for."

"I have already pledged to Leonardo that I will go with him. I cannot go back on my pledge." Ragaci's measured tone contrasted with the tremor of Donatina's agitation.

"You have also pledged that you will marry me. You know that the time is coming when you will need to show yourself to my father. That time is tomorrow and you will do as I have requested of you."

He refrained from pointing out that he had made no pledge of any kind to her. "I was asked by Leonardo to go with him to Arezzo – to help rescue his sister from a convent – if you must know. He needs me to be with him. Having agreed to go I cannot, nor will I, do otherwise."

Donatina was used to getting her own way and would not have the man who would be her husband contradict her. Suddenly, and without warning, she slapped him across the face, hard, and then again. Ragaci smarted from the blows but said nothing. His silent response further fuelled Donatina's anger. He sat and stared at her, suppressing his urge to slap her back and quelling his desire to forcibly eject her from his apartment. It would not take much more provocation from her for him to fully disclose the purpose of his trip to Arezzo.

"If you would abandon me now, when you know that I need you, how will it be once we are married?"

Ragaci stood and looked down at her. "I think that perhaps you should leave now," he said calmly.

"Leave now?" she yelled. "Not until I have accomplished my purpose."

"If your purpose is to persuade me to meet your father tomorrow, then that is a purpose that will not be accomplished."

Ragaci's defiance was a challenge that she had not expected to encounter. Curiously, it began to arouse her. She harnessed the passion of her anger and focused it in another direction. She put her arms around Ragaci and she kissed his lips and then his cheek where she had slapped him. He did not respond other than to continue looking at her impassively.

"Let's stop this fighting and go into your bed," she purred. "Yes?"

He shook his head. "No. I can't."

She looked at him querulously. "Pardon?"

"I said no. I can't."

"Why not? Don't you want me?"

"No, I don't. "

"What do you mean, you don't?"

"Just that. I don't want to take you to my bed."

"Well I want you to. I need to feel you inside of me," she protested.

"That's unfortunate. You won't and tomorrow I'm not coming to your palazzo. I'm going to Arezzo. That's final."

She grabbed hold of him and tried to push him to the ground where she might bestride him. He toppled backwards and knocked a chair flying. It made a loud crack as it hit the floor. She fell on top of him and started to run her hands down his body. She was strong and she had caught him by surprise but she was not strong enough to overwhelm him. He managed to roll onto his side and insodoing push her off him. It was his turn to kneel astride her and pin her down by her wrists.

"Get off me, you bastard! Get off me!" she shrieked.

"I will, but I want you to know that I will be away in Arezzo for a few days visiting Leonardo's family. I'm going to visit his sister who is a nun and in whom I have a special interest."

"What do you mean a 'special interest'?" she hissed.

"I used to teach her music and we were close friends. Leonardo is concerned about her state of being in the convent and thinks that I might be able to help her."

"How?"

"If I tell you, will you promise to stop making all this noise and then leave?"

"Answer the question."

Believing that the truth would out at some point and, having convinced himself that Maria would be his, he braced himself for the reaction that he knew would greet his confession.

"The fact of the matter is that if Maria Salcoiati realises that I am attached to her, she may be persuaded to renounce her vows and leave the convent where Leonardo believes her to be unhappy."

Donatina gaped at him. "You mean that you would have her and not me?"

"Whether or not she decides to leave the convent, I would do whatever it takes to make sure she is happy."

Donatina breathed heavily, narrowed her eyes and tried to push his hands up with her wrists. "You bastard," she said between gritted teeth. "You filthy, rotten bastard." Ragaci said nothing, but loosened his grip on her wrists and slowly stood up before helping Donatina to her feet.

"Do you realise what you have done to me?" she shrieked.

"I make no excuses for what we have done together, but at no time have I ever agreed to marry you."

"You lying bastard. You knew why I gave myself to you and if you do not make good the promise you made by taking my virginity, believe you me you will be punished. You will not have any satisfaction in anything, not with this Maria Salcoiati nor with anyone else."

"I can say nothing more on this subject. I would that I had not allowed it to happen, but it has."

"I curse you Giacomo Ragaci. I curse you from here to hell. I promise that I'll pray that you burn there for all eternity and I will do everything in my power to make sure that you do."

She grabbed her cloak from where she had left it draped across a chair and left. As she opened the door she saw the backs of a couple of women scampering away from her and towards the stairwell. Black with rage, Donatina slammed the door behind her and called after them, demanding to know what they had been doing outside Ragaci's apartment. They ran towards the staircase. Donatina decided not to give chase and, by the time she reached the top of the staircase, they had disappeared.

Paying the fleeing female figures no further attention, her thoughts returned to her primary concern, the impending announcement her father would make about her proposed marriage to Niccolo Tolosini. Her plan could not be made to work. Ragaci was all she had ever wanted in a man. At the same time, she could not understand why, when presented with the opportunity of a marriage to the most eligible woman in Florence, the musician had rejected her. Though he had not admitted an emotional attachment to the nun in Arezzo, he had said that he would do anything he could to make her happy. That, coupled with his refusal to make love with her, was enough for Donatina to know that it was pointless for her to build up any further expectations of him.

The line between the extremes of her emotions was finely drawn and, now, she felt nothing but disgust and contempt for him, that he could have treated her as he had. She would have her revenge and would turn her attention to that in due course. Her eyes were blazing with anger and with hatred as she reached the bottom of the staircase. A narrow corridor snaked around the back of that wing of the building before opening out onto the courtyard. She pulled the hood over her head.

As anonymously as Tazzi had disappeared when conducting her to Ragaci's apartment, he appeared from under an arch leading to the stable-block that was situated at right angles to the main building. He looked at her, anticipating that his expression alone would invite her to engage him in conversation, were it the case that she had something to say to him. His brooding presence drew her like a magnet.

With her head bowed, she crossed the courtyard towards him. He disappeared behind the arch and into a small room where Tolosini's sentries kept their belongings and rested in between duties. She followed him and shut the door after first conspiratorially glancing behind her.

"Signor Tazzi, I have a simple question to put to you."

She should have known better than to expect a verbal response. It was not necessary. He waited for the question to be put.

"My surmise is that you are not fond of Signor Niccolo."

Tazzi said nothing.

"Well?"

"I'm waiting for your question," he said gruffly. "I haven't yet heard one."

"Well, are you?"

"I am paid to work here. Keeping an eye on Signor Niccolo and keeping him out of trouble is part of what I am paid to do. Whether or not I like him is irrelevant."

"And how much are you paid for this task?"

Tazzi looked at her suspiciously. He had been standing in the corner farthest away from her, but now he stepped across to a table against which he leaned his buttocks. "My salary doesn't depend on my fulfilling any one of my many tasks, any more than any of the others."

"I see. So if Niccolo was to be incapacitated in some way, your livelihood would not thereby be affected?"

Tazzi permitted himself a rare smile. He understood her completely.

"I will not marry Signor Niccolo, not under any circumstances. The only way I can see myself free of him is if he becomes … well … incapacitated in some way."

Tazzi nodded. He waited for her to continue.

"And of course, were that to happen, a reward would be in order; a financial reward."

Tazzi considered the suggestion. "Presumably, the greater the incapacity, the greater the reward?"

"Of course," replied Donatina, almost without thinking. "Shall we say, fifty florins to ensure that he becomes unable to marry me?"

"A hundred."

She thought for a moment before proposing a compromise that favoured him, "eighty."

"Agreed."

"And, if you please, I would also like to engage you to deal with Signor Ragaci."

Tazzi looked puzzled.

"In the course of commissioning some music he …" She could never admit to anyone that she was no longer a virgin. "… sought to have his way with me. Naturally I resisted, but he needs to be punished. But there is no hurry. And of course there will an additional reward for dealing with him."

Tazzi had no strong feelings about Ragaci one way or another. The idea of Ragaci attempting to have his way with Niccolo's putative bride he found highly amusing. It appealed to his sense of irony. He would turn his immediate attention to Niccolo. It would not be difficult to conceive of a suitable treat for his master. That would be a routine matter. Punishment on the other hand would be something altogether more enjoyable and he would devise something that would not only achieve Signorina Castellani's objective, but also accommodate the perversity of his own imagination. Without saying another word Tazzi sauntered towards the door, opened it and ushered Donatina across the courtyard. He watched her leave the palazzo and walk along the street to her waiting carriage.

XX

Rescue

Arezzo. April 1517

An unexpected shower delayed their departure and left the rutted road out of Arezzo scarred by puddles. A strong wind chased the clouds that remained across an uncertain sky that was mottled with patches of blue and grey.

The previous afternoon, Good Friday, they had accompanied Leonardo's Aunt Bartolomea and her husband to the Church of San Francesco. The service included a number of meditations and readings as well as a musical recitation of the Passion from the Gospel of St. John. Two priests led the congregation in a dramatic rendition of the story of Jesus' arrest in the Garden of Gethsemane, his trial before Pontius Pilate and his subsequent crucifixion.

Ragaci found it hard to concentrate on the service. Descriptions of Christ's suffering in the Passion and the images of the cycle of frescoes that adorned the walls of the church fought with his own fears and imaginings. Each time he tried to forget the challenges of his own life and engage with the Passion as it followed Jesus along the via Dolorosa to Calvary, Ragaci became absorbed in the Legend of the

Cross that Piero della Francesca had painted on ten panels around the choir of the church. At the centre of the fresco cycle was a crucifix that reflected the climax of the Passion. Ragaci presently felt his own pain more than he could ever feel Christ's. Though it was only two days since his last encounter with Donatina, it seemed like an eternity. The vitriol with which she had laden the curse she had put upon him sat uneasily at the confluence of his conscious thoughts and his subconscious imaginings of Maria. The curse was no less vivid and its threat no less real than the pitted stone walls of the Convent of St Perpetua and St Felicitia that were so close he could almost smell them.

He barely slept. Not long before the cocks began to crow, he crept down to Aunt Bartolomea's kitchen, poured himself a cup of milk and started to strum his lute softly. He worked on some lyrics and a simple tablature for a short piece that had come to him as he lay awake staring at the ceiling, waiting impatiently for the day to begin. A short while afterwards, he was joined by Leonardo who was also finding it hard to sleep. As Leonardo entered the kitchen, Ragaci smiled at him and switched to a well known frottola by the master of the genre, Serafino dall'Aquila:

Tu dormi, io veglio et vo spargendo i pass
Et tormentado intorno ale tuo mura.
Tu dormi e'l dolor mio sveglia i sassi
Et fa per gran pieta la luna obscura.
Tu dormi, tu, ma non questi ochi lassi,
dove el sonno a venir non se asciura.

Perche ogni cosa da mia mente fuge,
Salvo la imagin tua che me struge

You sleep but I am awake and pacing
Distractedly about your walls.
You sleep, and my grieving wakes the stones
And makes the moon for pity veil its face.
You sleep, but to these weary eyes of mine
To which sleep is determined not to come.

For everything has fled my mind
Except your image which is torturing me.

And that was how he felt when he climbed into the carriage beside Leonardo and Gianetta Salcoiati.

At the last minute Aunt Bartolomea decided not to join them. A month earlier she attended the Mass that celebrated the lives and honoured the sacrifices made by the convent's patron saints and Maria had seemed fine to her. Aware of Leonardo's concerns about his sister's well-being, she decided not to get in his way. She counselled Ragaci and Gianetta against accompanying him and was upset at their refusal to countenance her suggestion. Nevertheless, she did not bear grudges and blessed them all as the carriage rolled forward.

It was some months since Ragaci last left Florence, though he was contemplating invitations to perform in each of Sienna and Bologna as word of his virtuosity spread. He returned home to San Gimignano to attend the christening of Bartolo Storioni's firstborn son and subsequently to celebrate the marriage of his brother, Cesare, to Lucia Gianbullari. He felt removed from both events, as if a mere passer-by who stumbled across them by accident. The destruction of the Palazzo Salcoiati and his decision to remain in Florence thereafter defined the final severance of his umbilical attachment to his home and all it symbolised to him. His past was an indelible part of him, but he no longer believed that he could play a functioning role in the lives of those he had left behind. His love for them was unconditional but his destiny required a single-minded commitment to his music and a way of life that none of them could ever imagine living.

It being Holy Saturday, a pregnant calm hung over the town. The silence of the streets was disturbed only by the rumble of the carriage wheels and by groups of unruly children playing outside their homes. Even they were less boisterous than normal. After a couple of wrong turns the driver found the Via Giotto that led to the Sansepulcro road. A few miles out of Arezzo there was a track that led northwards and wound its way up to the Convent of St Perpetua and St Felicitia.

In between scattered thickets of evergreens, the track climbed through jagged and uninviting rocks, at some points grey and at others a dirty white and in part cloaked with clusters of scabrous bushes. The peak of the Alpe de Poti dominated the mountain backdrop.

For Leonardo, the journey seemed to take longer than on earlier visits. The ground was heavy underfoot and he surmised that it slowed the horses down. Leonardo and Ragaci repeatedly took turns to lean out of the window as if that alone would hasten progress. The driver remained oblivious to his passengers' impatience.

Gianetta remained silent throughout the journey. Leonardo's concerns for his sister were her concerns as well. Though she had met Maria only twice, she was in total admiration for someone, especially a woman, who was able to choose her own path and stay true to it, while those around her would have had her do otherwise. The zeal of Maria's belief and the absence of sermonising and admonishment that accompanied it was refreshing. Brought up by a Humanist father who kept the excesses of church dogma at arm's length, Gianetta, too, had been encouraged to find her own path. Earthly reality and respect for all, no matter how humble, was as much a part of her philosophy as her faith in the unity of the spirit and an unswerving belief in God.

Leonardo had not explained to her why Ragaci was accompanying them. What little he had said gave her a clue. She tried hard to imagine Maria and Giacomo as a couple, but continually failed to do so. Irrespective of Leonardo's objectives and Giacomo's desires, her sense was that the musician and Maria Salcoiati could not be together. She readily understood that Maria's decision was not merely a way of avoiding a vow of marriage with which her conscience would not have been comfortable. In choosing the path of God, Maria had chosen a path to freedom. Her freedom was her religion and her conscience was her guiltlessness. Having made that choice and taken a vow, Gianetta was convinced that Maria would not relinquish it, even if others thought it convenient for her to do so.

A fast rushing stream on the right side of the carriage was a landmark that Leonardo recognised. He spotted the top of the convent's campanile rising above the line of the rocks.

"At last," sighed Leonardo, "we're nearly there."

Ragaci's excitement turned to apprehension. "I hope to God that the solemnity of the day and whatever rituals are observed here do not prevent us from seeing her." He had already made known to Leonardo his view that it was a mistake to have set off without first sending word of their impending arrival. Leonardo was quite insistent that their visit should be unheralded. If Maria was facing difficulties, forewarning the Madonna Suora of their visit might engender the creation of a smoke screen to assuage his concerns.

"Although the Madonna Suora is hardly the most hospitable of creatures, previous experience suggests she will not deny us the opportunity of even a short period of time with my sister after such a long journey."

"That's if we make it at all," sighed Ragaci. The carriage had ground to a halt. They heard the voice of their driver yelling something about moving out of the way. Gianetta's rueful look implied that an enterprise such as the present one would inevitably face obstacles. Once again, Leonardo and Ragaci leaned out of the windows. Their carriage had pulled up opposite a flat backed wooden wagon drawn by a single horse. It was driven by a heavily lined old man wearing a black floppy hat and a linen smock with unusual pleats. He sat hunched forward, gripping the reins tightly together with a horsewhip. He clenched a straw in his mouth that he alternately chewed then ground between his back teeth. The track was clearly not wide enough to let the two vehicles pass each other. One would have to give way. The old man seemed impervious to the logic of the coach driver who urged him to back up not more than a dozen braccia to a visible clearing and give way to the carriage.

Leonardo and Ragaci jumped down out of the carriage. "We can walk from here, Giacomo," observed Leonardo. "It won't take us long. We'll let these two sort out the rights of way between them."

Ragaci nodded in agreement and started to walk briskly ahead to the clearing from where he had a view of the stark, sombre walls of the convent.

Gianetta edged her way to the coach door and Leonardo

helped her down. As she gathered up her skirts to follow her husband towards the convent, she noticed a young girl sitting next to the wagon driver. She was about sixteen and wearing a rough, loose-fitting garment made of a sackcloth-like fabric that was smeared with dirt. There were weals on those parts of her shoulders that were visible and her face was bruised. Her hands were bound together and rested on her lap. Her thick hair was cut in an irregular shape and stuck out in spikes. There was something celestial about the young girl's demeanour, something that drew Gianetta towards her.

Leonardo squeezed between the side of the wagon and the trees and stopped to wait for Gianetta to catch up with him. The wagon driver turned away from Gianetta and from the young girl to talk to the coach driver who was endeavouring to explain the manoeuvres he proposed that would enable both vehicles to proceed.

Gianetta stopped level with the young girl who seemed to want to tell her something. "Leonardo?"

"Yes, what is it my love …?" said Leonardo.

It was not Gianetta who had spoken, but the young girl and it was Gianetta she had addressed and not Leonardo. Gianetta nodded, wide-eyed and waiting for more.

"Brother to Suora Maria?"

Gianetta nodded again.

"I thought so. They look alike," continued the girl. "Maria was my friend. They sent her away to die for trying to save me."

Gianetta furrowed her brow. "Who are you?"

"I'm Suora Graziella. But it's too late. It's too late."

"What was that?" called Leonardo.

Gianetta took a couple of paces towards her husband, stretched out her hand and beckoned him towards her.

"Suora Graziella, here, has just told me that Maria has been sent away?"

"What do you mean?"

"Come here! Ask her yourself."

"Ask who? What?"

"Suora Graziella."

"Who is Suora Graziella?"

"The young woman sitting at the front of this wagon."

"Eh? What are you on about? I don't see any young woman."

Gianetta turned around. What Leonardo said was correct. The wagon driver sat alone and turned towards them. He was waiting for them to move away from the wagon so that he could back it up to the clearing and let the coach pass. There was a long wooden box on the back of the wagon, but no young girl to be seen.

Gianetta blanched and the sudden palpitations of her heart alarmed her. "But Leonardo, there was a young woman there. She just spoke to me and I replied to her."

"I only heard you. There was no-one else."

"But there was!"

Leonardo put his arm around Gianetta's shoulders and turned her in the direction of the convent. "You must have imagined it. There's no-one there. Come on, let's go. Giacomo will be nearly there. They'll not let him in without us, as much as he would like to think they might."

Gianetta allowed him to lead her by the hand. They reached a bend in the track. She let go of Leonardo, stopped and turned around. The wagon driver was standing by the side of his horse, holding the bridle, clicking his tongue and exhorting the horse to back up.

Once again Suora Graziella was sitting at the front of the

wagon. She turned her head and waved at Gianetta and, as she did so, the sun emerged from behind a cloud and drew a ring of light above her head.

"Look!" shouted Gianetta chasing after her husband.

"What?" asked Leonardo, slowing down, but not stopping.

"She's there again. Suora Graziella is there," cried Gianetta. "Come back and see! Now!"

Leonardo turned and walked back. He rounded the bend to where she stood. "There's no-one there but the wagon driver. See for yourself."

Turning around again, Gianetta saw that he was right, "but … but …"

"Don't worry. Maybe you imagined it."

They continued along to the end of the track. Where it opened out, they saw Ragaci waiting for them by the gates to the convent.

* * * * * * *

They knocked on the outer gate and waited restlessly. A small panel opened and a veiled sister with a sad face looked at them suspiciously. When she heard who they were she promised to tell the Madonna Suora immediately. After some time the same furtive sister returned. She opened one side of the gate then led them into the main building and along a series of poorly lit corridors to the Madonna Suora's private study. Leonardo entered first followed by Gianetta and then Ragaci.

The small square room was sparsely furnished. Madonna Suora sat behind a bare, wooden desk. On the wall, to her left, was a naïf portrait of the late Pope Julius II and, to her right, a simple wooden crucifix. In front of the desk were four chairs, one of which was occupied by a young priest. He stood and bowed his head towards them. Madonna Suora remained behind her desk and motioned them to sit down.

"You won't mind if Father Alessandro joins us will you," she said.

"Not at all," replied Leonardo, the others nodding in agreement.

"I wasn't made aware that you were planning to visit us over Easter," she said sternly, "nor that you would be accompanied." She briefly looked away from Leonardo, who sat opposite her, to Gianetta and then to Ragaci.

"We thought we would surprise my sister while we were visiting my Aunt for the Holy Days."

"This is your wife who I believe has been here before, but who are you?" she asked Ragaci, peering at him coldly.

"I am Giacomo Ragaci, a family friend."

Madonna Suora received the information impassively. She bowed her head, closed her eyes, placed the palms of her hands together and prayed. Father Alessandro joined her and the others felt constrained to follow suit.

"Amen," said the Madonna Suora, opening her eyes and making the sign of the cross.

"Amen," they replied, following her lead and also making the sign of the cross.

Madonna Suora looked up and back towards Leonardo. It was apparent from the silence that followed that she expected him to speak.

"Will my sister be joining us, or should we wait for her in the refectory?"

Madonna Suora turned towards Father Alessandro. He cleared his throat. "Neither. Suora Maria isn't here." He spoke in a high-pitched voice with a regional accent that none of them could place.

"When will she be back?" asked Leonardo.

Father Alessandro looked towards Madonna Suora as if waiting for her to explain. She ignored the cue. He continued. "Suora Maria has left the convent."

"What do you mean, she's left the convent?" gasped Leonardo.

"She's left the convent to join a mission to Jerusalem. She'll not return here."

"Not return? I don't understand."

Ragaci did not understand either. He leaned towards Father Alessandro as if the movement alone might make things clearer.

"It's very simple," interjected the Madonna Suora curtly. "News reaches us that the Ottoman Turks led by Sultan Selim have defeated the Mamaluks. They have already taken Cairo and the rest of the Mamaluk empire is crumbling. Their rule over the Holy Land is at an end. Even as we speak, the Sultan's forces may have reached Jerusalem and brought it under his control. The pope has sent word that good Christians are needed at this time to support the work of the church in the Holy Land. Suora Maria decided that she wanted to be one of them."

"When did my sister leave?"

"Just over a week ago," relied Madonna Suora.

"Why did you make her go?" asked Gianetta innocently.

"I beg your pardon," said Madonna Suora indignantly.

"Why did you make her go?"

"I didn't."

"She volunteered," explained Father Alessandro.

"Are you sure?" asked Gianetta.

"During the course of confession, she made it clear to me that she didn't think that by remaining in this convent she could fulfil the goals she had set for herself."

"When did she make such a confession?"

"Perhaps three weeks ago."

"And she's gone to Jerusalem without letting me know?" said Leonardo, realising that the letter alerting him to Maria's state of distress must have been written at the time of the events that Father Alessandro related.

"The church's need in the Holy Land is an urgent one. Your sister was keen to answer the call immediately," said Madonna Suora.

"Did she leave any word for me? A note? A letter?"

Father Alessandro and the Madonna Suora looked at each other expressionlessly.

"As the Madonna Suora has said, the call was urgently made and answered immediately," added Father Alessandro.

Leonardo was perplexed, Gianetta shocked, Ragaci devastated.

"This doesn't sound like my sister. Was there something else? Perhaps something that affected her mind?"

"Or perhaps this convent wasn't to her liking?" speculated Gianetta, directing her remark to the Madonna Suora and at the same time endeavouring to gauge Father Alessandro's reaction to her hypothesis by observing his demeanour.

Both remained still and neither of them responded to her.

"Or perhaps," continued Gianetta, "she didn't volunteer but was sent away from here …"

Madonna Suora remained unmoved. Gianetta perceived the slightest of shifting by the priest in his seat.

"Sent away because she tried to save someone from

something," continued Gianetta. "Suora Graziella for example?"

Father Alessandro clenched his buttocks and sat up straight. His movement was clear to all of them, as was the sweat that was beginning to collect on his brow.

Madonna Suora narrowed her eyes. "What do you know of Suora Graziella?" she hissed.

"Only what she told me as we were approaching the convent."

Madonna Suora looked at Gianetta incredulously. "What blasphemy is this?" she snapped.

"Suora Graziella told me that my sister-in-law, Maria, was her friend and 'they', whoever that may be, had sent her away to die for trying to save her."

"Did either of you bear witness to this?" she barked at Leonardo and Ragaci irascibly.

Ragaci did not have a clue about what was being discussed and shook his head wearily. He was still gaping at the chasm into which his hopes had plunged upon hearing of Maria's departure. How and why it was precipitated were of little consequence to him. Leonardo knew that he had not witnessed anything personally, but was rapidly starting to believe what Gianetta had told him. He wished that he had been able to share in her experience directly.

"In truth, Madonna Suora, I neither heard nor saw anything myself, though I was not best placed to participate in the conversation that my wife had with Suora Graziella," said Leonardo truthfully.

Madonna Suora stood up, put her hands on the desk and leaned towards Gianetta. "Do you persist in this calumny?"

"It is no calumny. All I have told you is what I saw and what I heard."

"Then you are a liar, a blasphemer and should be tried for witchcraft."

"What do you mean by that?" shouted Leonardo leaping to his wife's defence.

"What I mean, Signor Salcoiati, is that Suora Graziella is dead. She died from illness the day before yesterday. She was removed from this place not long before your arrival to be transported to a pauper's grave. Suora Graziella displayed the traits of evil and Father Alessandro decreed that she might not be buried on holy ground."

"Is this true?" asked Gianetta.

"All of it," pronounced Father Alessandro, though Gianetta detected a hint of play-acting about the solemn tone of his voice.

"Then what did I see and hear?" asked Gianetta, bemused, but beginning to understand the true nature of her experience with Suora Graziella.

"Nothing but your imagination," said Madonna Suora. "And, if otherwise, you must be a witch. And if you are a witch then you have no place here and I demand that you leave immediately. All of you."

"I'm not a witch," said Gianetta, "but I think I'm beginning to understand what may have happened here."

"And even if my wife is beginning to understand, I'm not sure that I do and won't leave until I know the truth about my sister," added Leonardo.

"Are you suggesting that what you have been told by Father Alessandro and me is not the truth?" snapped Madonna Suora.

"I'm not suggesting anything other than the fact that knowing my sister as I do, I find it impossible to accept that she would leave for Jerusalem in the manner that you describe and not make any attempt to contact me or even her Aunt Bartolomea, who lives here in Arezzo and with whom you are personally acquainted."

"The circumstances were as I explained. If you won't believe me, then you should make a pilgrimage to Jerusalem where you may find your sister and verify the position. Now, I would be grateful if you would leave."

Leonardo was angry, Gianetta energised. They stood up. Ragaci remained seated. "If you don't mind, Madonna Suora, Father, I have hitherto held my peace, but I would like to say something."

"Make it quick," said Madonna Suora begrudgingly and the others sat down again.

Ragaci looked around at them, ensured they were all paying attention, then began to speak. "Signor Salcoiati came to visit his sister because he received a letter she had written to him from which he deduced that all was not well. Father Alessandro told us that that is as much as true, though the cause of Suora Maria's unhappiness still eludes us. Signora Gianetta is not capable of telling a lie and she is not a witch. Though I was not a party to her encounter with Suora Graziella, it is apparent that she has been blessed with a vision and, from that, we have learned more about what happened to Suora Maria than you have been prepared to tell us. That you may dwell in this House of God and wear the vestment of those who dedicate themselves to his service does not make you holy. That you wear the cross around your neck does not guarantee the truth of what you say. Nor does it absolve you from the sin you commit by concealing facts in the hope that those that remain will constitute enough of the truth to convince us of your honesty."

"I came here today to see Suora Maria in the hope that she might still be able to reciprocate the love I have for her and to declare it openly. Whether my frustration has been caused, as you say, by her removal to Jerusalem or otherwise is not relevant. I believe that Suora Maria's departure has been decreed by a greater force than any of us here may presently understand. What I do understand is that whoever amongst us that has spoken truthfully of these matters will be blessed and those who have distorted the truth, or who have concealed matters that touch or concern Suora Maria or Suora Graziella, or who may have done either of them wrong, will be damned."

Ragaci spoke in a slow and measured manner. His sincerity could not be doubted, neither could the pride that Leonardo and Gianetta felt in what he said and how he had said it.

Neither Madonna Suora nor Father Alessandro said a word. The look of worry on the face of the priest and that of disdain on the face of Madonna Suora told Ragaci all he needed to know. Ragaci stood up, walked to the door and opened it for the others who then followed him. "I will pray for your souls, too," he added. "Someone will have to, won't they?"

Before he was able to assess their reactions, Ragaci followed Gianetta and Leonardo out of the door. They retraced their steps and found a sister to unlock the front gate. Once outside they saw their carriage waiting and boarded it.

On their way back to Arezzo, they were quiet, each contemplating what had happened in the preceding hours.

Gianetta knew what she had seen and heard and felt blessed, even though the knowledge of the true cause of

Suora Graziella's death was denied to her.

Leonardo did not believe what they had been told at the convent, but knew not how he would be able to question the veracity of Madonna Suora's assertions, one way or another. He would pray for his sister's safe passage to the Holy Land or to wherever else they may have cast her out and that she might yet send word to him.

Ragaci castigated himself for having vested so much hope in the outcome of their visit and contemplated the ramifications of his rejection of Donatina Castellani. Damned that he had, damned if he had not, the prospects that would greet his return to Florence were not auspicious.

XXI

Settlement

London. May 1999

Matt Dayton never planned on staying in advertising. The unrelenting jostling for position played havoc with his ability to do the job and intruded too much into the time he wanted to spend on other things. Occasionally, during political in-fights, he was forced into taking sides. He survived and grew to enjoy what he did. Emerging as one of London's most consistently successful copywriters, he won awards for campaigns and developed a number of major accounts. He continued to prosper in spite of the vicissitudes of the economy and sustained a munificent lifestyle. He lived in a cottage on the edge of Hampstead Heath and developed an interesting circle of friends. Unfortunately, his relationships with women did not fare so well.

He remained convinced that destiny would ensure there was someone for whom he was intended, but, whoever she was, she had yet to show up. He had yet to meet his ideal and was not prepared to compromise. Serial monogamy with a best before end date was simply not for him. Inchoate friendships with intelligent and beautiful women with whom he did not fall in love were not enough. When he was unable to find someone who both stimulated him intellectually and also satisfied his other appetites, he would sacrifice one and go with the other. Either way the relationships would not work. As soon as the question of marriage or even living together arose, he retreated into his shell and began making less arrangements to meet. More often than not his romances did not come to a finite conclusion, but rather euthanased into friendship and then into nothing.

Reflecting on those he had been with, those he would like to have been with but had not and those he could have been with but chose to reject was one of those fruitless trains of thought that periodically occupied him. As the years passed the number of those in the first and third categories increased. Those in the second diminished, but he tried to keep tabs on some of them. There were always reasons why they were unavailable. Most of them eventually married – for better or for worse. Sometimes he could think of only one that he would like to have been with that he had not and that was Olivia Giorgianni. Wrong time, wrong place.

Fourteen years after his ill-fated attempt to hook up with her, sentimentality occasionally metamorphosed into the occasional bout of 'what if'? It could not have been more than three or four years since he went touring in New England with his then girlfriend, Naomi Matthews. They passed through Williamstown, Massachusetts, more by accident than design. He had not wanted to stop, but Naomi noticed a poster for a Paul Whiteman exhibition at the Williams College Museum of Art that featured the original 'soundie' of George Gershwin's Rhapsody in Blue. Having thoroughly enjoyed the unexpected opportunity of watching the rare Art Deco drenched footage, Matt kept finding more things for them to see and do in the town. A return visit to the Impressionists at the Clarke was followed by a shopping excursion in the quaint stores that lined Water Street. Amongst the bric a brac of an antique shop, he found a perfectly preserved large-scale model of an old Calliope, a steam organ, for which he bargained long and hard and then arranged shipping.

Eventually, Naomi became impatient. Vain hopes turned into unfulfilled longings and unreconstructed frustration. Whether or not Olivia was even still living in Williamstown was not beyond cavil. He left his memories of her behind once they returned to their car and crossed the county line.

By contrast, his career continued to go from strength to strength. Having survived the recession of the early nineties when those with lesser mettle failed, his agency was riding the boom as one of the top independents in London. Appointed to the board, Matt and his closest ally, Damian Robarts, had recently bought out the agency from the surviving partners who had originally established the business at the beginning of the nineteen-seventies. Snapping up every opportunity that came its way, the agency, now called GDFM Dayton Robarts, regularly won more than its fair share of pitches for new business. A continual stream of new talent was knocking on its doors, looking to join it, attracted by the reputation of its burgeoning creativity.

Fraser McKillop was a sleepy drinks firm that had recently been taken over by a dynamic group of young entrepreneurs. They raised new money to acquire some well-established but lesser known brands whose market profile needed improvement. Fraser's Highland Malt was the first. Matt was invited to lead a pitch for the account against a couple of other agencies, including the incumbent, Baker, Gaul and Osprey. If successful, another six or seven brands waited in the wings for a makeover. The potential for the agency was inestimable.

Matt was generally at his desk by eight-thirty and Greta Simons was never far behind. She had worked for the agency since its early days. Starting as a Girl Friday when the term was still in vogue, she progressed to personal assistant and sometime lover of Matt's mentor, Gordon Delaney. Delaney's untimely death on the golf course precipitated Matt's elevation to creative director and Greta had not needed any persuasion to stay on and help him.

Now in her middle fifties, Greta spent twenty-five years fooling herself that Gordon Delaney would eventually leave his wife. He never did. He also failed to make good his promise to make provision for her from his estate, so she was unable to give up work. Named by her mother after Greta Garbo, she had something of the star's bearing and posture. Bright, well-spoken, loyal and street smart, Greta ensured that Matt's life ran smoothly and kept his sanity intact.

"Anna-Lisa Condaletti wants to see you," she said, bringing in Matt a mug of his favourite Kenyan roast.

"Sure. When?"

"She was hoping you might have a few minutes before the Fraser's pitch meeting, but that's at nine-thirty, so maybe sometime between twelve and one."

"How about now?"

"Now?"

"What's wrong with that?"

"Nothing. I just don't understand why you need to go out of your way for her."

"What's everyone got with Anna-Lisa? She's not been here for a month and I keep hearing negative comments. She's always in on time, her work's good and she stays late if she has to. She graduated top of her class at St Martin's and has six year's experience at a couple of very good agencies. I also like the fact that she left Baker, Gaul and Osprey to join us. What else could anyone ask for?"

Greta knew how much competition there was between the agencies. Mark Gaul had been a contemporary of Matt's at Cambridge. Gaul had once made reference to their rivalry in an interview with an industry journal that had often been laconically referred to around the office. Even though Matt had achieved a first-class honours degree and Gaul only an upper-second, Gaul made a point in the interview that he had been the first to secure a partnership, which he had done, by establishing his own shop. There had never been much love lost between the two of them. Their mutual indifference had its origin in a disagreement over a punting trip, a blonde girl with a nose piercing whose name Matt could never seem to recall and a broken bottle of champagne. Though Matt had soon forgotten about the incident, its cause and effect had stayed with Gaul whose behaviour was often noticeably excessive.

"Something isn't right with that woman and I can't put my finger on it," said Greta assuredly.

"If you work it out, let me know."

"I will."

"In the meantime, ask her to come in."

Matt guessed that when she had been younger, Anna-Lisa Condaletti was the type to whom the phrase 'butter-wouldn't-melt-in-my-mouth' would have applied perfectly. The harsh realities of the commercial world had roughened some of the edges, but only as much as was necessary for her to ensure that she blended in with her surroundings. Beneath the veneer of her eagerness to please and the studied, almost academic thoroughness that she applied to her work, lurked an earthy sexuality. She permitted occasional glimpses of it when she thought it might do her some good, but she was always quick to bottle it up if there was any danger that it might lead into temptation those whose expectations she would never consider fulfilling.

Within a couple of minutes of Greta leaving Matt's room, Anna-Lisa knocked confidently on his door and did not wait to be invited to join him.

"Sit, sit," he said, tossing the half-read copy of Campaign to one side. "Shall I ask Greta to bring you a coffee?"

"No thank you, I've just had one."

"How can I help you?"

"The Fraser account. I'm interested."

"And I appreciate your interest, but we've already picked the team. Sunita Shah's going to be the art director."

Anna-Lisa went straight to her point. "Sunita just called in. We had lunch together yesterday and she didn't finish it. She felt ill and went home early. She said that she was going to the doctor. It appears that she has a bad case of gastro-enteritis and the doctor has signed her off for the rest of the week."

"I'm sorry to hear that. I'll have Greta send her some flowers," said Matt, seeking neither to query the cause nor the consequences of Sunita's indisposal. "But for you, I guess, it's right place, right time."

"I'm in?"

"You bet. Be in the presentation suite at nine-thirty."

* * * * * * *

Matt's team had the luxury of three weeks in which to prepare its pitch. His confidence in Anna-Lisa's abilities was not misplaced. Immediately she impressed her colleagues with a stream of powerful ideas. One of them formed the basis for the campaign they would propose. They decided to broaden the appeal of a traditional drink and reach a younger consumer by associating Fraser's Highland Malt with trendy pursuits. Hang-gliding in the Cairngorms and water-skiing on Loch Ness were the examples they would use.

It was the first project on which Matt worked with Anna-Lisa directly and he enjoyed the experience from the outset. Every morning on his way to the office, he found himself looking forward to seeing her. He maximised the time that he would spend reviewing her work. On a couple of occasions he took her to lunch at his favourite trattoria in Goodge Street.

Greta began to feel uncomfortable about Matt's intentions. "Don't you dare, Matt Dayton," she said in an unmistakeable tone of admonition. She had also noticed that ever since preparations for the Fraser pitch had shifted into top gear that Matt was making more effort with his wardrobe and was polishing his shoes every day. He even took himself to the hairdresser a week ahead of his previously scheduled appointment.

"Don't I dare what?" asked Matt disingenuously.

"You damn well know what."

"It's a Leicester Square preview and I have two tickets. Would you prefer me to go with my mother?"

"Actually …"

"Don't say it."

"I think I should," said Greta, as if scolding a disobedient child.

"Anna-Lisa happens to be free and I didn't have anyone else to ask."

"What about me? You could have asked me."

"But you don't like 'Star Wars' and besides it's a Monday and Monday is your bridge night."

"That's not the point."

"I've not got anything in mind. And even if I did …"

"And even if you did, don't. Trust me on this one, she's bad news."

"Greta, can I …"

But she was already out of the door. It was not her style to labour a point, but she knew what she had to do to ensure that he would accept her grave misgivings about Anna-Lisa Condaletti.

* * * * * * *

Whether or not he did have anything in mind he would not have given odds on what Anna-Lisa had in hers. Dutifully, she sat through 'Star Wars Episode 1: The Phantom Menace' and readily agreed to a post movie snack.

While they were chatting over the cappuccino about nothing in particular, she came out with it straight. "You don't have to persuade me to sleep with you."

Matt was not sure that he had heard her right. He made some quick mental notes. He liked her. She was sexually attractive – tall, good looking and with a slim athletic physique. She was unattached and so was he. She was the right age, late twenties, but they worked together. If that was the real nature of Greta's concern, and perhaps it was not, then it was laced with more than a little hypocrisy.

"Come on Matt, I think you want to and I want to – very much."

"Let me pay the bill," he said as casually as possible.

Often reluctant to invite any woman home until he knew her well and having never previously slept with anyone from work, Matt had no defence to making an exception for Anna-Lisa. The intensity of his desire not only eliminated the line of enquiry that he might otherwise have pursued about her domestic circumstances, but also neutralised the self-control that he usually exercised if even vaguely attracted by one of his female employees. Leaving cash on the table that provided a more than generous tip, he ushered her out onto the street and hailed a taxi.

* * * * * * *

Revelling in the passion that she normally concealed and giving free and unfettered rein to the desires of her flesh, Anna-Lisa opened herself up to Matt unconditionally. Stripping away any vestige of reserve to which he might have been inclined to cling, she unlocked a treasure chest full of delights in which he had not indulged for some little while. She pandered to every pleasure that he sought and in doing so ensured he knew that she was equally fulfilled by what, in turn, he gave to her. Once fulfilment progressed to the level of satiation they fell asleep, Anna-Lisa insistent that Matt lie on his back so that she could drape her arm across his chest.

Matt slept fitfully and half woke up on two or three occasions with blurred images from nightmares rapidly receding from his conscious mind. On the final occasion the image was clear. His body was drowning in a sea of blood, his severed head floating on the surface, his features frozen in a grimace of ugly terror. Anna-Lisa was nearby in a small boat. She had her back to him as she rowed towards the shore, a bloodied axe sticking out of the stern of the boat.

He sat up and saw that Anna-Lisa was no longer beside him. The ensuite bathroom door was ajar. He got out of bed and crept silently into the bathroom, but she was not in there. He gazed into the mirror at the bags that hung under his eyes, then splashed water onto his face. He took the robe from the hook on the back of the door and threw it on, hurriedly tying the belt.

Stepping quietly back into the bedroom he observed that her clothes were still strewn across the room in the places where he had excitedly removed them the previous evening. He shuffled onto the landing, stopped and listened. He tiptoed downstairs and saw that the door to his study was open. He peered inside. Anna-Lisa's naked back was facing him. She was standing in front of his desk but he could not see what she was doing there. He pushed the door open slowly. It creaked. She turned around. She was holding a glass of water.

"What's going on?" he asked suspiciously.

"I woke up and I was thirsty. I came downstairs to get a glass of water. I hope you don't mind."

"Not at all, but why are you in here?"

"When I was walking past this room, I couldn't help noticing that painting." She pointed to the piece that hung at a right angle to the desk. The background was graded shades of white. In the centre there was a beautiful young woman with thick, fair-golden hair that fell in wavy cascades to the middle of her back. She was dress in an opulent Renaisssance-style costume – a bright red full-skirted dress with white facing and decorated with hundreds of pearls and other small gemstones. She gripped a bloodied dagger in her hand. In the foreground there was a lute. Its body was cracked open and the strings tangled and broken; musical notes – quavers, crotchets and the like – poured out through the crack into a pile. Another woman wearing plain, dark robes and a white headscarf with a crucifix around her neck was picking up the notes and collecting them in a leather bag.

Matt declined to comment that, at the angle from which he had first observed Anna-Lisa, she could not have been looking at the painting. He was also not sure whether the study door was open before they went to bed. He observed that the power light on his computer was on, although it had not been booted up. Perhaps she had not had the time to do that. Perhaps he had left the power on anyway.

"It's very unusual," she said admiringly.

He was prepared to give her the benefit of the doubt. "The basic elements were in a dream. I mentioned it in passing to an artist friend who painted it as a surprise thank you for a good turn I'd done him."

"And then I noticed how pretty your garden is."

True enough, she could have been looking out of the window when he disturbed her.

"And then there were all the other things in here, like the model of that organ."

"It's not an organ, it's a Calliope."

"Calliope? I always thought that Calliope was one of the nine muses."

"She was and it was after her that this instrument was named, though I don't recall of what she was muse."

"Epic poetry and stringed instruments," said Anna-Lisa authoritatively.

Matt was impressed with her knowledge, though that was not all that struck him when she had mentioned the words 'stringed instruments' as though the phrase was a prelude to something else, something discomforting.

"Matt, you look worried about something."

"Me? No. I had a bad dream, that's all."

She put the glass down on the desk and walked across to him. She put one hand on his shoulder, drew him close and kissed him. She untied the belt of his robe with the other hand, then slid it down his body. Immediately she felt him begin to stir. "Then," she said, momentarily withdrawing her lips from his, "then, I thought, how nice it would be to make love in here in front of a blazing fire." She motioned towards the empty hearth. "Why don't we pretend … at least about the fire."

Unable to come up with a convincing reason not to accept her suggestion, Matt took her in his arms, lowered her onto the rug and fucked her in front of the empty fireplace.

* * * * * * *

"I hear the Fraser pitch team are going great guns." Damian Robarts' cheery smile was always a welcome distraction. Damian pushed his six foot plus frame through the door. Ruddy cheeked, flaxen-haired and blue eyes with a square jaw, he was bred to be a rugby forward. He had not disappointed his father, who had played full back for the Saracens second team, until one broken limb too many deterred him from playing rugby after university.

"Should be more or less done by Friday of this week. That'll give us a whole week plus two weekends if we need the time to tidy things up."

"Isn't Friday your birthday?"

"Indeed." Matt had not made a connection between the two events.

"Good time to celebrate."

"Could be."

"By all accounts this new girl, Anna-Lisa whats-her-name, is turning into a bit of a star."

Matt failed to suppress a grin. Damian raised an eyebrow. "And from what Greta tells me, she enjoyed the Star Wars preview, too."

"I hope so," said Matt as neutrally as possible.

"And how about the 'apres-ski'?"

"Pardon?"

"Matt. Come on. Level. Greta also mentioned that Anna-Lisa is wearing exactly the same outfit today that she was wearing when the two of you left here yesterday evening."

"Then I suppose the other one must be at the dry cleaner."

"Matt, be careful with that one. You don't know what you might be letting yourself in for."

"Please, Damian, don't you start."

"You know what they say, whoever 'they' may be."
"And what do 'they' say?"
"They say, 'don't shit where you eat'."
"I never have done, before."
"We're all tempted to at least once."

Matt looked at Damian with surprise. Six months after graduation, Damian married his college sweetheart and as far as Matt knew they had been together ever since.

"You mean you …?"
"That would be telling."
"Bet I can guess who with."
"Whatever may or may not have happened, it's all in the past."

"If you say so, but nothing is ever really in the past," mused Matt. The half thought triggered something in the back of Matt's mind. He was sure it had something to do with the image in his dream of Anna-Lisa and then seeing her looking at the painting in his study.

"Listen, Matt, you've got things on your mind and stuff on your desk and so have I. Let me know when you have the Fraser thing licked as I would like to take a look before you present."

* * * * * * *

The rest of his week was dominated by preparations for the pitch. Matt found himself drawn into discussing fine points of detail with various members of the team and working late into the evenings. During the course of Wednesday, Anna-Lisa signalled her intent by mentioning in passing that she had brought an overnight bag into the office. It was the prelude to another night of unbridled sex. Thursday the whole team worked till midnight and a fleet of mini-cabs arrived to take them their separate ways home. With the exception of the account director, he gave them Friday off. So it was a fairly exhausted, but satisfied, Matt Dayton who arrived at the office a little later than usual. He had overslept until eight when the customary birthday phone call from his mother woke him up.

Guessing by his tardiness that he would not have bothered with breakfast at home, Greta found someone to nip out of the office and pick up a couple of croissants. She took them into his office with his coffee and two flat packages that were gift-wrapped.

"Happy birthday." She put the tray down and went round to the back of his desk and kissed his forehead.

"Thanks. Thank you. What's all this?" Matt said excitedly.

"A birthday breakfast and two presents."

"And a card too," he said picking up the envelope and removing a card that was adorned by picture of a lesser-known Pontormo portrait. "Classy, very classy." He turned his attention to the larger of the two packages. "I wonder what this can be?" he said ironically. Manifestly from its shape and size it was a twelve-inch vinyl record. He removed the wrapping to reveal a 1972 pressing of 'Fragile' by Yes complete with original booklet insert. One of the tracks had been featured in a movie called 'Buffalo '66' that he had recently seen. He remembered the album from a friend's collection and idly mentioned it in passing to someone in the office.

"How thoughtful. Thank you."

"I hope you appreciate the other one too."

"I can't guess," he said, weighing the second package in his hand. "If it wasn't my birthday, I'd say it was some kind of a report or something."

"You're hot," she said.

Matt opened the package. It was a report. The cover had 'Magnum Private Investigators' printed on it. In the cut-out rectangle at the top that revealed part of the first page, two simple lines read 'Report on Ms Anna-Lisa Condaletti for GDFM Dayton Robarts'.

"What's this?"

"Read it and find out for yourself and I won't say …"

Matt's stomach began to churn. "Don't say it Greta, please don't say 'I told you so'."

"I'll let you read it in peace. And before you ask, I have given Damian a copy too. He's already read it and I expect he'll be in to see you shortly."

What the report contained made him feel sick. It was both disturbing and graphic. As he already knew, Baker, Gaul and Osprey was the incumbent agency for Fraser's Highland Malt. Anna-Lisa was Mark Gaul's lover and had been for at least two years. Much of the information obtained by Magnum had been provided by a disaffected female former employee who had recently left Gaul's agency. She had got to know Anna-Lisa well and been taken into her confidence. Gaul's relationship with Anna-Lisa was one that was not only properly categorised as 'sub-dom' but the lifestyle they lived paid more than just lip-service to some of its more extreme practices. Anna-Lisa would apparently do anything to please Gaul. In surrendering her will to him, she had also surrendered her body, so that it was his to do with as he pleased. Requiring her to screw Matt and simultaneously screw his agency appealed to Gaul's perverted sense of humour. That she had sex with another man was not an affront to him, far from it. The fact that she would do as he ordered amply demonstrated the extent of the power he was able to exercise over her.

The ideas that Anna-Lisa had fed Matt's team were largely based on suggestions made in the past that the Fraser board had already rejected. A hurriedly handwritten postscript to the report indicated that she had gone straight to Gaul's Kensington flat after the team had finished their late session the previous night.

Matt read the report a second time, all the while trying to understand how one in whose mouth butter might once not have seemed capable of melting, was able to have intensely climactic sex with him one night and then, presumably, turn it all on for her long-term lover the next. He had never previously encountered a woman who allowed the animal in her to take over from the animus so blatantly, nor one who was at once able to worship and suppress her libido in equal measures of calculated heartlessness. Either way, he felt badly used, dirty and cheated. He wondered how many of the screaming orgasms she had apparently reached were for real and how much of it had been put on.

A knock on the door heralded the return of Greta. She slipped into the room through the smallest gap she could make between the door and its frame, then closed it behind her. He dreaded what she was going to say to him.

"Damian's on the phone," was all. "He'll be in as soon as he can."

"Shit," uttered Matt under his breath. "I need him on this as soon as possible."

"This?"

"This Anna-Lisa business, but more especially the Fraser pitch. We need to jump into action straight away."

"I'm sure it's retrievable," said Greta sympathetically.

"So am I, but what I don't understand is how she could have done it."

"That's not the right question to ask," said Greta.

"It isn't?"

"No, the question to ask is how unlucky do you have to be to hire a sexually perverted fifth columnist at the time of pitching for potentially one of the most lucrative new accounts that has come the way of this agency since you and Damian took it over?"

"Luck didn't play a part," mused Matt. "For whatever reason, Mark Gaul has it in for me and it's obvious that he's prepared to stoop as low as he can to try and rub my nose in it."

Further discussion was interrupted as Damian came into the room brandishing his copy of the Magnum Report. "Now you know what you let yourself in for," he said.

"And everyone else, too," said Matt remorsefully.

"Don't think of it like that," said Damian. "It's pretty obvious that Mark Gaul doesn't like you. And according to this report and the way he lives his life, he doesn't like himself very much either."

The comment struck a chord with Matt whose scowl was replaced by a look of realisation. "Yes. You're right. I'd never thought of it like that."

"Anyway, Matt …"

"Yes, let's get it on and do, what we have to do."

Matt and Damian moved with ruthless efficiency. Immediately, they combed the agency's already overstretched resources and set up a second and secret pitch team to work around the clock. Weekends were cancelled with the promise of extra money and days off in lieu. The new team was moved down to the first floor where some empty space had been rented to await the firm's proposed expansion. Twenty-four hour security guards were brought in to restrict access to anyone outside the team. Then they turned their attention to Anna-Lisa.

Matt found time to meet her for Sunday lunch. He did not try to hide the fact that it was an urgent matter of business as much as pleasure that was on his agenda. He told her she was to go to Munich the following day. Dachsund, the electronics giant, was planning the launch of its fuelless car onto the UK market. He waved aside her protest that she would be needed for the Fraser pitch. He made it clear that Sunita Shah was fully recovered from her illness and that she was more than capable of doing what was necessary. Flattering her with compliments about the excellence of her work and the importance of her creative contribution, she was unable to refuse his request. Her apology that she already had another engagement following lunch so would be unable to go back to his house was gracefully accepted.

With Anna-Lisa safely on the plane to Munich and out of London for a few days, the second proposal came together on adrenalin and caffeine. Matt wanted to minimise any opportunity Anna-Lisa might have for interference. He called Frasers and persuaded them to bring the pitch forward from the Friday to the Thursday.

* * * * * * *

"Awesome, Matt, awesome." When Matt called him with the news the previous evening, Damian had put a bottle of Moet in the fridge. They drank it with smoked salmon bagels that Greta had someone bring in for a celebratory breakfast.

"Not bad really. Considering."

"What did you ever do to upset Mark Gaul that much?"

Matt shrugged his shoulders.

"And what of the lovely Anna-Lisa?" enquired Damian.

"I had someone at the solicitors draft her letter of dismissal. It's on their letterhead and on her desk with a gift from the team."

"And what might that be?"

"Come and see it."

They walked down the corridor towards the Art Department.

"Remember the early mock-ups we did for the Vermouth before we were told to concentrate on the malt scotch?"

"Vaguely."

"Anna-Lisa's original had a Daliesque landscape peppered with unconnected icons. On one side of the background there was a scary looking castle and in the foreground there was an attractive model wearing a bright red body suit pouring a glass of the Vermouth."

They reached the door of the Art Department.

"This is what I had Sunita prepare as a leaving present."

Prominently displayed behind Anna-Lisa's desk was a large-scale mock-up of her poster. The model's face was replaced with a photo of Anna-Lisa. The background had been altered so that instead of standing amongst the icons, Anna-Lisa's image was suspended from a gallows. The upright was a bottle of Fraser's Malt, the cross-piece an elongated crystal shot glass and the rope was symbolised by a stream of pouring whiskey.

"Good job," chuckled Damian. "That'll do nicely enough to settle the score."

"Pardon?"

"I said that'll do nicely enough to settle the score," repeated Damian.

"I thought that's what you said."

"Anything the matter with that?"

"No, not all. It's not something that I've ever really thought much about. I've never been much of one who had scores to settle. Though, now you mention it, I'm sure there was one, but I can't remember what it was."

"An old one?"

"Yes. Maybe something back in the past."

"Wasn't it you who said the other day that nothing's really in the past?"

"I did. And it's what I believe."

They looked at the poster again. "Maybe it's something to do with the picture itself," Damian suggested. "What about the castle?"

"I'm fairly sure it's not actually a castle as such, but the Bargello in Florence. It was used as a prison and a police station from the early sixteenth century. Executions used to take place in the courtyard."

Before Matt could connect his thoughts together, Damian noted, "talking of which, look who's coming down the hallway."

Anna-Lisa Condaletti smiled at them, as radiant as ever in a tight-fitting top, close-cut jeans, Prada sandals and sunglasses pushed back onto her head.

"Good morning, gentlemen," she called to them from a dozen paces away.

"Good morning," they replied in unison.

"Good trip?" asked Matt.

"Definitely, but I thought you would be on the Fraser pitch today," she said to Matt as she drew level with them.

"We brought it forward to yesterday."

"Oh," she said with visible surprise. "How come?"

"I think you'll work it out for yourself," said Matt mysteriously. "By the way, we won. Convincingly, too, so I am told."

"Great," she said with as much enthusiasm as she could muster.

"Anyway, thank you for your contribution," said Matt, without a trace of irony, "without which …"

He and Damian stepped aside and allowed her to walk into her office. They watched as she gaped at the poster then picked up the letter that was addressed to her from her desk. It was in an envelope with 'Marriott Harrison Solicitors' printed on the back.

"What's going on?" she asked coldly.

"We think you know," said Damian, stretching his arms behind him and resting them on his buttocks, Prince Charles style.

Nervously she opened the letter and read it. She started to tremble. They waited in the doorway until she had finished.

"You've got half an hour to tidy up your things. General office will help you out and call you a cab," said Damian.

"And give Mark Gaul our best," added Matt.

They walked back into Matt's office and continued drinking the Moet.

A short while later, Anna-Lisa walked past Matt's office on her way out of the building for the last time. She could not stop herself from turning her head and looking in. Their eyes met and in his look of calmness she sensed that Matt was at one with himself. The defeat of Anna-Lisa's attempted skulduggery and her exposure as a saboteur had infected her feelings and crushed her spirit. Something inside her was dying. Suddenly she began to feel very old.

XXII

Alone

New York City. June 1999

She adored New York City. No matter what her mood, the twenty-four hour a day throb of its heartbeat was a constant reminder that life was everywhere around her. She wanted to reach out and touch it for herself, to feel its warm embrace and to lose herself in whatever came her way. Her mind was urging her to let go, but Olivia Giorgianni had forgotten what to do. Perhaps the plain truth was that she had never been able to before and consequently did not know how to start.

The cosy familiarity of rural New England gradually lost the allure that it had when she originally sought to make her escape from the suffocating oppression of her parent's home on the Upper East Side. She found it increasingly difficult to complete her book on the politics of the early American presidents. A previous volume on the history of the Native American Tribes in the North-East, that established her reputation, was several years old. She had not published anything since.

Work had been her anchor. Cast adrift she began to flounder. Fighting against the current, she thought she would drown, but rescue was at hand. In 1995, at the beginning of the Fall Semester, the Faculty was joined by Ralph Bainbridge.

A patrician Bostonian with a stentorian voice, Bainbridge was a Mediaeval specialist who had spent some time at Yale. He looked to move somewhere that was less of a hot-house. Enthusiastically adjusting to the comfy parochiality of his new environment, he soon gained popularity with students and faculty members alike. Closer to forty than to thirty, he had never previously found the time or the space to reflect what his bachelor status truly meant. The relentless treadmill of writing papers and books, creating original lecture material, setting examinations and then marking them had taken its toll on his personal life. The carnage of the few attempts he had made to hold relationships together lay abandoned in the jetsam of his consciousness. The more vivid memories were of one-night stands with gullible undergraduates and zipless fucking with faculty colleagues and visiting academics.

Immediately attracted to Olivia and encouraged by colleagues who believed that she lived the life of an ascetic to spite her natural vivaciousness, Bainbridge set out to woo her. The alacrity of their romance surprised everyone. Within months they were married, within weeks of arriving home from their honeymoon they both knew that they had made a bad mistake.

After eighteen months of increasing misery, each of them was finally able to admit that they had married for reasons that were calculated and had little to do with romance, let alone love. For Olivia it was the hope that emotional fulfilment would kick-start her flagging career and reinvigorate her enthusiasm for her work. For Ralph, it was a beautiful, well-presented woman who would always be there for him, but whose own career commitments would allow him plenty of space and who, he suspected, would not mind too much what he did when he spent time there.

While the lawyers unravelled the not too complex financial ramifications of their divorce, Olivia fell into a chasm of depression. She berated herself for dropping her guard and allowing Bainbridge to punch his way into her life and to trample on her self-respect with his deceit and his lies. Her sense of failure was not in any way assuaged by friends and colleagues who attempted to comfort her with well-meaning invitations and pithy sentimentality. She had no-one to blame but herself. She had been a fool to relax her grip on the principles that had guided her since High School. As the depression deepened, she increasingly retreated behind the barriers that medication erected between her and normality. She conveniently forgot the rut in which her life had been stuck before Bainbridge had forced his way into it.

She spent days at a time alone, locked in the studio apartment to which she had fled from her husband. It was only ever intended to be temporary, but she needed distance from him and space to be on her own. Surrounded by rented tat and other people's decay, she trod back through the detritus of her memories. She put her failings and mistakes on trial and found herself guilty on all counts. Self-possession had become self-absorption, intelligent polemic had become self-serving sophistry, the barrier she constructed to protect her heart had isolated her ability to express her emotions on any level. Marrying Ralph Bainbridge only postponed the execution of her sentence. Splitting up with him meant she was condemned to serve her time when she could see nothing beyond the prison of her own failures.

After the second change of medication there was some light. She began to play dot-to-dot with the events of her life and the path they marked to the present whereabouts of her psyche. Some were positive, some negative and others neither, but significant as points of reference: riding her first bicycle through Central Park and chasing after her father; summer camp at Bucks Rock in Connecticut – balmy days trying to sculpt and developing black and white photographs, evenings rehearsing for her bit part in 'A Midsummer Night's Dream'; her confirmation at the age of twelve – there had never been time for religion in her life; all she could remember was the unrelenting dogmatism of her parents forcing her to blindly accept what they would never think of questioning for themselves; her first kiss and the revulsion she felt at having a teenage male tongue shoved down her throat; vacationing in Italy and spending time with her cousin Magdalena; she never would forget that wedding – all that food and now Magdalena had four children of her own. Then there was something else. Maybe it was connected by her thoughts of Magdalena or maybe it was propelled to the front of her mind by another route.

One afternoon, not long after she became engaged to Ralph, she had been hurrying across the campus to an appointment with the Dean. Determined not to be late, she took a short cut by the College Museum. The infrequent but regular exhibitions of material from the Paul Whiteman Collection were always a draw for students and tourists alike. She noticed a couple leaving the Museum, threading their way through a swarm of High School students clamouring to get in the entrance. She stopped to let the last clutch of students pass her and thought she recognised the male of the emerging couple. He reminded her strongly of Matt Dayton, the British student she had met on a flight to Florence and with whom she had subsequently corresponded for more than two years. She wondered whether or not it could have been him and, if so, what might have brought him to Williamstown.

With little time to spare, she had to make an immediate decision whether or not to test her theory. It was more than ten years since she had resisted his attempted conquest of her. Occasionally he had entered her thoughts, although she had always peremptorily dismissed any notion that that there was any reason for him to linger there. More often than not her memories of him surfaced when she came across the music box he had given her as a present. The mechanism that played the music had long since ceased to work. She kept it in a large carton of odds and ends that followed her from apartment to apartment and was only ever opened to add another item that she could not bring herself to dispose of. There was no logic behind the sudden desire that she felt to reach out towards him. Concluding that no harm could come of it, she made to enter the scrimmage of students when, suddenly, she felt herself pulled back.

"Darling!" The echo of Ralph Bainbridge's distinctive voice resonated like the blast of a ship's horn in the middle of a foggy sea. "I had a feeling I'd run into you some time today." He put his arms around her. She responded to his embrace with restraint. By the time she had pushed him away, protesting that he was preventing her from getting to her meeting in time, the couple had disappeared. All the way to the Dean's office she continued to look behind her, but could not spot them anywhere. Foolishly, after the meeting finished, she tramped around the town hoping that she might run into them. Once she returned home she questioned why she had done so. Even had it been Matt, he was not alone and, for all she knew and expected, the woman with him was his wife. Besides, she was also part of a couple and it was futile for her to think that, more than ten years down the line, an innocent student flirtation could have retained any meaning whatsoever for him. Nevertheless, images of Matt stayed with her for a few weeks afterwards. They faded again as her wedding day came into view.

With the medication reduced and her divorce finalised, she began to put some of the pieces of her life back together. There were enough of them in place to know that she had to move on. An opportunity to teach History to undergraduates at Columbia came her way. It was an opportunity that would enable her to pursue her long postponed doctorate. She did not hesitate to seize it. Formally released by her sympathetic colleagues at Williams, she moved back to the city as the sparkling spring days were replaced by the steamy humidity of summer in Manhattan. She found a one bedroom sublet on Riverside and 88th, an easy subway ride from the campus. Before she had time to readjust to the relentless pace of her hometown, she planned to complete her personal renaissance with a trip to Europe. A fortnight with Jennifer Monroe, a friend and former colleague from Williams, touring England and Ireland would be followed by another ten days in Pisa with her cousin Magdalena.

There were still a couple of weeks before she was due to leave. Without the routine of work, Olivia found the days beginning to stretch and the spectre of depression haunting her once again. Determined to hang onto her reconstructed sanity, she did what she could to keep her mind occupied. Her immediate priority was coming to terms with all that was going on around her and the part that she could play in it. The friendships of her youth were long since consigned to the past and she had not yet felt up to making the effort to get to know her colleagues at work that well. Her parents had each remarried and were both already involved in turf wars with their respective new spouses. Neither of them could relate to the depression from which Olivia had emerged and nor did they have much time to spend with her. She took long walks and visited galleries during the day and caught movies and the occasional play in the evening, but always alone. She managed to successfully tread the line that divided despair and composure, but it was never easy.

One morning, while wandering through Central Park, near the Turtle Pond and close to the statue of King Jagiello, she saw an old woman walking with a stick lose her footing and tumble over. No-one else was nearby. She sprinted across to where the old woman was sprawled on the ground, struggling to pick herself up. Olivia kneeled behind her, slipped her hands under the old woman's armpits and sat her upright. Slowly, she helped the woman to her feet, picked up the stick and made sure she was steady.

"Thank you, so much."

"Can you manage by yourself?"

The woman tried to take a couple of steps but faltered. "I'd like to say I can, but maybe I need to rest first."

Olivia guessed that the woman must have been well into her seventies, if not older. For all her apparent frailty, her face was animated and there was an energy about her that was infectious.

"Tell me where you live and I will walk you back there."

"Central Park West between 79th and 80th. Don't worry. I'll be fine." Her accent was unmistakably New York, her bearing one of someone who had learned how to survive in the face of all the bad breaks that life could throw at a person.

"It's no problem, Mrs …?"

"Gina will do, Gina Rosenfeld," she held out her hand to shake Olivia's.

"Olivia, Olivia Giorgianni." Olivia shook Gina's hand. They were close to a bench and sat down for a few minutes before Olivia gripped Gina by the forearm and steered her in the direction of the park exit on West 81st Street.

By the time they reached Gina's apartment on the twentieth floor, Olivia had heard a potted version of her life story. Born into a Jewish family in Germany in 1920, her parents had the foresight to leave during the worst years of the Weimar Republic. Three years old when she arrived in America, Gina remembered the Wall Street crash and her father's new found prosperity wiped out overnight. Herman Rosenfeld never let his setbacks bring him down. He made and lost a half a dozen fortunes and was on his way to mopping up what remained of the last when he passed away at the age of eighty-six, ten years after her mother. Married after World War II, Gina's husband died of cancer leaving three young children to bring up. Her eldest son was killed in Vietnam. The two younger ones were both married with families of their own; one lived in California, the other had recently moved to Seattle. Gina lived alone in an apartment stuffed full of framed photographs and family memorabilia.

"Barely a month goes by that someone I know doesn't die," she said as she organised a tray for tea. "Since Mrs Grossman across the hallway passed on we don't even have a four for Canasta. You don't play by any chance, do you?"

Olivia shook her head.

"Pity. It's not such a good game with only three. Tell me, what do you do? I've been doing all the talking. I didn't yet find out much about you."

"There's not much to say."

"I'm sure there is."

Olivia proceeded to tell Gina something about her work, her recent move back to New York and her academic ambitions.

"You speak about your work, but not who you are and what you do when you are not working."

"It's not very interesting."

"I'm not sure that's true, or at least it shouldn't be. But there is a sadness about you, Olivia and that's worrying. And such a beautiful woman, too."

"I'm fine," said Olivia. Talking like this to anyone, let alone a complete stranger, was not something that she did as a rule. Whatever she kept inside her was private. She made a lousy therapy patient and, since returning to the city, she had not bothered to find a new shrink.

"Something tells me that you recently split up with a boyfriend, a husband even." The kettle boiled and whistled insipidly. Gina insisted on pouring the water into the teapot herself, then ushered Olivia into her sitting-room that offered a stunning view over the park.

"Are you psychic?" asked Olivia guardedly.

"I don't think so, but I've always been intuitive about people."

"He married the wrong woman and I married the wrong man." It was about as much as Olivia was prepared to say but it was as much as Gina needed to know.

"But the right man's out there, somewhere," announced Gina assuredly while she poured out the tea. She handed a cup to Olivia and indicated that she should help herself to lemon or milk and sugar.

"If you say so."

"I know so. And if you have faith, you will know it too."

"Faith?" snorted Olivia, "what is faith?"

"Faith means having the ability to live with uncertainty."

"What do you mean?"

"Just that. You need to let go, take chances."

I did that with Ralph, thought Olivia, but she knew what Gina meant. There was a clear distinction between taking a chance on the one hand and walking open-eyed into something that, no matter how one tried to characterise it, was a calculated decision on the other.

"I wish I could," said Olivia ruefully.

"A wish is a dream from the heart," observed Gina. "What does your heart seek?"

"I'm not sure that it does."

"You've got to have a dream."

"I do, frequently. They're usually both disjointed and lengthy."

"I don't mean that kind of dream. I'm talking about the kind that a genie would make come true."

Olivia sniggered. "That'll never happen. Besides, I'm too old for it. I'm not even sure that I'd want it to."

Gina looked surprised, "don't be ridiculous. You're not too old to have a dream"

"Like what?"

"Like falling in love with someone."

"It's been years since I thought about falling in love, if I ever have."

The truth was that Olivia had always fought the notion that falling in love would be good for her. She had spent hours with therapists explaining her need to maintain control over her life, a need that was inconsistent with surrendering herself to an emotional entanglement with a man. For her, control enabled self-determination and self-determination enabled survival.

"I don't believe you've never wanted to fall in love," said Gina. Her tone was one of admonishment.

"It's never been high on my wish list."

"How about need? Maybe you married the wrong man before but maybe you never loved him," she speculated. "That's never a good basis for a marriage. Maybe you need to fall in love and to be with someone who is in love with you?"

Olivia felt uncomfortable with that suggestion and even more uncomfortable that it was made by someone who barely knew her.

"I'm not sure that there's time for that," she said defensively. "There never seems to be enough time to do even the things I want to do."

"Time may be overcome by love, you know."

Gina's thought reminded her of a painting, 'Time Overcome by Hope, Love and Beauty'. It was the painting that was reproduced on the lid of that music box. She had most recently come across it when moving back to New York. She half remembered her conversation with Matt Dayton on the meaning of the painting, something about love and hope and beauty being forces that existed outside of time.

"And by hope, too," she said under her breath.

"Exactly. Even if you don't have dreams, I wouldn't believe that you don't have hopes."

"I do, I do."

"Hopes are all about the future and making plans. Let time do as it will. Live your life in the moment, not the moments yet to come, otherwise you'll be so busy making plans you won't have time for anything of life at all."

What Gina said so closely described the way Olivia approached things that she was almost embarrassed to admit it to herself. Realising her need to seize hold of her life and to make more of what might come her way, she led Gina back into subjects of conversation that were less sensitive. After one last cup of tea, Olivia noticed that it was past noon. Declining the offer to stay for a bite of lunch, she exchanged telephone numbers and promised to stay in contact.

Olivia walked back onto the steamy sidewalk of Central Park West at the moment when the sky that had looked foreboding earlier on made good its threat. It started to rain quite heavily. The water bounced off the sidewalk. She spotted an empty cab and beat the competition to its passenger door.

"Bloomingdales," she said to the driver without thinking about it. As the cab gunned its way across the park and through the puddles that had instantly collected at the side of 79th Street, she planned a splurge on new clothes that she would take to Europe. She would start at Bloomingdales then work her way down Lexington. She remembered a beauty salon on Broadway near 75th. As soon as she returned home she would make an appointment to have her hair cut and restyled. Hell, while she was at it she would have a manicure and a pedicure and a facial.

Then there were a dozen and more other things in the city that Faculty colleagues had suggested she do and see before taking off for Europe. She might even call one of them and invite her over for dinner or suggest a movie and a drink in a bar.

It was late afternoon when she returned home weighed down with bags from a half a dozen stores and feeling better than she had about things for some time. She made some coffee and let it brew while she took a quick shower. Afterwards she started to put away her new clothes. There was not enough room on the floor of her closet to accommodate her new footwear – a pair of sandals, a pair of smart shoes and a pair of sneakers. She removed a large cardboard carton that was taking up space and put it into the living room.

Later on, while she was relaxing with a glass of wine and with Miles Davis playing on the stereo, she carefully emptied the contents of the carton onto the living room floor. On her knees, she started to sort through it, resolved to dispose of anything that was properly classified as junk. There were ornaments and buttons, Canadian coins and theatre programmes, branded baseball caps and photographs and a couple of High School Yearbooks. At the very bottom was the music box. She sat on the settee and, with a ceremonial flourish, placed it onto the coffee table. She lifted the glass of wine to her lips and sipped it slowly.

The box was about seven inches long, five inches wide and two inches high. As clear as the reproduction of the Vouet was, some of the detail was too small to be appreciated. She became absorbed by the virtual movement of Time's assailants and remembered what she could recall of Matt Dayton's interpretation was correct. There was a paradox between Time that constantly moved forward and changed the physical world through which it flowed and other dynamic forces that were eternal and existed and that mattered to a human life. She would stop living by rote and open herself up to the forces of the moment. There was hope and there was beauty around her and perhaps even love. She would let them into her life and free her mind to let them take her where they would.

She put down the glass and took the music box in her hands. It was years since she had kept anything in it – stud earrings and a sorority pin. She had not opened it even once since the mechanism jammed and the music stopped playing, and that must have been at least seven or eight years previously.

The clasp was slightly bent. She went into the kitchen where she found a screwdriver that she used to ease it open. The lid flipped up and, to her amazement, the music began to play. She clicked off the stereo with the remote. The quaint old tune sprinkled the apartment with a dusting of magic. The clockwork mechanism ran down half way through a third repetition of the melody. She looked inside the box and found the key and the yellowing leaflet that mentioned the lost lyrics, the ballad of the shepherd and the virgin who was devoured by a demon wolf disguised as a priest. She tried to work out what the plot of the story could have been. She did not get very far when she began to feel tired.

Before she went to bed she dusted off the music box and found a place for it on her dressing table. She wound up the mechanism then took a few pairs of earrings and arranged them neatly inside. She let the tune play once more before she went to sleep, perchance to dream of hope and love and beauty.

Whatever may have been on her mind before she went to sleep, the dream that came was one she had had before, though not for some time, and was imbued with anything but hope or love or beauty. She was standing on the street where her parents had lived before their divorce. It was in the upper eighties between York and the River. The apartment block had been totally destroyed by fire. There was nothing to indicate that any kind of structure had been there except the party walls of the neighbouring buildings that were completely black with soot. All that was left was an empty lot. In the centre of the lot was a large crucifix. It was made of black granite, rough and unpolished. A man was nailed to the far side of the crucifix. His head was slumped forward so that it was propped up on the horizontal beam of the cross. His mouth was moving. She guessed he was trying to say something.

She ventured slowly towards him but the cinders that covered the ground were still hot. They began to melt the soles of her shoes and burn her feet. She moved forward gingerly, determined to find out what he might be saying. She got as close as she could to the cross. The man's head was four or five feet above her so she had to strain to hear what he said. He was completely naked and his face was one that she knew but could not place. He repeated a single word. Instead of speaking he moaned in a way that suggested a melody of irregular metre.

The word was 'previty'. She recognised the word from other dreams, but did not know what it meant. She checked it out in dictionaries and encyclopaedias, but could not find it anywhere. Preview? Previse? No, it was definitely 'previty' and it conveyed a sense, a feeling, an understanding, an interpretation of things that were yet to happen but which had their roots in past events.

The dream recurred during each of the three following nights. It began to antagonise her but she would not let it interrupt the course that she had set. She was determined not to loosen the grip she had taken on her life. By the time Jennifer Monroe arrived to spend a couple of days with her in New York before they set off for Britain, the dream stopped and, once again, its memory began to fade.

XXIII

Betrayal

Florence. April 1517

They remained in Arezzo longer than originally planned. The coach driver's mutterings about wanting to be back home before he lost his mind were pacified with a few florins and the recommendation of a rough little taverna on the other side of the town, where the wine was cheap and the women were loose.

Aunt Bartolomea's contacts discovered nothing about Maria's departure from the convent other than what had been alleged by Madonna Suora. With Easter three days past, Leonardo began to believe that, even if the cause had been neither fully nor frankly disclosed, Maria was en route to the Holy Land. Gianetta Salcoiati did what she could to help Aunt Bartolomea around the house and generally said little that was not directed towards soothing her husband's vexation. At night she dreamed of Suora Graziella, though it was sometimes hard for her to distinguish those dreams from what she believed could have been further visitations from the restless spirit of the hapless young nun. She made a half-hearted attempt to locate the whereabouts of Suora Graziella's grave. The paupers' cemetery was some distance away. She accepted the received wisdom that it would be one of many recent graves, freshly dug and unmarked and that it would be a matter of guesswork to identify it accurately.

Ragaci was composing an instrumental piece for a grand banquet to be thrown by his patron, Ignazio Tolosini, to mark the May celebrations. He worked assiduously in a small room behind Aunt Bartolomea's parlour, imagining the opening crescendo blasted out by a chorus of trumpets. While he laboured, he pushed to the back of his mind what might await his return to Florence.

For the rest of their time in Arezzo, he and Leonardo comforted each other in the knowledge that, if not her body, at least Maria's soul was in safe hands.

On the Saturday following Easter they returned to Florence. As the familiar skyline came into view, dominated by the magnificence of Brunelleschi's dome, Ragaci's mood darkened. He thought back to his arrival at the Palazzo Salcoiati, nearly two years earlier, how much his first breaths of the city's air had filled him with optimism and excitement. Images flashed through his mind in quick succession, of beauty and of happiness and of camaraderie that were first obscured, then blotted out by others - distrust and hatred and evil and death. Perhaps it was the right time for him to move on.

He had never previously contemplated making a pilgrimage to the Holy Land, a desire to witness the cradle of the faith did not motivate him. The possibility that Maria might be there would be enough to guide him, his ability to earn his way by singing and playing for his supper enough to sustain him. Even were he not to find her there, he might escape the immediate threat posed by Donatina's curse and the impending wrath of her father. There was no reason to delay. He would seek an audience with Tolosini the next morning and make his decision known. There was no indenture to keep him tied and, within a short time, he could be on his way.

* * * * * * *

It was already dusk when Ragaci arrived at the Palazzo Tolosini. Happy with the decision he had made, there was nothing he could yet do to implement it. He ate the evening meal with other members of the household, then returned to his apartment. His new piece was more than half done and he was keen to complete it quickly. Not long after he settled down with his lute and a manuscript book, there were three sharp raps on the door. Dreading that it might be Donatina returning to haunt him with her threats and curses, he waited in the hope that his visitor might be deterred by the silence and go away. The second and more insistent series of bangs on the door demanded a response. He put down the lute and stepped tentatively towards the door and opened it. He was faced with the unprepossessing countenance of Adamo Tazzi. Thickset, ugly, uncompromising and plain dangerous, Ragaci guessed that, whatever the reason for his appearance, he would not be required to sing anything romantic. As was ever the case, Tazzi waited to be spoken to before identifying the nature of the summons.

"What is it, Tazzi?"

"Your presence is required by Signor Niccolo," he said gruffly. "You don't need to bring anything."

"Let me put some shoes on."

Tazzi thought about the request. His inanimate belligerence indicated that Ragaci might do that before following him through to the main part of the palazzo.

Niccolo's grand suite of rooms was one level above the ground floor and overlooked the splendid gardens at the rear of the palazzo. Now there was darkness and the shutters were closed. Tazzi showed Ragaci into a small salon where Niccolo reclined on a chaise longue, propped up on one elbow, a silver cup in his other hand, a flagon of wine on a small table in front of him. He nodded at Tazzi, who then retreated to stand in front of the door.

"Sit down, musician, sit down." He waved at a couple of low chairs that were arranged on the other side of the table. Ragaci chose one that had its back to the shuttered windows but from which he could maintain a clear line of sight towards Tazzi.

Niccolo stared at him with the benign somnolence of a drunk about to collapse. Ragaci tried to see past the intoxicated gaze and to check the layout of the room. There was another door on the far side that, from its situation, he assumed to lead to an internal room from which there was unlikely to be access to a corridor. On the near side there was another door behind a screen that he suspected led to Niccolo's bed chamber but nowhere else.

"You know why you're here, don't you, musician," slurred Niccolo.

Ragaci could guess but preferred to be told and waited accordingly.

"While you absented yourself, a deed was notarised. It was a deed that set out the terms of a dowry. The dowry in question is that of Signorina Donatina Castellani. The man she will marry is me." Niccolo blinked at Ragaci then took a good long swig from his cup. "With me so far, musician? Are you hearing me?"

Ragaci said nothing.

"Speak when you're spoken to," growled Tazzi from the shadows.

"Yes, I'm with you," said Ragaci expressionlessly.

"Presently, my father and Signor Feduccio Castellani, my father-in-law to be, are visiting Venice together on matters of commerce. They will return within the next ten days at which point there will be the public meeting between our male kin and those of the bride; the ring day will follow shortly afterwards. These events are set in train and no-one shall interfere with them. Understood?"

Ragaci wanted to be the first to congratulate him, but confined his response to an uncontroversial "understood."

Niccolo took another slug of wine.

"This intelligence does not seem to bother you, musician. Perhaps you knew about it already? Perhaps there was a spy who disclosed our secrets to you even before the ink was dry on the indenture?"

"I was unaware until this very moment that you were contracted to marry Sigorina Castellani," said Ragaci truthfully.

"Nevertheless, Tazzi here tells me that you have developed a great fondness for my intended wife."

Ragaci said nothing.

"Remaining silent will not guarantee your innocence. You see, I have proof of your guilt."

Ragaci swallowed hard. He knew not to what Niccolo might refer. Niccolo swung his legs down onto the floor, leaned forward and put his cup down on the table. He motioned towards Tazzi who went over to a bureau in the corner and removed two pages of manuscript. He gave them to Niccolo, then returned to his post in front of the door. Niccolo selected one of the pages, perused it briefly then handed it to Ragaci.

"This was written by you I believe."

Ragaci recognised the manuscript straightaway. "This is a frottola I was commissioned to write by Signorina Castellani to celebrate her father's birthday. She paid me for it and this is the manuscript copy of the piece that I gave her."

"It was during the course of working on this commission that you made amorous advances to the Signorina."

"No. Not all," lamented Ragaci. "That's not true. I made no advances towards her."

Ignoring his protest, Niccolo continued. "More than that, I'm told that you laid your hands on her and that you tried to force yourself on her."

"What?" gasped Ragaci.

"Two maids heard a commotion coming from your apartment. They looked through the keyhole and saw you sitting astride her and pinning her wrists to the floor with your hands."

Ragaci rapidly decided that it would be better if he said nothing and not try to explain the sequence of events that led to his bestriding Donatina in an attempt to restrain her, rather than any attempt to have his way with her.

"Answer me, musician."

"Answer him," snarled Tazzi.

"That's not right."

"I think you're lying. I think your intentions towards Signorina Donatina are thoroughly disreputable. I believe that you would use her like a cheap whore, dishonour her and her family, then throw her away when you tire of her."

"No. No. Not at all," said Ragaci indignantly.

"Then what do you say to this?" Niccolo handed him the second page of manuscript. It was a letter addressed to Donatina in which the author declared his undying love for her in florid terms. It condescended to some detail about the nature of certain physical acts in which the two of them might collectively participate and was signed 'Giacomo'.

Ragaci puffed out his cheeks, exhaled sharply and shook his head.

"You look puzzled, musician. Is this not your doing?"

"I've never seen this letter before."

"But it is written in your hand, isn't it?"

"It looks a little like my hand, but I assure you it is not."

"Give it to me." Niccolo reached across the table and snatched the two pages of manuscript out of Ragaci's hands. He was already familiar with them, but gave them a cursory glance before screaming, "of course it's your fucking handwriting, musician! They're identical. You know it and I know it, too. They were brought to Tazzi by Signorina Castellani herself who attested to the provenance of both."

Ragaci continued to protest and to remonstrate, but Niccolo stood up and stepped in front of him, grabbed him by the collar and dragged him to his feet. Ragaci immediately took hold of Niccolo's wrists and started to struggle with him. This was a cue for Tazzi to rush across the room and to pounce on Ragaci from behind. The force of Tazzi's challenge sent both Ragaci and Niccolo flying. In the melee that ensued, Tazzi managed to haul Ragaci away from Niccolo enabling his master to stand up. Ragaci landed a couple of punches, but Tazzi was too strong for him and made short work of his resistance. Wrestling Ragaci to the floor, Tazzi subdued him with his full body weight. Niccolo then assisted in pulling Ragaci to his feet. Tazzi held one of Ragaci's arms up his back, with his other hand he gripped the musician's collar, pushing his knuckle hard into his victim's neck.

Niccolo put his face close to Ragaci's and snarled, "you listen, musician, and you listen well. This is a warning. You will stop contacting Signorina Donatina. This finishes now. Do you understand me?"

Tazzi's grip on Ragaci's collar tightened. The best that Ragaci could do was to choke out the words, "yes, I promise."

"And I will make sure you keep this promise. My father will be informed of these events before his return and so will Signor Castellani. They will not witness your disgrace though, because I'm telling you that your tenure here is terminated forthwith. You will go back to your apartment and remain there until the morning when Tazzi will escort you and your belongings from the palazzo and deposit you, with them, on the street."

Momentarily, Ragaci's instinct for self-preservation deserted him. He wanted to protest the decision, the downright unfairness of it. He reined in his rebellious side. Though his reputation might suffer from the ignominy of his dismissal, what had happened was a blessing in disguise. He gave thanks that at least Donatina had not disclosed the full extent of their intimacy. It would not have suited her immediate purposes, but that could change. By the time Feduccio Castellani returned to Florence and before Niccolo, if sufficiently sober, might realise that Donatina was not a virgin bride, Ragaci would be gone.

Tazzi escorted him back to his apartment. Neither spoke. Tazzi closed the door behind Ragaci who then locked it from the inside and put the key on the table in the middle of the room.

Even though he was exhausted by the events of the day, he found it hard to get to sleep. In ordinary circumstances he would have picked up a lute and played for a while. These were not ordinary circumstances. He sat on his bed in an upright position and pondered what he would gain by staying the night. He reasoned that he would be better to pack up his things, then leave immediately for Leonardo's house and spend the night there. Leonardo might then accompany him in the morning to pick up whatever he was unable to carry with him.

He hurried about collecting his belongings together. He packed his leather bag that he would be able to manage with two lutes. He blew out the candles and unlocked the door. He pushed it open but was surprised to find his way blocked by two large men. One of them, Lapozzi, was more usually to be found working in Tolosini's stables. The other was Tebaldi, a great hulk of a creature with three fingers missing on his left hand, a bodyguard who answered directly to Tazzi.

"Where are you off to?" enquired Lapozzi.

"I'm going to the house of my friend, Leonardo Salcoiati. I will return in the morning to pick up the rest of my things."

"I'm sorry but that won't be possible," announced Lapozzi firmly.

"Why not?"

"Because we have been instructed to ensure that you don't leave the palazzo until further notice."

"What? That's ridiculous!" cried Ragaci. "My tenure here has been terminated. I've been told to leave by Signor Niccolo and that is precisely what I intend to do."

"Not until morning, you're not."

"Come on, Lapozzi, you know me better than that. I'm going to have to come back anyway. I can't manage everything now - not without a carriage of some sort." Ragaci tried to push his way past them, but Tebaldi stood firm, preventing him going anywhere by virtue of his sheer size.

"This is crazy, you will not stand in my way." Laden with his bag over one shoulder and a lute in each hand, Ragaci's ability to manoeuvre quickly was impaired, but he turned sideways and started pushing against Tebaldi with his other shoulder.

"Giacomo, please go back into your apartment. I do not intend to hurt you, nor even to touch you, but you must understand that I have my orders from Tazzi whose orders, in turn, come from Signor Niccolo himself. If you continue to make it difficult for us to obey those orders, then Tebaldi will have to physically restrain you."

"Then that's what he's going to have to do then," snapped Ragaci, redoubling his encumbered efforts to push his way past them. He got no further than half a head in front of Tebaldi who caught him around the neck with his arm. Tebaldi then smashed his knee into Ragaci's thigh, expertly dead-legging him. Ragaci fell back, dropping one of the lutes that clattered onto the floor. Lapozzi steadied Ragaci and then, together with Tebaldi, ushered him back into his room. Tebaldi stood in the doorway while Lapozzi picked up the dropped lute and returned it to Ragaci.

"Giacomo, please don't make this more difficult than it need be."

Given a choice that was, effectively, no choice, Ragaci had little option but to remain where he was. He began to wonder why he was being cooped up in his apartment when he had already been told to leave the next morning. There was no logical reason for it and that, of itself, bred suspicion. He redoubled his determination to get away from the palazzo immediately, sensing that to remain any longer would expose him to danger, the nature of which was, as yet, unknown. He went across to the window and opened it. He looked from side to side and then straight down. It was a sheer drop of perhaps twenty braccia and there was nothing even close on either side to grab hold of. He looked around the apartment and considered whether or not there were things from which he might fashion a rope that he could use to escape, but there were not.

He lay down on his bed again, fully-clothed and resolved to wait a while before trying again to leave through the door to his apartment. No doubt his guards would be relieved from duty at some point and, when they were, he would try a more unctuous approach with their replacements. Alternatively, it was possible that sooner or later the guards would need to take a nap and he would use the moment to make his escape.

Periodically he looked through the keyhole, but there was no change outside. After sitting upright on his bed for another two or three hours, Ragaci found himself fighting to stay awake. He lay down and decided to close his eyes for a little while. It would be enough to enable him to wake up feeling sufficiently alert. It was the second plan of the night that was not to be realised. Exhausted after his long journey from Arezzo and by what had followed, he fell into a deep sleep.

* * * * * * *

That he slept later than he might usually have done was apparent from the strength of the sunlight that pierced the shutters. The pounding on his door was pointlessly violent. It succeeded in its object of waking him up. The cries of 'open up!' reminded him that he would be leaving soon. He stared at the pile of his possessions and wondered if someone would help him carry them over to the house of Leonardo Salcoiati. His intention was to remain there only for as long as it would take him to organise his departure for the Holy Land, stopping first for a brief visit with his family in San Gimignano.

"Open up, or we will smash the door down." The voice was unmistakably that of Tazzi.

Ragaci would not accord the demand even the courtesy of an acknowledgment. They could smash the door into pieces for all he cared. He picked up the key from the table and went over to the door where he slipped it into the lock. He turned it, but it would not move. He could have sworn he had locked it the previous evening; the evidence was to the contrary. He opened the door to admit Tazzi and whoever accompanied him, wondering why they had not simply walked in without all of the fuss.

Tazzi stood at the door with three others wearing the uniform of the Militia.

"Is this really necessary?" snapped Ragaci. "I'm more than happy to leave as quickly as I can."

"You're going nowhere," barked the oldest of the militiamen, the adornments on whose uniform revealed his rank as captain. "Hold him," he ordered the others, each of whom pushed their way into the room and took hold of one of Ragaci's forearms.

"What is all this about?" shouted Ragaci, trying to wrestle himself out of the grip of the officers.

While Ragaci was held still, Tazzi and the captain snooped around the room.

"Over here captain," said Tazzi gesticulating towards a music stand in the corner of the room. Ragaci strained to see what Tazzi had identified, but was pulled back sharply by his guards. The captain picked up the object and waved it in front of Ragaci. It was a long, steel dagger with an ivory handle and a sharp blade, covered in what looked to be dried blood.

Ragaci gazed at it in disbelief.

"Your guess was right Signor Tazzi," said the captain.

"What in heaven's name is that?" exclaimed Ragaci.

"That is what we believe you used for your handiwork last night," continued the captain.

"Handiwork? What handiwork?"

"Signor Ragaci, I am placing you under arrest for the murder of Niccolo Tolosini."

"The what? There must be a mistake". Once again, Ragaci tried to break free from the officers' grip, but they held firm. "I've not murdered anyone!"

"Signor Tolosini was found dead in his bed this morning by a servant. His body was punctured by a number of stab wounds and covered with blood. It appears that he was murdered last night."

"Last night? Then that clearly proves I'm innocent."

"How so?"

"I've been confined to my apartment ever since Signor Tazzi escorted me back here at a little before midnight. When I tried to leave, there were two guards on the door – Tebaldi and Lapozzi. They will tell you themselves."

The captain looked at Tazzi, "well?"

"Tebaldi and Lapozzi were here until about three of the morning when they had been told they could leave. There was a misunderstanding. Others were supposed to have taken their place, but clearly failed to turn up."

"I did not murder Signor Tolosini. I am innocent!"

"You can protest your innocence all you like. In due course you can protest it to a magistrate, though I doubt that it will do you much good. Signor Tazzi here told us that you had a disagreement with Signor Tolosini last night, that you resented being told to leave his intended wife alone and that resulted in him dismissing you from your position."

"That's not what happened!"

"We have seen the evidence. We have seen the letter you wrote to Signorina Castellani. We have seen the body. We have listened to Signor Tazzi's account of events and now we have found the murder weapon in your apartment."

"That letter is a fake. It's all lies. I did not make advances on Signorina Castellani."

"Signor Tazzi says otherwise. He tells us that Signorina Castellani was physically assaulted by you. Apparently there was a commotion between you and the signorina in this very apartment about ten days ago and it was overheard by two maids. I've already spoken to one of them. She told me that they looked through the key hole and saw you astride the signorina, pinning her arms to the floor."

Once again, Ragaci tried to free himself from the grip of the officers who held him. He shouted "but that's not …"

The captain was not interested in listening to anything that Ragaci had to say and pushed him hard in the chest with the flat of his hands. The other officers stood firm and tightened their grip on Ragaci.

"Shut up prisoner. I've not yet spoken to Signorina Castellani herself, but Signor Tazzi assures me that she will verify the account."

"Then Signorina Castellani is a liar," yelled Ragaci. "And so is Signor Tazzi. I'm no more capable of committing a murder than he is of composing a frottola." Ragaci continued to struggle. With an enormous effort he managed to free his right arm and elbowed one of his guards in the stomach, briefly winding him. He turned to try and punch the other, but Tazzi stepped in and deflected Ragaci's fist. Simultaneously, the captain grabbed hold of Ragaci's right arm and brought it hard round his back.

"I reckon you owe him one, Luccheto," said the captain to the guard. Luccheto stood up and had recovered his breath sufficiently to thump Ragaci hard in the stomach. Ragaci doubled over and lurched forward. On a signal from the captain they let him fall onto the ground, hitting his head which then started to bleed.

"And there's more of that if you don't learn how to behave," sneered the captain. "Take him to the Bargello."

* * * * * * *

Ragaci persisted in telling the truth and would not be intimidated into making an admission that could have shortened the process of his prosecution. He explained to the investigating magistrate how Donatina had made advances towards him with a view to thwarting the marriage that had been proposed for her with Niccolo; how, he realised that he was being played off against her father's intentions for her and made it clear that he rejected her; the curse she had put on him and the forged letter. He studiously avoided any mention of her seduction of him.

The Castellani closed ranks behind Donatina. Not a word was said by any of them about how Donatina expressed her intention to marry a man of her own choosing and her rejection of her father's choice of Niccolo. No-one thought to ask Egidia Colesi about what Donatina had told her of her designs on Ragaci. The investigating magistrate would likely not have cared less. There was more than enough evidence to convict and that was more than enough for him.

Ragaci languished in the dank cells of the Bargello for the best part of a month. There were few visitors. Gianluca Cavaliere and Angelica Margherita were among the first. After leaving him they went straight on to the Taverna del Cielo.

"How did he look?" asked Nurchi as he poured drinks for the group that were huddled around the table nearest the bar.

"Tired, hungry and dirty," said Angelica Margherita despondently.

"And how was his disposition?" continued Nurchi.

"Strangely enough, he was in good spirits," observed Cavaliere. "He has persuaded them to let him have a lute. He even played us a couple of tunes. It was as if he was trying to say that life goes on."

"Though in his case, not for much longer, I warrant," lamented Nurchi, following the remark with a hearty slug of wine.

"The true culprit may yet be found," said Cavaliere hopefully.

"Though there is little sign of anyone else being arrested," added Nurchi.

"Whoever could have wanted such a thing to happen to such a sweet, gentle soul?" moped Angelica Margherita.

"Did Giacomo say anything of his own suspicions?" enquired Nurchi thoughtfully.

"He was unable to say much as we were constantly being watched by the guards, but what he did say is that the accusation that he made advances to Signorina Donatina Castellani is false; that it was she who put him in a compromising position. He stated that Niccolo Tolosini had many enemies, especially amongst those in his father's employ." Cavaliere paused to drink and looked searchingly at those around the table for a reaction. They each sat expectantly. "In order for the murder weapon to have been planted in his apartment, the murderer, even if not a member of the household, would have needed the close acquaintance of someone with unlimited access to all areas of the palazzo."

There was a silent pause while they supped at their drinks and absorbed what they had been told.

"We should endeavour to find out the truth ourselves that we might assist in bringing the real culprit to justice," interjected Turrichio, who had finished his complimentary cup of wine and looked at Nurchi with a hang-dog expression that he hoped would be enough to persuade the taverner to pour him another.

"Has it occurred to you that perhaps the true murderer is already rotting in prison?" The question was posed by a relative newcomer to the del Cielo regulars, Aloisi Delvigna. On several occasions, the young tailor had expressed views that were generally neither welcome nor accepted. Rotund and inclining to corpulence, Delvigna's unhealthy appearance was not improved by his left eye that continually twitched in a way that suggested that he was permanently impatient, which was not, in fact, the case.

"What intelligence abounds that would make you believe that?" enquired Castellani.

"Only the intelligence that was passed to the officers of

the law, repeated by the banditori and which I anticipate we may also hear when sentence is finally passed on Ragaci."

"You mean you take at face value the charges made against Giacomo?" asked Angelica Margherita.

"What else is there? All this talk of waiting for the real culprit to be found is no more than just that; it's drinking talk. The reason why no-one else has been found or arrested is quite simple."

"And that is?" asked Nurchi.

"No-one else did it. Ragaci is clearly the murderer."

Delvigna's remark met with a dumbfounded silence. Eventually Cavaliere broke it. "How can you say such a thing when you have never even met Ragaci?"

"It stands to reason. Ragaci had a motive – the proposed marriage between Niccolo and Donatina, apparently the object of Ragaci's affections. He had the opportunity. Apparently Ragaci was in the palazzo throughout the evening in question. And the most important part of the evidence, the murder weapon, was found in his apartment still dripping with Niccolo Tolosini's blood."

"No-one, but no-one who would have committed such an act would have left the evidence where it could be so easily found," asserted Cavaliere, "and so obviously intended to point to one upon whom those responsible wanted to pin guilt."

"It is said that when one man murders another, his mind is no longer sane, that in order to commit an act of murder that is so obviously pre-meditated, the guilty one is no longer capable of exercising reason. If that is so, then it is hardly surprising that Ragaci would have returned to his apartment bearing the murder weapon," said Delvigna with an air of assurance that bordered on the pompous.

"And not leave it at the scene, where it would not be obviously linked to anyone in particular?" queried Cavaliere.

"Even were that to have been done, the other circumstances point to only one culprit. And it is a view that is shared on the street," said Delvigna. "You should be careful not to make too much publicity for your defence of Ragaci.

"Is that intended as a threat," asked Nurchi, quizzically. "For, if it is so, you will surely not be welcome in this taverna again."

"It's no threat," said Delvigna, defensively, "merely a warning. However much acclaim and admiration Ragaci may have collected, he is now regarded as nothing much more than a cowardly murderer who must surely pay for his crime in the only way that is prescribed by the law."

"Which is?" asked Angelica Margherita timorously, but knowing the answer full well.

"With his own life."

Hearing this stated so baldly was more than she could bear. She started to sob.

"Cry your tears, wench, and dry them quickly. For if you are seen to weep for Ragaci in public, your association with him will do you favours with your customers."

"That's enough, Aloisi!" shouted Nurchi, reaching across and grabbing hold of his tunic. "You may think what you like. We know that Ragaci is innocent and don't want to hear any more of your foul-mouthed stupidity."

Nurchi began to drag the hapless tailor towards the door to the street.

"And please do me a favour and take your custom elsewhere."

Delvigna started to flap his arms and whimpering, "let me at least finish my drink."

"Here, I'll bring it for you," called Turrichio, putting down his own cup and picking up Delvigna's. "Hold him still, Bruno."

Nurchi stopped at the door and turned Delvigna towards the oncoming Turrichio who threw the wine straight into the tailor's twitching face. "And have this as well," he added, launching the heavy pewter cup at Delvigna's testicles.

"Argh!" yelled Delvigna, lurching forwards as Nurchi pushed him out through the door and onto the street, where he landed heavily on his backside.

The rest of the group gathered around the doorway and watched a couple of bemused passers-by help Delvigna to his feet.

"Don't worry, Nurchi," Delvigna yelled, "I'll find somewhere else to drink and, when I do, it'll be a taverna that has something better than the watered down piss of an excuse for wine that you serve and somewhere that isn't full of a bunch of morons who like to be associated with murderers."

Nurchi made to chase after Delvigna who began to walk swiftly down the street as they continued exchanging insults.

As much as they persisted in their belief that Ragaci was not capable of murder, it was a belief that was at odds with the majority view on the street. Most were reviled by the descriptions they heard of the cold-blooded slaying of Niccolo Tolosini while he slept and which descriptions became more lurid as the days passed.

Each of those who Ragaci had counted as friends had livings to earn. Even the principled Cavaliere could not afford the possibility of negative association with the unfortunate Ragaci. Along with the others, he began to distance himself from Ragaci's plight.

By the time of the second week of his incarceration, Feduccio Castellani and Ignazio Tolosini had returned to

Florence; public frenzy demanded the speedy execution of the murderer.

Only Leonardo and Gianetta continued to visit Ragaci regularly. They needed no convincing of their friend's innocence and accepted his explanation without question. Simply stated, Donatina, angered by Ragaci's rejection of her, made good the promise of her curse. Disgusted with her father's choice of Niccolo Tolosini, she had hired Tazzi to commit the murder and put the weapon in Ragaci's apartment, having engineered the set up with the forged letter and the termination of his patronage in its wake. She had calculated that there was enough of a motive and more than enough evidence to keep the authorities happy. Nobody would believe the word of an itinerant musician against that of a grieving young woman who had had matrimonial bliss snatched away from her so cruelly, nor that of Tazzi, a trusted servant who had once been a loyal soldier.

The day before Ragaci was scheduled to appear before the Court, Leonardo visited him alone. Earlier Gianetta had announced to him that she was pregnant. She was feeling unwell and asked him to apologise for her absence. In deference to Ragaci's predicament, Leonardo tried to suppress his joy, but simply could not.

"Life is there to be lived," said Ragaci. "Enjoy it. Enjoy it while you can, for once you give in to the unjustified expectations of others and what may be required of you against your free will, there is nothing."

"I hear you, my friend, I hear you."

"I am still alive, Leonardo and I am still living. They agreed to remove my chains and they brought me my lute. I still have choices; whether to play or not; whether to compose or to play a song written by another; whether or not to sleep; whether or not to engage with the guards. It's not much, but it is better than nothing. I am alive and whole and while I am alive there is hope."

"What do you hope for?"

"I hope that the true culprit will be brought to justice and that I am freed. I hope that I may once again walk the streets of this city that I have grown to love and to play my music to its people. I hope to see your portrait of me completed. I hope that I may live to see Gianetta bring your baby into this world and above all …"

"Yes?"

"… above all, I hope that I may once again see your sister Maria, that I may fall on one knee before her, take her hand in mine and ask her to marry me, even if she were then to decline my request."

"I would like to see that too. Even to hear from her and to know that she is alive and flourishing would be enough."

"Had it not been for these false accusations, it was my intention to follow her to the Holy Land."

"Why didn't you mention that to me before?"

"There seemed little point. Although I have hopes, I am resigned to my fate; but, if you are able to contact Maria, I would like you to let her know that my last wish was to be with her."

"I will, Giacomo, I will." But for all the good intentions of Leonardo's promise, he sensed that he would never see his sister again.

Leonardo managed to send word of Ragaci's unfortunate situation to his family and friends in San Gimignano. Mosciano Vannozzi read between the lines of the carefully worded letter and figured out something close to the truth, but he was struck with illness, bedridden and unable to travel. Bonaccio and Cesare Ragaci, Giacomo's father and brother, made arrangements to leave the farm for a couple of days, though his mother was too distressed to contemplate seeing her son condemned and shackled.

Even knowing him as they did, Bonaccio and Cesare Ragaci had a simple notion of justice and of law and order. Overwhelmed by the size and the bustle of the city, they could not bring themselves to believe that the authorities would seek to incarcerate and convict an innocent man. By the time they reached the Bargello, they were concerned not to show too much sympathy for Giacomo, the murderer, lest they be visited with some penalty for so doing. When they were finally led into his cell, Bonaccio could only say, "how could you have done such a thing?"

To which Ragaci could only reply, "how can you believe that I would have done?"

"I know that's what you say, but how could you have done such a thing?"

Having completed this cycle of remarks three or four times, Ragaci looked at his brother who, too, was overwhelmed by the circumstances. Unable to think of anything more to say than "I'll pray for you, brother," Ragaci was at least able to extract some idea of how everyone was doing, that his baby nephew was sitting up and gurgling and that the farm was prospering. All the while his father sat looking at his feet and shaking with distress.

* * * * * * *

On Thursday 4th June 1517, two years to the day after his arrival in the City of the Medici, Giacomo Ragaci was found to be guilty of the murder of Niccolo Tolosini. He was sentenced to be hanged, then to have his body burned and his ashes scattered outside of the walls of the city.

He was granted one last request. He was permitted to perform for those assembled to witness his last moments of life, one final frottola that he had composed for the occasion. On the morning of his execution he was taken from his cell to the yard at the back of the Bargello. In front of the gallows, a tiered stand had been temporarily erected that was occupied by members of the Signoria, the investigating magistrate, the captain of the Militia who had effected his arrest and a number of others. There were also family members of the Tolosini and the Castellani, including Donatina, who was suitably garbed in black.

Ragaci was escorted up the steps of the ladder to the tiny platform then given his lute. There was no chair, so he stood at the edge of the platform and rested his foot on a wooden strut that held the ladder in place. He picked out Donatina in the crowd and fixed her with his gaze as he sang:

Crudel et despietata, che n'arrai
quando davantia te me vederai morto?
Forse che la mia morte piangerai;
alor pensando havermi occiso a torto.
Non te vara se ben te pentirai
esser sta causa del mio viver corto,
che a chi a stagion sua crudelta non smorza
tanto li val quanto pentir per forza.

Cruel, heartless, woman, what will you gain
by seeing me dead before you?
Perhaps you will mourn for me,
realising that you have killed me wrongfully.
It will do you no good, even if you regret
being the cause of my early death.
For if cruelty is not tempered at the right time,
it is worth no more than repentance under duress.

As the echo of the final notes swirled across the yard, a priest climbed the ladder to the platform to hear Ragaci's final confession and to administer the last rites. After hearing the confession he blessed him "… in nomine pater, filius et spiritus sanctus." He made the sign of the cross, then withdrew slowly down the rungs of the ladder to retake his place with the dignitaries.

The hangman stepped across and began to weight Ragaci's body with chains, linking them together until they were secure. He raised his arm to a uniformed drummer standing at the foot of the gallows who began to play a roll. Using a cord, the hangman pulled the rope in from where it was suspended over the edge of the platform. He had Ragaci move to the edge of the platform and face his public. He slipped the noose around Ragaci's neck and tightened it. Signalling to the drummer, he readied himself for the end of the roll. The last snap of the drumsticks was the cue for the hangman to push Ragaci off the platform. The crack of his breaking neck as the weight of the chains pulled him sharply downward was enough for the hangman to know that he had completed his task successfully.

Ragaci's lifeless body swung gently from side to side. Several of those who watched were unable to hold on to the contents of their stomachs. Donatina Castellani was not one of them. She took in the proceedings impassively and dismissed the message of the frottola as nothing but idle and otiose sentiment.

After fifteen minutes, the hangman and his assistant built a fire on the platform. They sprinkled gunpowder on it so that once it was set alight, the sound of explosions rent the air. Those who passed through the courtyard could observe Ragaci's burning body. Gradually his limbs dropped off. The rest of his mortal remains clung to the chains from which they were then separated, burned to ash then sprinkled outside of the city as ordered by the magistrate.

XXIV

Confession

Paphos, Cyprus. 1517

⚜

The journey was long and tortuous. Attacked by pirates in the Tyrrenhian Sea, struck down by fever on the island of Cyprus, robbed by bandits on the road from Tyre, it was eight months before Maria arrived in Jerusalem. Protected for part of the way by a quartet of Papal guards accompanying a group of pilgrims, they left her for dead in Cyprus. She had been too sick to continue with them. Taking pity on her as she gasped for breath and sweated her guts out on the quayside in Paphos, an elderly widow took her in and nursed her back to health.

After recovering from her illness, Maria stayed with the widow for nearly four months and was tempted to remain permanently. The widow lived a simple life that she was only too pleased to share with Maria who she came to regard as the daughter with whom she had not been blessed. Once the widow had cares of her own, but age and the passing of many of those who mattered to her had removed them. The widow supported herself as a seamstress. Two or three times a week, her only surviving son and two grandchildren would come to visit her and on

Sundays she went to church. At first, the eastern service felt strange to Maria, but she soon became familiar with its distinctive features. Grappling with the Greek language was a challenge to which she also rose. She began to pick up on conversations and learned to make herself understood and even began to conquer the idiosyncrasies of the curious alphabet.

The unexpected break in her voyage gave her time to reflect on everything that had happened to her since the age of fourteen, when her proposed marriage to Guido Castellani fell apart after the Medici's return to Florence: her family's move to the grand palazzo on the Lungarno Terrigiani; the entry into her life of the musician, Giacomo Ragaci; the threatened union with Niccolo Tolosini; her removal under cover of night to the convent; the destruction of her family by the fire at the Palazzo Salcoiati; the brutal punishment she suffered for expressing her thoughts on the testament's view of women; the betrayal of her confidence by the treacherous Father Alessandro; her presumably failed attempt to save Suora Graziella from the clutches of the evil bishop and his accomplice, the untrustworthy Madonna Suora.

Given the option of joining the order's mission in Jerusalem or facing the likelihood of further regular punishment for any perceived infraction of the convent's standards as determined by Madonna Suora, she chose the former. With no more than two hours in which to make her decision, she extracted assurances from her tormentors that Suora Graziella would be protected. It was not until after she sailed from Livorno that she realised the stupidity of the mistake she had made. None amongst those with whom she was travelling, neither pilgrims nor the Papal guards, had any knowledge of a Benedictine Mission in Jerusalem. Although she was on her way to a place where the Madonna Suora believed she might be able to do some good, her primary intention was that Maria would be in a place from which she would likely never return. Maria also suspected that the sealed letter she left for her brother explaining what had happened, had been read by Madonna Suora and not passed on.

Deceived by those who betrayed the beliefs they sought to serve, the constants of her own faith were severely tested. She considered returning to Florence and seeking out her brother Leonardo and asking his advice. She could predict what that might be. Leonardo knew that love had touched her heart and that that love was for a mortal man. Memories of Giacomo Ragaci were alive within her – his music, his mind, his touch, his very essence coursed through her spirit, sometimes uncontrollably. There was no force more powerful than love, yet there was no love more powerful than the love of God. It was to God that she had made her vows and they were vows that she could not break for any mortal man. God had led her onto the road to the Holy Land from which there was no turning back.

She arrived in Jerusalem on Christmas Eve, 1517. She immediately made her way to the Church of the Holy Sepulchre where she joined in the celebration of the Midnight Mass. Her habit and the rest of her garments were worn and ragged but she was still recognisable as a Benedictine nun.

She was invited to stay in a hospice on the Mount of Olives that was run by Italian women. It was not attached to any particular order and not all of the women who lived there had taken vows. Immediately she felt at home and was offered the opportunity to remain, which she did. Abandoning any pretence of a connection with the Benedictine or any other order, she adopted a modest form of dress that seldom varied with the season – plain, dark robes and a white headscarf. Nevertheless, she continued to wear a crucifix around her neck. She performed the work of God and spread his word while looking after the pilgrims who came and went and who left her their gratitude and their blessings.

They arrived from all over Europe and from North Africa and even from as far as India, young and old, healthy and infirm. Some came in the belief that by doing so their redemption would be assured, others to fulfil a lifelong ambition to tread the path that Christ had taken along the Via Dolorosa to Calvary. Some would turn up at the door to the hospice with a letter of introduction or mentioning the name of someone they met who had suggested that a bed might be found for them, others were discovered alone and lost in the city, tired and hungry and in need of assistance. Maria would regularly spend her afternoons in the heart of the Christian quarter offering succour to those whose souls were enriched and fulfilled by the fact of their arrival in the Holy City, but whose physical appearance suggested they needed help.

Periodically she would write letters to her brother and send them with pilgrims returning to Italy. She was not to know that none of them were ever delivered. She realised that Leonardo could not have been aware of her precise whereabouts, though assumed he had discovered that she had 'volunteered' to go to Jerusalem. She could not know that Leonardo had written to her and that his attempts to reach her had also failed.

Occasionally a pilgrim arriving from Florence itself would be full of the doings of that great city – good and bad. Hearing descriptions of the places in which she had grown up filled her with the longing to return and to once again see it for herself. She imagined visiting her brother and his family. She was convinced that Leonardo had become a great artist and that he and Gianetta would have been blessed with beautiful children. But however much she projected and imagined, she knew she was not intended to be permitted to return. Besides, was it not also the case that the only other person her heart desired to see, the musician, Giacomo Ragaci, was no longer there? She sensed that in some way his provincial naivety had led him to be deceived and that though she knew it was not so that he, too, had been consumed by the flames that had devoured her family.

He often came to her in her dreams. More often than not he would be playing his lute and singing 'Non e tempo d'aspectare' and inviting her to join in. Sometimes she would even hum a refrain or two, half awake, but then lured back into the dream by the promise it had to offer. Every time, the dream ended in the same way, with a lit taper in a gloved hand. It was the taper that had started the blaze that destroyed the Palazzo Salcoiati. It was the same taper in the same hand that consumed her visions of Ragaci with fire too. Eventually, she discovered the identity of the culprit who, in the dream, held the taper and ignited the conflagration. When the dream finally rolled forward to reveal that it was she, herself, that had been responsible, she would wake up shouting and shaking.

Sometimes there were questions and anxieties and on other occasions there were doubts. With each passing year there was no diminution of the frequency with which the doubts took hold of her. When they came, they were often intense and possessed her totally. She became unable to think, unable to reason and could only turn inwards and to no-one else for help.

There were doubts about the decisions she had made and the path she had taken as a consequence and, most painfully, doubts about herself. Outwardly, she tried to act normally and to give away as little as possible of the pain by which she was affected. None of those with whom she lived would pry, though, as they got to know her, each of them was aware when all was not well within her. She had told them little of her past or of her background. In the beginning there had been no need to and, as time went on, no point in doing so at all. Any attempt to comfort her would yield no response other than a polite shrugging of the shoulders or the muttering of a well-tempered platitude. They respected her need to be left alone and prayed that God would bestow her with sufficient inner strength to enable her to ride the storm of her internal turmoil and to emerge at one, not only with herself, but with everything that defined the life she had chosen to lead.

Even when she was duelling with her demons, Maria never slackened her dedication to her tasks. If it was her turn to clean the hospice, the floors would be swept until there was not a single speck of dust to be seen and the surface of every piece of furniture sparkled. If there were foot-weary and hungry pilgrims who arrived after journeys that were often measured in months rather than weeks, their blisters would be dressed and their stomachs filled to the point of satisfaction. Whatever the task, Maria set about performing it with genuine altruism and always with God in her heart.

The hospice had been founded in 1498, coincidentally within a few weeks of Maria's birth, by Isabetta Velluti. A childless widow at the age of twenty-eight, Isabetta resisted the pressure of both sides of the family to take the hand of her late husband's younger brother and left her native Padua to make a pilgrimage to the Holy Land. With what money she was able to recover from her dowry, she bought a plot of land overlooking the city of Jerusalem and engaged local craftsmen to build the hospice upon it. Those who were invited to live there, never more than four or five at any one time, were all women, predominantly Italian and all were devout followers of the Christian faith.

There were no corresponding restrictions on those who might be invited to stay. They came from far and wide, spoke in many different tongues and had many different beliefs. In addition to Christian pilgrims, there were occasionally Jews who had fled the Inquisition in Spain and Portugal and Moslems from many far-flung corners of the rapidly expanding Ottoman Empire.

Those who remained at the hospice to help Isabetta inevitably moved on after a while – to take orders, to serve the sisterhood in one or other of the convents on the Via Dolorosa or to return to the places of their birth. Maria remained and became as much a part of the hospice as the bricks and mortar from which it had been built. She was able to practice her religion, help others and was sufficiently sheltered from the harshness of life without being cut-off from the benefits of living in a community. She had nothing much in the way of material possessions, she had lost her family and would never bear a child herself. These deprivations were compensated for by the companionship and the love that she shared with all of those who lived in the place that she began to call home and the ability to give to others whose travels or plight brought them to the sanctity of the hospice.

In her sixtieth year, Isabetta began to suffer from a number of ailments. Her slightly-built frame became more delicate, the permanent expression of contentment more frequently began to reveal a trace of disquiet. Individually, her ailments were nothing serious or unusual; shortness of breath, failing eyesight and arthritis in her legs. Their cumulative effect suggested to her that she may have little time left. There was one last important thing that she had to accomplish before God took her.

"When I go, it is you who I want to take on the responsibilities of this house," she said to Maria. It was not long after they had returned from the morning service at the Church of the Holy Sepulchre.

"I would that I was worthy enough to do that," replied Maria, whose melancholy mood of the previous few days had reached a level of transparency. Isabetta thought that by making her intentions known, Maria might be moved from the trough of self-doubt to a more permanent level of self-belief.

"That you are, is clear to me," said Isabetta reassuringly. They were sitting together in the kitchen, preparing a meal. Isabetta started cutting a pile of peeled potatoes into neat slices.

Though Maria's mood gave her the appearance of being careworn and sad, there was still a look of contentment about her that defined a woman who had reached a destination from which she knew she would never move. "I wish that anything in my life was clear," sighed Maria, keeping her head down and her focus on the carrots that she was scraping clean.

"Of all of those who have remained with me for any length of time, you are the only one who has shown by her actions that she is both capable and dedicated enough to take over my mantle when I pass on, or even beforehand if I become too infirm to continue as I have done these past thirty-one years."

"I pray that it may be many years before that comes to pass." Maria looked up from the table. Isabetta's usual kindly expression was fighting wistfulness and even fear.

"May the Lord God hear your prayer, but the truth is, Maria, that I fear that the day when I am taken from this place may be sooner than you might wish."

There was neither bitterness nor anger in her voice. Isabetta spoke as if the revelation she had made to Maria was one that she was divinely intended to share with her. Maria understood that Isabetta did not seek reassurance or contradiction. She put the knife down on the table, bowed her head and closed her eyes for a moment or two of silent prayer. When she finished she made the sign of the cross. She looked up and Isabetta, too, was praying. Maria waited for her to finish before she picked up the knife and resumed scraping the carrots. Isabetta nodded at her and carried on slicing the potatoes.

"If you will not succeed me as I wish," she said carefully, "there is no-one else here who might."

Maria nodded solemnly. "Then what is to happen? Although I have been here for fifteen years, I am not able to say that I will be here forever, whether you survive for many years yet, or otherwise."

Isabetta looked at her questioningly. "I have never once pried into your past, Maria, and, as God may be my witness, I do not intend to start now. I may never truly understand the events that transpired that led you to come to this holy city. But I am sure as I can be that the path you trod that brought you to my door was one that was intended by God."

Maria smiled, but it was a smile that was thinly drawn and lost in the confusion that closed in around her like a fog.

"If you are unable or unwilling to take over my mantle, there is only one other who might."

"And who is that?" said Maria, raising her eyebrows.

"Her name is Ana Sani and presently she lives in Damascus."

Maria had heard Isabetta mention Ana Sani on previous occasions, though knew little about her.

"Ana stayed with me some little while before your arrival. Since then she has journeyed and lived in many parts of the Holy Land. From time to time she writes to me from the convent where she lives."

"She is in orders?"

"No. She would never take orders. Like me she was once married. Having once been wed to a mortal man, she feels unable to pledge herself to God in the way of a virgin. Her husband fought for the Venetians and was killed at the Battle of Agnadello. She had two children, of whom a son survives and is a merchant in Treviso."

Maria had finished scraping the carrots and started to cut them and put the pieces into the bowl with the potatoes. "What does Ana do in the convent?"

"She works as a cook for which she receives a very modest stipend and a room of her own. It is some years since I last visited her when she was living in Nazareth. I will ask you to go to her and take her a letter that I will write this very day."

"And in this letter you will invite her to return to Jerusalem in preparation for the time when you may no longer have the strength or will to continue with your work here?"

"Exactly. If I was well enough to travel I would go myself, but I fear that my strength is not enough for such a journey."

"So you would have me do it instead?" Maria was almost embarrassed to be vested with such an important mission.

"Yes, and it may not be easy to persuade her. Ana is a woman who has plotted an unusual course in life and whose motives I have never always understood."

Maria did not pick up on the thinly disguised irony of Isabetta's comment. She put down her knife and considered the request. Since her arrival in Jerusalem the farthest she had been was to the port of Jaffa in the west and to Bethlehem in the south. She was comfortable where she was. A journey that would take four or even five days was not something that she would have chosen to do. But she could hardly refuse the request that Isabetta made, especially having turned down the invitation to take over the running of the hospice herself. After all, if not Maria, someone had to succeed Isabetta.

"Very well. I will do that, I will go there for you."

Isabetta smiled broadly, her mouth puckering where her teeth had fallen out. "And I would that you leave here as soon as we may make the necessary preparations.

Maria fully understood the importance of the task she had been set. Forewarned that Ana Sani may not be at all interested in returning to Jerusalem, Maria resolved to do her best to persuade her of the importance of accepting Isabetta's invitation.

* * * * * * *

The dry stillness of the deserted road echoed as the old wagon rumbled over loose rocks and avoided the boulders that occasionally blocked their path. Once beyond the Sea of Galilee, the small villages and settlements became fewer and further between. It had been nearly three hours since they had last stopped and she felt tired and dirty and her back ached from the jolts and bumps of the journey. From time to time a vapid breeze picked up swirls of sand that blew into their faces and made them cough.

For nearly four days she had sat patiently beside Sulayman Humam, the old hunchbacked driver who Isabetta had hired at the Damascus Gate. He had been sitting at a low table with a group of other wagon drivers, sipping an aromatic infusion and discussing the fact that the aqueducts that had recently been repaired were bringing water into the city. When Isabetta had interrupted them, Sulayman had been the first to respond to her proposal. He seemed honest enough and Maria had expressed herself happy with the choice.

Maria understood Arabic better than she could speak it and was content to listen to the loquacious Sulayman recounting anecdotes about his life on the road, the places he had been to, the events to which he had borne witness and the people he had met. Occasionally she would open the small book of psalms that she had brought with her, but the motion of the wagon made it hard for her to concentrate without feeling sick. She would close the book and clutch it to her chest, as if physical contact would be enough to enable the power of the words to feed her soul.

The mood of doubt that had affected her in the days before her departure still hung heavy on her and continued to hold her powers of reasoning to ransom.

As the sun began to drop in the translucent late afternoon sky, Sulayman pointed out the peak of Jabal al-Harah. He advised Maria that they would not be able to reach Damascus by dusk and that they would need to find somewhere to spend the night. She hoped they would reach the next village soon, because, as the light was fading the sporadic breeze had been replaced by a steady wind that was beginning to increase in strength and bluster. As the dust and sand began to blow around them, they had to cover their faces and the horse was becoming upset by the change in the conditions.

Sulayman brought the wagon to a stop and jumped to the ground. Shielding his face from the brunt of the storm, he tended the horse and tried to calm him down.

Aware that Sulayman was not beside her, Maria opened her eyes a little. She was blinded by the dust storm that blotted out the last glimmer of the sun as it fell below the horizon. Unable to see, unwilling to move, Maria sat quite still, alone with her thoughts and praying that the storm might end soon and that they would be able to find their way safely to Damascus. With the force of the storm continuing to increase, she put her hands up to her face and periodically squinted between her fingers. She could see nothing and there was nothing for her to see. The roar of the wind and the hiss of the sand as it blew across the forlorn landscape were the sounds of evil. The unrelenting lamentation of their cacophonous disharmony began to frighten her. She prayed hard and promised that if she reached Damascus unharmed that she would find Ana Sani and do as she had been asked to ensure that the future of the hospice would be safe-guarded.

After two hours, the storm began to relent, the wind began to recede and then, finally and without any warning, subsided almost completely.

Maria opened her eyes and turned around. In the visceral darkness she could make out the figure of Sulayman lying asleep in the back of the wagon in between the barrels of olives that were stashed there.

Anticipating that they would leave as soon as the sun was up, she lay down along the front of the wagon and slept as well as she could.

* * * * * * *

Though there were many convents in Jerusalem, in all her time, Maria had not once stepped foot inside any of them. It had taken the road to Damascus to bring her to enter a convent in the Holy Land. In contrast to the maze of crooked alleys by which it was approached, the Convent of St Theodora was situated on a road that was straight. A little after three in the afternoon, Sulayman left Maria at the gate. If not before, he arranged to pick her up at nine o'clock on the morning after the following day to take her back to Jerusalem.

Maria was welcomed into the convent by an elderly nun who spoke only Greek, but in an accent that was altogether more guttural than the one with which she had become familiar in Paphos. She was able to explain in a mix of broken and half-forgotten phrases and some sign language who she had come to visit. The nun showed her into the kitchen where, she was told, Ana Sani would soon join her.

Maria drank water from an earthenware cup and noted how basic everything was compared to the kitchen in the hospice, where Isabetta had imitated what might have been found in a townhouse in Padua or Venice.

When Ana Sani eventually arrived she immediately recognised Maria as an Italian and started to speak to her as if she was an old friend. The warmth of her greeting was worthy of Isabetta herself. Ana was short and round, ruddy-cheeked and hovered rather than stood, suggesting that she was one who never sat and relaxed and was forever looking for things to keep herself occupied. Probably no more than fifty, Ana Sani had already lived many different lives. The detritus of her experiences fused together in the wrinkles that lined her face. The warmth of her heart showed through every time she smiled, which was often.

Maria wanted to find out how an Italian woman from Padua ended up living with Greek Orthodox nuns in Damascus, but before she could say very much, even explain why she had been sent, Ana went to a cupboard and took down a jar of biscuits.

"Please have one. I baked them only this morning," she said, shaking the jar in front of Maria, who had not eaten much since earlier in the day.

Maria took a biscuit and placed it in front of her. Having exchanged pleasantries, Maria reached into the plain linen bag in which she had packed a few items for the journey, picked out Isabetta's letter and handed it to Ana who opened it eagerly.

She read the letter carefully, occasionally looking up and squinting at Maria, then returned to the text. Maria munched the biscuit, repeatedly trying not to stare at Ana. Having finished the letter, and clearly having read it for a second, and perhaps third, time, Ana folded it into her lap and looked at Maria querulously.

"You have been living at the hospice for a long time then?" asked Ana rhetorically.

"It will be fifteen years at Christmas."

"You must know its ways and the ways of my dear friend, Isabetta Velutti, as well as you know your own."

Maria smiled but said nothing.

"I think that you know what this letter requests." Again, Ana's tone was rhetorical.

"I believe I do, though I have not read it."

"I question why Isabetta would send you all this way with a letter for me, knowing that I am unable to do as she asks, when it would seem that the one who might most appropriately fulfil the role is you."

"Isabetta has already asked me and I have already turned her down."

"But why?"

Maria could answer the question easily, but quickly shifted the focus of the discussion. "Isabetta said you might initially reject her offer, but not for reasons that have anything to do with what you may consider to be my suitability to take on her mantle myself."

"It matters not what reasons I would give for not returning to Jerusalem. Suffice it to say there is nothing, not even my love and respect for Isabetta, that would change my mind. You may launch at me every argument that you may have, but my answer will remain the same. The question is not why I will not return to Jerusalem, but, more, why must I remain in Damascus?"

"And why is that?"

Ana narrowed her eyes, then stood up and fetched a jug

of water and another cup from the far side of the kitchen. She topped up Maria's cup and then poured one for herself. They each sipped in silence.

"You were going to tell me why you must remain in Damascus," said Maria prompting her.

"It is a matter of no moment," sighed Ana.

"It will be if I am unable to explain it."

"You won't need to."

"I won't? Why ever not?"

"Because, when you return to Jerusalem, you will tell Isabetta that you will accept the offer she made to you."

Maria smiled and shook her head.

"But first I must understand why you are so reluctant to fulfil a role for which you have been intended for some time," said Ana.

Maria's answer was the same as she would give anyone who invited her to assume a role that was intended to be permanent. The reason both fuelled and was fuelled by her doubts. It was a reason that she had never previously articulated to another, though, in truth, there had been no occasion on which nor reason for her to do so for the last fifteen years. She felt compelled to explain it to Ana Sani, even though she was a complete stranger. Without understanding what motivated her, Maria began to talk.

"You must understand that whenever I have been faced with making a decision in circumstances intended to dictate the course of the rest of my life, the decisions I have made have resulted in events taking a different turn. Time and again I have been blown off course and the lives of others have been affected badly as a consequence. If I accept the role of running the affairs of the hospice once Isabetta is no longer able to do so, my fear is that something bad will happen."

"Something bad? What do you mean?"

"I believe that there is a malevolent force that affects my life and that it will cause something bad to happen – either to others who live or stay at the hospice or to the hospice itself."

"For the fifteen years that you have already been there, has anything happened to you or to those around you?"

"No, but then I never made a decision to seek out the hospice. Isabetta invited me to stay when I first arrived in Jerusalem and I have been there ever since." She picked up the cup and drank some water.

"These bad things that happened were long ago. Time has overcome that period of your life. The opportunity that has been give to you is not one that you sought. It has been offered to you by Isabetta who has shown you love. Turn your back on the past and approach the future with hope. Open your eyes and see the beauty of life and how you might fulfil yourself by accepting what Isabetta has offered you."

Maria began to understand what Ana meant, that the ravages of her past could be overcome by love and by hope and the sheer beauty of life itself. Was it ever thus? Once she had had that faith in life herself; it had been shaken by the events by which she had been affected. Isabetta was showing faith in her and that faith deserved repayment.

Ana stood up and walked around the table to where Maria sat. She put her hands on Maria's shoulders and said, "in the same way that Isabetta sent you here that you might persuade me to see my future in Jerusalem, I have been sent to you that you might remove the mask that has been preventing you from seeing what is so clearly in front of you."

And Maria began to see and to see clearly that the path that had led her to Jerusalem was the path that she must continue to take. She would do as Isabetta had asked.

"Fear not, Ana, I will do my best to succeed Isabetta and I will tell her as soon as I return to Jerusalem.

Ana bent forward and kissed Maria on the forehead, then took a step back and made the sign of the cross.

"Are you hungry?"

Maria nodded and Ana set about preparing her something to eat. She put a loaf of bread and some meat on the table and they ate together.

Maria spent the next two nights at the convent and attended services with Ana and with the sisters of the Convent of St Theodora. On the second morning following, Sulayman came, as he promised, and they began their journey back to Jerusalem. On her return, Maria broke her news to Isabetta.

"What did Ana say to make you change your mind?" she enquired, though she spoke in a tone that suggested she was hardly surprised at all.

"Perhaps that is as much between her and me as the content of the letter that you wrote is between you and her," said Maria mischievously.

"Why? Whatever do you mean?" asked Isabetta weakly, almost disingenuously.

"It means that what Ana said to me should be of no more importance to you than the content of the letter is to me."

The reasoning behind Maria's decision was debated no further. Within a couple of months Isabetta was no longer able to physically continue looking after the hospice and passed away not long afterwards. Maria fulfilled Isabetta's wishes and took control over the hospice and continued to run it for the next forty-five years.

At the beginning of her eightieth year, Maria suddenly became ill and complained of pains in her stomach and in her kidneys. There was nothing that could be done to ease her suffering and the time came for a priest to administer the last rites.

In her final confession, she was able to offload the burden that had weighed her down for most of her life. She found it hard to speak. The words emerged in breathless spurts and the confession took time as she lapsed in and out of consciousness.

"Father, I have sinned. I have sinned against my family and against the will of God. My family first. I disobeyed my own father. I ran away from a marriage that he proposed for me. In saving myself from the man he would have me marry, I condemned my father and the rest of my family to suffer untimely and unseemly deaths."

"I sinned by abandoning a young nun who placed her trust in me. She put her faith in me by seeking my help to prevent her from being further abused and shamed by those who were evil but who pretended to be good. All I succeeded in doing was to save my own skin."

"And then I sinned by ignoring the desire of my own heart and forsaking the true love of a man, a good and honest man, a loyal man who would have given everything to make me his wife. I loved him as much as any mortal woman could love a mortal man. 'Delight yourself in the Lord and he will give you the desire of your heart.' I have always taken delight in the Lord and he chose to give me the desire of my heart, but I rejected it when it could have been mine. Thus I was exiled to this holy place where I have sought to follow his word and to do his bidding. I wish that … I wish that … I wish …"

Before she could complete her last sentence she lapsed into semi-consciousness. By the time the priest had concluded his words, the breath would no longer come to her lungs and her heart beat for the last time.

XXV

Hibernation

Pistoia. December 1899

At the far northern boundary of the estate, not far from Pistoia, there was an empty house. Abandoned for many years, its decaying grandeur and the redundant dreams of those who built it were fast disappearing. Much of the roof had collapsed and its timbers were rotting away.

The house had been built at the beginning of the sixteenth century by a horse-dealer. Together with his progeny, he lay buried in the family crypt, an overblown marble structure located in the middle of an area wooded with firs and pine. It was to be found half-way between the old and the new, altogether grander, house on the south side of the estate that was completed in about 1850. The incumbent owner of the estate was an industrialist from Milan. He had recently extended the grand mansion that occupied beautifully landscaped grounds abutting the winding road to Piastre. He frequently threw extravagant weekend parties for his friends and business contacts. Politicians and opera singers, local dignatories and foreign ambassadors were usually to be found on the guest list.

The basement of the disintegrating house was not entirely deserted. Heavy wooden doors to an underground storeroom had been sealed for more than a hundred years. While time moved on and left behind innumerable wars and intrigues and a legion of romances, the hope and beauty that inspired previous generations remained alive but often neglected.

Some time before the old house began its disintegration it was acquired by the members of a Jesuit-inspired sect who eschewed all things of temporal beauty. They packed away the trappings and fripperies they found around the house and even items that had practical functions if they were adorned with sinful images. Eventually the sect faded away and the estate was abandoned until the middle of the nineteenth century. Those who bought it soon realised that the old house was beyond restoration and thus had started work on the new.

With a new century about to dawn, the industrialist resolved to pull down the ruins of the old house and to replace it with a smaller villa where his recently widowed mother might live out her days in a degree of comfort and not three hundred metres from her son and six grandchildren.

A demolition team was hired to raze the old house to the ground. They arrived early one cold winter's morning with carts loaded up with ladders and every type of pick and hammer and axe imaginable. Their first act was to break open the front door that had long been barricaded to prevent occupation by vagrants. The industrialist and his eldest son followed the demolition team into the building and viewed it from top to bottom. Eventually, they came to doors that led down to the basement. They were locked. For the second time one of the workmen swung his pickaxe to break down doors, but they remained as they had been. Another workman joined in and, after a couple of minutes of heavy battering, the wood began to splinter and access was gained. Lanterns were lit and a flight of stairs revealed. Gingerly, they clambered through the doors and then down the stairs and into the bowels of the building.

Holding up the lanterns, they soon saw that the basement covered an area that was equivalent to that of the entire ground floor of the house. What was more, much of it was filled with what looked to be the entire contents of a home, most of it very old.

Amongst the decaying furniture and chipped and cracked crockery and glass were the icons that had once adorned the walls of drawing rooms and salons, and sculptures that had looked across neatly-trimmed lawns. There was a wooden chest that revealed gold and silver plate and even an exquisite necklace that had once lain on the milky white breast of an Eastern European princess.

Two portraits leaned against each other in a far corner, face to face. The spirits contained within them were in a state of repose. Occasionally, they had stirred but were not yet ready to be liberated. They responded to the sound of the melodies that, now and then, had been summoned from the walls around them, the call of an earthy baritone – the response of a heavenly soprano. The harmonies they aspired to sing together had already been composed. They waited patiently to hear the tap of the conductor's baton that would awaken them from their slumber, the signal that would indicate that the moment for which they had each been created had arrived and that they could, at last, be together as one.

Once the inspection was completed, the industrialist had the contents of the basement removed. Much of the trove was useless and was burned. Of the rest, most was sold at auction, some of the paintings were kept. The two portraits were eventually cleaned up and placed in the newly built villa. The portrait of the musician was hung in the salon, that of the young woman over the landing on the stairs between the ground and the first floors. There they remained until the death of the industrialist's mother that coincided with her son's bankruptcy. The portraits, together with the other pictures, were then acquired by a collector of the work of Pier Paulo Forzetti, the artist who had painted them. They would remain in the hands of the collector's family for some considerable time afterwards.

XXVI

Recognition

London. July 1999

◈

This time it was him. She was absolutely certain. He was with a much older woman and they were sitting a few tables away. She would never have seen them but for the fact that Jennifer had spotted a small counter where ice creams were being sold. Olivia turned around to look where Jennifer was pointing but her attention was immediately diverted away from her friend's craving for ice cream.

"Oh my God!" she gasped.

"Oh my God, what?" responded Jennifer, all flat New England vowels and Laura Ashley calf length summer frock.

It was their last night together before Jennifer was due to fly back to Boston and Olivia would go onto Pisa. They had enjoyed two wonderful weeks, barely pausing for breath from the moment they had landed in Dublin. Four days in Ireland were followed by visits to Oxford, Bath, Stratford-upon-Avon and, finally, London. Olivia had managed to obtain tickets for a new production of the John Osborne classic 'Look Back in Anger', at the National Theatre. On their way, they took a leisurely stroll along the Victoria Embankment, excitedly pointing out the profusion of landmarks, then they had walked across Waterloo Bridge. Arriving at the theatre with time to spare, they were sitting in the large bar, drinking bottles of mineral water and reading the theatre programme.

"Oh my God, what?" repeated Jennifer, trying to make out what had caught Olivia's attention.

"Someone I know. Over there. I must go and say hello to him. I simply must."

"Oh. Ok. Sure. Shall I come with you?"

"Please. No. I mean. It's ok. No."

In two weeks of travelling they had inevitably caught the attention of various men. Jennifer was engaged to be married yet still enjoyed flirting with and then rejecting the approaches of those who were not dissuaded by the ostentatious way that she brandished her engagement ring in front of their noses. She had also enjoyed mentioning Olivia's single status and watching the reactions of those who were attracted by her good looks and slim, well-proportioned body. Jennifer was pleased at how much progress Olivia had made in herself since moving back to New York. But for all Jennifer's playfulness, she also respected the fact that Olivia was not yet ready to face the unrelenting vicissitudes of another relationship with a man so soon after finalising her divorce, even a meaningless holiday fling.

"When you've said hello, if there's time, maybe you could get me an ice cream. I'll stay here and hold onto the table."

Olivia did not hear her. She was already up and navigating her way through the packed tables to where he sat with the older woman who, as she got closer, she assumed to be his mother, the same blue eyes, the same line of the jaw.

"Excuse me for interrupting, but aren't you Matt Dayton?"

Matt put down the glass from which he had been drinking and looked at her. "Olivia?"

"Yes." Not knowing quite what to do next, she held out her hand towards him.

He waited momentarily then shook it as he stood up and gasped, "Olivia Giorgianni."

"Once more," she replied, immediately regretting the remark.

He looked puzzled.

"I mean … well … I was married for a while. But I'm not any more." Shit, she thought. Too much information and she had said nothing yet that was worth saying.

"Olivia, how wonderful to see you again. This is my mother, Ruth Dayton. Mother this is Olivia. We met years ago when I visited Italy during my degree course."

"And again in Williamstown, Massachusetts, when I was studying there," added Olivia, keen that Matt should know that she had not forgotten their second encounter. "We used to write to each other as well."

"Indeed," said Matt, nonplussed.

Ruth Dayton stood, too, and shook Olivia's hand. "And you're just here on a visit?"

"Yes, it's my last night."

"You've made a good choice of play. Michael Sheen is supposed to be a wonderful Jimmy Porter. You know, I saw the original production at the Royal Court in 1956 when I was in the sixth form at school." Ruth knew no inhibition where people were concerned and was always happy to share her observations and recollections with anyone who would listen.

"Really?" said Olivia.

"Yes. It's not one of my husband's favourites though, so I was able to persuade Matt to join me. It's the first time we've been to the theatre together for simply ages, isn't it dear?"

"Yes, mother. So, Olivia, what brings you to London?"

"Vacation. Just blowing out some cobwebs. I'm here with a girlfriend," she added quickly, emphasising the 'girl' in girlfriend and gesturing towards Jennifer who waved at them. "And you?" she said, desperate to keep the conversation going while she gathered her thoughts and worked out where she was expecting the encounter to lead.

"I'm still here in London. Still working in the advertising business. The same agency as before."

"Except now he owns it," announced Ruth proudly. "He's done very well in his career.

"Yes, thanks," said Matt, confidently predicting that his mother would move on to make some pithy comment about what she saw as his lamentable single status and the absence of any grandchildren. "And you?"

"I've recently moved back to New York. Columbia. I'm working on finishing my PhD at last and still teaching undergrads." The words emerged without shape or meaning while she pondered what to say that would engage his attention.

There was something about Matt that she did find fascinating, that did intrigue her. It was there the first time they met, when she had consciously not let herself be swayed by it. It was there the second time, too, but she had not let him breach the barrier she had erected around her emotions. It was still there and she wanted to find out more about him and to ask all of the questions she had left unasked. She wondered whether he remembered the music box and what he had said about it. She wanted to know if he was still passionately interested in art. Perhaps there might be time to have a drink with them after the play finished. While she worked out how to telescope her wishes into a single sentence, Ruth wittered on about Matt's career. Then the Tannoy system bellowed into action. "Please take your seats in the Lyttleton for tonight's performance which will start shortly."

While Matt waited for Olivia to say whatever it was that was plainly on her mind and while his mother filled the space with words, he thought back to the last image that he had in his mind of Olivia. It was the faculty party to which she had taken him with her then date. He wondered whether or not it was that particular man that had become her husband. The defences that she had constructed around her thoughts and feelings during the course of that weekend were nowhere in sight. Though his mother's interjection meant that Olivia had said very little, her emotions were exposed for him to see. She had been married and divorced and he guessed that she had no children. She was on vacation with a girlfriend who he noted was walking over towards them. For once his mother's loquaciousness may have provided some benefit. Had he been alone he might have asked her to join him for a drink after the play. Maybe the initial excitement he felt when she came over would have sustained and evolved, and maybe not. The circumstances made it impossible for him to know or even guess. Besides, he had trod the path once before, made the emotional investment and got hurt in the process. He had more than enough to contend with, without the prospect of resuscitating a transatlantic romance that, for years, he had come to accept had only ever been one-way. Before he could articulate a polite exit line, Jennifer arrived at their table.

"And you must be Olivia's friend," said Ruth.

"Jennifer Monroe. I guess we better move on in. The show's about to start."

"Indeed," said Ruth, slightly perturbed that Jennifer would refer to a great work of drama as a 'show'.

"This is Matt Dayton, an old friend of mine, and his mother Ruth," said Olivia, not moving her eyes away from Matt.

"It's been so nice to see you again," he said politely "I'm flattered you even recognised me after so many years."

"You haven't changed," she said and wanted to add that he had become more handsome with maturity.

"You too," he said, decidedly pushing back any thoughts that he might have had to extend their renewed contact.

"Lovely to meet you both," said Ruth, organising her handbag and the jacket that she had hung across the back of a spare chair.

"Enjoy the play," said Matt.

"Yes, you too," replied Olivia and Jennifer in unison.

Matt started to escort his mother towards the theatre door and watched the two American women as they made their way towards the stairs that led to the upper level. He was relieved that they would be sitting in a completely different part of the theatre.

The production was dynamic but Matt's interest gradually began to fade and he started to shift in his seat. Jimmy Porter's angry young man began to annoy him with his self-indulgent diatribes. As pusillanimous as his wife may have been, there was something fundamentally incompatible that should have been apparent to both of them before they had contemplated marrying each other. At least each of them had been able to make enough of a commitment to get that far in a relationship. He wondered whether or not he would ever get that far himself, whether or not there would be someone who could love him for the person he was and not what he was or represented or what she might want him to be. His thoughts drifted back to Olivia who, though out of sight, was probably no more than a hundred feet away. He regretted that when the chance had been there for her to find out more about him that she had not taken it. What if it was not too late? Was he being no less silly than she had been all those years before by passing over the opportunity to find out whether the bond he had once believed had existed was real? After all he was fundamentally the same person that he had been at the age of twenty, just older and more beaten up by the world and the crap that life regularly threw at him. She was as beautiful as the day he first saw her, just made wiser by some shitty marriage into which she had presumably allowed herself to drift, no doubt pressured by family and the thought of being alone forever. He cogitated about it all as Osborne's drama reached its climax.

After the play had finished, he hurried his mother out of the auditorium, in the hope that perhaps he would spot Olivia in the foyer, but the crowds were dense and neither she nor Jennifer were anywhere to be seen. His mother babbled effusively about the play and how impressed she was with the production, while Matt's heart flailed out in anguish.

They walked out onto the terrace that overlooked the Thames, the magnificent vista of London's landmarks gently lit in the background by the failing twilight. To their right was the dome of St Paul's, to the left the Palace of Westminster. Matt imagined walking arm-in-arm with Olivia soaking it all up before taking her in his arms and holding her body close to his.

As they turned in the direction of where he had parked, Matt looked back at the theatre in anger, anger with himself that he had failed to seize the moment.

XXVII

Awakening

Florence. August 1999

࿇

Olivia Giorgianni's trip to Tuscany was her first for many years. Unlike modern America where urban landscapes could change unrecognisably over a matter of months, she marvelled at the stillness of the history that preserved the Tuscan towns and cities. The only visible alteration to Pisa that she noticed was the installation of steel cables to keep the Tower from toppling over. If only something as simple as a steel cable could have been put in place to have stopped her from falling apart after she had made her unfortunate marriage to the ghastly Ralph Bainbridge.

The first week was filled with the joys of her extended family and day trips hither and thither. As ever, Magdalena was keen to make a match for her, but Olivia firmly rejected both of her suggested introductions to apparently eligible males. She tried to put her brief encounter with Matt out of her mind, but it stayed with her and she accepted that his image would hang around until it would eventually fade with time. She rationalised it too. The break she had made with her past when leaving Williamstown was all-encompassing. The existence of Matt in her life was technically part of her Williamstown era. Matt was part of the past.

Persuading Magdalena of her need for some time on her own, Olivia decided to take the train into Florence. Although she had visited the city on previous occasions, there were some lesser known palazzi and some new and out-of-the-way exhibitions that had so far escaped her attention.

Emerging from the Stazione Santa Maria Novella she started walking in the general direction of the Duomo. She soon spotted the pinnacle of Brunelleschi's dome overlooking the city with unchallenged authority. She stopped for a moment to check her guide book. It was not the most profound of texts. She had bought it in a hurry from a bookstand at the American Airlines Terminal at JFK. She giggled, as she had on previous occasions, when she noticed the blurb on the back cover.

'Considered by many to be one of the most romantic cities in the world, the streets of Florence ooze with history and its many ancient buildings are dripping with art.'

Romance was not what she was looking for, but she wanted to experience some of the 'oozing history' and the 'dripping art'. She crossed over towards the Via degli Avelli with her mind open and a sudden lightness of spirit.

* * * * * * *

Arriving at a luxury boutique hotel overlooking the River Arno was altogether different to his previous experience of visiting Florence. The upholstered opulence and spectacular view were a far cry from the modest pensioni where he had stayed during his student days. The dynamics of Matt's agenda had radically changed as well.

Then it was a couple of weeks devouring the artistic content of the Uffizi, the Palazzo Pitti, the Galleria dell'Accademia and others. This time, clients were paying him to spend a few days developing ideas for a campaign for a range of pre-cooked pasta sauces.

The concept that he had developed with his team was not stunningly original but the client had bought it. Setting Italian food in context gave him the opportunity to revisit Florence, something that had been at the top of his agenda for a while

As the sun began to dip he sat out on the balcony with a cold drink. He looked across to the south bank of the river. It was less crowded than the north bank, yet it still had its fair share of tourists wearing the international uniform of t-shirts and baseball caps. They wandered aimlessly along the embankment as the late afternoon shadows began to lengthen. Gradually, as he watched them, the crowds began to change. The men were wearing long gowns and soft hats, the women ankle length skirts and headscarves. Horse drawn vehicles and handcarts replaced the cars and scooters that only minutes previously had been inching their way through the pedestrian traffic that spilled onto the roadways. He surveyed the buildings all of which bore hallmarks of the Renaissance and earlier.

Suddenly, directly opposite, on the Lungarno Terrigiani, he heard a series of explosions following which a blaze broke out in one of the imposing palazzi that overlooked the river. Great swathes of fire clawed at the sky. The roar of the conflagration was deafening, as though the match by which it was lit had been struck in hell. The screams of the inhabitants of the building began to pierce the air in a cacophony born of fear, but fuelled by helplessness. One by one their spirits rose from the flames, escaping the fiery grasp that tried to grab them. Matt stretched out his hand and tried to help them. They looked towards him, but were powerless to respond to his entreaties. As the spirits disappeared above the roof of the darkening sky, Matt began to sing in a powerful baritone.

Non e tempo d'aspectare
Quando se ha bonaza o vento,
Che se vede in un momento
Ogni cosa variare.
Non e tempo …

Se tu sali fa pur presto.
Lassa dire chi dir vole.
Che non duran le viole
E la neve al caldo sole
Sole in aqua ritornare.
Non e tempo …

Quando se ha firmato el piede
Et in tutto intorno visto
Muta por fortuna sede
Che non val contra al provisto
Che gli e ben da pocho e tristo
Chi no sa col tempo andare
Non e tempo …

Non aspecti a volti questa vota stabilita
Molti sono stati accolti nel condur della
lor vita.
Non e tempo …

Though it was not his own voice that sang words he did not fully understand, he sensed that the lyrics contained messages of hope. As the final stanza evanesced into the early evening sky, he stood motionless, holding the railing and watched a crowd of people stop to stand and stare as the imposing palazzo was transformed into a spectacular funeral pyre.

He continued to observe the devastation until all that remained was a burnt out shell, roofless, the outer walls blackened with soot. The immediate area was covered by an umbrella of smoke that shrouded the fading daylight. Hypnotised by the speed with which the majestic grandeur of the palazzo had been devoured, the horror of the destruction touched something deep inside him. He opened his mouth, as if to scream, but no sound emerged and he began to cry, in silence. The tears obscured his vision but he was unable to move his hands, so could not wipe them away. Eventually harnessing his emotions, he stopped his sobbing and blinked through the mist that clouded his eyes.

The crowd of onlookers had thinned out. A few uniformed officers were milling around in front of the main entrance to the palazzo. They stopped anyone from walking into the smouldering carcass of the building and trespassing against the souls of those whose lives had been taken. A carriage pulled up outside of the palazzo. Two men, one younger the other older, jumped out and started to hurry towards the officers. They were too far away for Matt to make out their features, but, for a brief moment, the younger man stopped moving. He turned away from the palazzo and looked towards the balcony where Matt was standing. Matt felt as if the young man was reaching out to him and saw in a moment that everything was beginning to change, not only in the life of the young man but in his own life as well. He wanted to find out who the young man was and to speak to him. Matt sensed that the young man had a message for him and he wanted to find out what it was. If he was going to act, Matt knew that he would need to do so quickly.

"In the same way that violets do not last and snow in the hot sun returns to water, there's no time for me to wait," Matt found himself saying.

Later on, when Matt tried to recall precisely what he had seen and said, he was certain that, when he had spoken, he had been standing on the balcony and, therefore, could not have been asleep and dreaming. He was not clear if it had been the words he spoke or the ringing of the telephone that had brought him back to the moment, but he did know that his spirit had been disturbed.

The phone stopped ringing before he became sufficiently aware of his surroundings to be able to answer it. Emerging from his reverie he heard himself speaking again, "silent fortune still sits and doesn't go against what's meant be."

He shook his head and closed his eyes for a few moments. When he opened them he was relieved, if not a little frustrated, to see that the ancient buildings were all intact and further reassured by the throngs of tourists who continued to walk along the banks of the river.

Once again the phone began to ring. He turned around, walked from the balcony back into his room and picked up the receiver. It was Sunita Shah who, together with her assistant, had taken a later flight. She let him know that they had checked in at the hotel. Knowing of his love for Art, they had booked a table for nine at La Taverna del Bronzino. Apparently the Florentine painter of that name had connections with the palazzo in which the restaurant was housed. Matt looked at his watch. There was just enough time for a quick shower and to return to the twentieth century. He undressed, went into the bathroom and started to sing Santa Lucia.

* * * * * * *

Although it was Friday afternoon, Matt still had plenty of time left in which to wander around. The three-day visit had been tiring, though punctuated with wonderful food and a chance to look at some of the sights in the cause of his client's campaign. The others had already gone to the airport. The weekend beckoned and there were parties and clubs waiting for them in London. Matt was not in that much of a hurry and had decided to extend his stay through until Sunday evening. He found a small café in a side street near the Duomo. He sat down at a table outside and ordered a plate of pasta and a Moretti. While he waited for his meal to arrive, he scanned through the notes that he had made for his client's campaign.

The pasta was tasty and a second Moretti was followed by a large capuccino. He asked for the bill and stood up to take in the scene. He noticed a banner hanging from a building on a bend that was further down the street. He could just about make out what it said. 'L'arte di Pier Paolo Forzetti'. He paid the bill and started to wander towards the banner. He was certain that he had heard of Pier Paolo Forzetti, but at that moment could not place any of his works.

He paid the entrance fee and entered the first of the rooms of the exhibition. The story of Forzetti's life was related on a series of large plastic boards illustrated by contemporary iconographical material. Apparently Forzetti had enjoyed the patronage of several wealthy families. He was ultimately murdered by a nobleman who found him in bed with his wife. Much of his earlier legacy had been lost until the end of the nineteenth century when a cache of his work was discovered in the basement of a ruined old house on the outskirts of Pistoia. Most of what was on display was on loan from a series of private collections as there was little of his better work in permanent exhibitions at museums.

Matt ambled slowly through the next two floors. There were sketches, a couple of not particularly distinguished sculptures and a few portraits. The larger panels betrayed evidence of the movement often referred to as Mannerism. In its deliberate stylisation it attempted to take the balanced proportions typical of the earlier Renaissance artists and look at the subject matter in an exaggerated way. The larger panels often contained fewer figures and not crowd scenes. Forzetti laid emphasis on the grace and languor of many of his figures, though brought out less palatable qualities in some of his subjects. One in particular caught Matt's imagination. 'Venus and her Lovers' showed the Goddess in a pose of pure eroticism, yet the usual look of understated absorption that was generally associated with her was replaced by one of wanton lust.

At the end of a corridor was a narrow staircase that led to the top floor. It was not clear whether the exhibition continued that far, but, after a moment's hesitation, Matt decided to check to see. At the top of the house bright sunlight poured through a dormer window in incandescent torrents. Matt looked out across the rooftops of the city. Viewed from any angle, the vista was energising. Half-closing his eyes in the silence, it was easy to transport himself a few centuries backwards and breathe air that was enchanted by the magic of the Renaissance.

He imagined himself to be the owner of the house, a prosperous merchant and a patron of the arts. He would have his own private study up here, away from the rest of his household. It was the place where he could keep his own company, somewhere he could read and contemplate, somewhere he could write and keep a carefully composed journal of his daily life. One day it would serve as a living testament to the most golden of eras of man's existence.

There were two rooms with open doors. They were smaller and more intimate than the rooms lower down the house. He looked briefly from one to the other and selected the room to his left. It contained only two paintings, each about twelve or fifteen feet across. The first was a banquet scene. A number of prosperous looking people sat along a table. In the centre was a young woman wearing a simple white robe. Her face looked upwards. An angel's halo in gold shimmered above her head. Two places to her left an imposing man stared outward. He was magnificently dressed and looked to be the host of the table. To her immediate right an older woman, altogether more modestly attired than the rest of the company, sat with her head bowed. To her left there was a younger man whose features were similar to her own, the same green eyes, the same strong jaw, his hair a swirling mass of copper curls. In front of them, posed in profile, was a musician, playing what looked to be a lute. On the ceiling of the room, just visible, was the face of Christ. His kindly countenance concentrated on the young woman almost to the exclusion of the others.

The other piece showed a group of nuns kneeling in prayer in a small chapel. Another nun stood away from the group. She was bareheaded and bore a striking resemblance to the young woman in white in the other painting. She held a picture in front of her. It was a portrait of a handsome young man who looked holy, but not religious. She was close to the door and looked as though she was about to leave.

Matt spent some minutes looking at each of the two paintings. They flooded him with an intensity of emotions. Although creating scenes from the past, they conveyed a feeling, an understanding, an interpretation of events that were yet to occur and in which he was directly involved, a feeling of 'previty'.

He crossed the landing and entered the second room. Matt was a little surprised to see a woman standing with her back to him. She wore a straw hat, a plain pale blue top and a smart, navy, knee-length skirt. He thought he had been alone. He had not seen or heard anyone join him in the eaves of the building.

A row of four portraits lined the walls to either side. The woman was looking at another two that hung on the wall that was farthest from the door. Two rows of sixteenth century faces beckoned him to walk past them. They were not bothered if he did not stop to make their acquaintance. He had an appointment in front of the two who waited at the end of the room. The appointment did not appear in his diary, though it was one that had been made a long time before.

Matt acknowledged the welcome of his eight hosts and walked slowly towards the woman. When he reached her, he stood slightly behind her. He looked at the two paintings, to the left 'Ritratto di Musicisa' and to the right 'Ritratto di Maria Salcoiati'. The woman was reading a catalogue of the exhibition. He wanted to see what it said about these two paintings but the print was too small for him to make out from where he stood. In any event, he found it hard to turn his attention away from the two faces that stared at him from a distance of nearly five hundred years. One was an unnamed musician with a book of manuscripts on his lap. He looked as though he was about to make a change in the life that he had led up to the point at which his portrait had been painted. The other was a young woman, beautiful in an ascetic way, but modestly attired and holding what looked to be a holy book. A beatific look imbued the composition with a feeling of tranquility. Yet, despite this, the artist conveyed a sense that she was inwardly troubled, perhaps affected by self-doubt.

"They are really beautiful, aren't they?"

The woman spoke in a hushed tone, almost reverential. She looked up from the catalogue and at the paintings again. She did not turn towards Matt. She knew that she did not have to.

"Yes, they are. Quite the best of them all. But I wonder why they've been hung together like this?" he replied

"There's something about these two that they need to be with each other." She spoke very slowly as though speculating as to whether what she said might not be right, but secretly confident that she was.

"You think so?" Matt wanted to think about what she said, but began to concentrate on the voice that he thought he had recognised instantly and of which he was now certain.

"Oh yes," she said. "I sense that they have waited a long time to be together."

Matt turned his attention away from the paintings and looked at the woman. She was wearing reading glasses that she removed and placed on the crown of her hat. She leaned forward and slightly across him to look more closely at the painting of the musician. As she turned her face slightly towards him, Matt knew that what she said was true.

He reached his hand across and laid it gently on her shoulder.

"Olivia."

She acknowledged him with a smile. They looked at each other but their attention was drawn back towards the two paintings.

The musician rose, placed the book of manuscripts on his chair and greeted his lady. Maria Chiara Salcoiati closed the holy book and put it down. She turned towards him. The musician held out his hand towards her and she took it. The sound of a lute began to fill the room. The delicate melody was one with which they were both familiar. Maria smiled at the musician and returned his embrace. They walked towards and through Matt and Olivia as though making their way to the door.

Matt and Olivia turned around. They saw nothing save for the eight dead faces staring at the space in front of them. The music began to subside.

"Now I remember what it was that I never got round to asking you," said Matt.

Olivia looked into his eyes. For the first time in her life she knew what she really wanted and it was well within her grasp. She would not let it slip through her hands this time. She reached forward to stroke his cheek.

She responded without waiting to hear the question. "I quit religion school after my confirmation, when I was twelve. I was never much one for all that dogma and I know that I made the right decision. They crammed it down my throat at home and the nuns who taught me were always strict and intolerant. I've always believed in God though."

"Always?"

"Yes."

"And the divine will?"

"Not always, but I think that I may do now. In fact I'm sure that it is entirely possible that it exists."

"And destiny?"

"This time I will take the right fork."

"Right," he said. And then trying to think of something else to add, he said it again, "right."

"Right, Matt!"

They moved together and kissed, softly, tenderly, and with all the feelings they had been saving for the moment.

The spirits of the past that were living within Matt and Olivia were at peace and at one with each other as it was always intended that they should be.

Gently they pulled away from each other. Without turning back, they left the room and went down the stairs. Hand in hand, Matt and Olivia walked out on to the ancient streets. The rest of eternity was theirs and there was nothing in this world or beyond that would stop them from spending it together.

Addendum and Glossary

Many of the following terms and references appear more than once in the text. The chapter references are the first occasion on which each respectively appears. This addendum and glossary is in no way intended to be a comprehensive reference work, merely a guide to assist readers in acquainting themselves with some of the terminology that is used and the material that forms part of the background to the novel.

I Arrival

palazzo: a grand house; many of the great palazzi in Florence were built by and served as the principal residences of the leading families for many generations

ricercari: a musical prelude, sometimes with the characteristics of a fugue

frottola (pl. frottole): a secular form of song, particularly popular in Italy in the late fifteenth and early sixteenth century

braccio (pl. braccia): a unit of measurement, the precise length of which varied from one city to another. In Florence a braccio was equal to 58.36 centimetres or slightly less than two feet

signor: man; form of address of a male; the equivalent of mister or 'Mr.'

saltarello: a form of dance music

piva: up tempo form of dance music

benda: a length of silk or linen veil used for covering, wrapping around or plaiting the hair

signorina: unmarried woman; form of address of an unmarried female the equivalent of 'Miss'

II Dream

signora: married woman; form of address of a married female; the equivalent of 'Mrs' *piazza*: square or large open area; often used for public gatherings or meetings; the Palazzo Vecchia, the seat of the Signoria and the Consiglio Maggiore, is situated on the Piazza della Signoria, the largest of Florentine piazzas

banditori: town-criers who would read proclamations and decisions of the Signoria and the Consiglia Maggiore in the public piazzas and who would similarly disseminate important news

the process of marriage negotiations: the ritual surrounding the contracting of a marriage was of crucial importance to Italian Renaissance society; most, if not all marriages, especially between those in the upper echelons of society, were arranged between the fathers of each of the bride and groom and only took place after a potentially lengthy period of negotiation and ritual of which there were four principal stages. Firstly, the negotiations for the dowry would be conducted between representatives of each party, often someone trusted outside of the family, a consigliari (or advisor). The ability of a family to provide a dowry for its daughters was hugely important. The size of a dowry would partly determine the status of the husband that night be attracted. A less wealthy family, with many daughters and unable to afford more than one or two dowries, would often be forced to send younger daughters to nunneries. Once a preliminary agreement was reached there followed a series of three rituals. The first of these was a public meeting between the male kin and friends of each of the bride and the groom at which the dowry terms were legally notarised in a written deed. At the second stage, popularly referred to as a 'ring day', a ceremony took place at the bride's family home where, with the assistance of a notary, the groom, attended by close members of his own family, would place the ring on the bride's finger and then present gifts not only to his bride but also to important members of her family. At this point the bride's father would provide a celebratory banquet. The final stage was the formal move by the bride to her husband's home. Suitably attired in the finest of her outfits, the bride, either on horseback or in a fine carriage, would be part of a procession that would very publicly wend its way to her new husband's home. At the beginning of the sixteenth century an Italian marriage was regarded as an entirely secular affair and it was not, therefore, celebrated as part of a religious service.

Signoria: the governing body of Florence consisting of nine members

Il Magnificente: literally 'the Magnificent', by which name Lorenzo de' Medici (1449-1492) was also known

III Vows

Humanism: a philosophy based on human ethics and the recognition that right and wrong may be determined by application of innate human qualities; Humanism in its purist form emphasises self-determination and rejects concepts that relate to the supernatural or depend on the divine. During the Renaissance there emerged in Italy the concept of Christian Humanism which placed value on earthly experience provided that it was combined with the acceptance of the Christian faith

tastar de corde: chord sequences, often used by lutanists to warm up at the beginning of a performance and which they would use as the basis for improvisation

IV Harmony

cappella: chapel

V Portents

consigliari: advisor, counsel

gonfaloniere: the head of the Florentine government; elected annually though, during the period of the Medici exile and following the removal of Savonarola, the ascetic monk who was executed in 1498, Piero Soderini proclaimed himself gonfaloniere for life. Soderini was removed from office and exiled consequent upon the return of the Medici in 1512

canzone (pl. canzoni): the Italian word for song or ballad

strappado: instrument of torture; the victim's wrists are tied behind his back which are then secured to a rope that is tied to a hook or some other fixed point; the hook will be located in a position that is raised from the ground. The victim is then pushed from the height causing major stress to the extended arms leading to dislocated and/or broken shoulders

VI Preparations

campanile: bell-tower

chiaroscuro: artistic effect that achieves light and shade in two dimensions but which suggests three

divisions: variations and/or ornamentations based on an existing musical theme

mantilla: a triangular headscarf made of cloth or lace and worn by Catholic women when attending religious ceremonies

X Devotion

the process of becoming a nun: although practice varied from one convent to another, in early sixteenth century Italy a series of ceremonies took place that reflected the fact that the attaining of the status of a fully-ordained nun was a gradual process rather than a single event. Although there were many younger daughters of families who could not afford a marriage dowry who were consigned to becoming nuns, it was generally the case that the family of a novice was expected to provide some form of dowry upon their daughter entering the convent. The first of the ceremonies was the acceptance into a convent; secondly, there was the ceremony of vestition when the nun would put on the habit of the convent for the first time; thirdly, profession, when the nun would make a series of public vows and, lastly, consecration and veiling which would mark the formal integration of the nun into her community

Suora: sister

Madonna Suora: Mother Superior

XII Ambition

viol: stringed instrument, forerunner of the violin and the cello

shawm: woodwind instrument, forerunner of the oboe

XIV Seduction

tabor: drum-like percussion instrument

eventi del passato favoloso: fabulous events of the past

pensiero saggi: wise thoughts

pre-marital sex as a basis for marriage: evidence suggests that a couple who had sex together before marriage without their families knowing might then marry without rancour provided, of course, that the match was with a suitable partner. Such occurrences were normally to be found amongst artisans and those of the lower classes; such an event would be rare amongst the well-to-do and those with aspirations to social advancement.

About the author

Anthony David Morris was born and brought up in Portsmouth, England. After graduating in law from Manchester University he qualified as a Solicitor. He has spent the last thirty years in private practice in London, specialising in Media, Entertainment and Intellectual Property Law. The author of many published articles and commentary pieces in the legal, industry and national press, 'The Musician and Maria Salcoiati' is his first published novel.